The Stars at Night

MERRIN CAMERON

Ark House Press
arkhousepress.com

Cataloguing in Publication Data:
Title: The Stars at Night
ISBN:978-0-9756331-2-0 (pbk)
Subjects: Fiction

Design by initiateagency.com

Dedication

For the beautiful young women in my life;
Chrissa, Mieke, Leacia, Bianca and Emilie.
May you always look heavenward and be blessed.

Part One

*Look up into the heavens. Who created all the
stars? He brings them out like an army,
one after another, calling each by its name.
Because of His great power and incomparable
strength, not a single one is missing.*
Isaiah 40:26

CHAPTER 1

Flying High

"He said "Love...as I have loved you."
We cannot love too much."
Amy Carmichael 1867-1951

The howling wind rattled the old tin roof. Loose sheets of iron banged loudly as they tried to break free from the rusty nails barely holding them in place. A high-pitched screeching came from the drooping branch of the old pepperina tree as it scratched wickedly along the side wall. The hens huddled silently together on their perches, tense and alert.

Spiders moved about hurriedly in their dusty webs, seeking prey to devour. Mice scurried to and fro, intent on feasting on the grain and scraps scattered on the wet ground. Rats raced around on the rafters above, squealing in panic, while a long, fat python hissed in anticipation.

A dirty figure lay in the mud and filth, curled into a tight ball; shivering from cold and a dreadful, all consuming fear. Smoke began to creep in, its silver-blue wisps reaching out menacingly in the enclosed area. The wind increased its ferocious attack as clouds covered the moon; the darkness adding to the terror.

There was a beast outside, steadily drawing closer, roaring in rage. Suddenly, the door was flung open; the old hinges squeaking hideously. The woman drew back against the wall in horror, impaled by the bright light that filled the old shed; her scream sending the chickens into a wild, cackling frenzy.

* * *

Kath sat bolt upright in bed, gasping for air with her shoulders heaving, her scream still ringing in her ears.

"Hey, it's all right. You're safe. Just a dream. Shoosh now, you're fine, shhh."

Strong arms encircled her in a warm embrace, work hardened hands caressed her back. Warm breath fanned her neck. Slowly, Kath became aware of her surroundings. She was in the bedroom, with Sam.

"Just breathe deeply, slowly. You're safe. I'm here," he kept repeating the comforting phrases until she relaxed against him, her heart rate slowing.

"Sorry darling," she whispered.

"It's okay, just a bad dream. Nearly scared the life out of me though," he chuckled quietly, kissing her forehead tenderly before turning on the bedside lamp. "Okay now, sweetheart?"

"Yes, I'll be fine.

"Was it the same old dream?"

"Yes, the same old dream," she replied in disbelief. "Haven't dreamt it for ages. I wonder why now?"

"In the past it's always been triggered by you getting upset or anxious. Are you worried about something, love?"

Kath sighed loudly. "Well yes, I suppose I am. The plane ride."

"The flight with Jillian? But that's next week, isn't it? I didn't think you were worried about it?"

"She called last night and asked if we could go today because her pilot friend has to go to Sydney on business next week. Apparently today is going to be perfect for flying, and it'll be the last opportunity for a while. Then on the news last night there was a story about a small plane crashing..." her voice trailed off.

"Why didn't you tell me any of this?" Sam enquired.

"You were home late and looked so tired. I thought I'd talk to you this morning at breakfast." She turned to look at her husband. "I don't think I can do it Sam," she cried with tears spilling down her cheeks.

"Nonsense, of course you can do it. It'll be fine. You'll love it."

"But what if I don't enjoy it? What if I get air-sick and throw up everywhere? That would be mortifying!"

"Kath, really? You don't get sea sick, you don't get car sick, and the times we've flown you have never been air-sick."

"But I've never been in such a little plane, and I don't want to embarrass Jillian."

"You'll be right," Sam asserted more forcefully. "Don't talk yourself into having a bad experience. Keep thinking about how wonderful it'll be, and the photos you'll take and be able to paint later. Come on darling, relax, it'll be just fine."

Kath kissed his whiskery cheek. "I know you're right but I can't help being nervous."

"Nervous is okay but," he hesitated, "what's that saying of Bryce's about concrete?"

Kath rolled her eyes. "He would tell me to take a spoonful of concrete and harden up princess."

"Yeah," laughed Sam. "That's it, and Jess has one about big undies or something."

"Oh Sam, you're hopeless," Kath giggled. "Jess would tell me to put on my big girl pants and go for it."

"Well, there you go, words of wisdom from all directions." He smiled, patting her leg affectionately.

"Thanks honey, I do feel better but I don't think I'll be able to go back to sleep though."

"That's okay, it's nearly morning. Let's just stay here and watch the sunrise, hmm?" he said quietly as he turned the lamp off.

She nodded and they settled back, with Kath leaning into Sam's broad chest, his tanned arm around her shoulders.

"I'm sorry, love, I know I've been a bit pre occupied lately."

"It's okay; I know you've been busy. I'm just a bit jittery. I went to sleep thinking about the plane ride, and then I suppose my subconscious kicked into gear and the dream came again."

"We need to get you into a more trusting frame of mind then, don't we?" He smiled and kissed her again before continuing. "You know Jillian is a control freak with absolute attention to detail? She would never have suggested this if she wasn't sure the plane was safe and the pilot was good. Right?"

Kath nodded.

"She would also have checked the weather herself to make sure it really was going to be fine today. Agree?"

Kath nodded again, a little smile playing around her lips.

"And way up there in the sky, you'll be so close to Heaven, if anything does go wrong, I'm sure God will send an angel or two down to help."

Kath's laugh was silenced when Sam rolled over and held her in his arms, capturing her mouth in a deep kiss.

* * *

Later that morning, Kath and Jillian stood together at the little Dalby Airport, looking at the small aircraft parked beside the runway; one woman still with feelings of apprehension, the other bubbling with excitement. Neither one of them had ever been up in a small plane before.

"I sure hope this is a good idea. That plane looks very small," whispered Kath nervously.

"Of course. It's a great idea," laughed Jillian. "I can't wait to take off! Don't worry, we'll be fine. I know Barry and he's a great pilot, very experienced. Come on, he's waving to us."

They walked over to the Cessna aircraft.

"Good morning, ladies. Beautiful day for flying. Isn't it?" smiled their pilot. "G'day Jillian, good to see you again, been awhile." He gave her a cheery handshake and then offered his hand to Kath adding, "And you must be Kath? Great to meet you, my brother used to play soccer with your husband years ago."

"Oh, really?" Kath answered vaguely. "Nice to meet you, Barry."

"Sorry about the short notice but its great weather today and I didn't want to disappoint you. I can't get out of my trip next week. Now just give me a few minutes to complete my pre-flight inspections and we'll be off."

Barry proceeded to walk around the little plane making notes on a clipboard. The safety check complete, he returned to his passengers to give them the required briefing about the weather, flight conditions, safety equipment and emergency procedures. Noticing Kath's nervousness, he said kindly: "Nothing to worry about Kath, this little beauty may look small but she's efficient and very safe. Conditions today are very good, so just relax and enjoy the scenery and don't forget to take plenty of photos." He then told them where to sit and gave them each a set of headphones to wear.

Before long they were taxiing down the runway, with the little plane increasing in speed until suddenly they were taking off into the air. Kath, fear churning her stomach, felt herself being pushed back into her seat as she stared out the small window at an immense blue cloudless sky. Her wide-eyed face with her mouth forming an anxious 'O', gradually relaxed and her mood changed to one of tentative exhilaration; she was flying! They flew over the town with Barry pointing out landmarks and sharing some local facts and history. He then banked the plane gently and Kath was a little unnerved by the change in movement but relaxed again as she took in the panoramic view. It was amazing! Barry even flew out over the farm and she was able to look down on her house, easily recognisable by the tree-lined driveway and red-roof. They turned slowly and headed towards the Bunya Mountains, Barry telling them some of the history of the area,

"The local Aboriginal people would invite other groups up here. They used to gather the huge nuts from the Bunya pines and feast on them. In the late 1800s the early settlers began milling the Bunya pines in the forests. It was declared a National Park, over 9,000 hectares, in 1908. Today, it's a cool and shady haven. It's great to come up here when the temperature on the surrounding plains is soaring in the summer months, but I especially love it during the winter time when the fog and mist roll in. There's nothing like sitting in front of a log fire in one of the chalets. Of course, the park is a sanctuary to an abundant array of wildlife including wallabies, possums, king parrots and satin bowerbirds."

Kath knew most of the history as the mountains were one of her favourite places to visit, but she was hoping to get some great photos of the high country and rainforests from the air.

Jillian and Barry chatted away; or rather Jillian prattled on and on as she did when she was excited, and Barry seemed to have mastered the art of nodding in all the right places. Kath smiled to herself, listening to her friend while she sat in silence, holding tightly to her camera. She tried not to think about how far away the ground was and that she didn't have a parachute. She could feel the plane vibrating all around her and didn't know whether to be comforted by the constant vibrations which, if she let herself relax, were strangely reassuring, or to worry that something was working its way loose.

Slowly the tension eased from her body and her fears dispersed as she marvelled at the scenery below, quickly grabbed her camera and started taking photos. The view of the Bunyas was spectacular, the vivid green of the rainforests contrasting starkly with the brown landscapes of the surrounding countryside. Everything looked so small, far away and beautiful. She no longer heard the others talking; becoming totally engrossed with the endless views, the colours and the thrill of being so high in the sky. She snapped pictures quickly, trying to capture as much as possible on her digital camera.

Kath could feel the adjustments that Barry was making as he piloted the little aircraft, and was startled when the plane was jolted by turbulence. She was suddenly terribly afraid. Screwing her eyes shut, she gripped the edge of her seat with clammy hands as beads of cold sweat broke out on her forehead, her heart racing. The screeching noise from the nightmare, not so long ago, filled her ears. She was about to scream when Barry's calm voice came through her headset.

"Sorry ladies, these little planes are quite susceptible to changes in the wind, nothing to worry about. We'll start heading back now, might be a bit bumpy for a little while."

Jillian turned and gave Kath a comforting smile and a big thumbs up, frowning slightly when she noticed the pale face looking back at her, but Barry began speaking again so she turned her attention back to the pilot. As the plane turned for home it gently rolled, and Kath once again felt the centripetal force push her back in her seat. Fear returned for a few moments and she had to force herself to concentrate on the view out of her window. The words of an old hymn sprang into her mind and she sang the chorus quietly to subdue her anxiety:

"Safe in the arms of Jesus,
Safe on His gentle breast;
There by His love o'ershaded,
Sweetly my soul shall rest."

She smiled at the childhood memory of her mother singing those words to calm her night terrors. Thankfully, there was no more turbulence and the flight back to the airport was smooth and uneventful with more interesting commentary from the pilot. It was surprising how quickly the time passed and Kath, totally absorbed in taking in the sights below, jumped again when Barry's voice crackled through her headphones.

"We'll be landing in a few minutes, should just be a little bump."

Jillian was looking forward excitedly, but Kath couldn't help but be alarmed when she saw how quickly the hard surface of the runway was rushing up to meet them. Barry did a splendid job, however, and landed the aircraft gently, bringing their first flight to a textbook perfect ending. After thanking him for taking them flying, the women walked towards the car park, Jillian laughing and talking excitedly about their wonderful experience.

Kath was more subdued but was still able to truthfully say, "That was amazing! I can't wait to check out the photos I took. I know there are some that'll be jumping out at me to paint them. Thanks so much, Jillian. I nearly chickened, you know? And, I must admit, I had some anxious moments up there, but I'm very glad I went through with it. It was wonderful!"

"It certainly was a thrill. I did notice you looked rather pale at one stage, but I'm glad you enjoyed it. And what beautiful weather! We could see forever! Can't wait to tell Dave and the boys! We'll have to have a coffee together soon, but I've got to dash now. Bye."

"Thanks so much for talking me into it, Jillie. It truly was amazing," Kath replied hugging her friend.

Jillian laughed. "I knew you'd love it," she called over her shoulder, as she walked quickly to her blue Honda and was soon driving away.

Kath walked in a daze over to her silver Mazda CX5 parked under a shady tree. Opening the car door, she settled herself behind the wheel and started the engine. She closed her eyes, images from the flight filling her head while she sat still waiting for the air con to lower the temperature before she buckled up, closed the door and slowly drove in to town, still feeling elated from the flight and pleased with herself for overcoming her fear.

✶ ✶ ✶

Kath headed for home, to the farming area where she lived on the Western Darling Downs of Queensland, about 20km from Dalby. The exhilaration from the flight had not worn off and she smiled as she remembered the amazing views. Suddenly, she noticed red and blue flashing lights in the rear-view mirror and, groaning out loud, she put on her left indicator and pulled over to the side of the road. She waited for the police officer to walk to her window and turning to look at him she gasped, "Oh no!"

It was Ricky Miller, a good friend of her sons, now Constable Richard Miller with the local police force and, to make matters worse, he had pulled her over for speeding only three weeks ago.

"Mrs. Wilmont," he smiled. "We meet again. Is there any reason for speeding this morning?"

"Oh, Ricky. What can I say? I'm so embarrassed. I've just had my first ever plane ride and I was still thinking about how wonderful it was. I just didn't realise that I was going too fast."

"Well, I know flying can be a real buzz but you were going 9km over the speed limit, and I did let you off last time with a warning. I'm afraid I'll have to write an infringement notice today. I'm sorry, Mrs. Wilmont."

"No need for you to be sorry, Ricky. You're only doing your job. I promise I will be more careful. How's your day going?" she enquired sweetly.

"Fine thank you, Mrs. Wilmont. I'll just be a minute or two," he replied politely, before heading back to his vehicle to check her licence details. Kath closed her eyes and shook her head imagining what Sam and the boys would say this time; they would happily torment her for days, weeks even. Ten minutes later with her speeding fine issued and the reprimand about road safety from the young officer duly noted she continued her journey.

The road was quiet and driving sedately, she soon arrived at her home, a farmhouse on a 600-hectare grain property. It was prime agricultural land with rich black soil plains that were renowned for growing high yielding crops. She stopped to check the mail box, an old cream-can hanging by short chains below a sign which bore the property's name 'Yallaroo'. The sign and the vintage can had been there when they first bought the property, and she had painted them both bright yellow to make a cheery welcome. Yallaroo was an aboriginal word, she had discovered after some research, that meant beautiful flowers. She always endeavoured to have something flowering in the house yard so that the property could live up to its name.

The driveway was lined with western white gums that always seemed to welcome Kath home, with their graceful branches and shiny green leaves waving over the gravel track. She parked the car in the carport attached to the old weatherboard home and stepped up onto the verandah that wrapped around the house on three sides. A happy yipping bark sounded from within, and then a little toy poodle shot out through the doggy door to dance around her mistress's feet, greeting her with an exuberant welcome as usual. The small dog had been a gift from Kath's family two years ago and had arrived on her bed on Christmas morning. The puppy had been a tiny ball of soft black fur, wearing a red collar with a bell on it, and so she became Tinkerbelle, or Little Tink for short.

Kath removed her shoes and tossed her car keys on the kitchen bench. Opening the fridge she poured a glass of cold water before walking out on to the verandah. Leaning on the railing, she gazed over the sorghum crop toward the Bunya Mountains, some 100 kilometres away. *'I've just flown over there',* she thought happily. This was her favourite view from home. The mountains were soothing to her soul, bringing back happy memories of family picnics, bushwalks, camping weekends and cosy fire-places.

She pulled her dark hair loose, letting it fall thick and silky below her shoulders. Standing 166cm tall, she had a trim figure that was the envy of many of her friends. The sun had sprinkled light freckles over her nose and cheeks despite regular application of sunscreen, but she had learned to live with them. She had inherited her mother's soft, plump lips, long lashes and beautiful hazel eyes of soft honey brown infused with green hues. If she wanted to highlight her features, she applied a touch of mascara and her favourite plum lipstick; otherwise a natural foundation and lip balm completed her simple makeup routine.

Kath taught part-time at one of the schools in town and had been job-sharing a Year 3 classroom for the last six years. She had a great working relationship, as well as a personal friendship, with Jenny her co-teacher. Kath had been teaching in some capacity since her graduation from university many years ago, juggling the responsibilities of being a wife and helping her husband, Sam, run their grain farm, while raising their three children. She had been employed in various capacities, including full-time, part-time and supply, depending on her stage of life and the time she had available. Seasons in the country could vary from being very good, to very tough when drought set in, necessitating some form of off-farm income. So, Kath worked as a teacher, while Sam managed the property and farming requirements, and it all seemed to balance out.

The sound of a vehicle approaching startled her, and she smiled when she recognised Sam's beaten-up old farm ute coming up the track from the back paddock. He pulled up at the machinery shed and carried something inside, his faithful red cattle dog, Nipper, following him in. Sam and Kath had been married for nearly 30 years and she had never thought it possible to love her husband more than she had on their Spring wedding day. But their love had deepened with time, and they shared a special bond that was strong and comfortable.

It was Sam who had rescued her from a miserable upbringing, and shown her that the world could indeed be a happy place where she was loved and appreciated. Together they had raised their children – Jarrod, Bryce and Jessica – in a loving supportive home. Sam was the one who had enabled her to grow into an accomplished woman, and she would be forever grateful to him for that. He had natural charisma and intelligent blue eyes that missed very little. He was not overtly handsome, although his light brown wavy hair, square jaw line and aquiline nose did him no disservice.

Kath's thoughts skipped back to Jillian and their adventure together in the sky that morning. Jillie worked as a Chaplain at the same school where Kath taught, and had given her many unofficial counselling sessions over the years, usually at one of the cafes in town, with strong coffees on the table between them. Her role provided a valuable service to the school community, becoming involved in the children's lives by simply listening, supporting and encouraging them. Although at times Jillian never seemed to stop talking, she was actually a very gifted communicator who was quick to pick up on moods and body language, intuitively knowing just when to speak and what to say. She had been a godsend to Kath and other teachers over the years, not to mention to the countless children she helped. Kath felt truly blessed to have her as a close friend and confidante.

Nipper's excited barking again interrupted her thoughts, and she looked up to see the crazy dog chasing pigeons that had been startled in the shed. A few minutes later she heard Sam's sharp whistle and Nipper immediately changed direction and raced back to the ute for the short ride to the house. Kath watched Sam walk back to the ute and get in behind the wheel, Nipper jumping in the back, barking happily at a flock of noisy corellas flying overhead. A small trail of dust followed the vehicle's progress to the front of the house yard where an old jacaranda tree gave welcoming shade beneath its thick green foliage.

"Look at you! You're filthy! I thought you were just going to clean up the machinery shed this morning?" admonished Kath, looking at his mud-covered clothes as he walked up the path.

"Well, that was the plan," he retorted, kissing her cheek before stopping to take his muddy boots off and dropping his battered felt hat on the verandah floor. "The pipeline behind the shed was leaking so I had to dig it up and do some repair work. All fixed now and, besides, a bit of mud never hurt anyone," he winked.

"Well, better mud than grease or oil, I suppose. How about you have a quick shower and I'll put the kettle on?"

"What? No hug?"

Kath pushed him away with a chuckle. "Definitely no hug! But you might get a biscuit or two with your coffee if you're lucky. Hurry up, I've got lots to tell you!"

"Ah yes, the plane ride, how was it?"

"Shower first and then I'll tell you. Scat!" she smiled.

Kath walked into the kitchen humming happily, looking forward to telling Sam all about her flight. She turned on the coffee machine and found the biscuit tin full of the jam drops she had baked yesterday. The kitchen was a favourite place for all the family and was a very welcoming room, with natural light from the large window over the sink that looked out over the northern verandah to the garden beyond. A large silky oak table and chairs sat in the centre, proudly bearing the scars of many years of use. An electric stove had been a welcome addition in the kitchen remodel many years ago. However, the old wood stove was left in place. It had warmed many a cold body and there was nothing better than the smell of a beef stew slowly cooking on the hotplate on a bleak winter's day. A potted fern sat elegantly on top of it during the summer months adding to the bright happy atmosphere of the room. A framed verse hung on the wall:

> *Love the LORD your God with all your heart and with all your soul and with all your strength. These commandments that I give you today are to be on your hearts. Impress them on your children. Talk about them when you sit at home and when you walk along the road, when you lie down and when you get up.*
> *Deuteronomy 6:5-7*

Kath, bursting to tell Sam about her plane ride, was sitting on the verandah with hot coffees and a plate of biscuits ready on a tray, when she heard his footsteps echoing down the hallway from the bedroom. When he joined her, she was surprised to see that instead of clean work clothes, he was wearing his good RM jeans, boots and checked shirt. He also wore a frown on his face and, when their eyes met, he said, "Sorry, change of plans. I've got to go to Toowoomba."

"What? Why?"

"The spare parts' mob just called. They've got the parts for the header I've been waiting for, and the fellow I want to talk to is finishing early today."

"Surely you can ring him and get the parts sent out by courier?"

"It's not that straight forward. He wants to see the old part and make sure its compatible, so I've got to take it in."

"Well, that sounds strange. He must know what you need. He is a machinery dealer, after all!"

"Kath, I have to go. Now!" he responded curtly. "Just pour my coffee into a travel mug and I'll drink it on the way. You can tell me all about your flight tonight," he added in a softer tone.

Kath stared at him questionably. "Tonight? But if you're only picking up parts you won't be home late, will you?"

"I've got a few other things to see to so I may as well do them all while I'm there."

"But Sam, today is Jarrod's birthday, and everyone's coming here for dinner. Remember? Jarrod and Majella, Bryce and Sally, and your parents," she listed them off.

"Oh yeah, I had forgotten about that," he replied another frown forming on his face. "I'll be home as soon as I can. Gotta go." With a quick kiss on his wife's unhappy face, he hurried down the verandah steps.

"Wait! I'll put your coffee in a travel mug."

Five minutes later, Sam was driving down the driveway in his Mazda BT50 ute, with Kath standing despondently on the verandah watching him disappear. She was still trying to make sense of it all, wondering why it was suddenly so urgent to get the parts today of all days. Harvest was still weeks away, and he was planning to go to Toowoomba in a couple of days anyway. Nothing made sense.

She turned and sat back down in her chair reaching for her coffee, mulling over everything in her mind, troubled by Sam's unusual behaviour. Little Tink came and curled up by her feet, sensing the tension in the air and looking enquiringly at her mistress and whimpering. Kath placed the untouched coffee back on the table and reached for her little dog, hugging the warm furry body. It was all so out of character for Sam, he seemed quite rattled about something and rarely did he get stirred up over anything, let alone picking up machinery parts.

The birthday dinner for Jarrod had been his idea in the first place and he had even rung everyone and invited them all, so how could he have forgotten all about it? They had been talking about it on the weekend and he knew Kath had been planning the menu for days and making preparations; another reason why having the flight this morning had been stressful for her. Thankfully, she had just finished making Jarrod's favourite dessert of chocolate mint cheesecake when Jillian had phoned yesterday. All she really needed to do was tidy the house, set the dining-room table and cook the roast beef and vegetables. Sam's strange behaviour had upset her and had really put a dampener on her exuberant mood. Even the speeding ticket had not spoilt her day, although she was still dreading telling Sam and the boys about it. They would tease her mercilessly as she had the worst driving record in the family.

Standing abruptly, she unsettled the little dog which had to quickly jump to the floor.

"Sorry Tink, but I think I need to go for a little walk in the garden. Coming?" The little dog yipped in reply, bringing a small smile to Kath's troubled face. "Let's go then."

Together they walked slowly around the garden, at least Kath strolled unhurriedly, Little Tink ran around excitedly, happily chasing shadows and butterflies. The path led around the back of the house to an old wooden building with a bright yellow door. Kath turned the handle and stepped inside. This was her special place, her retreat, her haven, her very own art studio; the place where she let her creative juices flow, where she had re-connected with her gift for painting. For many years she had purposely denied herself the joy of art, but now it was an important part of her life and brought her immense pleasure. Thanks to Sam's gentle encouragement, she had been able to rekindle the passion that had been so savagely extinguished.

The building was once the old wash house which had ceased being used when a new laundry was added to the house soon after she and Sam had moved in. The old shed was then used for storage until Sam and his father had worked together to renovate it. They had succeeded in totally transforming the old shed into a light and airy workspace. Once the main structural work had been completed, Kath had delighted in choosing the colour scheme and painting the ceiling and walls, searching second-hand shops for furniture, and buying the necessary art supplies to get started. The room was alive with colour, the aqua-themed walls, decorated with shells and pieces of drift wood, announced Kath's love for the beach. Colourful pots with indoor plants were placed throughout the well-lit interior, and posters and seascapes adorned the walls. Bright cushions and curtains completed the makeover.

She had been both excited and nervous to have her own space to paint in. She was worried that her old skills, not used for so long, may have deserted her and all the hard work of the renovation would have been in vain. But, with Sam's help, she had been able to overcome the painful memories associated with painting and quickly became immersed in all sorts of little projects.

Her love for art returned, and her skill improved as she experimented with new techniques and media. Now she supplied the Information Centre in town with hand-painted cards and small water-colour landscapes, and they sold quite well, much to her amazement. It was a wonderful release for her stress and frustrations; never failing to relax her tense muscles and calm her fears and worries. Such a blessing to have artistic talent with therapeutic benefits! The feeling of accomplishment she experienced when her artwork sold always thrilled her. *'No time to start anything now'*, she thought, resisting the urge to pick up a paintbrush. She knew she would become engrossed and lose track of time completely, and as much as she would like to paint, she did have a birthday dinner to prepare.

Her eyes were drawn to an old chair positioned in a corner so that an uninterrupted view of the distant mountains could be enjoyed through the window. She had purchased the old 1930s Genoa lounge chair after a winning bid at a clearing sale many years ago, and it was now a prized possession in what she now referred to as her studio prayer corner. The chair was covered in a rich mahogany brocade and was still firm and supportive, and oh so welcoming to sink in to. It was here that she often sat to read her Bible, or unburden herself, pouring out her heart to the Lord, seeking His will and guidance but, most of all, His comfort. A beautiful canvas with one of her favourite Bible verses written on it hung on the wall as a reminder of God's faithfulness.

Do not be anxious about anything, but in every situation, by prayer and petition, with thanksgiving, present your requests to God. And the peace of God, which transcends all understanding, will guard your hearts and your minds in Christ Jesus. Philippians 4:6-7

As her gaze lingered on the verses, she wondered how many times had she sought solace nestled in the beautiful old chair? How often had she felt wrapped in the arms of Jesus, the Holy Spirit covering her like a hen covers her chickens with her wings? This was the comfort and reassurance she sought now; that Jesus knew her heartache and would walk with her, giving her strength to endure whatever was brewing. She felt that something was not quite right; something was going on with Sam but she just couldn't figure it out. She turned her thoughts inward to her Heavenly Father, and prayed quietly for a while until she felt the peace that only God can give, settle her racing mind.

CHAPTER 2

Family

*"O Lord that lends me life, lend me a
heart replete with thankfulness."*
William Shakespeare 1564-1616

Jack Wilmont sat in his favourite squatter's chair and chewed thoughtfully on the end of his glasses as he watched his wife Edith happily
water her beloved garden. He had recently celebrated his seventy-seventh
birthday and still had a very sharp mind. He stooped slightly and walked
with a limp from an old knee injury, but remained quite active. His greying hair was thinning and, although having spent most of his life working
outdoors, he had managed to avoid the weather beaten look of so many of
his counterparts.

It was his eyes that really commanded attention, however, as they were
a deep piercing blue that seemed to look right into one's soul. His children
had all discovered at a very early age that it was impossible to look into

those eyes and say anything but the absolute truth. They had also realised that, more often than not, there was a very definite twinkle of mischief lurking in them.

Sam was their middle son, with Nate being the oldest, and Josh their youngest son, followed by their daughter Rosemary. Jack had been delighted to have three sons and often joked that he had scored a hat trick, to which his quick-witted wife would reply that he only sent them in, she had done the hard work of getting them out! The birth of a beautiful baby girl had completed their family perfectly.

They were a close-knit family and remained so, even though Nate and his wife Angela had moved to South Australia with their three children. Angela had grown up on a wheat property on the Eyre Peninsula, but had moved to Queensland after she married Nate. Their return to SA had been precipitated by Angela's father's decline in health which had rendered him incapable of farming the land any longer. Consequently, he and his wife had moved into a retirement home in Port Lincoln while Nate and Angie had moved their family into the sandstone-block homestead and taken over running the property.

Sam's younger brother Josh was not a farmer, although he loved the country and was proud of his heritage. He was the academic of the family, and had moved to Brisbane after finishing high school to study law at the University of Queensland. He had then worked for several years in the city where he met and married Bronwyn, an optometrist. They moved to Toowoomba when Josh was offered a position in a law firm and, after a frustrating few months, Bronwyn also found employment in her chosen field. They settled in the beautiful garden city perched on the top of the Great Dividing Range, raising their three daughters there.

Rosemary, the quiet daughter after three rowdy boys, was adored by parents and brothers alike. She was equally capable of driving the farm trucks and tractors as she was at cooking a three-course dinner. She had gained employment at a large electrical firm in town after she finished Year 12, and worked happily as an Administrative Officer for several years before marrying the boss's son, Craig. Now they ran the business together, living in town with their four children. Rosemary was still a great help to her parents, who lived only a few streets away. A heart attack had slowed her father down while her mother suffered from arthritis.

Edith was still a keen gardener, although some days it was quite a struggle as she battled against her stiff and painful joints. She stepped up on to the verandah carrying a small watering can. Not very tall, only 160cm, she was thin and somewhat fragile in appearance. Her silver wavy hair was held back from her oval face by two side combs, which emphasised her big brown eyes. She had a kind face and a ready smile which seemed to generate a peaceful aura around her. Jack and Edith had enjoyed a long marriage and still shared a deep bond of respect for each other; their love having endured many ups and downs over the years. They were totally devoted to each other and Jack knew that he was blessed indeed to have Edith by his side. Her calming influence and quiet strength and wisdom balanced his somewhat tempestuous nature.

"Better finish up now, love. Time we were leaving."

"Oh, really? I have lost track of time now, haven't I?" she smiled.

"You always lose track of time when you're in the garden. I'm sure those plants are more important to you than I am," Jack teased.

"Now you know that is not true, you old rascal," Edith replied swatting him playfully on his shoulder, "How ever do I put up with you?"

They were the first to arrive at the farm for the birthday dinner, parking at the rose-covered archway at the front gate at 5pm on the dot. Of course Edith did not come empty handed, and carried a pumpkin pie and a jug of homemade custard. Her cooking was renowned in the area and she had won many prizes at the Dalby show over the years. Jack followed her up the path to the verandah carrying a gift for their grandson's 26th birthday, chatting to the little dog who danced excitedly around their feet.

"Tink, come here," called Kath from the verandah. "Careful she doesn't trip you up!"

"She won't do that, she's just happy to see me. Aren't you, Little Tink?"

Kath went down the steps and reaching out took the jug from Edith before greeting her with a kiss on her powdered cheek, saying affectionately, "Hello, Edith."

Calling her mother-in-law by her Christian name had seemed the natural thing to do once she had married Sam, and Edith fully understood the special place that Kath's own mother held in her heart. She made no attempt to usurp that position. Edith's relationship with Kath could not have been closer, regardless of what she was called.

"Hello Kath, my dear. What a pretty blouse. That shade of blue really suits you."

"Thank you. You've had your hair cut since I saw you last."

"Yes, it was driving me crazy now the days are warming up. I'll just go and put this pie inside."

"Sure. Hello, Dad." She greeted Jack with a kiss on his clean-shaven cheek. It had been so easy to start calling her father-in-law 'Dad', as she had never used the term in her whole life. Jack was a true father-figure to her and filled the void that her own father had left dark and empty. Jack had never failed to treat her like his daughter, although she always respected the special relationship he had with Rosemary. However, both women had developed a close bond, each becoming the sister neither one had ever had.

"Hi love, how are you?" he enquired placing his arm around her shoulders.

"Just fine, thanks. Have you had a good weekend?"

"Pretty quiet. Caught up on some chores and dug up the veggie garden ready for planting. Where's Sam? Not still out working?"

"No, he had to go to Toowoomba to pick up some parts and he's not back yet. He shouldn't be far away."

"Oh, he told me he was going to Toowoomba on Thursday."

"Yes, that was the plan," smiled Kath, a little sadly. "But suddenly he had to go today."

She was determined to hide her true feelings, but Jack wasn't one to be easily fooled, and noticed the hesitancy in her voice and the slight change in her expression.

"Well, I'm sure he must have had good reason." Wisely changing the subject, he continued. "It's a shame Jessica can't be here tonight."

"Yes. She's tied up with meetings at work, and just couldn't get away."

"She works too hard, that girl! Reminds me a lot of Edith as a young woman; very independent. Quiet, too. Such a pretty thing, our Jess, looks a lot like her mother, you know," he winked. "I sure hope that accounting firm appreciates her!"

"I believe they do. She received a raise recently. She loves her apartment; it has a nice outlook over a park. It's rather small, but she's happy there. Considering she only finished Uni last year, she's doing very well for herself."

Nipper suddenly started barking loudly behind them, with Little Tink joining in with her high-pitched yapping. They both turned to see Jarrod and Majella coming up the driveway in their silver Prado.

"Ah, the birthday boy," smiled Jack.

"Come sit on the verandah, Dad. I'll bring some drinks and nibblies out."

Jack turned and followed Kath up the steps to sit on the cool verandah where he could look out at the garden and down the long driveway to the road. Soon his eyes were focused on the couple walking up the path towards him. He smiled warmly at Jarrod and Majella, calling out: "Hello, you two!"

"Hi, Grandad," they chorused back in unison, laughing at their shared greeting they turned and kissed each other on the lips. They were a striking couple, very much in love and not afraid to show it, kissing and cuddling constantly with a repertoire of endearments that were a constant source of amusement to the rest of the family. There was no mistaking Jarrod was Sam's son; he was leaner and a little taller at 188cm, but had the same blue eyes and wavy hair. His whiskers were darker and rather unkempt compared to his father's neatly trimmed moustache but his mannerisms and voice were just like Sam's.

Majella was the daughter of cane farmers from Tully in Far North Queensland. Her dark eyes, shiny black hair and olive complexion giving no doubt to her Italian heritage. They had met when Jarrod was an agricultural science student at the University of Queensland's Gatton campus. He had travelled to north Queensland on a study tour where his group had spent a week visiting properties in the Innisfail area.

He had fallen for Majella quite literally, she liked to joke. During a visit to her family's sugar cane property the skies had opened up in a torrential downpour, not uncommon in the summer months and, with his head down running for shelter in one of the sheds, he had run straight into Majella as she too sought a dry place out of the rain. They both landed in a tangle of arms and legs in the mud, fortunately with her on top. Struggling to stand up, they both slipped and fell again. Jarrod finally managed to stand and, with an embarrassed grin, helped the drenched and mud-covered beauty to her feet and into the shed where they both could not help but laugh.

Majella's father, Angelo, had witnessed the whole scene, and also found it extremely amusing. He called his wife Dafne out onto the verandah to describe the incident to her in rapid Italian. Dafne, not one to miss an opportunity on her daughter's behalf, insisted that Jarrod have a hot shower to clean up, and assured the bus driver that the student would be delivered back to the motel after he had joined them for dinner. Angelo, being a devoted husband and father, simply agreed to the plans of his beloved wife and settled down on the verandah, ready for an evening of good food, wine and conversation with their guest. And so Jarrod and Majella began their friendship which blossomed into love and, two years later, they were married in the old Catholic church in Innisfail.

After honeymooning in the beautiful Whitsundays and, with very tearful farewells to her parents, five siblings, and large extended family, Majella journeyed south with her new husband to begin their life together. They settled on Oakleigh, the original family property which still belonged to Jack and Edith. Oakleigh adjoined the property that Sam and Kath had purchased when they first married. When the older folk retired to town, Sam had taken over running Oakleigh, as well as Yallaroo.

The house on Oakleigh had been rented out, but the tenants had left so it was the perfect place for the newlyweds to live. It had been well maintained but Majella had wasted no time adding some modern touches to make the old farmhouse an enviable showcase of shabby chic on a shoe string. Kath had been a constant source of inspiration, and a great help tidying up the large established garden which was evidence of Edith's green thumbs.

Majella worked at one of the banks in town, but her aim was to run a small book-keeping business from the farm and she already had a couple of clients. Not enough to quit her job yet, but she hoped to grow her business and be able to work entirely from her home office within the next 12 months. She was very tech savvy, using multiple platforms to grow her business. Jarrod had worked for a company in town as an agronomist but now worked full-time in the farming business with his father.

Nipper's loud barking caused them all to turn to see who was coming up the track next. Kath was hoping it would be Sam, but the Toyota ute with the big spotlights and bull bar undoubtedly belonged to Bryce. The vehicle roared in, causing a cloud of dust to rise up behind it.

"Glad that wind is blowing away from us," remarked Jack dryly shaking his head. "Does he always drive in that fast?"

"That's slow for him, Grandad," laughed Jarrod.

"Yeah," added Majella. "You should see him coming up our driveway; he literally flies over the grid!"

They were still chuckling when Bryce and his girlfriend entered through the gate and started up the path.

"What's so funny?" asked Bryce, hand-in-hand with Sally.

"Just glad to see you, that's all," replied his brother, elbowing Majella.

Bryce just grinned and looked at them all questioningly with the same blue eyes as his grandfather, father and brother. He was shorter and stockier than Jarrod, but not by much, and his hair was darker. He had a strong muscled body that he kept in shape playing rugby. He also exercised in the gym in town after he finished work at the machinery company where he worked as a diesel mechanic. He was keen to be a full-time farmer too, but his parents had insisted that both boys gain a qualification and work experience off-farm first.

Sally was slim and athletic looking, with straight blonde hair hanging down her back, and baby-blue eyes. As a couple they were the epitome of health and fitness. They had been seeing each other for about 12 months. Sally was a nurse at the Toowoomba Base Hospital, but had worked at the local hospital in town for a few months before that. A mutual friend had introduced them and, after a rocky start, they had become an item, although with her shift work and the 100km distance between them, it was something of a long-distance relationship. Sally was a city girl through and through, and had never been west of Brisbane before starting her nursing career. Her lack of knowledge about farming and country life in general was a constant source of amusement to the boys. Fortunately, she had a good sense of humour and usually managed to laugh at herself also. She had certainly been on a steep learning curve with regard to life on a farm but, with her quick mind and great memory recall, she was more than up to the challenge.

After welcoming hugs for Jarrod and Majella, Kath went down the steps and greeted the new arrivals with a kiss and a hug. "It's lovely to see you again, Sally, it's been a while."

"Yes, I've had crazy shifts lately, but I've got three days off now so I can relax a bit."

"Well, that'll be nice." Turning to her youngest son, she added, "And what's your excuse Bryce? I haven't seen you for a while either?"

"Oh, c'mon Mum. I had lunch with you in town last Monday!"

"That was two weeks ago, Bryce!"

"Oh, was it? Well, I'm here now. Came out just to see you," he added, giving Kath another hug.

She laughed at his ploy. "I thought we were gathering for your brother's birthday?"

"Nah, it's all about you, Mum!"

Kath cuffed him playfully on his ear. "Pour Sally a drink, love. I've got to check the roast."

Friendly greetings and conversation followed Kath into the kitchen where she went immediately to check her mobile phone to see if Sam had called or messaged. No messages and, when she tried to ring him, it went straight to message bank. *'That's odd,'* thought Kath, *'why would he have his phone turned off?'* Shaking her head, she went to the oven to check the meat and veggies.

"Everything under control, dear?" enquired Edith coming up behind her.

"Yes. Not quite done but nearly. I'll just make some gravy and steam some carrots and greens. Hopefully, Sam will be here by the time everything is ready." Just as she finished speaking Nipper barked again and she could tell it was his happy bark indicating the arrival of his master.

"Well, about time!" muttered Kath.

Edith looked at her in surprise. "Everything okay? You seem a little upset."

"Oh, it's nothing, really, I've just been worrying about Sam. He's so late home, and I haven't been able to reach him all day. All good now," she finished with an over bright smile.

Edith took the saucepan Kath was holding. "I'll make the gravy; you go and say hello."

With a smile of thanks, Kath disappeared out the door, Little Tink hot on her heels.

Sam had driven around the back of the house and was just getting out of his ute when she arrived. Unbeknown to his wife, he had actually been parked out of sight on a side track, a few miles up the road, for twenty minutes or so as he composed himself for his arrival at home. His day in Toowoomba had been fraught with delays and frustrations that had affected him more than such things usually would have. Slow traffic, red lights, appointments running behind schedule and finally his conversation with Rose had left him feeling like he was spinning out of control. He had pulled the ute over, braking fiercely, and slammed his fists down hard on the steering wheel, quite uncharacteristic for him. He took a few deep breaths and got out to walk around the vehicle, kicking the tyres unnecessarily hard.

He had to pull himself together. No one must know, not yet. The charade of happy, contented family man must continue, specially tonight with everyone gathered together for Jarrod's birthday. He had tried so hard to find a solution to his dilemma, but there just wasn't one. Every time he closed his eyes, Rose's face swam before him, her eyes big pools of sadness. She had been kind but firm. No matter what he had said, the outcome remained the same. Every suggestion he offered was dismissed for various reasons. Surely, there was something he could do, he had asked in desperation, but she simply shook her head, her long black hair falling back over her shoulders and down her slender back. An air of finality filled the space between them.

"You must accept it, Sam," she had said as she ushered him out the door. But he wasn't ready to do that.

* * *

"Hello beautiful!"

"Hi darling, you look tired. What took so long?"

"Just a lot of running around." He reached back into the ute and lifted out a bouquet of flowers, "Sorry for rushing off this morning, and now I'm home late."

"Oh, they're beautiful and smell heavenly!"

"Am I forgiven then?" he asked pulling her into his arms.

"Have I ever managed to stay mad at you for long? You are a worry at times though. Is everything okay?"

"Yes, everything's fine. I just like to keep you on your toes." He smiled before kissing her.

"You are incorrigible, Sam Wilmont! I know where the boys get their cheekiness from!" Kath scolded. "Now come on, everyone's here and your poor mother is making the gravy for me."

"My mother could make gravy with her eyes closed and both hands tied behind her back!"

Laughing, they walked hand in hand towards the waiting family. The evening that followed was relaxed, with easy bantering around the table, and at last Kath was able to share about her plane flight. The home-cooked meal was devoured with gusto, not leaving any leftovers for the next day, a fact noted and bemoaned over loudly by Sam. He was not given any sympathy by his sons however, who were renowned for their hearty appetites.

"I'm sure Mum will manage to feed you tomorrow, Dad," commented Bryce as he finished his second helping of dessert.

"Yeah, what are you worried about, there's not even a slice of cheesecake for me to take home! And I am the guest of honour, after all!" Jarrod lamented.

More conversation followed before Bryce and Sally cleared the table and offered to clean up the kitchen while the others enjoyed the cool air on the verandah. Jarrod and Majella left first as they had an early start planned in the morning, followed soon after by Bryce and Sally. Sam looked exhausted, a fact that his mother was quick to point out, but he laughed it off and blamed his busy week and long day. Jack and Edith studied him carefully but neither made any further comment and they, too, decided it was time to head back to town.

Thanking Kath for the lovely meal and family evening together, they bid farewell. No sooner had they started their car when Sam declared he really had to go to bed. He drew his wife into his arms for a goodnight hug and kiss, and then walked slowly down the hallway to their bedroom.

"I'll read for a little while, won't be long," Kath called after him. He waved his hand in acknowledgement as he disappeared around the corner. Kath was not sure what to make of his early departure, as normally they would sit in the lounge room and chat for a little while and discuss the day, or the evening as it were, before retiring.

"Strange," she spoke quietly to her little dog. "But he has been busy this week."

Kath sat in her favourite chair, her eyes resting on the family portrait hanging on the wall above the fire place. It had been taken last Christmas and had captured them all beautifully; each one looking happy and relaxed. Jessica's resemblance to both her mother and grandmother could not be missed, and provided a strong link between the two older women. She was similar to her mother in many ways but she had the same brown eyes and wide smile as Edith and Rosemary. The family resemblance amongst the men was even more evident. Three generations of Wilmont men, with Jack being a wonderful patriarch and mentor for them all. He was so full of kindness and wisdom and was deeply loved and respected.

It was Jack who had been responsible for helping Kath find her worth, and fully understand how loved she was by God. Many years ago, before she had married Sam, he had noticed her looking sad and wistful one day when she was sitting with Rosemary on the verandah. He had gently enquired if she was okay, which had resulted in a torrent of words escaping from her quivering lips. In between hiccups and sobs, she had explained how alone and undeserving she felt. Being from a very dysfunctional family, she had never experienced so much kindness. She was trying hard to fit in, but she was afraid she would let everyone down. Jack had sat with the two young women and told Kath the story of Esther, a young Jewish girl, an orphan, who was taken from her uncle's home to become a part of the king's harem at his palace.

"Can you imagine how frightened and insecure she must have felt?" he asked before continuing. "But God had His hand on her and she found great favour with the king, eventually becoming queen and saving the Jews from destruction."

Jack had explained that it doesn't matter what your past is, or where you came from, we are all beautiful in God's eyes and He can lift us up to become royalty. He had told them they were both children of God, daughters of the King, beloved and cherished by their Heavenly Father. Kath smiled now at the memory of that night. She had asked Jesus to become Lord of her life some months earlier, but that night cemented the fact that God considered her worthy, so precious in fact that He had died for her. That was how great the Father's love was for her. She was part of a much larger family now, a worldwide one with many brothers and sisters in Christ and, best of all, Jesus had promised that the Holy Spirit would be with His children always as a constant helper, friend and guide.

A tear slipped slowly down Kath's cheek at the memory. Esther was now one of her favourite books in the Bible; a soothing reminder that she was not alone and never would be. A verse from Proverbs reiterated the value of her worth:

> *Her value is more precious than jewels*
> *and her worth is far above rubies or pearls.*

With a grateful heart she stood quietly, switched off the lights and walked peacefully to the bedroom where she could hear her husband snoring.

CHAPTER 3

An Unfair Life

"Hardships often prepare ordinary people
for an extraordinary destiny."
C.S. Lewis 1898-1963

*A*lthough she had succeeded at becoming a teacher, and had enjoyed a successful career in education over many years, Kath had never realised her dream to focus solely on her art. It had simply become a wonderful past time, a great hobby, and she happily painted as often as she could. She loved visiting galleries and art shows, and had visited many with Sam, who went along with her just to keep her company. He always did a quick walk around giving all the exhibits a cursory glance before finding a quiet spot to read a book, or pull out his phone. Kath didn't mind, she was just thankful he always made time to fit 'her cultural excursions' as he called them, into their business trips or holiday schedules. Of course, a good meal at a fine restaurant afterwards always sweetened the deal for him.

Kath was more than content to wander around galleries and exhibits by herself, taking her time studying each piece carefully, taking mental notes on the colours, textures and techniques employed, the different medias used, noting the artists' names and individual styles.

She yearned to commit more time and energy to her own art, wondering if she actually had any true potential waiting to be revealed; a masterpiece waiting to be painted, perhaps? Or would it always be just a creative leisure pursuit that would never amount to much? It saddened her to admit that she would be a much better artist now if she hadn't stopped painting for many years. Was it too late? That was the question. Kath sat back in her chair and stared out the window, as memories of her upbringing began crashing in.

* * *

William Baxter was a formidable man. As a child, Kath had been terrified of him. He was big and heavy-set, with bulging biceps and large hands. His hair was jet black; his eyes so dark they appeared black as well. He had a dark complexion reflecting back to his Lebanese grandmother. His overall appearance was menacing but, when he smiled, revealing his white, albeit crooked teeth, his countenance was transformed, making him almost handsome. He was proud of his powerful physique and kept himself in good shape. Having a big family with many sons was very important to him, and he never thought for a minute that he would not father strong boys to work on the farm and continue his legacy.

William grew up in the North Burnett area and met Suzanne Marriot when he was sent to his Uncle George's property near Bell to help when the old man became ill. Suzanne's appearance was a total contrast to his own, as she had golden blonde hair, fair skin and, as William thought to himself, hips that looked well suited to child bearing even if she was a bit thin. George Baxter passed away the following year, leaving his property, Chadwick, to William's father, Stuart, who told his son to continue managing it. After a brief courtship, where he presented as an ideal husband, William and Suzanne were married. Their union had been well received in the district as George had been known as a kind and hard-working man, just as his nephew appeared to be.

And so began their married life together and right from the start the pressure was on Suzanne to have a baby, or more specifically, a baby boy, as William considered this the primary reason for having wed his beautiful wife. William was ecstatic when, only a few months later, he learned that she was pregnant. Sadly, the joy quickly evaporated when Suzanne miscarried. They were both utterly bereft but Suzanne was further hurt and shocked when her husband snarled at her, "How could you let this happen?"

Try as she could, she could not make him see that it was not her fault. He was only consoled when she promised to try again for another baby as soon as possible. Further heartbreak followed when the next baby was also lost. The doctor was caring and sympathetic, and encouraged Suzanne to rest to allow her body to recover both physically and mentally from the trauma of the two miscarriages but, of course, William was adamant that she should give him a son as soon as possible. The third pregnancy was successful in that a son was born, but absolute disbelief and heartbreak followed when he was delivered still born. William just glared at his heartbroken wife blaming her for failing yet again.

The doctor at the hospital was shocked to witness the look on the distraught father's face, but was astute enough to suggest that Suzanne return to her parents' property to recuperate and give them both time to grieve. He knew Suzanne needed time to recover, and he was not convinced her husband would provide the love and support he knew the young woman required. He kindly suggested to William that he make an appointment to see him so that they could talk through his grief, but the man merely snorted, saying menacingly, "I hold you just as responsible for the death of my son as this useless woman here." He pointed a large finger at Suzanne's weeping face. "Next time we'll have another doctor, someone who knows what he's doing."

With that he rose, stomped across the room and slammed the door shut behind him. The doctor stared after him, shaking his head sadly before returning his gaze to look at his stricken patient and enquiring, "Perhaps you'll give me your mother's phone number, and I'll arrange for someone to come and fetch you? I will also make enquiries for the baby's burial. Just give him time. You both need time to grieve."

A week later a sobbing Suzanne stood beside her parents, her mother's comforting arm around her shoulders as the baby's tiny coffin was lowered into the cold, dark ground after the simple graveside service. William did not bother to attend. It was nearly 12 months later when Suzanne discovered she was pregnant again. She was both excited and concerned by the knowledge. She knew William would be pleased, but what if she lost this baby too? She doubted she could bear the anguish again and, as for William, she was frightened to think how he would behave if she failed to produce a son this time.

William had never seemed to recover after the loss of their baby boy, and their marriage had been under terrible strain ever since. Certainly nothing she had done or said since that heartbreaking time had pleased him. He had become distant with her, obviously blaming her for their childless marriage. He criticised everything she did, and everything she said, constantly putting her down and pointing out her failures. There was the briefest of smiles on his face, however, when she did work up the courage to tell him the news, but it quickly disappeared as he stood over her and shook his fist in her face saying softly: "Well, you had better get it right this time, hadn't you?"

It was a difficult pregnancy and, even though Suzanne was constantly feeling weak and tired, there was no respite from her daily regime of home duties and farm chores. If anything, William expected more from her, thinking to toughen her up rather than allowing her to take the rest she so desperately needed. What thought processes went on his mind, Suzanne could only wonder, as she plodded through each long demanding day, helping to feed out hay, move stock, milk the house cow and tend the large vegetable garden they relied on, not forgetting to make butter, bread and prepare the huge meals her husband expected. So, it was no surprise when she felt the first contractions several weeks early. After a short but intense labour the cries of a tiny infant could be heard. With great hope and trepidation Suzanne asked the doctor what sex it was.

He smiled broadly. "You have a beautiful baby girl, Mrs. Baxter. Small, but seemingly strong by the noise she's making."

The exhausted woman smiled feebly, tears falling gently down her pale cheeks as she wondered just how badly her husband would react this time. Once she was comfortable, the doctor left the room to give the father the good news, but he returned a few minutes later frowning and shaking his head.

"Your husband has left. Gone to spread the good news I presume," he stammered in confusion, not telling Suzanne that William had sworn profusely at him, cursing his wife and his newborn daughter.

Suzanne, however, saw the look on the doctor's face and could well imagine what had transpired outside in the little hospital waiting room. A feeling of dread besieged her, as she thought about what life would be like when she returned home with the baby. But then a nurse appeared and placed a tiny bundle in her arms and gazing down at her daughter's face, a love like nothing she had ever felt before overwhelmed her.

"What are you going to call her?" the nurse asked gently.

"Kathleen," was the quick reply. "After my little sister who died when she was 12. I adored her, and I miss her still."

"How lovely," the nurse replied as she quietly left the room to allow mother and baby to get acquainted.

Although, the baby girl was only 2.4kg in weight, she thrived, growing stronger in her mother's tender care. Their bond had been instantaneous, and Suzanne never doubted that this child would survive.

William had come back two days after the birth to collect his wife and 'the child', as he referred to the baby, and was taken aback when the doctor informed him that he was keeping Suzanne and the baby in for another two weeks to make sure there were no complications with mother or baby. William argued that he needed his wife at home, and that lying in bed for so long would only make her lazy. The truth being he was already tired of batching and wanted his wife to come home and cook for him and take on her chores again.

However, the doctor was adamant, and stared the selfish man down with a look that broached no further argument. Without even speaking to his wife, or looking at the baby, and knowing better than to make a scene in such a public place, William abruptly left. Suzanne was alarmed by what the doctor had said and spoke up as soon as the noise of the heavy footsteps and slamming door had subsided.

"But doctor, you said we were both fine, what are you concerned about?"

Turning, the doctor smiled and said reassuringly, "Why nothing at all, you are both doing very well indeed Mrs. Baxter, I just thought a little more rest would be good for you. It's far too early for you to go home yet." And with a meaningful look and a wave he left.

Suzanne sighed and cuddled her little daughter closer, whispering to the sleeping babe, "What a kind man the doctor is, my darling. I think he knows what we'll be going home to. But don't you worry; I promise I will look after you and keep you safe."

Exactly, two weeks later William appeared again and curtly told Suzanne to hurry up and get ready. The staff all knew that there was no reason to keep her or the baby any longer and, with heavy hearts, they wished her well and watched the popular young woman leave with her odious husband. The drive home was tense, but thankfully the baby slept. William was lost in his own thoughts, still mortified that his only surviving child, after years of loss and heartache, was a girl. He was only interested in sons, big strong healthy boys who would grow up working on the farm. Big strapping boys who would become big manly men, just like him.

Suzanne was starting to doze off when William's loud voice startled her. "We'll call her Victoria, Vic for short, after my father," he stated without bothering to look at her.

Suzanne replied quietly. "Her name is Kathleen, after my sister."

He thumped the steering wheel. "No, the name is Vic."

"I know you wanted a son called Victor, and I'm sorry that wasn't to be. You didn't come to visit me so we couldn't discuss it so, on the forms for her birth certificate, I put Kathleen Victoria. It's done. We'll call her Kath."

She waited for the outburst but surprisingly he said nothing, just stared at the road ahead, his face turning red. So, Kathleen Victoria it was, and it was one of the few battles Suzanne ever won with her belligerent bear of a husband. William showed little interest in the baby except to complain if the care of the child meant his meals were not prepared on time, or his wife was not available to help him when he instantly required her assistance. The idea of discussing what his plans were for the day, and letting her know when she would be needed, never occurred to him. She was his wife and she was expected to be at his beck and call, baby or not. No other child was ever forthcoming, and he berated her often about her inability to bear him a son who would ensure the farm and his family name would continue.

Little by little he wore Suzanne down with his constant criticisms and ridicule. William Baxter made bullying an art form and, once his daughter was old enough to understand, she too was victim to his vicious verbal and mental onslaught. Sadly, both of Suzanne's parents had died within months of each other when Kath was only a toddler, and William would not let her visit any of her other family members, so there was no one for her to turn to for support. He rarely raised a hand against either his wife or daughter, but he threatened constantly. He was very good at throwing things that would crash into the wall within inches of their faces, causing them to jump in fear, much to his great satisfaction. He also enjoyed threatening them with his clenched fist, or his thick leather belt which would thump ominously against a chair leg or the door when he felt the need to assert his authority further. Slowly, day by day, he chipped away at their self-esteem and confidence. It was only her mother's love and gentleness that gave Kath any comfort or hope, and it was her mother who sheltered her as much as possible from her father's loathing and quick temper.

It happened when Kath was about six years old, that she forgot to lock the hens in, a necessary chore to keep them safe from hungry foxes. Her father had noticed the chook-house door open when he drove past on the tractor on his way home for dinner. He entered the kitchen like a raging bull and dragged Kath forcefully from the table where she sat quietly waiting for the evening meal. She had cried out in fright as he dragged her outside by her arm, growling obscenities at her and telling her she would be punished for her laziness. She tried to escape but he merely thrust her under his huge sinewy arm and marched up the hill in the cold windy darkness to the old building. He threw her inside and with spittle flying from his evil mouth said menacingly, "You stay there all night and learn yourself a lesson about doing your chores! Stupid, useless girl!"

He slammed the bolt in place on the outside of the weathered door and thundered off back to the warm house. Alone and very afraid, Kath had curled up in a ball on the filthy ground below the perches and nesting boxes, shivering in the cold and weeping in total misery. She eventually fell asleep and was woken sometime later by her mother calling her name and pushing open the squeaky, old door. Half asleep, Kath looked up in fear and saw her mother's face framed in the torch light, looking like an angel.

"Come, Kathleen. Let's go home," she said defiantly, against the cry of the wind.

Together they had hurried back to the warm kitchen where Suzanne washed and dried her daughter in front of the wood stove and dressed her in clean pyjamas. After a cup of warm milk and some mutton stew, Kath was bundled into her bed with her mother sitting by her side comforting her. She fell asleep to the sound of her father's loud snoring coming through the wall of her tiny bedroom, and her mother's soft, trembling voice reciting something over and over. After straining to hear, she had managed to recognise the verses of Psalm 23 that her mum had taught her:

> *The LORD is my shepherd; I shall not want.*
> *He makes me to lie down in green pastures;*
> *He leads me beside the still waters.*
> *He restores my soul;*
> *He leads me in the paths of righteousness for His name's sake.*
> *Yea, though I walk through the valley of the shadow of*
> *death, I will fear no evil; for You are with me;*
> *Your rod and Your staff, they comfort me.*
> *You prepare a table before me in the presence of my enemies;*

You anoint my head with oil; My cup runs over.
Surely goodness and mercy shall follow
me all the days of my life;
And I will dwell in the house of the LORD forever.

Kath woke up the following morning to the sound of her father shouting. She huddled deep under the blankets, terrified that he would come into her room. She finally wriggled out some time later after she heard the kitchen door slam shut so forcefully the walls rattled. She dressed slowly and ventured out to find her mother sitting in a chair by the stove, rocking slowly back and forth her arms clasped around her waist.

A large bruise was already showing on her right cheekbone and her eye was swelling shut. Kath walked slowly over and, kneeling down, lay her head in her mother's lap, knowing full well that this injury was the punishment for rescuing her last night. How she loved her mother, but oh, how she hated her father. That was the first time William Baxter had struck his wife. Sadly, it wasn't the last…

CHAPTER 4

A Whole New World

*"We must accept finite disappointment, but
we must never lose infinite hope."*
Martin Luther King 1929-1968

*K*ath was nervous and excited when she caught the school bus for her
first day of school. She had never been to a playgroup, or kindy, or
socialised with other children at all, so she had butterflies dancing crazily
in her stomach. However, she needn't have worried.

She soon discovered that going to school was like visiting another planet,
there was laughter and playtime, and the teachers were kind, patient and
encouraging. She hurried through her morning chores at home, grabbed
her lunchbox off the table, packed her school bag, and peddled as fast as
she could on her old bicycle down the driveway to the mailbox. She always
worried she would miss the bus and have to stay home, because she knew
her mother would never be allowed to drive her to town if that happened.

It was her daily escape to freedom for five days of the week. She went to a place she loved to be, where her mind was like a sponge, soaking up information and experiences, enthusiastically engaging in everything offered, looking in amazement at her friends who complained about having to attend school. She excelled in all her subjects in primary school, and the years seemed to fly by. Soon she was wearing a new uniform and going to high school. Despite the heavy workload at home before and after school, she managed to keep up with her schoolwork.

Kath had always loved to draw, and first started when she was given crayons by her mother when she was very little. Then, one Christmas when she was eight years old, she received a water-colour paint set. Nothing could have pleased her more. From that moment she was fascinated by all artwork, and created her own childish paintings. Her skill developed, and she would often escape to her tiny bedroom to sketch and paint when she could.

Her favourite past-time, however, was to sit somewhere outside on the farm, in a spot where she wouldn't be seen, and draw pictures of the sky, the crops, the birds, whatever captured her fancy. Her teachers encouraged her, and she entered pieces into the local show and the school fete. She was thrilled when she won first place one year. Her mother even took her to the Dalby Show, and she was incredulous when she saw the blue ribbon hanging on her painting of the wheat crop with the Bunya Mountains in the background.

As she progressed through the year levels, school became more demanding and she often struggled to find the time at home to complete all of her required assignments and assessment pieces on time. Most of her teachers happily granted her extensions as they knew she was bright and hard-working, and guessed that her home life was difficult, although Kath never complained and was always quick to assure them that everything was fine.

Her mother was her proud supporter and encourager while her father only wanted to know if she had done all the jobs he gave her to do. He took little interest in her schooling, expecting her to leave after her 15th birthday so she could work on the farm. It had been a bitter battle between her parents that went on for some weeks, but eventually Suzanne persuaded her husband to allow her to stay on and complete Years 11 and 12. Kath never knew what really transpired between them, but she didn't believe that her mother's broken arm and bruised face were the result of her falling off a ladder in the shed. The incident was never clarified; she was simply told by her mother that she could go to school for another two years, as long as she did the additional chores her father had added to her already heavy workload.

As she advanced through high school, her painting skills developed further. It was a wonderful escape for her, and time would pass by unnoticed when she was absorbed in her artwork. One afternoon, after she had placed a casserole in the oven for dinner, she went into her bedroom to finish a painting for her art class the next day. Unfortunately, she lost track of time, totally forgetting to set the fire place with kindling and fill the wood box with the split wood her father had chopped. Her bedroom door was thrown open and there stood the menacing form of her enraged father.

"You useless girl!" he roared. "Wasting time on this nonsense and not doing your work!"

He picked up the nearly finished painting and, ripping it apart with his big brutish hands, he continued slowly. "There will be no more painting, do you hear me?" His face was so close to hers that she could feel his hot breath and smell the foul odour of the tobacco he smoked. He looked at her walls, at the paintings and sketches stuck all over them, and slowly, one by one, he pulled each one down, watching Kath's horrified face as he tore them up.

"No more," he repeated in a low growl. "The sooner you finish school the better. Learning is a waste of time on a stupid girl. You better be prepared to work here full-time, or have a job before this year ends. Time you started contributing some funds for your keep, or there'll be hell to pay!"

Kath was now staring at him with her mouth gaping open. She couldn't remember when he had last spoken so many words to her. He usually spat out succinct orders or harsh criticisms. Theirs was a mostly quiet house, with little conversation except between Suzanne and Kathleen when they were alone. Once William had destroyed everything he could see – thankfully Kath's pieces for her final assessment were under her bed out of sight – the wind seemed to leave his violent egotistical sails and he merely said quietly, so quietly that Kath could barely hear him: "Any more painting in this house and you'll be sorry. You and your wretched mother. You'll both be sorry."

He turned, slamming the door behind him as he always did when enraged. He threw a kitchen chair over, as he stomped outside.

William Baxter's narcissistic ego had suffered a crushing blow when he was denied male children. It was something he had never been able to reconcile. The fact that it was not a personal affront, and neither was it a deliberate act by his wife to humiliate him, never crossed his mind. He believed he was totally justified in feeling cheated and, worse, he did not think he was respected as the strong and virile man he believed himself to be. He had continued to blame his wife from the day their daughter had been born over 16 years ago, daily regretting his decision to marry her. He had thought Suzanne was a good strong country girl and would be excellent at child bearing, but now he saw her as a pathetic failure. Strangely enough though, deep within him, at odds with his other irrational thought patterns and behaviours, he believed in the sanctity of marriage. They had been married by a priest in a church, and that was that.

He believed his treatment of his wife and child was completely justified. He totally dominated them, as his father had dominated him, his brothers and their mother. It was the only parenting style he had known. At least he didn't take his belt to the child, he thought valiantly. Regular beatings had been the norm in his family. His mother had been nearly as rough as his father, but at least she had borne five healthy sons. That William had never physically abused his daughter was something Suzanne daily thanked God for.

When both William's parents drowned trying to drive across a swollen creek the year Kath was born, William was fortunate to inherit Chadwick. His younger brothers received equal shares in the family property but decided to sell it, along with the machinery and stock, and divide the proceeds. The youngest boys disappeared to Victoria, while the two remaining sons bought a property together and moved to New South Wales. All contact was lost between the brothers as communication within the family had never been a priority. There was no love lost between any of them; all they had ever known was hard work and violent tempers.

Suzanne knew the tirade in Kath's bedroom, culminating in the destruction of her precious artwork, would be a cruel and bitter blow to her daughter. When she saw the farm ute speeding down the road, she went quickly to comfort her. Kath sobbed into her mother's shoulder, trembling badly with reaction to her father's wrath. Finally, when she had calmed, she lifted her tear-streaked face and asked her mother the question she had voiced many times over the years.

"Why don't we leave, Mum? We could work out a plan and escape. I know we could," she pleaded.

"He would not rest until he found us. And then I hate to think what he'd do, to you as well as me. I must protect you. I married him for better or for worse, I just never imagined it would be this awful. But you, my girl, must leave as soon as you graduate. Somehow I'll prevent him from finding you."

"No, Mum. I won't go without you. Either we both go, or we both stay."

Their desolate tears mingled as they hugged. Kath knew her mother would never leave. Perhaps years ago she might have seriously considered it, but now she was too defeated, too tired and too terrified to try. And so they both stayed. As she surveyed the mess in her room, Kath vowed to finish high school, and then find a job in town so she could stay and support her mother as best she could. Her father's cruel condemnation of her art, and his ultimatum that she never paint again or he would harm her and her mother, felt like it was burned into her inner being. Part of her died that day.

Suzanne aged considerably during Kath's schooling years. She worked hard on the farm; feeding pigs, hammer milling grain, whatever her husband demanded. She was obedient and submissive for she knew the penalty for being argumentative. William hired contractors to assist with harvest, and a workman was employed to help out during other busy times but, regardless, there was never any respite for his wife. She managed to shield Kath as much as possible from William's violent and spiteful nature, and was grateful that he was quite dismissive of his daughter. As long as she completed her rigorous list of chores, he left her alone. She was like a thorn in his side, a constant annoyance, so it was best she kept a low profile and stayed out of his way.

She had been expected to do all the cooking and cleaning for several years now, as well as the washing and ironing, although thankfully there was not much that needed ironing. Kath also had to clean the kitchen up after each meal, which her mother always intended to help with but she was simply too tired at the end of the day. William kept them all well fed at least, with money enough to stock the cupboards and he made sure they were well dressed as keeping up appearances was paramount to him. Not that they went to town very often or received visitors. Kath was forbidden to bring any friends home and neither was she allowed to visit anyone.

They rarely socialised but, when they did, they were expected to play 'happy families'. And William was happy; his farm was well run and productive, the seasons had been good for several years now, his wife and daughter were totally under his control and, though he never commented, he did know that Kath was doing well at school and was secretly proud, not of her, but that a Baxter was going to complete high school. He made their lives a misery and, although most people were aware that he was a hard man, they didn't begin to appreciate just how appalling the lives of his wife and daughter were.

With the end of the school year quickly approaching, Kath considered her options. Although she had promised to stay at home and support her mother, more than anything, she wanted to leave and study to become a teacher. Suzanne knew this and bravely raised the topic of tertiary studies with her husband as she wanted her daughter to break free from his power. But of course, William was furious when he learnt that Kath wanted to continue studying instead of working on the farm or getting a job in town. He ranted relentlessly, his voice loud and scathing at the idea of a university course. He would not consent, and issued all sorts of vile threats against them both if Kath dared to leave the farm.

It was a tumultuous time all through Kath's final exams and during the lead up to her graduation. She'd learned to survive on limited sleep, as it had been necessary to do her homework and assignments late into the night after her chores were completed, so somehow she managed to satisfactorily complete Year 12. Her results would have been much better if she had been allowed time to focus on her studies but, to her credit and determination, they were good enough to consider studying Education at the University of

Southern Queensland in Toowoomba. She was not allowed to attend the School Formal but her mother was permitted to attend the graduation ceremony and see her receive her Year 12 Certificate. Unbeknown to William, Suzanne still encouraged her daughter to apply for the university course.

Deeply disappointed that her desire to go to university was not to be, Kath began looking for work in town. Her manner and results were well regarded by potential employers and she was, much to her surprise, offered two jobs almost immediately. She accepted a position as a receptionist at a busy medical practice in town, and commenced work just before Christmas. In January she was both thrilled and saddened to receive an offer of placement in the Bachelor of Education course at USQ. The only one she shared the news with was her mother, who hugged and congratulated her. After a brief discussion, Kath decided to defer for a year, as it seemed more positive than the dreadful reality of declining. Kath settled in to her new job and enjoyed her role at the clinic. She was diligent and hardworking, and more than met her employer's expectations, but it was not a fulfilling role for her. She ached to become a teacher. She thought about it constantly, and kept the dream alive in her heart.

CHAPTER 5

The Circle of Love and Life

"He who counts the stars and calls them by name is in no danger of forgetting His own children." Charles Spurgeon 1834-1892

*K*ath met Sam Wilmont properly when he came into the surgery late one afternoon with a deep gash on his lower leg. He had crashed his motorbike on the farm. It was a rather embarrassing accident as he had ridden straight into a wire gate that he himself had closed just an hour before. He simply told the doctor that he was hurrying back to the shed, going a bit too fast, with the Sun in his eyes. His mother smiled knowingly, but made no comment.

Kath recognised him from school, although he had been a couple of grades above her. He seemed more handsome now than ever, even if he was covered in mud and blood. His eyes were alive, and his wide-open smile showed white teeth against his tanned skin. He seemed to know who she was, and was very appreciative of her assistance in showing him and his mother to the surgical room to wait for the doctor to tend his wound.

Two days later a yellow rose and a thank you note were left at reception for her when she was on lunch. The note simply read: 'Thanks for your care and attention the other day, Sam'.

The other staff teased her good naturedly, and she blushed crimson, but was very happy to receive the thoughtful gift. The following week he appeared at reception again.

"Hello Sam. Your stitches aren't due for removal yet," she smiled shyly.

"Yes, I know, but I was wondering what time your lunch break is?"

"Oh!" she could feel herself blushing again. "It's between 1 and 2. Why?"

"Well, I was wondering if you would have lunch with me?"

That was the beginning of their friendship. They talked long and easily, feeling very comfortable with each other. Sam, who was nearly finished his apprenticeship as a mechanic, was outgoing and a terrible tease, Kath quiet and introverted, but they clicked and their relationship blossomed. Suzanne was her only confidante, and her mother was pleased that Kath had met a nice boy. Her father of course flew into a rage when he eventually learned that Kath was going out with Sam Wilmont. Not that he had anything against Sam personally; he didn't even know him or his family. He simply didn't like anything happening outside of his control, and he certainly wasn't going to allow Kath to reduce any of her workload at home to spend time gallivanting around with a boyfriend. It was not easy for Kath to hold down a full-time job, run the family home, and make time for a relationship, but somehow she managed it.

Sam was in awe of all she did but shocked to discover what her home life was like. It was such a stark contrast to his own carefree upbringing. When Kath first visited Sam's home and met the rest of his family, she just sat quietly observing their friendly behaviour, revelling in the peaceful atmosphere. There was so much laughter and multiple conversations all happening at once, teasing but, above all, kindness and respect. There was no yelling, cursing or angry demands, just a group of people who obviously cared about each other and enjoyed being together.

It was at the end of winter that year, just after Kath's 18th birthday that her mother became ill with a heavy cold. Kath encouraged her to rest as much as possible but, of course, William demanded she get out of bed and help him outside. The south westerly was icy and tore through her old coat as if it were made of tissue paper. When Kath returned home from work that evening, she found Suzanne collapsed on the kitchen floor. She managed to wake her and help her to a chair when her father came storming in. Kath wanted to call an ambulance but he would not hear of it. However, when Suzanne again passed out after another coughing fit, he relented.

"If you're so worried, you drive her in!" William growled and unceremoniously picked his unconscious wife up and carried her out to Kath's little Toyota Corolla. Without a backward glance he hurried back to the warm kitchen.

The hospital staff were very efficient, and Suzanne was quickly bundled inside. The diagnosis was pneumonia but Kath sensed something worse, a foreboding fear wrapped itself around her anxious heart. She visited every day, before and after work, and grew increasingly alarmed as there was little improvement, the antibiotics seeming to have little effect. Her mother seemed to stop fighting, she was weak, frail and exhausted. She had nothing in reserve and was without the will to live. The doctor rang William but the conversation was one-sided. William did not bother to go to the hospital as requested. His mood had been worse than ever with Suzanne away, especially when Kath was home late each evening and he had to wait for his dinner. Nonetheless, he showed no concern for his wife's failing health.

Early one afternoon, Kath received a call at work from the hospital asking her to come immediately. She rang Sam as she feared the worst and knew she would need his strength, but his mother answered the home phone and explained that he was working out of town for the day.

"What's wrong Kath?" a concerned Edith then asked, responding to the evident distress she detected in the girl's quavering voice.

"Oh, Mrs. Wilmont. It's my mum. She's not doing well and now the hospital has rung telling me to go there straight away. I just don't think I can do this on my own..." her trembling voice broke.

"Then how about I meet you there, my dear? I would be more than happy to," the older woman suggested compassionately.

"Oh, really? Would you? That would be lovely, thank you," was the soft reply.

"I'll be about 30 minutes though."

"That's fine. Thank you so much."

Kath didn't know Sam's mother all that well, but knew she was a kind Christian lady and the thought of her comforting presence at the hospital was a great relief. Declining an offer by one of her colleagues to drive her, Kath hurried to her old car and drove the short distance to the little country hospital. When she saw her mother, tears once again filled her eyes. Suzanne lay still, her face the same colour as the white pillows she was propped up on. Kath sat beside her bed and reached for a frail work hardened hand as she bent over her mother and cried despairingly, "Mum, please try to get well. I need you. Please don't leave me."

Suzanne opened her tired eyes and smiled wanly at her daughter. Her breathing was laboured and she was being given oxygen. She closed her eyes and seemed to doze. Kath just sat quietly watching her, tears flowing down her cheeks. A nurse came in briefly to check on Suzanne, but left quietly after patting Kath gently on her shoulder and saying gently, "She's very weak but she's comfortable, not in pain. Just talk to her, she's been asking for you. The doctor will be in soon to speak with you."

Kath nodded and tried to talk, but the words would not come. It was all too hard, so unfair. Her mother had never deserved the harsh treatment she had endured for so many years, but she had borne it all bravely, paying the price to keep her daughter safe and well cared for. Kath had always hoped that one day she could take her mum away, let her enjoy the rest of her life, and not be afraid, but now she could see that dream disappearing. Kath was lost in her thoughts and didn't realise Edith had arrived until she felt her hand on her shoulder.

"Oh, Mrs. Wilmont," she cried. "She's not getting better."

Edith pulled another chair over to sit beside the distraught young woman and put her arm around her shoulder, which was Kath's undoing as she couldn't help but sob into the older lady's shoulder. After a few minutes when Kath had calmed, Edith asked quietly:

"Have you spoken to the doctor?"

"The nurse said he would be in soon."

Right on queue the doctor, a man of similar age to Edith walked in, obligatory stethoscope hanging around his neck.

"Hello Kath," he spoke quietly, before turning his attention to Edith and offering her his hand. "I'm Dr. Newell. Are you a friend of the family?"

"Well yes, sort of. Kath is my son's girlfriend and, as he's away at present, I offered to come and be with her."

"Very good," he smiled sadly, focusing his kind eyes on the obviously upset younger woman, "I'm glad you have someone here to support you, Kath. I did ring your father but he said he was busy."

"He won't come," Kath said quietly. "How ill is my mother? Please tell me the truth doctor."

"She is very weak and her heart has been affected. You need to prepare yourself for the worst, I'm afraid. I don't think she will last much longer."

Kath held her mother's hand tighter, and cried softly as the doctor nodded sombrely to Edith then left the room. About half an hour later, after some prompting from Edith, Kath was speaking quietly to her mum trying to recall some happy times, and telling her how grateful she was for everything she had done for her over the years. Suzanne stirred and opened her eyes focusing on her daughter's face.

"So glad you have Sam now, darling. He seems such a good young man, just right for you. I've seen how happy you've been." She spoke so quietly, slowly and with great effort that both Kath and Edith leaned closer to hear her words. "Leave the farm, Kathleen. Don't go back. Leave!" she said as forcefully as her weakened body would allow her. "Break free, please my girl," she implored looking fiercely into Kath's eyes now. "I want your life to be so different from mine. I love you so much, my bright and shining star. You're what kept me going all these years. I love you," she gasped finally, relaxing back on the pillows, eyes closed.

"Oh no, Mum! Oh, Mum! How will I go on without you?"

Edith watched Suzanne's chest move slightly with each tortured breath. "Hush now. She's sleeping. That was a huge effort for her." She placed her arm around Kath's shoulder once again. They sat quietly for another two hours, speaking softly, with Edith also quietly praying for both Suzanne and her heartbroken daughter. Kath told her that her mother had a little Bible hidden away at home, and had read it to her every so often throughout her childhood. She had taught her to pray the Lord's Prayer and to recite Psalm 23 and John 3:16.

"How lovely to know those beautiful scriptures, my dear. Shall we say them now? It might be a comfort to your mother?" Kath nodded in reply and, together, the two women from different generations, families and backgrounds, drew strength from the ancient words they recited softly from memory beside the dying woman's bedside.

Kath then began to sing Amazing Grace, also taught to her by her mother when she was very young, and Edith readily joined in:

Amazing Grace, how sweet the sound
That saved a wretch like me
I once was lost, but now am found
Was blind but now I see
'Twas Grace that taught my heart to fear
And Grace, my fears relieved
How precious did that Grace appear
The hour I first believed
Through many dangers, toils and snares
We have already come
'Twas Grace that brought us safe thus far
And Grace will lead us home

They concluded with John 3:16, one of the key verses in the Bible:

For God so loved the world that He gave His only begotten Son,
that whosoever believes in Him shall not perish but have eternal life.

Afterwards, they resumed their faithful watch, speaking softly to each other and to Suzanne. The nurses came regularly into the room, careful not to intrude more than necessary on the final precious moments before a death that would soon separate a beloved mother from her precious daughter. Suzanne did not open her eyes again and her breathing grew slower and shallower until with one final shudder she breathed her last.

Kath cried out and fell on her mother's still chest and sobbed uncontrollably while Edith wiped tears from her own eyes, privileged to have been able to comfort Kath at such a time and deeply saddened as she began to understand what the home life for these two women had been like. Her fervent prayer had been that Suzanne was at peace with God. From what Kath had told her she believed she was, and had been taken to Heaven to be with Him. One day mother and daughter would be reunited again. No sickness, heart ache or pain; just happiness and joy in the Saviour's presence.

* * *

Later that evening, back in her home on the farm, and after the dishes were done, the kitchen tidied and the house was quiet, Edith entered the lounge room smiling secretly at Jack as he looked up from where he sat reading in his favourite chair. She stood quietly; searching through her book case, beaming with pleasure when she found what she knew was there. Within moments, she had opened the well-worn book to the correct page and, with glistening eyes, slowly read one of her favourite poems that seemed to perfectly reflect the life and death of Suzanne Baxter.

Gently closing the book, she wiped her tears away, turned and looked tenderly at Jack, who responded with a wink, not saying anything to interrupt her mission. He then watched her gather her stationary set and favourite pen from out of the old bureau that sat in the corner, before slowly exiting the room, leaving him to ponder what she was up to. He knew she would share with him later when she was ready, for they had no secrets. With his mind full of loving thoughts for his kind, caring and sometimes mysterious wife, he returned to reading his book, a tiny smile flickering across his face.

When Edith returned to the kitchen she sat down at the table and selected a sheet of cream coloured paper from her stationary compendium, decorated with doves and lilies. She kept the beautiful paper for special occasions like this; or for writing thank you notes or letters of encouragement for friends and loved ones. Opening the little book of anthology, she copied the words in her own beautiful handwriting. After reading the poem once more, she folded the sheet of paper and tucked it in a matching envelope before writing Kath's name on the front.

She placed it on the mahogany sideboard that matched the table and chairs; a beautiful suite of hand-crafted furniture that adorned the large kitchen. Probably the most important room in the old farmhouse, it is the heartbeat of the home; where countless meals had been shared and many heart to heart discussions held. Everything seemed better when accompanied by a hot cup of tea and a piece of cake. Tempers cooled, heads cleared, troubles eased, and minds, both young and old, discovered new ideas and ways forward. Grace and forgiveness offered and received. Reaching to turn off the light, Edith thanked the Lord again for His goodness and mercy, and asked that the beautiful words in the poem would comfort the grieving young woman presently residing in the guest room down the hall.

Perhaps
she will land upon That Shore,
not in full sail,
but rather,
a bit of broken wreckage
for Him
to gather.

Perhaps
He walks Those Shores
seeking such,
who have believed
a little,
suffered much
and so,
been washed Ashore.

Perhaps
of all the souls redeemed
they most
adore.

CHAPTER 6

Bringing in the Sheaves

"When we work, we work. When we pray, God works."
James Hudson Taylor 1832-1905

*I*t was a perfect autumn day in March. Sam smiled, thankful for such a great start to the sorghum harvest. The big machine he was driving moved quickly down the rows of rust-coloured stalks standing straight and tall before the big harvester. After several years of poor rainfall and poorer crops, this one was a beauty, and Sam knew the yields would be good.

The spring rains last September had resulted in a good moisture profile ready for the planting in October. The rain then seemed to fall just when it was needed throughout the growing season, the seeds sprouting quickly in the fertile black soil, with green shoots soon reaching upwards towards the sky. Sorghum and cotton were the main summer crops grown on the Western Downs. Wheat, barley and chick peas predominated the winter growing season.

Nothing pleases a farmer more than seeing his crops flourishing and forming full heads of grain. Well, nothing except getting the harvest completed and the money in the bank. Sam loved his work; taking care of the soil, managing the water, controlling the weeds, planting the seeds, growing crops that supported his family by providing grain for a variety of local markets and for export.

Heavy dew had fallen last night so it was after 11am before he made his first short run in the header, as the combine harvester was commonly called. The moisture meter in the big machine registered below the maximum of 13.5% permissible for safe storage of the grain, so he was right to go. The sorghum would continue to dry out as the day progressed so, barring any mechanical breakdowns, the harvesting could continue late into the night, stopping only when the moist air descended and the moisture reading went up again.

Sam was grateful that Jarrod was now working with him full-time, and Bryce was able to have time off from his job to assist with the harvest, as it was always 'all hands on deck' when the grain was ready. He would hate to waste one moment of the fine weather they were presently experiencing so, with the three of them available and working together, they were making great progress. He was still amazed that they were having such a dream run without any breakdowns and, as Bryce hadn't been called away by his boss, he could only assume that others in the district were also going well. It would do wonders for the community in general to have a good harvest, as it would lift the spirits of the hard-working farmers who had really been doing it tough during the previous years of drought.

"How're you going, Dad?" The radio interrupted his thoughts, but he smiled to himself as he thought of his youngest son and Sally.

"Going well thanks. Won't be long and I'll need you to pull up here so I can empty the bin."

"Righto, just tell me when. Me and Sal are waiting back here behind you."

"Okay, I'll give you a call shortly."

Bryce and Sally were sitting quite happily in the cab of the big tractor, eating fruit cake for their 'smoko'. They were enjoying having their morning tea together in the confined space.

"Why did your dad say he would need you to pull up there? I thought that when the header is full of grain your dad will come here and empty it somehow into the trailer?" Sally asked with a puzzled look on her face.

"Well, you're nearly right," Bryce responded. "The grain will need to be emptied into the bin we're towing, but he keeps going and we drive up to him."

"Really?"

"Yep, when the bin on the header is nearly full, Dad will call on the radio and tell me so I know it's time to drive up beside him and position the chaser bin, that's the trailer you mentioned, in the right spot so he can transfer the grain into it. Then the header doesn't have to stop and can keep on harvesting while augering the grain out at the same time."

"What do you mean augering?" Sally was confused.

"Well," said Bryce thinking how best to explain the process to a girl who had never been involved in a grain harvest before, and certainly wasn't familiar with all the machinery necessary to operate a successful farming business. "Do you remember watching that old movie the other night about the hijacked plane, and they refuelled up in the air?"

"Of course. But what has that got to do with this?" she asked perplexed.

"Be patient," he admonished, dropping a light kiss on the end of her nose. "I'm trying to explain."

"Okay, so explain what planes have to do with tractors and a grain harvest, Mr. Farmer."

Grinning, Bryce continued. "It's really quite simple. The plane carrying the extra fuel pulled alongside the jet with the bad guys and the hostages on it and a flexible hose was sent from one plane to the other and then the fuel was pumped across, while each plane flew at the same speed. Remember that?"

"Yeah, of course!"

"Well, same principal here. The header keeps harvesting and Dad hits a switch to move the auger, it's like a big pipe, out to 90 degrees and, when I have the chaser bin lined up directly below the auger, he hits another switch and the grain is augered out of one bin into the other. Both machines move along at the same speed and, when the header bin is empty, Dad positions the auger back in place and keeps harvesting. I then drive the chaser bin back to the mother bin and the grain gets augered into it. It stays in the mother bin until it's loaded into a truck and taken back to the silos or to the grain depot."

"Mother bin! You've got to be kidding me?" Sally chortled.

"No seriously, we call them mother bins. They're a huge mobile storage bin, like a big trailer that sits in the paddock so the chaser bin doesn't have to wait for a truck to arrive to empty into; makes the whole process much more efficient. Of course, if the truck is handy, the header will just empty straight into it. All bases covered." He smiled.

"Wow, I suppose farming really is a big business; so much land, all the big machinery."

"So much work, so much debt!" groaned Bryce, rolling his eyes.

"Well, you obviously love it, or you wouldn't be here helping out; counting down until you can quit your job and farm full-time. You've grown up with it, and respect the land. I've just taken my food for granted. I guess I just go to the supermarket and buy what I want. I really am impressed you know," she added sincerely, looking deep into Bryce's eyes. Her focus was just moving down to his mouth when the tender moment was interrupted by the radio.

"You there, Bryce?"

"Yeah, Dad." He smiled ruefully at Sally.

"Come on down when you're ready. Bin's nearly full."

"Righto. On my way." Giving Sally a quick peck on her cheek he put the big John Deere tractor into gear and headed north from the gravel pad, where the silos stood beside the machinery shed, down a well-worn track bordered on each side by paddocks of sorghum.

"There you go, Sal. That's the mother bin." He pointed to the big blue grain storage bin sitting by the track as they drove past it. "It's about 4m wide and 15m long and it'll hold about 130 tonnes of grain, while the little bin we're towing will only hold about 20 tonnes, and the bin on the harvester holds about 12 tonnes."

"You sure know your stuff, Bryce. I would never remember all that."

"Well, like you said, I've grown up around this sort of machinery and, like most farm boys, I love it. You, on the other hand, are very knowledgeable about what you do. I could never be a nurse; I hate the sight of blood!"

"Well, no wonder you became a diesel mechanic then. How come your boss gave you time off for the harvest?"

"He's an old mate of Dad's. He's given me time off as long as I stay on call 'cause there's bound to be plenty of call outs for breakdowns. So I'll just help as much as I can. Dad and Jarrod can manage on their own, no worries, but I like to be involved too. Here comes Dad. Now you'll get to see it all in action," he grinned happily.

* * *

The harvest continued with early starts, long days, and clear starry nights. The machinery performed well, with no breakdowns, which in itself was miraculous for many harvests have been disrupted with breakdown after breakdown, with parts soon in short supply, and servicemen run off their feet. But for the Wilmonts, this harvest was a dream run. The grain was taken off and transported to the silos for storage, with moisture content in acceptable levels. What had so far been delivered to the receivable depots had all been given excellent grades. The men were all in good spirits finding it hard to believe everything was going so well. Although it was an exceptionally busy time, and everyone was bone tired at the end of each day, they were grateful for all that they were able to achieve, and for the good weather and especially that the end was in sight.

Kath was worried about Sam though. He looked extremely tired and had developed a cough but, of course, he said it was nothing, just too much grain dust and not enough sleep. He wasn't running a temperature so she didn't think he was ill, but even so she tried to keep him hydrated and resting whenever he had an opportunity. He seemed to have lost his appetite but, with driving the header, managing the logistics of trucks, chaser bins, silos, augers and off farm deliveries, Kath knew he was stretched to the limit. It was the same every harvest. Even with Jarrod and Bryce both more than capable of handling pretty well anything, Sam was always involved with everything. And so it became a very long, demanding period.

Towards the end of the harvest, with only about 30 hectares left to go, the accident happened. Sam had stopped for lunch but remained in the cabin of the header, his thoughts immediately turning to Rose. She was a beautiful woman. Born in Australia, her Indian parents immigrated from New Dehli when they were very young. The words from their last conversation haunted him day and night. He knew he should be stronger, rely totally on God, but he seemed to be stuck in a black vortex of denial. He didn't want to hurt Kath or the children, but how could he prepare them for what he had to say. He groaned inwardly, desperately wanting to confide in someone. But he wasn't ready to just yet.

Agonising over his quandary, he opened the door to climb down the steps but, being consumed by darker thoughts, he missed the first step, lost his grip on the rail, and slipped. He fell heavily down the steps of the big machine, bouncing off each metal rung to land on the hard compacted gravel below. Jarrod was sitting in the tractor about 20m away and saw his father pull up and open the door and, when he looked back a minute or two later, he was horrified to see his father's crumpled body lying on the road.

He quickly turned the tractor's engine off, jumped to the ground, and sprinted over to where his dad lay in the dirt. Blood was flowing freely from a large gash on his forehead, and he was unconscious. Thankfully, Jarrod could see his chest rising and falling. Speeding up the steps into the cab he grabbed the first aid kit and flew back down to his father.

"Dad! Dad! Can you hear me?"

No reply and no movement. Quickly pulling a cotton pad out of the kit, Jarrod placed it firmly on the bleeding wound and did a rough job of securing it in place with a bandage. He then sped back up the steps in to the cab and called Bryce on the radio, having left his phone in the tractor.

"Bryce! Dad's fallen out of the header and knocked himself out. There's blood everywhere. Call an ambulance!"

"What?" gasped Bryce in surprise. "Where are you?"

"Down behind the pump shed. Hurry!"

"How'd he do that?"

"Later Bryce. Just call a bloody ambulance. Quick!"

"Right, right. I'm on it."

Ten minutes later Bryce roared up in the old farm Toyota and, braking hard, covered Jarrod and Sam in a blanket of dust.

Jarrod looked up angrily. "Did you have to do that, you idiot?"

"Sorry, sorry, just a bit freaked out," responded Bryce hurrying over. "There' so much blood!" he added, going pale.

"Yeah, he's got skin off everywhere. Why don't you go wait at the gate and show the ambos the way in?" Jarrod spoke more gently to his younger brother.

"Sure, good idea," agreed Bryce, turning away quickly from the sight of his unconscious father.

Fortunately, living only 20 minutes from town meant Jarrod could soon hear a siren approaching. Although, to the two young men waiting anxiously, it seemed like hours before two paramedics were kneeling beside Sam's inert body, checking his condition. He had slowly regained consciousness, but was very groggy and obviously in a lot of pain. Jarrod and Bryce were relieved to step back and let the professionals take over. They were very efficient and, after examining Sam's injuries, they re-bandaged his head, splinted his arm, placed a brace carefully around his neck and then gently placed him on a stretcher before moving him into the ambulance. It wasn't long before the man, who had introduced himself as Mike, came over to speak to the brothers.

"Well boys, he's sure knocked himself around a bit. He could have a bad concussion to go with that head wound, a broken wrist, and maybe a few damaged ribs as well. We'll get him to the hospital and they'll do some x-rays and go from there. I'll need a few details from you before we go, if you wouldn't mind?"

"Sure," replied Jarrod.

They had just finished talking when the other paramedic, an older man with a kind face and soft voice, joined them and patting Jarrod on the back said, "Don't worry; we'll take good care of him. You did a good job with your first aid, by the way," before settling quickly into the driver's seat and heading off down the track. Once they were on the main road the lights and siren were turned on and they sped off towards town and the hospital.

Jarrod and Bryce both stood in the hot sun, arms akimbo, watching the receding vehicle and said simultaneously, "We'd better call Mum."

Turning, they gave each other a sad little smile and, holding his hand out for Bryce's phone, Jarrod stated, "I'll do it."

* * *

Kath was busy supervising a craft activity with her young students when there was a knock on her classroom door. She smiled when she saw Warren, the Principal, standing in the doorway. But her welcoming countenance quickly changed when she noticed the worried look on his face and a feeling of apprehension stole over her. She'd been working with Warren for many years, and they had become close friends.

"Please continue quietly," she instructed her class as she hurried outside.

Warren put his hand on her shoulder and said quietly, "Jarrod just called. Sam's had an accident."

Kath gasped, and covered her mouth with her hand.

"Now, he's all right," Warren added quickly. "But he's on his way to the hospital in an ambulance."

"What happened?"

"Apparently he slipped when he was climbing down from the header, and knocked himself out. I'll ask Stacey to drive you to the hospital."

"No, it's not far. Thanks for the offer, but I'll be fine."

"Well. If you're sure? Stacey can take your class for the rest of the day then. Here she is now," he added, as a young teacher aid arrived. "Off you go."

Kath hurried back to her desk to gather her handbag and car keys. Stacey followed her in and said quietly, "I'll tell the children you were called away. Don't give work a second thought."

"Thanks."

Kath walked quickly to the car park, fumbled with her keys, and stopped to take a deep breath before unlocking her car and getting in. She prayed a silent plea for help to her Heavenly Father before driving to the little hospital, her hands trembling on the steering wheel. She quickly parked her car, not very straight but now was not the time to be pedantic about parking lines, and hurried to the emergency entrance, pushing the lock button over her shoulder as she went. Of course, her old school friend, Leanne, was working at the reception desk, but her welcoming smile changed to a 'Kath, what's happened?' question, as she took in her friend's anxious face.

"It's Sam. He's had an accident. He's being brought in by ambulance."

"You sit down for a minute. I'll grab his file and see if he's arrived." Leanne pointed to the row of plastic chairs in the waiting room.

She returned promptly. "He's just arrived, and they're wheeling him in, so give them a few minutes and then I'll take you through. Would you mind coming to the counter and we'll check if his details are all up to date?"

Kath nodded absently to Leanne's questions about personal details, health insurance, and so on. A few minor details needed changing but it was all basically correct, and she began to feel faint as she recalled the last time she had filled out hospital forms for Sam; the awful memories flooding back in a dark torrent. Leanne was a good friend and an observant medical receptionist. Noticing Kath's sudden pallor, she quickly led her back to the waiting room chairs.

"Sit down, Kath. Deep breaths now. I'll get you some water."

Thankfully, the emergency department was not very busy, and the other receptionist needed no help handling the front desk, so Leanne sat down beside Kath and handed her a plastic cup with cold water in it.

"Come on now, don't think the worst. This is probably just a bump and a scratch. We know how tough he is."

"Yes, I'm sure you're right, but just being in here brings it all back. I nearly lost him then," she whispered, tears in her eyes.

"Now, now, that's all in the past." Leanne patted her hand reassuringly before rising. "I'll go and see what I can find out."

Kath sat upright in the waiting room chair, praying fervently that Sam was okay. She could feel her neck muscles tensing with worry. She tried to relax, but couldn't, and was about to rush down the corridor to find Leanne when she saw her friend returning with a smile on her face.

"You can come through now. He's asking for you. He's got a nasty cut on his head, and he's covered in blood, so don't get a fright," she warned.

The strong hospital smells of antiseptic assailed Kath's nostrils. Almost squinting in the bright light reflecting off the squeaky-clean floors, she hurried into the triage room and, despite being warned, she was shocked to see her husband with so much blood on his face, shirt and hands.

Sam spoke first. "I'm okay," he said. "Don't worry, just need a few stitches."

"You look terrible!"

He was very pale, and looked anything but okay. He closed his eyes after his initial greeting, coughing and grimacing in pain. Kath wanted to touch him, but his left arm was in a splint, his head bandaged, neck brace in place, and a nurse was busy checking his vital signs. All she could do was touch his leg reassuringly. Sam responded with a tired little smile and, before she could say anything, the doctor returned. He was young, but spoke kindly and efficiently as he conversed with the nurse before turning to address Kath.

"Mrs. Wilmont?" he enquired with a lift of his brows.

Kath could only nod.

"I'm Dr. Heswell. Your husband is a lucky man. He doesn't appear to have any major injuries but, before we remove the brace, I'd like to perform some tests and, of course, a number of x-rays, namely head, chest and arm. We're giving him something for the pain but I am concerned about the wheeze in his chest, and his BP does seem a little high, but that of course could just be because of the recent trauma."

Another nurse hurried in and spoke urgently to the doctor in a low voice. Nodding, he turned his attention back to Kath.

"I'm needed elsewhere, but I'll return once your husband's x-rays are completed and we'll go from there."

With that he hurried from the room, the partitioning curtain flapping noisily behind him.

Kath moved closer to Sam's bed again, and saw that he was looking at her.

"Stop worrying," he rasped. "I'll be fine. Looks worse than it is, they're just being cautious. A few stitches and a bit of plaster on my arm maybe, and I'm outta here." He smiled feebly but she knew he was just trying to set her mind at ease.

"Oh Sam, you really scared me. I should have made you stop and let the boys finish the harvest; you've been so tired and coughing all the time. Just listen to your breathing now!"

"Kath, stop!" he said with as much authority as he could muster lying on his back in a hospital bed, still shaken up and hurting. "It was just a silly accident, not your fault at all. I should have been more careful."

Kath did not reply as he started to cough again and, with his injured ribs, the pain was obviously excruciating. She was standing there feeling terribly helpless with tears rolling down her cheeks, when two orderlies bustled noisily in to the room. Seeing her distress, they stopped and apologised for interrupting before explaining they were ready to take Sam to the x-ray department. The taller of the two men was very loud, but he was also a very happy character and it was difficult not to appreciate his sunny disposition. As they were wheeling Sam's bed out, he looked at Kath kindly as she wiped away her tears.

"Don't worry love, we'll look after him."

Kath smiled thankfully and blew Sam a kiss before he was whisked away. She turned and surveyed the small room, empty now except for various items of medical equipment and emergency paraphernalia, most of which she had no idea what they were used for. She was not comfortable in hospitals, but resigned herself to wait. She had just sat down on the nearest chair when her phone sounded the arrival of a text message. It was from Jarrod.

"What's happening, Mum? Is he okay?"

She shook her head at the phone, the boys always sent texts, rarely calling, but for once she was glad to receive a text message as she really didn't feel like talking. She always asked her children to ring not text, but they just laughed and called her old fashioned, to which she always responded that they were typical of young people today, afraid of one-on-one conversation. It was a common source of teasing in their house. Jessica was her most frequent caller, and sometimes the boys surprised her, but not often.

"Just gone for x-rays. Hopefully nothing too serious."

"Okay. Talk soon," was the quick reply.

"How does he type so fast?" she asked herself, shaking her head again. Exhaling loudly, Kath settled down to wait for Sam's return, her thoughts flitting from one thing to another. She tried to remain positive but it was difficult, almost as if some negative force was trying to pull her in a direction she did not want to go. She fought to remain calm, and desperately prayed for God to be her strength and give her courage, and for the x-rays to reveal nothing too serious. She focused on her breathing, and all the positives in her life, the many things she had to be grateful for, and gradually she regained her inner calm. "Thank you, Lord," she whispered knowing she was not alone.

It was still a very long 45 minutes before she recognised the voice of the cheery orderly, and heard the sound of the bed being pushed back to where she waited. She stood as the men arrived, looking anxiously at her injured husband.

"Don't look so worried. It's just a badly sprained wrist with a bit of a cut on it, and a few cracked ribs," Sam advised.

"What about your head? Look at the size of that lump! I can see it under the bandage!"

"Yeah, well. Head's a bit sore, I'll give you that. But haven't I always said I've got a thick skull? X-ray lady said no damage to my ol' noggin." He ended the sentence with a coughing fit.

"Well, that's good news but you still look awful."

"He's tougher than he looks, I'll wager," the cheery orderly smiled. "We'll leave you to it. All the best, Sam."

"Thank you, gentlemen," Kath said as they left the room and another nurse came in.

"Hello Mr. and Mrs. Wilmont, I'm Candice. Dr. Heswell has been called away to an emergency but he has checked your x-rays, and asked Dr. Yates to suture your wounds and bandage your arm, Mr. Wilmont. Then he'll come and see you as soon as he's free. He'd like to discuss your x-rays with you."

"But what does he want to discuss? Is there something wrong with Sam's head?" Kath asked, concern rising in her voice.

"Just standard procedure, Mrs. Wilmont. Dr. Heswell is in charge of the ED and he was your husband's admitting doctor, so he would like to speak with you. In the meantime, we'll get treatment started," she explained efficiently and then, with a bounce of her ponytail, she walked out of the room in her super-quiet shoes.

"So professional. But she looks so young!" Kath smiled at Sam. "Or are we just getting older?"

Sam just smiled tiredly in reply. "Don't hang around here waiting, Kath. Take a break. Go tell my parents before they hear some dramatic story from Bryce. You know how he loves to exaggerate. Oh, better ring Jessica too."

"But I don't want to leave you here alone."

"I'm feeling really drowsy, must be the pain meds they gave me. And who knows how long 'til the first doc comes back. Besides, I'm sure you don't want to watch them sewing up my head? You'd pass out!" He smiled. "Off you go, love, I'll see you later."

"Well, if you're sure? And you're right about your parents. I'd better go see them. And I completely forgot about poor Jessica, unless one of the boys thought to let her know. But I won't be long, my poor darling." Bending down she kissed him goodbye on his pale cheek.

Sam closed his eyes, thinking how much he cared for his wife. He didn't want to hurt her, and his resolve nearly crumbled. '*Am I doing the right thing?*' he wondered for the thousandth time in the last few months?

"Oh Lord, I'm so sorry. Please forgive me. Give me courage. I know I'm doing this all wrong," he whispered. He felt so very tired, but thankfully his troubled mind was silenced as sleep stole over him.

CHAPTER 7

A Change of Plans

*"Sir, my concern is not whether God is on
our side; my greatest concern is to be on
God's side, for God is always right."*
Abraham Lincoln 1809-1865

After watering her treasured ferns, Edith turned and smiled at her
husband.

"You look a million miles away, Jack. Everything okay?" she enquired, a
light frown replacing the smile.

"Everything is just fine, love," he replied. "Just thinking how lucky I am.
The good Lord has certainly been kind to me. I have a beautiful wife and
four children that make me very proud. We have our health, our home and
our grandchildren. What more could a man ask for, eh?"

Edith walked slowly over to him. He knew she could see right into his
heart and mind, and had realised that something was amiss. *'How does she*

do that?' he wondered as he had done so many times over the years. He had never been able to keep anything from her, she had an uncanny knack of knowing when something was afoot.

"What's troubling you?" she queried softly as she sat down beside him and took his work-hardened hand in her softer one.

He looked into her eyes, all at once relieved to share his thoughts. He had been wondering whether he should tell her about the disturbing dream he just had.

"I dozed off and had the strangest dream. It's rattled me a bit, love. I'm not sure what to make of it and I don't want to think the worst."

"Tell me about it, and let's see if we can't nut it out together."

"Well, it's about Sam. We were walking through the back wheat paddock, just checking out the crop, and suddenly, he was gone, disappeared down a huge crack in the black soil. I looked down and I could see him about two or three metres below. So I yelled out for him to wait while I went to get a rope. But when I got back, I looked in and he was gone. And this is where it gets really strange, next thing I'm driving back to the shed and I see him climbing up the ladder on the big silo, you know, the one with the little safety platform halfway up?"

Edith nodded her head, totally engrossed in the story.

"Well, he stops at the halfway mark, stands on the little platform, and waves at me, a big smile on his face. But he doesn't come down, he turns around and keeps climbing higher up to the next level, and then I couldn't see him anymore, and I woke up. It was the strangest dream, yet it felt so real, like Sam is going somewhere and was waving goodbye."

Edith was quiet for a few moments, and then said, "Well, you know Sam's been talking about going to South Australia to visit Nate and Angie? I did hear you ask him on the phone the other night when they were going away. Maybe your mind is playing around with that?"

"Yes, I did ask him about the trip, but somehow I feel there's more to it. Pray with me love, would you?"

"Of course," she smiled.

And there, in the cool of the wide verandah, they bent their greying heads, closed their eyes and as they had done for decades, prayed together for their family, Sam in particular, asking their Heavenly Father to bless them all and keep them in His care.

When they had finished, Jack felt more at peace and squeezed his wife's hand.

"Anything else, dear?" she raised her eyebrows in question.

"No, nothing more, except some lunch perhaps? You don't want me to fade away now do you?" he questioned cheekily.

"You'll survive another ten minutes, I'm sure!" she countered with a laugh and, standing slowly, she disappeared into the house.

Jack sat on the verandah for a little while longer, thinking about his disconcerting dream and, then shaking his head, stood wearily and joined his wife inside. A minute later Rosemary arrived to have lunch with them as she often did. Jack joined in the easy chatter with the two women, but his thoughts kept returning to Sam and Kath. Little did he know that his daughter-in-law was just slipping past reception at the hospital, hoping she wouldn't be noticed as she left to drive to her in-laws' home. She didn't feel up to talking to Leanne just at present, her compassionate nature would be her undoing so she decided she would catch up with her when she returned.

Much to her relief the reception desk was quite busy, and she was able to walk by unnoticed. On settling in the car, with the air-con blasting, Kath rested her head on the steering wheel and gave way to the tears that had been threatening to overwhelm her for the last hour. She needed the emotional release, especially before visiting Sam's parents. She loved her in-laws dearly, but knew she would never hold herself together in their caring presence.

Kath was not surprised to see Rosemary's red vehicle parked in their driveway, as she knew Rosemary visited frequently to check up on her parents. She didn't need to knock as Jack had heard her arrive and now stood on the verandah to greet her, but his welcoming smile faded when he studied her face and noticed her puffy red eyes that indicated she had been crying. He felt a flutter in his chest, knowing something was wrong.

"Why Kath love, whatever's the matter?"

"You don't miss much, do you Jack, still as observant as ever." She smiled feebly before kissing his wrinkled cheek. "Sam's had an accident, but he's okay," she added quickly.

"Oh Lordy me, come inside so Edith and Rosemary can hear too. Mother!" he called urgently, "Rosie! Kath's here!"

The two women hurried from the kitchen, hearing the anxious tone in Jack's voice, one an older version of the other, leaving no doubt of their relationship.

"Jack, whatever's the matter?" Edith echoed his earlier statement.

Then both women looked at their visitor and blurted out in chorus,

"You've been crying! What's wrong?"

"It's Sam," Jack interjected. "Let's all go and sit down and let the girl speak."

Kath told them about Sam's accident, emphasising several times that he would be fine. He'd just need some rest and time to recover from his injuries.

"Oh, thank the Lord that it wasn't more serious," Edith spoke at last in a quivery voice. "Those machines are so big, and so high. It's a long way to fall, let alone bouncing down the steps!"

"Yes, poor fellow," Rosemary added. "The boys must have been worried sick waiting for the ambulance to arrive! But Kath, have you had anything to eat? We're just about to have lunch and there's plenty. You need to keep your strength up!"

"I'm fine, Rosie, really. I was just so worried." She burst into tears again.

"Come, my dear, the worst is over, he'll be fine. We all know how tough he is," Edith gave her a hug, before rising and adding, "I'll put the kettle on and make you a cuppa and a sandwich, can't have you passing out on us too." She smiled kindly at her daughter-in- law.

"Do you have to pick him up, or are they going to keep him in for a couple of days?" Rosie wanted to know.

"His doctor was called away, but he arranged for another doctor to see to his wrist and the stitches, but the first doctor, I forget his name, wants to meet with us to discuss the x-rays so I can't stay too long."

"You know how long these things can take," said Rosemary. "Relax for a bit and have some lunch. You'll feel better then, and be right to go back to the hospital. I can drive you up if you like?"

"Thanks. But I'll be fine, really."

Kath knew they were right and she should eat, and she also knew that she had no hope of leaving before the obligatory cup of tea and sandwich had been consumed. Once they ganged up, the Wilmonts were quite a force to reckon with, but they always had the best of intentions at heart. She knew from past experience how strong and protective they could be, and she loved them all the more for it. Sometime later, she looked at her watch and gasped at the time. Phone calls to Jarrod and Jessica had taken longer than she expected, on top of sitting around the kitchen table chatting to Jack, Edith and Rosemary while they ate lunch together.

"I've got to go, I don't want to miss the doctor," she blurted out rising to her feet and looking for her keys and phone. After hasty goodbyes to everyone she was soon on her way back to the hospital ED. On arrival, she found a lady she didn't know working at reception and, after introducing herself and explaining the situation, Kath was once again escorted to Sam's bed in the treatment room.

He looked up and smiled as she entered, looking a little brighter than he had earlier, but still very pale.

"All stitched and wrapped up," he said indicating the large dressing on his forehead and a snow-white bandage on his arm. "Nothing too bad at all."

"How are you feeling?" Kath enquired after a brief kiss hello.

"Better thanks, no pain at the moment as long as I don't move too much. Bit dizzy though. Ribs are pretty sore, Doc said three are cracked, bit of bruising, but nothing broken." He lowered the sheet to the ugly red and blue patches on his chest.

"Has the doctor been already? I wanted to hear what he had to say about your x-rays?"

"Now, don't fret. He just rushed in and had a quick little chat, and tore off again. Says I've got a bit of concussion, otherwise my head and neck are fine."

He lay back into his pillows obviously in pain.

"Well, you don't look all right to me. I hope they have the sense to keep you in for a few days."

"As a matter of fact they are keeping me in overnight, just until this headache eases. And I must admit, I feel a bit crook too. Doc says the concussion could cause dizziness and nausea."

He closed his eyes, breathing quickly.

"Oh Sam, you look dreadful! I'm glad they're keeping you in, I'd be so worried if you came home." Kath settled into the chair beside his bed to wait with him until he was transferred to a ward. Sam squeezed her hand and, before long, she could tell by his breathing that he had dozed off.

As she watched her sleeping husband, Kath offered up a silent prayer of thankfulness, grateful that he would be okay. His body would mend but, she knew, he was also physically exhausted from the busy harvest. Plus, she couldn't understand why he kept driving to Toowoomba chasing various parts instead of having them sent out. It made no sense to her, but he always became very terse and defensive whenever she mentioned it. '*Poor Sam*', she thought to herself. '*You have really worn yourself out, no wonder you lost concentration and had an accident.*'

The dilemma now would be trying to get him to rest and fully recover. She knew he would never completely relax at home where he could see work to be done outside every window or, indeed, in his office. Even with Jarrod taking over much of the workload, Sam would find something that he should be doing. Thankfully the boys could easily finish the harvest and manage the delivery of the grain to the depot, and Majella was very capable and organised, and could help Jarrod out with any office work. All that remained was to convince her stubborn workaholic husband to take a holiday and recuperate properly before returning to work. How hard could that be? Kath almost laughed out loud as she looked lovingly at the sleeping form in the bed.

It occurred to her that they could accept the wedding invitation they had received to their friend's son's wedding in Adelaide, and then hire a car and go on to visit Nate and Angie. Sam had mentioned recently that he would like to visit them, so they could easily drive to their property after the wedding. Her scheming was interrupted when an orderly arrived to take the patient to a ward. Sam was gently woken up, assisted into a wheelchair and, grimacing with pain at the movement, was wheeled along the corridor with his protective wife following along. Once he was settled into a bed between crisp white hospital sheets, he looked sadly up at Kath.

"Please go home now, love. I'll be fine, just want to sleep now." And to himself, he thought *'without your worried face watching my every move'*.

Kath smiled sadly, realising that she did feel quite drained and, knowing that Sam was in good hands and needed to sleep, she agreed. "Okay, I'll see you in the morning. I'm so glad you'll be okay. Love you," she added, kissing him on the lips.

"Love you too," he whispered, patting her hand. "See you tomorrow, drive safe."

He winked and she smiled back, knowing his teasing tone where her driving was concerned.

"Slow and steady, my darling. I promise."

As she was driving home she quietly sang along to one of her favourite songs on the local Christian radio station. The words were so apt. Sam's life was her miracle and she was so grateful to God for giving him to her as her husband for all these years.

We sing, come alive in the name of Jesus
Come alive in the name of Jesus
This is a house of miracles
We bring everything to the feet of Jesus
Everything in the name of Jesus
This is a house of miracles

* * *

Kath arrived home to a very dark house, empty except for Little Tink who barked excitedly as usual. Kath walked slowly down the hallway and into the main bedroom, trying not to think about Sam not being home. She entered the ensuite where she turned on the shower, before stripping off her clothes and dumping them in an uncharacteristic pile on the floor. With a loud sigh she stepped into the large tiled space and let the hot water pour over her in a relaxing cascade. She soaped her tired body and shampooed her hair, feeling most of the tension and worry of the day's events wash away. Finally, emerging from the steamy mist, she rubbed herself dry on a soft towel before putting on her favourite pyjamas and blow-drying her hair. Feeling warm and relaxed she finally acknowledged her rumbling belly and padded softly back to the kitchen. Ten minutes later she sat down to a quickly assembled omelette and, as an afterthought, rose and poured herself a glass of shiraz. She rarely drank alcohol, but tonight she really felt the need for some red wine.

She didn't feel like talking to anyone so she sent a group text to her three children, updating them on their father's condition. She then sent another one to Rosemary, updating her and asking her to let Nate and Josh know about Sam's accident. She felt guilty about her lack of personal communication with each of them, but knew they would not think twice about receiving texts. She did, however, ring Jack and Edith, and update them of their son's condition and hospitalisation. All duties dealt with, she took her wine glass and retired to the lounge room to sit in her favourite chair. She leant back and relaxed, thanking God once again that Sam had not been seriously injured. He could have easily broken his neck; she shuddered at the thought. She had felt physically sick when she had first arrived at the hospital, her mind immediately taking her back to a dark period in their lives six years ago. The same terrible fear of losing him had engulfed her once again.

Sam had been diagnosed with bowel cancer, after a number of digestive issues had finally led to a colonoscopy. This procedure had found some advanced polyps and abnormal tissue, which the surgeon had removed, but the pathology tests came back positive. He then needed surgery followed by several rounds of chemotherapy. The care he had received in the private hospital in Toowoomba had been exceptional, but the effects of the chemo had been dreadful. No matter what they administered, and they tried several different drugs, he suffered terrible side-effects. He seemed to have little tolerance for the medications and endured endless nausea and vomiting, insomnia and then, when he did manage to sleep, horrific nightmares.

Finally, when he said he had had enough and would have no more chemo, his doctor gave the good news that the latest tests had come back clear and no more chemo was necessary. What wonderful news! Gradually he had built up his strength and regained the weight he had lost. Slowly, the old Sam had re-emerged from the frail skeletal man he had become. His return to health had been quite amazing, and they had all been very thankful to God for answering their prayers. It had been a very trying time for the whole family, but the insidious disease had been beaten and they all breathed a collective sigh of relief. Life on the farm had finally returned to normal. So, in comparison, today's accident was nothing major after all. She still had her best friend, confidante and mentor. The man she relied on for advice and support, a sounding board for her crazy ideas, a strong shoulder to lean on, and an even stronger hand to pull her up when her confidence faded and her knees shook.

Her eyes settled on Jarrod and Majella's wedding photo, remembering the happy day with a smile. They had both been 24 when they married over two years ago. It had been a beautiful day in the middle of winter which, for Innisfail, meant mild temperatures with warm sunshine and clear blue skies. This particular photo was of the bridal couple standing with Jack and Edith, Kath and Sam and Bryce and Jessica. No mistaking the family resemblances amongst the Wilmont clan, with Majella's stunning Italian features standing out in contrast. They all looked so happy and relaxed.

His health scare a thing of the past, Sam was back to a healthy weight, looking tanned and fit once again. She shuddered again at the memory of his illness, and moved her thoughts along, refusing to be drawn back to that worrying time. *'Oh Father, how grateful I am to have this man in my life. How blessed am I?'*

Her eyes grew heavy, and she relaxed further into the depths of the leather upholstery, its smell comforting her like an old friend. Little Tink jumped up onto her lap and snuggled in, and sleep soon claimed them both. She woke from a deep sleep well after midnight, feeling disorientated and cold. Rising slowly, she remembered where she was and, carrying the sleeping dog, she turned off the lights and walked slowly to the bedroom. Placing Tink in her doggy bed on the floor, she pulled back the quilt and crawled between the sheets. It wasn't long before she was once again sleeping soundly. When next she woke it was to the morning sounds of the birds in the garden. However, as the Sun had not quite risen, she rolled over and tried to go back to sleep, but that proved futile as her hand failed to find a warm body beside her. Her eyes flew open and her thoughts went instantly to Sam in hospital.

The bed was so big and empty without him! They always went to bed together and, after a good morning kiss and cuddle, sometimes more, they rose together. Sam always put the kettle on and made a pot of tea, while Kath cut up some fruit and made toast; an everyday routine that they had followed for decades. Sighing sadly, Kath rose and stretched, before letting Tink out through the French doors into the garden. Dressing quickly, she combed her hair and headed for the kitchen. She made a cup of tea, cut up an apple and, taking both, she went outside on to the verandah and sat quietly, enjoying the freshness of the morning air. Her view took in the house yard garden where little wrens darted in and out of the bottlebrushes and grevilleas, and a beautiful new spider web glistened in the early sunlight. In the distance were her beloved Bunya Mountains.

The mountain air would be just what Sam needed, she thought, another place I should take him while he's recovering. Glancing at her watch, she realised it was still very early, too early to ring the hospital, so she wandered along the verandah and stepped down the side steps onto the narrow path that led to her studio. She had painted a number of photos from the day she went flying with Jillian, and her latest effort was still sitting half-finished on her easel. She looked at it longingly, but resisted the urge to work on it. Instead, she watered her indoor plants from the old tin watering can she had painted bright nasturtiums on and, smiling in satisfaction at the healthy foliage and bright airy room, she left, closing the door behind her.

The smell of fresh toast and coffee soon filled the air. Jessica called to check on how she was this morning, and Kath was pleased to have a leisurely chat with her about yesterday's events. Checking the time, as she tidied the kitchen she decided on reading for a little while before calling the hospital. She sat in the early morning sunshine, and opened her Bible to Psalm 46.

The first verse caught her attention, giving her strength and courage for the day:

God is our refuge and strength, an ever-present help in trouble.

Such timely words of comfort and reassurance. After a short time of prayer, she felt ready to take on the day. Her quiet time was broken by her phone ringing.

"Hello."

"Good morning, love."

"I was just about to call the hospital. How are you today?"

"Much better, ready to come home. The doc's been and given me the all clear. What time are you coming in?"

"I can come in anytime. Are you sure you're right to come home, you looked pretty terrible yesterday? Did you sleep okay?"

"Hard to sleep in here with all the noise, and they kept coming in to check on me. I'll rest better at home. Come and get me, please love," he pleaded.

"Okay, don't fret. I'll be there shortly." She smiled into the phone. "Although I did hope to talk to your doctor, he must have come around early? I wonder if I can track him down?"

"There's no need for that, no serious injuries for you to worry about. He probably came in early so he could go play golf or something, it is Saturday you know. I just need some of your TLC and I'll soon be right as rain."

"Oh dear, I think you're going to be a difficult patient but, don't worry, I'll come and get you. Oh, and Sam?"

"Yes?"

"There will be rules for your recuperation!"

Sam chuckled quietly. "Now don't go bossing me around like a school teacher. I'll be good, I promise."

"I'm not so sure about that! See you soon, bye."

Kath entered the hospital about 30 minutes later, with a spring in her step and a smile on her face. She walked purposefully down the empty corridor to Sam's room, and entered to stand beside his bed, a frown forming on her brow.

"Hello, love," he greeted her.

"Hi," she kissed his cheek. "You still look very pale. Are you sure you're right to go home?"

"Yes, yes, get me out of here! I'll be much happier at home. You know how much I hate hospitals. Did you bring me some clothes?"

"Of course." She patted her big shoulder bag. "Shall I call a nurse to help you change?"

"I think between the two of us, we'll manage. Just help me up, would you?"

He held out his good hand, the other arm secured in a sling, and slowly moved to a sitting position on the side of the bed, wincing in pain. A nurse walked in carrying his discharge papers, and some scripts for pain medication and antibiotics.

"Here, let me," she offered with a smile. "I can help him dress, Mrs. Wilmont, while you go to the pharmacy for his medication."

Less than an hour later, Sam was being pushed out to the car in a wheelchair by the same nurse. They chatted about the weather for a few minutes while they waited for Kath, who had stopped to chat with Leanne in reception. Actually, the friendly nurse talked nonstop, while Sam sat with his eyes closed, soaking in the warmth of the sun and breathing in the fresh country air, while listening to bird calls and the sounds of a truck rumbling along the Bunya Highway. Once Kath arrived and unlocked the car, the nurse settled Sam in the front seat and gently buckled him in, giving them some more friendly advice and reminders before waving them off. Kath drove home very leisurely which her husband could not resist teasing her about.

"I'm not going to break into pieces you know. It's okay to go a bit faster."

"Just want to get you home safely, without causing you any more pain."

"Thanks, but you could at least drive to the speed limit. Going this slow must really be a first for you," he grinned.

"Do you want to walk instead?" she asked with a wicked smile.

"No, not at all, I'm getting used to slow and steady, little old lady style." He settled back more comfortably in his seat, leaning his head back and closing his eyes. "Wake me in an hour or so when we reach the farm."

"Very funny! You'll be there in about 15 minutes. I should have left you in the hospital with friendly Nurse Have-A-Chat," she teased.

"Love you darling." He smiled, not opening his eyes and they travelled the rest of the way home in an easy silence.

Their arrival was loudly announced to absolutely no-one by a very exuberant cattle dog, and an extremely over-excited poodle.

"Hello boy. Settle down now, I haven't been gone that long!" Sam patted the ever-faithful Nipper once he had managed to climb slowly out of the vehicle. Little Tink was spinning crazily on the other side of the gate, nearly deafening them with her high-pitched yapping.

"Oh, my goodness, what a welcome you two!" laughed Kath. "Tink! Tink! That's enough! You're hurting my ears!"

Once both dogs had been acknowledged and patted, they calmed down, obviously very pleased by their exhibition and still madly wagging their tails. However, they allowed Kath and Sam to pass by and happily followed them up the path to the house. Sam made a beeline for his favourite recliner chair in the living room and sank slowly into its welcoming leather.

"Comfy?"

"Yep, this is good, thanks."

"Righto, I'll go make us both a coffee then." Kath kissed him on the forehead.

Sam didn't leave his chair for long during the following days. It provided the most comfortable position for his bruised and battered body. He even slept there at night, preferring it to his bed, much to Kath's chagrin, but she was thankful that he was able to sleep and mend. She kept a vase of fresh flowers from her garden on the table near him and, once when she filled the vase with fragrant roses, she was surprised and pleased to hear him mumble in his half-asleep state, 'Rose'. Normally, he didn't take much notice of her flowers.

By the time she drove him back into town to get his stitches out 10 days later, he was much improved and was moving more freely, albeit still rather gingerly. Kath was very surprised at how good a patient he had been, and that he was content to take it easy at home. He spent quite a bit of time in his office catching up on paperwork, and seemed to make a lot of phone calls during which he closed the door. When Kath enquired who he was talking to she felt he just fobbed her off. When she hesitantly raised the subject of flying to Adelaide for the upcoming wedding, she was absolutely gobsmacked when he readily agreed.

"That must have been some bump on your head," she teased. "You never want to go away, at least not for longer than a weekend!"

"Ahh well, I think it would be nice for us to spend some time away together, and I'd like to see Nate and Angie again."

"Well, that's just wonderful. Another month or so off work will do you the world of good. You're still not your old self, are you?"

"No, I'm afraid that fall did knock me around a bit. You shouldn't have taken time off work to look after me, though."

"Actually, I was glad to have an excuse to stay home; I think I needed a break too."

"All good then, I'll ring Nate and let him know we'll be coming down, and I'll check out some flights too."

Kath was in the garden watering her plants a little while later, still marvelling at how agreeable Sam had been about going to South Australia for the wedding, and then to visit his brother and sister-in-law. She couldn't help but smile, excited about going away together on a holiday. The boys would keep an eye on the farm and, with harvest over, it would be the ideal time to take an extended break. Humming happily to herself, she turned off the tap and made her way to her art studio. Through the window she could see Sam resting his eyes, family code for snoring softly in a sound afternoon nap in his recliner chair. She decided to paint for a while, and eagerly sought out another of the photos she had taken during the plane ride of a beautiful Bunya pine. She wanted to capture the majesty of the forest giant surrounded by the vibrant green rain forest, with the clear blue sky as a contrasting background.

She was feeling very content, knowing that Sam was recovering, and they were planning a holiday together. Life was full of ups and downs, and she was thankful that the worry of the last few weeks was behind them and an adventure beckoned. More photos, she thought, more beautiful scenes to paint while enjoying time away from the farm with Sam. He'll be able to switch off and relax, not having to worry about anything. Happy days ahead!

CHAPTER 8

Ageless Wisdom

*"We will never be released from emotions such
as hatred or jealousy until we realise that other
people are not responsible for our happiness."*
Neil Eskelin 1938-2018

Old Tom leaned back in his chair, gently rocking to and fro. His skin was pale and wrinkled, with fresh scars on his face where some suspicious spots and dry patches had been treated, not surprising for a man in his late 80s, especially one who had spent most of his life working outside in the harsh Australian sun. His pale blue watery eyes seemed to be permanently squinting, as if hot rays of sunshine still beat down on him.

Kath had met old Tom on one of her visits to the nursing home where he resided. Meeting Tom Kennedy had been a life changing event; one she knew had been orchestrated by the Master's hand. Her Heavenly Father had used Tom to bring about healing, and the release she had long sought from the hold of her cruel, abusive parent.

She had escaped from her father when she married Sam, having nothing to do with him since. He may as well have been dead as far as Kath was concerned, as she had not one pleasant memory of him. He seemed to be glad to be rid of her as well as he never attempted to contact her. Their paths never crossed, probably because her father rarely went to town but instead chose to drive to Toowoomba or Kingaroy for his business, even though it was a greater distance for him to travel. He was never far from her thoughts, however. He seemed to haunt her, and always overshadowed the memories of her mother and her own upbringing. She could not help but compare him to Sam or Jack, or indeed any other man she knew.

William Baxter always fell far short. Kath often wondered why she had been given such a heartless father; why she and her mother had suffered such a terrible existence with him. Why was life so unfair? She knew it was not because she was unlovable, her mother and Sam had shown her that. She also knew she needed to forgive her father, but she struggled with forgiving someone who was not sorry for his actions, who did not even comprehend that he had done anything wrong. She tried to bury the past, but it proved impossible; a constant struggle deep within her.

It had come as quite a surprise one cold winter's morning to receive a phone call from the local hospital saying her father had been brought in by ambulance. He had collapsed while delivering grain to a neighbour's property. The neighbour knew William well enough to be able to give Kath's name as next of kin.

What a dilemma, how could she go and face her father after all these years? Why should she? He had never cared for her, or her mother. What good would going to the hospital do? She anguished over all these questions until Sam came in for smoko. He had left early, when the frost was still lying on the ground, to get ready for planting the wheat crop and she hadn't been able to discuss the phone call with him yet. He could tell she was upset as soon as he stepped into the kitchen, going immediately to the wood stove to warm himself.

"What's up, love?" he asked as he backed up closer to the stove, pulling his wife into his arms.

"A nurse from the hospital rang early this morning."

"Oh, what's wrong? Who?" he quickly asked, worried about his parents.

"No, it's okay, your folks are fine. It was about my father."

"Your father? Really?"

"Yes, apparently he collapsed and was taken in by ambulance. A neighbour gave the ambulance officers my name."

"Is he alright?"

"I don't really know. They want me to go in and see him, but I don't know if I can, if I even want to…" her voice trailed off.

"Well, I guess we can't just ignore the hospital. How about you give me half an hour to finish up a couple of things in the shed, and then we'll go in together? It must be serious or they wouldn't have contacted you."

"Yes, you're right. We should go. I'll ring them back and tell them we'll be there in about an hour. Coffee first, hey?"

"Of course. Coffee first," he smiled. "And don't worry, he can't hurt you anymore, and I'll be right there with you." A kiss on her worried forehead allayed some of her fears, but not all.

When they arrived at the hospital, Kath was required to complete some paperwork concerning her father, a task with which she had great difficulty. Actually, it didn't take very long because she knew nothing of her father's medical history, blood type, allergies, medications, and so on. The only thing she did know was his birth date, the 1st of August, the day celebrated as the horses' birthday in the Southern Hemisphere. Kath had once seen a drawing of the devil riding a huge black stallion, with red coals for eyes and fire coming from its nostrils, and she had thought it quite a fitting representation of her father.

Once the ordeal with the paperwork was completed, they were ushered into a small room where they met with the doctor taking care of William. He was brusque, and obviously in a hurry, but nevertheless sat for a few minutes to explain her father's condition. He had suffered a stroke which had left him paralysed down one side and unable to speak. It was hoped he would recover, but to what extent was uncertain.

The doctor encouraged them to ensure all William's affairs were in order, and assured them they would give him the best care possible, but he also informed them that he had other health issues. His liver was diseased from alcohol abuse, and he had a chest infection, for which it would seem he had not sought medical attention, and this would further impact on his recovery. He then enquired if Kath had Enduring Power of Attorney, to which she replied that she didn't think so.

They were then escorted to a room where a wizened man lay on a bed, with an oxygen mask covering his face. Kath was shocked to realise that the patient was actually her father! He certainly bore little resemblance to the frightening man whose image was burned into her memory. She just stood in shock staring at him; at the frail old man he had become.

His face was a pasty white, his hair mostly grey and his muscles withered away. She could not believe the change in him in since she had last seen him before she was married. His eyes were closed and did not open when a nurse came in to take his observations. Sam just stood wide eyed and silent by his wife's side holding her hand.

After what seemed an eternity, another nurse came in and invited them to sit with him until he woke, but Kath quickly shook her head saying, "No, thank you, we have to go."

She pulled Sam's hand and walked quickly from the room, tears streaming down her cheeks.

She stopped abruptly and turned to look at Sam. "I know he's very sick, and possibly dying, but I can't sit there watching him. I just can't. He's brought all this on himself."

The nurse from his room came up to them and, mistaking the reason for Kath's tears, said compassionately, "Take heart Mrs. Wilmont, he may well recover and you'll have your father back again."

Kath's eyes opened wide, but she did not reply and the nurse continued gently. "We'll phone you if there's any change."

Sam thanked her and, placing his arm around Kath's shoulders, led her from the building to their car. After helping her in and then getting in behind the wheel, he asked quietly, "Do you think he made a will?"

Kath looked at him shrugging her shoulders. "I have absolutely no idea. How would we find out? He's going to have medical expenses now too, and how do we pay for those?"

"Good thing I have a brother who's a solicitor. I'll give him a ring later and see what he suggests."

They drove home in silence, both lost in their thoughts about a man named William Baxter, the life he had lived, and the condition they had just seen him in.

Sam's brother, Josh, proved to be a godsend. He knew exactly what to do and, in no time, had all the information they required. There were more surprises in store for Kath. Her father had indeed made a will, which was lodged with a firm in town, and had even nominated Kath as his EPOA. She could scarcely believe it. The documents still awaited her signature, but he obviously expected her to make decisions on his behalf concerning his health and finances!

This latest development made no sense at all. How ironic that Kath now had the responsibility of caring for the man who had failed her and her mother so miserably when they had needed him. She struggled to understand why he had entrusted her with his care in his old age and ill health but, as Josh explained, he probably didn't know where his brothers were and his wife was deceased, so that left his only child, his daughter. Besides, Kath thought to herself, he was always so arrogant she doubted he ever thought he would be in a position that required someone else to look after him.

So, Kath went to the solicitor and signed the documentation, and then found herself making decisions for her father, who never fully recovered from his stroke and was placed in the local nursing home. He never walked again and was wheelchair bound, and he spoke only occasionally and with great difficulty. He knew who Kath was, but showed little appreciation for anything she did for him, and so she only visited him when necessary. His farm Chadwick, was leased out in a share-farming agreement to another family in the area.

On a particularly cold windy August morning, Kath had arrived at the nursing home to deliver some new clothes that the staff had said her father needed. She was not in particularly good spirits, after having had some stressful days in the classroom with a new student who seemed to delight in pushing all her buttons, while disrupting the rest of the class. The last thing she felt like was visiting her father. She had walked up the path with the freezing westerly seeming to blow straight through her thick coat, and was at least thankful to step into the warm foyer. She looked at the doors that opened into the corridor that led to William's room but just couldn't bring herself to walk through them, so she turned and walked to the little sunroom opposite, to sit with a loud sigh in a chair beside a huge bay window.

She was massaging her temples with her eyes closed when a soft voice said quietly, "Never did like westerlies, specially at this time of year. Looks like it could blow a dog off the chain!"

Kath looked up quickly to see an elderly man sitting beside her in a wheel chair, surprised she hadn't heard him arrive.

"Oh, hello."

"Didn't mean to startle you, love. Tom Kennedy," he introduced himself, holding out his hand.

"Pleased to meet you Mr. Kennedy," Kath smiled shaking his hand, blue veins standing out starkly against his soft, papery skin. "I was just gathering my thoughts."

"No harm in taking a breather. Come to visit someone, I see," he added pointing to the parcel she held on her lap.

"Yes, my father."

"Aah, he'll be pleased to see you, I'm sure."

"No, not at all," she answered shaking her head sadly. "He has never been pleased to see me, not once since the day I was born."

"Oh, come now. I find that hard to believe!"

"You would not believe the things I could tell you about him."

"Why don't you try me?" he asked leaning forward, his blue eyes suddenly bright. "I've got nothing but time on my hands. My old mum used to say a problem shared is a problem halved." He patted her arm reassuringly.

And so they sat side by side enjoying the sun's warmth through the large glass window. Kath spoke quietly, telling Tom some details of her childhood, not sharing everything but enough for him to understand the type of man her father had been. He interrupted occasionally asking a question or seeking clarification about a detail, or just shaking his head in disbelief. When Kath had finished he was holding her hand in his while she stared stonily out the window. They sat in silence for a while before Tom spoke.

"You know, one of the hardest things to do is to forgive someone who isn't sorry, not the least bit remorseful. But, if we want to be free of ill feelings and bitterness, it's up to us to make it happen. By being angry we're allowing the other person to continue to have a hold on us, we're giving them power they certainly don't deserve. You know what I mean?"

"Yes, my husband, Sam, has said something similar to me but I just haven't been able to completely forgive, and certainly not forget."

"Now forgetting is something different entirely. Just work on forgiving for starters and maybe the forgetting will come along later. It's between you and God, my dear, not you and your dad. Only our Heavenly Father can give you the strength to do what needs to be done."

Kath looked at Tom. "You're very wise, Tom, and you seem to be speaking from experience."

"I don't know about being wise, but I've sure made my share of foolish mistakes. My dear wife, Nellie, God rest her soul, taught me a lot about forgiveness. Now she was a right godly woman and had the patience of a saint, that's for sure. Needed to, with a hothead like me for a husband," he chuckled before continuing. "She taught me that real strength comes from accepting an apology that was never given. Took me a long time to understand that, but eventually I did and it stopped me from being eaten up by bitterness. It was my brother, you see, stole a lot of money from me and made my life very hard. He made life for my Nellie very hard too, that's what really got me riled up. She should never have suffered because of him. But she just said, '*Tom, he's your brother, don't let his selfishness destroy you. Forgive him and let God deal with him. We've got each other, we'll be fine.*' Nellie knew her Bible well you know and she often quoted Jesus saying:

> *Love the Lord your God with all your heart and*
> *with all your soul and with all your mind*

and with all your strength. This is the first commandment.
And the second is this: 'You shall love your neighbour as yourself.'
There is no other commandment greater than these.

"It's in the Gospels, can't remember where but I've never forgotten those verses. And you know what? She was right, of course." Tom smiled. "I stopped being angry and stopped holding a grudge against my brother and just decided to get over it. I finally forgave him. I couldn't change the past, but I did change my future; had a whole different outlook I did. I probably didn't love him the way I should have, but I stopped hating him, and the bitterness went away and we had a reasonable relationship right up until he died. The good Lord helped me do it, of course. Couldn't have done it without Him, or my sweet Nell. We worked hard, me and Nellie, bought our own place in time, and had our kids, and we were happy. We were married for over 65 years. Good years they were too."

Kath looked at Tom with tears in her eyes. "You know, Tom, I've known for a very long time what I should do, but I just haven't been able to overcome all the hurt and disappointments. I know God has been chasing me down about it, but I've been ignoring Him too. But, today, I really feel I can try to overcome the terrible feelings I have for my father. I don't think I'll ever have any real affection for him, but I need to forgive him and, like you said, break the hold he has over me once and for all. I'm so glad I met you today, Tom. You said just what I needed to hear." She leaned over and kissed his cheek. Tom looked at her in surprise before giving an embarrassed chuckle. "My pleasure, love."

Kath stood then and walked with new resolve through the doors, and towards her father's room. She stopped at the nurse's station and gave the nurse on duty the new clothes to be tagged with her father's name, before boldly walking into his room. He was awake and watched her enter, but made no movement. She looked directly at him and, in a strong but quiet voice stated simply, "Father, I forgive you for the way you treated me and Mum. I will never understand how you could be so awful to us, but I'm going to forgive you anyway. You have no power over me and I am not going to let you drag me down any longer."

William continued to stare at her with his piercing dark eyes, a look she remembered only too well. Turning abruptly, she left the room feeling like a huge weight had been lifted from her shoulders. She had finally forgiven her father just as God had forgiven her for all her wrongdoings. Old Tom was nowhere to be seen, but that day marked the beginning of a long friendship with him. She went every few weeks to visit him, and to briefly look in on her father. She loved listening to Tom reminisce about his younger days; he had so many stories to tell.

"You're looking very smart in that shirt, Tom," Kath remarked as she sat beside him in the sun room as usual when visiting another day. "You look like Robert Redford in *Butch Cassidy and the Sundance Dance Kid*," she teased.

"Is that so? Must still have my good looks, after all." The old man chuckled. "I've got a lot to thank my mother for. I've got her fair skin, you see? But I always covered up and always wore a hat," he added pointing to his shiny bald head. "Mother never let us leave the house unless we had on a wide-brimmed hat and boots, and of course a pair of strides and long-sleeved shirt. That habit lasted all my life. Sun still burnt me a bit but it could've been much worse. Worked hard back then we did," he continued, looking out at the cloudy sky, seeming to forget Kath's presence. "Up at dawn to gather the horses. We kept 'em hobbled at night in the house paddock, but it was still a fair size and we didn't want 'em to go too far. Then we had to milk the cows before going in for breakfast. Always had eggs and bacon, or lamb chops washed down with hot tea. Then we took a cut lunch out to work with us, usually too far to come back to the house. Just bread and meat and we'd boil the billy for tea. By the time we finished at sundown we were so hungry we could eat a horse, shoes and all." He smiled a toothless grin, rubbing his whiskery chin at the memory. "The boss' wife was a great cook," he continued. "Just plain food, mind you, nothing fancy but lots of it. Roast beef or mutton stew, with lots of spuds and gravy. Didn't always get sweets, but we sometimes got bread and butter pudding, or rice pudding and cream. I'm going back a few weeks, mind you." He turned to look at Kath, eyes twinkling. "They were good times, we worked hard for an honest dollar. The boss was fair too."

Tom continued rocking, lost in thought of days long gone and, when Kath looked again, he was fast asleep, mouth agape, bare gums exposed. She smiled and tucked the knitted rug more tightly over his bony knees noticing his wedding ring, loose on his thin finger. He often spoke about Nellie, whom he had lost some years ago. They had been devoted to each other throughout their long marriage, weathered many a storm together, Tom said.

Kath had heard him humming softly one day, and asked what the song was, and he had told her it was Nell's favourite waltz tune *Goodnight Irene*. They had often gone to country dances and twirled happily around the dance floor together. How wonderful, Kath had thought, to be able to share a lifetime with one person, your life's partner. She stood to leave but, on noticing that it had started to rain, she sat back down. Taking Tom's hand in her own, she leaned back in her chair, closing her eyes as her thoughts took her back to when she was a young woman of 20 and about to be married.

* * *

The day had dawned bright and clear, no sign of the clouds of the previous day which had seemed to be heralding inclement weather. She had fallen asleep wondering how she would keep her beautiful white gown and new white heels clean and mud free. It had taken her ages to save up for them. She had tried to reassure herself that it would still be a wonderful day, even if it did rain. However, her worries were totally unfounded as she was woken by the bright sunshine beaming in through her bedroom window. An excited smile of anticipation lit her face; it was her wedding day! It was finally here! There was a nervous feeling in her stomach, the usual butterflies fluttering about, as she contemplated making the biggest commitment of her life. She knew that Sam was the only man for her, and she was undeniably madly in love with him and she knew he felt the same but, nonetheless, she still felt a little anxious; what if she failed as a wife? Her dream was of a happy marriage full of laughter and adventures, and everything that was the opposite of her parent's woeful wedded life together.

A heart-to-heart with Rosemary and Edith had reassured her, and the pre marriage counselling with their pastor had given her confidence that she, and Sam, could work through any issues together if they kept their communication channels open, and kept God in the centre of their relationship. It all sounded so easy and positive, in theory, but she had still whispered her concerns about disappointing Sam to her soon to be sister-in-law.

"Nonsense." Rosie had smiled. "He adores you and you'll work things out together. That's what marriage is all about, two promising to become one. Just be honest with each other, and try to talk about everything. You'll see, it'll be fine."

"Relax and enjoy your wedding day, it will hold special memories for you for the rest of your life," added Edith. "Besides, making up after a little lover's quarrel can be quite fun." She grinned cheekily causing her daughter to laugh out loud, and the bride-to-be to blush.

When the time came for Jack to walk her down the aisle, something he had felt very privileged to be asked to do, Kath felt like she was walking on clouds. No longer apprehensive, her fears having all evaporated. She knew with absolute certainty that this was the right path for her. When the groom turned to stare at her, she dazzled him with a beautiful smile that reflected all her joy. It all felt so very right and she was just amazed that little nobody Kathleen Baxter was about to marry the popular, charming and oh so handsome, Sam Wilmont. It was her very own fairytale.

The service seemed to be over in no time and, before she knew it, she was presented with her new husband as Mr. and Mrs. Sam Wilmont. Rosemary, who was her Matron of Honour, was the first to congratulate them before they were both embraced by Jack and Edith. The reception, held in the church hall, was small yet filled with warmth and happiness. Kath had no family on her side present and, of course, did not invite her father. She had a number of friends from work and church, but the rest of the guests were family and friends of the Wilmonts. She felt very welcomed by them all and was thrilled to be officially part of a large loving family at last.

Their honeymoon was spent in the beautiful Gold Coast Hinterland where they delighted in each other, and the beautiful mountains and rainforests, as well as driving down to walk hand in hand along the white beaches below. When they returned to the Darling Downs, it was to begin their new life together at Yallaroo, the property next to Oakleigh where Sam had grown up. His parents had helped him purchase Yallaroo the previous year and had combined the land into their farming enterprise. An agreement was now in place for Sam and Kath to repay the loan as they farmed the property. It was the ideal place for the twosome to make their home, and it enabled Sam to work full time as part of the family farming business.

The following year, Kath finally went to university and obtained her Teaching Degree, something Sam had strongly encouraged her to do. On completion of her studies, she was offered a position in town, and commenced her career in education as a Year 2 teacher. And she loved it. She was totally committed to her young students, and was completely focused on ensuring that she enabled them to achieve their very best, whatever that may look like for each individual student.

She looked forward to having a child of her own, but wanted to teach for a couple of years first. When she and Sam decided the time was right to begin their family, they were both excited and were quite taken back when, after 12 months of trying, no pregnancy had occurred. Kath began to wonder if motherhood was something she would be unable to achieve, and she worried she would follow in her mother's footsteps of despair and disappointment.

Sam understood his wife's distress, and tried to comfort her. He was not too concerned and believed they just needed to be patient, a sentiment that was echoed by her doctor when she visited him for a checkup. He felt confident that there were no problems, and she simply needed to relax and try not to worry. 'That's easy for him to say' Kath thought, but she committed her dreams of a baby to her Heavenly Father, and prayed fervently that they would soon become parents. Thankfully their prayers were answered when Kath was least expecting it. The school year had finished, and all the final activities, including school plays and presentations, were behind them when she was stricken with a gastro bug that was going through the school community. Relieved that at least she had managed to get through the final school week, she was still quite unimpressed to be ill as she had much to do to prepare for Christmas.

Despite feeling tired and nauseous, she determinedly dragged herself out of bed early one day only to crawl back in at mid-morning. Nothing would stay down and she felt terrible. When she managed to walk out to the kitchen that afternoon she promptly fainted into Sam's arms when he came in for his afternoon tea. He panicked and quickly carried her to the car and drove her straight to the hospital. They were astonished and delighted to learn some time later that she didn't have gastro but was suffering from severe morning sickness. Kath had not even considered being pregnant, which was surprising, as she had thought of little else for the past year except becoming a mum. Sam was also guilty of not considering the obvious, and the family teased them both about their lack of perception while also sincerely congratulating them on the good news.

Kath stayed in hospital for a few days to rest and rehydrate before returning to the farm. She hoped and prayed that the pregnancy would be trouble free, but she need not have worried as once the morning sickness settled down, and the weather cooled, she had a dream pregnancy and a straightforward delivery of a healthy baby boy. They were further blessed with two more pregnancies resulting in beautiful healthy babies, each labour getting shorter and quicker. Bryce was born in the foyer of the hospital emergency department, and Jessica was delivered by her father in the bathroom at home on the farm, while Edith cared for the other two children in the front yard as they waited for the ambulance to arrive.

Together, Sam and Kath had built a strong marriage, one they intended would stand the test of time. Their love for God, and for each other, provided a firm foundation but, still, they worked hard at strengthening their bond and overcoming issues as they arose. Kath, smiling, roused from her musings, so grateful for the blessings of her family.

She gently placed old Tom's hand under the blanket on his lap, careful not to wake him. What a gift this old man was to her. She had learned so much from her time spent with him, and respected him for the loving husband he had been. '*Nellie had been one lucky lady,*' she smiled to herself. She was so grateful for her own marriage, and could imagine sitting in the sun with Sam, many years from now, rugs over their knees, skin sagging and wrinkled, holding hands and laughing; their hearts still full of love for each other.

> *Be devoted to one another in love.*
> *Honour one another above yourselves.*
> *Romans12:10*

CHAPTER 9

Fish and Salt Spray

*"Someone has altered the script.
My lines have been changed.
I thought I was writing this play."*
Madeleine L'Engle 1918 -2007

S am woke early and lay still, listening to Kath's even breathing beside
him. He was pleased he had booked the quaint little cottage in Cowell,
a coastal town on the eastern side of the Eyre Peninsular in South Australia,
instead of the cabin in the caravan park he had first considered.

Kath had been thrilled with their accommodation in a two-bedroom
sandstone cottage. It had been totally renovated, with all the modern con-
veniences, but still oozed all the charm of yesteryear. The fridge contained
champagne and gourmet treats and luxurious towels, soaps and bath salts
sat on the shelf in the tiny bathroom, alongside two fragrant candles.
She had been very impressed that he had booked such a delightful, and

obviously expensive, place for them to stay but, when she remarked on it, he had just winked at her and said he wanted this trip away to be really special. She certainly didn't object! He had smiled to himself with satisfaction.

The drive from Adelaide to Nate and Angie's property had been unhurried and enjoyable. They only spent two nights in the city, and left the day after the wedding, both keen to get out in to the country again and see Nate and Angie. The week spent staying with them had also been relaxing, with plenty of time to catch up on family news, and to see the improvements they had made on their property since they had last visited a couple of years ago. The fact that they were also going to spend a week alone in the nearby town came as a complete surprise to Kath, and Sam was again very pleased with his forward planning and arrangements.

Outside, he could hear stirrings in the street, as the town's early risers started their day, and the dedicated fishermen began their final preparations prior to hooking their boats onto their vehicles and heading off towards the boat ramp, ready for a day on the water. Kath stirred and rolled over, snuggling into Sam's bare chest. He kissed her forehead.

"Good morning."

They always woke within minutes of each other, seemingly in sync with each other's body rhythms.

"Is it morning already?" Kath whispered. "It's still dark."

"Not really. Piccaninny dawn, you know," She could hear the smile in his voice. "Nate and me want to get an early start and be out on the water at first light. Wanna come? It'll be a beautiful sunrise," he teased.

"No, no, I'll be fine here. I'm still recovering from yesterday's icy winds. It's too cold for fishing, Sam."

"I'll dress warmly, I promise. But remember darling, it's all about the tides and when the fish are biting! The plan is to bag out early and head back before it gets too windy."

"Such optimism," Kath yawned. "But, being the good fisher wife that I am, I'll get up and put the kettle on. I should go for an early walk; I've been pretty lazy of late without Tink to motivate me. I hope she's behaving at your folk's place."

"Good idea. You'll see the sunrise after all, and I'm sure that little dog is being spoilt rotten."

Kath kissed his smiling mouth and stroked his whiskery face.

"I hope you have a great day, and bring home some lovely fish for dinner. Oh, and some crabs for lunch would be good too." They both hopped out of bed grinning.

Not long after, Nate's ute pulled up out the front of the cottage and the men headed off towards the marina, towing the boat trailer to the boat ramp. They were in good spirits, and laughed about a time, years ago, when they had launched the small aluminium boat, usually called a tinny, and set off happily, only to realise a few metres out that they had forgotten to put in the bungs. Water had started flooding in through the two drainage holes in the stern, necessitating a quick turn around and a fast trip back to the ramp.

Today, they carefully did a final check of safety gear and, ensuring they had remembered their rods and bait, and of course to put the bungs in, they quickly launched the boat. Sam waited by the ramp holding the rope secured to the tinny's bow, while Nate parked the ute and trailer and walked back. Sam felt totally relaxed and excited to be going fishing again, a moment of anguish washed over him when he realised that this may well be his last ever fishing trip.

He shook his head to clear his mind of such thoughts, and smiled as Nate punched him lightly on his arm.

"Ready to go, little brother?"

"Sure thing. Hope you're ready to be well and truly out-fished?"

"Hopeful words from an old grain farmer, who doesn't even live near the water, let alone own a boat!"

"Don't worry Nate, old boy; I'll give you a fish, or maybe two, so you can at least have a feed tonight."

Both laughing, they settled into the tinny which measured just over 4.5m, very comfortable for two men, and headed towards the rising sun. There was no wind, so the water's surface was just like a mirror, beautifully reflecting the sunrise and the orange rimmed cumulus clouds that dotted the horizon.

Sam breathed deeply and inhaled the crisp salty air, which made him cough, but still he smiled at its freshness. He relaxed back into his seat, facing forward, content to watch the morning sky and the water scenes around him.

"Perfect morning to go out," called Nate.

Sam only just heard the comment over the noise from the motor, and the squawking gulls that nested along the shoreline. He raised his hand in response, as Nate opened up the throttle and increased speed, now that they were out of the 4-knot speed zone which ran the length of the long jetty. Two dolphins rose quietly from the deeper water and dived, their graceful motion at one with the calm water. Sea birds called noisily, disturbed by the 30-horsepower motor, but quickly resuming their search for small fish in the water. The rush of cold air increased, threatening to blow Sam's cap into the water, so he quickly pulled it off and tucked it under the bow where the anchor, emergency gear, raincoats and, of course, their thermos of hot coffee and container of biscuits were kept.

After about 20 minutes of motoring, Nate backed off the throttle and left the main channel in the harbour, heading towards shallow water near an old oyster lease. The rows of posts stood out in the low tide. They were no longer used by the oyster farmers to tie the black plastic mesh baskets on used to house the shellfish. New oyster leases had been obtained further along the harbour, and new wooden infrastructures put in place. It was further for the oyster boats to travel, but the big purpose-built aluminium boats were propelled by two powerful 150hp motors, sometimes bigger, that allowed them to race effortlessly through the water.

It was amazing how the oyster farmers and the grey nomads co-existed on the harbour water ways. The oyster farmers, and their employees, were fit and active with busy schedules to keep as they worked for their livelihoods while, in contrast, the grey nomads were generally older, slower, enjoying their retirement and golden years while in their 60s, 70s and even 80s. It was a tricky dynamic, as even though the fishermen in the smaller boats tried to keep clear of the much larger oyster boats, they sometimes caused a lot of congestion on the three-lane ramp. The oyster farmers tended to be polite and considerate to the recreational fisherman, recognising that these people, for the most part, had worked hard their whole lives in a huge cross section of careers, and were now enjoying their hard-earned retirement. However, sometimes frustrations boiled over when too many people, some quite slow or inexperienced, were trying to launch or retrieve vessels at the same time. Nevertheless, if someone from either group needed help, many hands readily offered assistance.

Nate skilfully motored around the oyster lease and, after a few minutes, found what he was looking for; shallow water, only about 60cm deep, a big sandy area with weed beds growing around it. It was a nice location to fish for the yellow fin whiting they were targeting and, if they were lucky, maybe even a flathead. He jolted Sam out of his reverie by calling: "Hey mate. You're the deckhand, so you better throw the anchor out!"

Smiling broadly, Sam got the anchor and, after a brief discussion about tides and currents, they agreed where to place it and Sam dropped it over the side, ignoring the pain in his chest area as he did so. The chain rattled against the side of the tinny before submerging, and pulling the attached anchor rope down.

"That'll do, decky, tie her off there," directed Nate, and Sam quickly tied off the rope at the required length on the rail on top of the bow. Both men then wasted no time baiting their hooks and casting over the side onto the sand, careful to avoid the weed but hoping to entice some whiting with the little pieces of squid and blood worm on their shiny sharp hooks. They settled back to wait, knowing that fishing could be very tedious and much patience was required. In the quiet that followed, Sam said, "I'm still bit weak, mate, so I don't know how good a decky I'll be today."

"Oh yeah, sorry. I forgot you banged yourself up. I shouldn't have asked you to throw the anchor out. No worries, pass the rope back here and I'll tie it off near me so I can pull it in when we're ready to go."

The anchor and rope duly sorted, they had no sooner settled back into their seats, when Sam felt a tug on his line. He wound in quickly and let out a whoop of joy when he saw he had a double hook up. Their lines were rigged with two hooks about 30cm apart and he had a good-sized whiting on each one. He pulled the fish into the tinny and, after removing the hooks, measured them and was pleased they were good sized, well over the minimum legal limit of 24cm long.

"Well done, brother!" complimented Nate. "You're off to a flying start!"

They fished in happy camaraderie, enjoying each other's company as they always had, although Sam was quieter than usual and more withdrawn, a fact that did not go unnoticed by his brother.

As the fish seemed to have gone off the bite they decided to move to another spot. When they were once again anchored up, Nate looked at his younger brother with concern and asked, "You don't seem your usual self, Sam, are you feeling all right?"

Sam was staring out across the water and Nate was about to repeat his question when Sam turned to him and said quietly, "It's back, Nate."

Nate looked at him in confusion, wondering what he was referring to when it suddenly dawned on him, his eyes widening in surprise, he asked, "No! Surely not the cancer? That was years ago and you got the all clear!"

"Well, apparently it never really went away, and now it is back with a vengeance. It's right through me. I have tumours everywhere and it's in my lymph nodes too."

Nate was speechless. He opened his mouth twice to say something but no words came out. He turned his head and stared out across the water as he tried to digest the shocking information.

Finally, still not looking at Sam, he stated, "Kath seems to be handling it pretty well."

"She doesn't know."

"She doesn't know?" repeated Nate incredulously, turning quickly to look at his brother. "You haven't told her? But why? How've you kept it a secret from her?"

Sam just shrugged. "I haven't been feeling well for months now. She knows that and she did send me off to see the doctor. He gave me some antibiotics and said my BP was a bit high and, you know, come back if I don't pick up. Anyway, long story short, he finally sent me for a whole gamut of tests. You know scans, x-rays, blood tests, the whole works. I've been seeing an oncologist in Toowoomba again. We've considered every option, from every angle. All they can offer is palliative chemo. Just to try and slow it down. I'd rather spend what time I have left at home as well as I can be, not crook from some concoction of drugs that aren't really going to help me much anyway."

"It's really that bad?"

"It's terminal, Nate, its spread too far, inoperable."

"But how on earth have you kept all this from Kath?" he asked again.

"I told her I was going to Toowoomba chasing spare parts and such, and attending field days. She was busy at school and I just kept up the white lies. I've never kept anything from her before. I feel so bad, I really do, but I just haven't been able to tell her yet."

"But why? Why not tell her? She deserves to know, Sam."

"I know, I know, but it's taken me all this time to come to terms with it and I know it will tear her apart. I know she can be strong, but this will really knock her around. She doesn't have a lot of self-confidence, and we're such a team. She'll have to adjust to being on her own, and I just couldn't figure out how to prepare her for what's going to happen. I don't want to hurt her any more than necessary, and I know she'll want me to do chemo again or drink some naturopathic swamp juice or some such thing. I don't want to do any of that. I trust my doc, and I've discussed every possibility with her. I've got another appointment next week when we get home, and I'll take Kath along and let her explain it to her. I know it's been gutless of me. But I've had a lot of time to think since the accident and I've asked God to forgive me for being so weak, and I know now that He'll give me the strength to talk to Kath. I decided to get away from the farm and tell her down here, so she can absorb it all a bit before we face the kids. I'll tell her tonight after dinner," he finished sadly.

The two men sat facing each other in the small boat; their identical blue eyes locked together, both faces filled with sorrow. In unison they reached forward and clasped hands, then Nate leant further forward onto his knees and enveloped Sam in a bear hug. The younger man leaned on his brother as tears rolled down his cheeks, trying to absorb his strength.

"What do you need me to do?" Nate asked gently, leaning back, his hands on his brother's shoulders.

Sam gulped a few times. "Just be there for Kath and the kids, Mum and Dad too. Help me to make them understand that I never meant to hurt them, and I don't want to leave them, but it's too advanced this time. I'm not going to fight it. I don't want them to see me die by degrees. It's taken me a lot to come to terms with it, but now I've made my peace with the disease and dying. It's apparently my time to go." He shrugged despondently, raising his hands in the air and shaking his head. "I don't know why and I don't want to go, but it is what it is. I've really struggled with it all, but I do trust God and I'm now at peace with Him too."

They sat in silence for several minutes, each man lost in his own thoughts. Nate's head was spinning as he tried to process everything his brother had told him. He couldn't believe it. How had the cancer come back so stealthily, and advanced so quickly that it pronounced a death sentence without any hope of the verdict being overturned? On his brother no less, and he, Nate, who would do anything for Sam, could do nothing to correct this great injustice. He was powerless to do anything at all. His emotions ranged from incredulous disbelief, to anger, to overwhelming sadness. He banged his balled fist down hard on the side of the boat, causing the tinny to rock, and Sam to look up at him sharply. Their eyes locked but neither one spoke, what more could be said? They knew each other well enough to know what the other would be thinking. With heavy hearts the two fishermen tidied the boat and prepared to head back to shore.

"Let's go for a run around the harbour before we go in. I know I need some speed and fumes right now. Clear our heads, and find a nice sheltered spot for smoko," Nate suggested.

"Good idea," agreed Sam as he watched his brother pull up the anchor and start the motor.

They zoomed around on the water for a while, before slowing pace in a little bay and, realising they were over a nice clear patch of sand, they decided to drop their lines once more and try for a fish while they had their coffee. It proved to be a good idea as they each pulled in a couple of nice fish, but they had little joy in fishing now and, what had been a gentle breeze when they pulled up, was strengthening quickly, causing little waves with white caps to dance on the water, a sure sign that it was time to go in. The day had well and truly lost its beauty as great sorrow enveloped them.

Just before he pulled the anchor for the final time, Nate looked at Sam and, with a heartrending smile, said, "Let's just pray together before we head back. We'll surely need God's help to get through this. We trust Him in the good times and we need to trust Him now."

And so, the fishing trip ended with the two men bowing their heads in prayer; asking their Heavenly Father to give them strength and wisdom to navigate the terrible road ahead.

* * *

Sam stood on the pontoon, holding the rope tied to the bow of the little tinny. Nate walked up to the car park to bring his ute and the boat trailer back so they could retrieve the boat. It was still sunny and cool and, although the wind had come up and made them head for home, conditions had been absolutely perfect for fishing in the harbour. For those more adventurous, it had been calm enough to go out through the entrance of the harbour to the ocean waters beyond and try for some King George Whiting. They were the largest of the whiting species, and usually required more patience and skill to catch.

Nate and Sam had been happy to stay in the harbour and fish for the smaller Yellow Fin Whiting. They were more than satisfied with their combined catch of 8 legal fish, the smaller ones being thrown back in the water. Sam was looking forward to a meal of freshly fried whiting fillets, and he knew Kath would love the sweet moist fish. He didn't care that they hadn't caught many. He had really only wanted to go out on the water one last time with Nate.

The wind continued to grow stronger, and the fishermen knew the window for fishing in calm waters had closed, so there were lots of little boats making their way in to shore. Sam hadn't mentioned to Nate that he was feeling incredibly tired and worn out after their time on the water, the dull pain in his chest gathering momentum. He was wondering how long Nate would be when a noise behind him caught his attention.

A fully laden oyster boat was motoring slowly towards the boat ramp, observing the 4-knot speed limit. Another oyster boat was about 50m behind the first one. Turning his head back towards the car park where the familiar sound of a tractor beckoned to his farmer ears, Sam watched the big machine swing around and begin to reverse its trailer, with an empty oyster boat on it, back towards the water. 'It's all happening here,' he thought to himself. 'Launching and retrieving oyster boats and grey nomads coming in with their hauls.'

He looked back towards the other approaching boats, and saw that they had stopped well back. The first one obviously waiting for the empty boat to be launched and leave the boat ramp area, before it moved up to be loaded on to the same trailer. The drivers of both the tractors and the oyster boats were experienced and adept at launching and retrieving the big boats. Sam turned to look back along the pontoon from where he was standing. Another tinny had tied up behind him, while yet another was just entering the 4-knot area. He watched an older lady with white hair scramble onto the pontoon and hold the boat steady. The man who had been driving, stepped out carefully and, taking keys out of his pocket, wandered off to get his vehicle and trailer.

Sam, catching the woman's attention asked, "How'd you go today?"

"Not bad. Nice crabs and squid. Got a bit windy though. What about you?"

"Caught a few whiting," he smiled. He was about to say more when the oyster boat that had just been launched into the water started its powerful twin motors, and the water immediately churned and waves rocked the nearby boats and the pontoon.

Holding on tightly to Nate's tinny, Sam watched the big boat being propelled backwards past him. He turned to watch its progress when, to his horror, he saw the older woman a few metres further along from him, lose her balance and topple head first into the swirling water. She disappeared quickly beneath the surface and Sam lost sight of her.

He quickly looped the rope he was holding around the mooring cleat, and waved his arms at the fellow driving the waiting oyster boat to get his attention. The driver waved back to him, but Sam had no idea if he had seen the woman fall. Sam stared into the water which had calmed considerably now that the launched boat had moved away, and saw the woman's dark shape below.

The water was only about three metres deep, but she was weighed down by the coat, track pants and shoes she was wearing. Her eyes were wide-open in shock and her mouth was also open as if in a silent scream. She was making no effort to swim to the surface, seemingly paralysed by fear. Unfortunately, she had removed her life jacket while standing on the pontoon.

Sam tore off his own life jacket and locked eyes again with the oyster boat driver before diving cleanly into the icy water to the body below. He reached her quickly and grabbed her around the waist and pushing his feet off from the sandy bottom, he began to pull her upwards.

His head broke the surface, followed by the woman's. Confused bystanders, who had seen him dive into the water, suddenly realised what was happening. A backpacker, a young fit man who was standing with the oyster boat driver, quickly dived in from the side of the oyster boat, swimming easily to help the two bodies struggling in the water.

Sam was really working hard now; his sodden clothing hampering his efforts. The woman was a heavy weight, and was now coughing and struggling. Sam too was trying to gulp air, but could not seem to get enough breath, and felt his strength quickly leave him. He could hardly keep his own head above water now, let alone the woman's. Thankfully, the back packer took hold of the woman and pulled her to shallower water where they could stand.

But Sam was still in deep water, and knew he was in real trouble as he felt himself sinking, the salt water burning his throat and lungs. Suddenly he felt a strong grip on his arm and he was pulled forcefully towards the surface. Nate's face appeared inches from his own, determination etched into his every feature.

"Relax, I've got you." Rolling onto his back, he allowed his big brother to pull him to the shallow water at the bottom of the slippery boat ramp. Other men quickly came to help Nate carry the limp body up to the level road. Sam could not get enough air, he was coughing and gasping, the pain and pressure in his diseased lungs was immense. His sight blurred, he couldn't see Nate although he knew he was there, still holding him in his arms.

"Kath," he mouthed tiredly. "Where's Kath?"

Just before he passed out, he heard someone shouting: "Call an ambulance!"

* * *

The whirring sound grew louder, muffled voices sounded all around him, and when finally he managed to open his eyes, bright light pierced his throbbing head and he quickly closed them again. Every laboured breath hurt; his throat was on fire. Then he heard Kath's familiar voice.

"Sam! Sam! Wake up, darling," she pleaded.

With great effort, he turned his head in the direction of the voice, and slowly opened his eyes again.

"Where am I?" he whispered through dry lips.

"In the little hospital here in town. But don't worry; the Flying Doctors are coming to take you to Adelaide."

"Water," he gasped, managing a little sip before coughing and Kath's eyes widened in alarm when she saw the blood on his lips. A nurse reached over and wiped his mouth.

"Leave me here! Need to talk to Rose."

"What? Who? Sam, you need to be in a bigger hospital with specialists and the right equipment. Just relax, I'll make sure they take good care of you."

"No! Need Rose," he repeated louder this time, causing Nate to move back a bit from where he was standing so that Kath could talk to her husband.

"Sam, I don't know who Rose is. Do you mean Rosemary? You need to go to Adelaide."

Sam shook his head, before searching the room for Nate.

"Nate, listen!" Sam lifted his hand, and his brother quickly came closer again and grasped it firmly, "In the cottage. In my computer bag. A document. Hurry!" His voice faltered, and he started to cough again.

Nate and Kath looked at each other in bewilderment.

"I have no idea what he wants and I certainly don't know why he keeps asking for Rose, whoever she is," Kath said quietly, tears in her eyes.

"I'll go look; it must be important to him. Give me the key." Within minutes Nate was running through the car park to his ute. He had unhooked the trailer with the tinny on it in the marina car park, and a mate was taking it back to his place in town.

It was only a short drive to the cottage on the foreshore, and Nate quickly unlocked the door and found the computer bag in the bedroom. Opening it, he looked through the contents and found a document titled: *Advanced Health Directive for Samuel Matthew Wilmont*.

The significance of his find was not lost on Nate, and scrubbing his hand through his salt-encrusted hair, he groaned inwardly before taking the document, locking the door behind him and racing back to the hospital. He hurried in through the reception area and down the corridor, to where Sam and Kath were. Thankfully the doctor on duty, Dr. Franks, was back in the room and Nate handed him the document simply saying, "He has an Advanced Health Directive."

"A what?" exclaimed Kath in confusion, looking from Nate to the doctor and then back to Sam.

"Give me a few minutes please," said the softly spoken doctor, leaving the room.

"Nate, I don't understand. What's going on?"

'Oh God, how am I going to tell her? God, help me!' he prayed silently. He placed his hands on Kath's shoulders. "The cancer is back, Kath. Sam was going to tell you tonight. It's really bad, there's nothing they can do. I'm so sorry."

Kath just stared at her brother-in-law. She felt like he had slapped her, so great was the shock.

It made no sense. Sam would have told her. He told her everything. He could never keep the smallest of secrets, let alone hide something this serious.

"But, but how? When? How do you know and I don't?"

"He only told me today out in the boat. He didn't know all this," he indicated the hospital room, "was going to happen. He's had x-rays and scans with his oncologist in Toowoomba. Said he told you he was chasing spare parts or something."

"Well, yes, he's been going to Toowoomba for all sorts of reasons, and I knew something was up, but I never imagined it was for medical appointments."

They both just stood beside the bed, staring disbelievingly at Sam.

Dr. Franks returned a short time later and looked from Kath to Nate and back to Kath again.

"Mrs. Wilmont, I have just spoken to your husband's oncologist in Toowoomba, Dr. Rose Maitrey-Yuzuvendramisi." He stumbled over the long name. "She confirms the contents of this document."

Kath just stared at him in horror, unable to say more than quietly whisper, "Rose is his doctor?"

Nate put his arm around her shoulder.

"Doctor, Sam hadn't told Kath about his illness, in fact he only told me today, so we're both quite stunned by all this. We know very few details about his condition except that the cancer is back, and Sam said there was nothing that could be done."

"Oh, I see." He looked at them in surprise. "Forgive me; I obviously thought you were aware of his condition. Come sit in my office." He led them to a small office just down the corridor, and offered them both a chair and a glass of water.

"This would indeed come as a terrible shock for you, Mrs. Wilmont". Looking across at Nate, he added, "And for you too, Mr. Wilmont. Let me explain what I know. Sam was diagnosed with Stage IV metastatic colon cancer approximately ten weeks ago by his oncologist in Queensland. I understand he was treated for bowel cancer some six years ago and, unfortunately, this present situation seems to have arisen from that. Basically, some of the cancer cells survived the surgery and chemotherapy, and have spread. He has a large tumour on his right lung and smaller tumours on his left lung and his liver. The surrounding lymph glands and blood vessels have all been affected as well. He was offered palliative care to manage his symptoms, and to try to slow down its progress, but he declined all treatment except for pain relief. There is little more that can be done. Hence, Sam had the Advanced Health Care Directive drawn up outlining what his wishes are concerning his final treatment. Basically, the document says he simply wants the illness to take its course with no other treatment other than pain medication. I am so sorry."

"But he didn't know about this accident. Can't he recover from today and still have a few months left?" Kath's voice was barely audible. "Can't you ask his original oncologist? I don't know anything about this woman, Rose."

"Dr. Maitrey-Yuzuvendramisi explained that your husband's previous oncologist, Dr. Simpson, is working in London at present, and she has been handling all his patients. As her surname is a somewhat difficult one, she encourages her patients to simply call her Rose. Her younger patients call her Dr. Rose, I believe she said. As for your husband recovering from today's trauma," he paused before adding, "well, unfortunately, his lungs were put under enormous pressure and, as they were already compromised, the damage has been quite severe and is irreparable. I think the larger tumour may have ruptured and he is haemorrhaging internally. He may have a better chance in Adelaide, but he has indicated he doesn't want to be transferred and we have his final wishes to consider."

"This is a nightmare!" Kath sobbed. "How can we just sit here and watch him die?"

Nate pulled her closer to him. "He told me today that he just wants to slip away, that he doesn't want to be kept alive by tubes and machines. He wanted his final days to be calm and peaceful, at home on the farm, with you. He was going to take you to see the doctor next week and get her to explain it all, but now this has happened."

"But I've been with him the whole time since the farm accident, and he didn't say a word about it to me! He's mentioned Rose a few times but I thought he was referring to my garden, or Rosemary!"

Nate just shrugged, shaking his head, the enormity of it all nearly too much for him to bear also. His brother was dying.

"Please use my office for as long as you need, I know it's a lot to take in." The kindly doctor rose from his chair behind the desk, and left them alone.

"We have to respect what he wants, Kath, and he has obviously thought all this through."

"Oh Nate, I just can't believe this is happening! He's never lied to me before."

"He's never been in such a terrible situation before either. Faced with death, and leaving his family behind. At least last time he knew he had a chance. This time there is no hope of recovering."

Kath was overcome with a wretched sorrow that made it hard to breathe, hard to think straight and even harder to comprehend what her sweet man was going through. Turning, she buried her face in Nate's shoulder sobbing uncontrollably. Sometime later, after visiting the rest room and washing her face in the cool tap water, Kath, her eyes puffy and her face still drained of colour and masked in pain, walked back to her husband's bed, her knees shaking. She sat beside Sam, and taking hold of his hand whispered, "Oh Sam, what have you done?"

Sam looked directly at his wife. "My darling," he wheezed. "Please forgive me. Try and understand. I don't want to die in a city hospital full of strangers." He closed his eyes to rest before continuing. "I'm dying, Kath. Sooner than I expected, but you need to let me go. Let me die here in this beautiful fishing village, with you and Nate beside me." He spoke slowly with frequent stops. "Don't send me away. It's my time. I know it is. Let me go." He lay still, exhausted from talking.

"Oh, Sam," she cried. "Why didn't you tell me sooner?"

She thought he was asleep, but he answered her question.

"Because, I love you. So very much. I didn't want to hurt you more than necessary."

She knew that was true, he had always been there to protect her, right from when they first met and he realised what a hard man her father had been. Dear darling Sam was always there when she needed him, her knight in shining armour. She couldn't believe that a crazy act of daring, to save an old woman from drowning, had fast-forwarded the inevitable. Why, oh why, did he have to be the hero? Why didn't he call for someone else to dive in?

He had thought they would have more time together. Perhaps there was a new treatment he could have tried or a trial of some sort, Kath wondered miserably. Too late now, the final card had been played. There was no sound in the room except for his slow rattly breathing, a nurse returned to check the monitors and adjust his oxygen mask.

"He's sleeping," she said quietly before leaving the room.

The doctor returned, and both Nate and Kath looked at him with enquiring eyes.

"There's another factor at play, unfortunately, as we now have a major weather factor to contend with. A dust storm is fast approaching; unusual for this time of year, but it does happen. There's no way the Flying Doctors could assist us until it blows over. But, as I explained earlier, we are bound by Mr. Wilmont's Health Directive, so it really doesn't matter."

In a panicky whisper, Kath asked, "So what do we do?"

"We are only a small facility, as you're aware, but we do have a private room where we could move your husband to, where he won't be disturbed. We have already administered pain relief. So let's make him as comfortable as we can, and see what happens, hmmn? I'm going to confer with my colleagues in Adelaide while we wait."

Kath knew she should be praying, asking God for help, to give her peace, to be her comfort, but she couldn't. She couldn't even think clearly. She could barely breathe, let alone speak or put forth coherent requests to her Heavenly Father. Somewhere, in the dark recess of her mind, she knew there was some scripture about the Holy Spirit interceding for God's children in extreme times, but she couldn't think what it was, much less where it was from. So, she just sat at her husband's bedside, praying, "Oh, dear God, please help."

When we don't know what to pray for, the Spirit prays for us in ways that cannot be put into words. All our thoughts are known to God. He can understand what is in the mind of the Spirit, as the Spirit prays for God's people. Romans 8: 26-28

CHAPTER 10

Overwhelming Reality

"I shake, but my rock moves not."
Charles Spurgeon 1834-1892

*K*ath sat in the quiet little room at the end of the hall where they had moved Sam. It was tastefully decorated, with seascapes on the walls and a large bay window which overlooked a well-kept garden. She barely noticed any of it. The whole situation was surreal.

Sam's secrecy left her totally bewildered; it was so out of character for him. Sam, who told her everything, who could never keep the smallest of secrets, had been to Toowoomba for x-rays, scans and oncologist appointments; all under the guise of hunting for spare parts while she was at work.

The worst part was that he even had a legal directive outlining his wishes for his final care and treatment, and she knew nothing about it!!! Why had he planned to tell her on this trip, and not before? How could she not have known? How had he hidden such terrible mind-blowing news from her?

Her husband had terminal cancer which had been silently spreading, undetected for goodness knows how long; with any symptoms wrongly presumed to be the flu, or hay fever, or grain dust, or tiredness, or whatever excuse Sam could come up with. She was utterly dumfounded by his duplicity. They had always shared everything, done everything together. They should have talked about this together, cried together, discussed options together, and ultimately battled this together. Together they could have overcome it again, surely?

The shock of the day's events was overwhelming her. She glanced over at Nate, who sat on the other side of Sam's bed. He was watching Sam's breathing, the slow rise and fall of his chest, and she realised that his face was almost as white as Sam's. He, too, had experienced a terrible shock. It was bad enough that he had only just learned that Sam was terminally ill, then to witness him nearly drown and have to pull him out of the water, and now to see him here in the hospital in such a serious condition with a dust storm howling outside. The whole situation was inconceivable; she could scarcely take it in let alone process all the information.

"Where's Angie?" Kath whispered.

"She'll be here soon, slow going in the dust," he replied softly. "We have to abide by his wishes Kath. He's obviously thought this through and, I know you don't think so now, but he was only trying to spare you more pain." Nate looked up at her, his eyes moist. "He adores you, Kath. Always has. He doesn't want you to see him die little by little, suffer through chemo again, slowly fade away. He knows there's no point fighting this now. Try and understand, and let him have the death he's decided on." Nate wiped his eyes on the sleeve of his shirt, one of Sam's. He had quickly changed out of his wet clothes into some of his brother's when he picked up Kath after the ambulance left the marina. "I'll wait outside for Angie." Standing, he walked around the bed to Kath and held out his arms, she did not hesitate to return his warm embrace, more tears on his shirt.

"My two most favourite people," a hoarse whisper came from the bed. They both looked at Sam and returned his weak smile.

"I'll leave you two together." Nate disappeared out the door.

Kath carefully lay beside Sam on the narrow bed, she couldn't help but cry quietly against his shoulder.

"Oh Sam, why didn't you tell me?"

"I'm so sorry, love. I wanted to, I really did, but I just couldn't." He spoke very quietly, and with great effort. "Please forgive me."

"Oh, Sam. I love you so much," she whispered. "How will I live without you?"

"You won't be alone… my darling girl; I'll be cheering you on… from above." His speech was broken with coughs and gasps. "And we've never… been alone… have we? We've always known… that God is with us… His Holy Spirit… guiding us. And you'll have… the family." He stroked her hair and kissed her forehead gently. "I love you… with all my heart, always have… you know that. Tell the children… I'm sorry… and that I'm… so proud of them. I thought we'd have more time. Really did… Sorry love. I'm so sorry."

Kath choked back a sob, her heart was breaking, this couldn't be happening.

"Be brave… my darling… Kath… be strong. I know you… don't think… you can… but I believe… in you."

He stopped talking, and lay wheezing and gasping for breath. Just as Kath was about to push the buzzer for help, his breathing settled and he opened his eyes again, and winked at her, a larrikin to the end. They smiled sadly at each other, knowing that their time together was quickly running out. Even though it felt like they were shrouded with a heavy cloak of sadness, a sense of peace slipped through suddenly, like a ray of sunshine in the dust storm, and they were both comforted and reassured. Sam drifted off to sleep, while Kath lay beside him, trying to pray but unable to blot out the frightening sounds she could hear within his chest and airways; her mind consumed by swirling thoughts and images.

Her Sam, her rock. He had become so grateful for every new day that dawned after recovering from his illness last time. He took nothing for granted, believing that he had been given extra time on earth to spend with his family and friends. He was always willing to help anyone, anytime, and was actively involved in his church family and the local community. Nothing was too much trouble. He was a devoted family man. He encouraged them all in every aspect of their lives, wanting them all to be the best they could be. He had developed a close relationship with each of his three children, and tried to keep up to date with their comings and goings.

But there was to be no reprieve this time, no second chance. There was nothing to be done except to let a good man die as peacefully as possible, knowing he was loved and that he would never be forgotten. At least it would not be forever, as she knew without doubt that Sam would be going home to Heaven, and they would be reunited again one day. But that didn't really help at the moment. Oh, the pain of saying goodbye. How it hurt!

Kath wondered if she would have the will to go on alone. She could see nothing but emptiness in front of her, despair, loneliness, sadness… Her thoughts were spiralling downwards and, with great effort, she forced herself to stay in control, to be brave for Sam, now, when he needed her most. He mumbled something incomprehensible and she stroked his forehead, crooning to him like she had to their children when they had been small. He lifted his hand, searching for hers, and she grasped it and held it between her own. He settled then, a little smile on his face. She watched him sleeping, but had to move after a while as her arm was going numb.

Carefully she eased off the bed and sat on the edge of the chair again, leaning over his sleeping form, frowning at the sound of his forced breathing.

She must have fallen asleep as she was woken by a gentle touch on her shoulder and, straightening stiffly, she found Nate and Angie standing beside her. Angie was staring at Sam with wide eyes, evidently shocked by his appearance and the sound of his breathing. She turned to Kath who rose to embrace her sister-in-law.

"Oh, poor Sam! He looks so dreadful. I can't begin to imagine how you're feeling, Kath. It's just devastating. I'm struggling to understand what's happening."

"I know, Angie. It's all so hard to fathom."

"Just know that we're here for you. And for Sam, of course. We won't leave you. Can I get you something to eat?"

"No, nothing. I couldn't eat a thing."

"I'll get you a cup of tea at least. Coffee, Nate?"

"Ta, love."

Angie left the room quietly, and Nate moved to resume sitting on the other side of the bed. "Would you like me to call Dad and Jarrod? They need to know what's happening, and to prepare for the worst. They'll let the others know. Dad can contact Pastor Bob too. The more people praying the better."

"Yes, of course. Thanks. But what do people pray for? He's not going to recover, Nate," she answered with a quiet sob, as more tears slipped down her face.

"I know he's not, but we all need God right now. There's no way we'll get through this without Him. Remember, Kath, that all our days are numbered. God knows exactly when each one of us will die. He has His reasons and He'll be our strength, and comfort us in our grief. I know that doesn't really help much right now, but I know it's true and I've got to keep reminding myself of that right now." Nate, too, wiped more tears away, looking sadly across the bed at the distraught woman, before leaving the room for a short time to make the phone calls.

Angie returned with their hot drinks, and they sat together for the rest of the long afternoon and evening, speaking quietly to Sam and reading scripture passages to him, unsure if he could hear them or not. Worship music played softly on Angie's phone. Sam stirred from time to time, and finally opened his eyes. He looked first at his wife, and then at his brother and sister-in-law. He weakly held his hand up, and Nate took it in his own strong right hand, his other hand clasped over the top.

"Love you, brother," whispered Sam. "Look after... these two... won't you?"

"You know I will," Nate replied, gently shaking hands with his younger brother one last time.

Sam nodded and turned his attention to Kath. "My darling... love you... so much. So... very... sorry." His chest rattled once more and he closed his eyes and exhaled his final breath.

Kath sobbed loudly, and threw herself on his lifeless body, while Nate watched on holding his own weeping wife against his chest, his face contorted with grief. A nurse came in, and quickly left to summon the doctor. After he had made his brief examination and quietly spoken his condolences, he left the three bereft family members. They stayed together in the hospital room for some time, before Nate and Angie quietly left Kath alone to farewell her husband for the heartbreakingly final time.

Nate put his arm around Angie's shoulders and together they left the hospital building and walked the short distance to the motel where Angie had booked a room for them. In silence they entered, and Angie immediately turned into her husband's embrace and cried again into his warm shoulder. When she had calmed, he pulled her down on the bed and they lay there together, seeking comfort in each other's closeness, both feeling desolate, neither speaking. So many thoughts running through their minds.

When Nate realised that Angie had fallen asleep, he lay quietly for a long time, mulling everything over in an unbelieving kaleidoscope of emotions that threatened to smother him. Finally, he rose slowly, pulled a blanket over Angie's sleeping form, and took a long hot shower to clear his head.

When he returned sometime later, Angie was awake and had put the kettle on. They found the packaged biscuits that the motel supplied, and ate them with their cups of hot tea. In their present states, neither felt able to eat anything more substantial. They spoke softly of all that had transpired at the hospital, both still struggling to fully comprehend the tragedy that had taken place. How could Sam be gone? How could Kath not have known? So many questions that neither one could answer. When Nate looked at the clock, he was surprised to see that it was after midnight.

"I think I should go check on Kath," he told Angie.

"Yes, of course. It was good of them to let her stay with Sam. She may well be asleep, so don't wake her if she is."

Nate nodded, and kissed her cheek. Grabbing his car keys, he left the room, closing the door softly behind him.

There was a young male nurse at the reception desk who Nate had not seen before but, when he introduced himself, and asked if he could check on Kath, the man quietly said, "Of course, Mr. Wilmont, go on down. I'm sorry for your loss."

"Thank you," replied the older man before walking slowly to Sam's room.

He stood for a moment readying himself before slowly opening the door. He was surprised to see Kath standing at the foot of the bed looking at the form of her dead husband.

"Kath," he quickly asked. "Are you okay?"

She started at his words, but gave a little nod, and replied ever so softly. "Yes, I'm fine. I've talked to him, kissed him goodbye, hugged him, and laid beside him, and cried, and prayed, and cried some more. Now I'm just not sure what to do. People to ring and things to organise, I guess. The things that Sam would usually take care of..." She stopped on a whimper.

Nate went quickly to her, and put his arms around her. "Right now you need to get some sleep. I'll take you back to the cottage. Everything can wait until morning, and I can do a lot of them for you. Few good decisions are made between midnight and dawn. It's time to let him go. He's not here; he's up in Heaven with the Lord now."

She nodded, but returned to Sam's side. She stroked his face and kissed him one last time before turning and walking out the door that Nate held open.

"Just give me a moment," he murmured before returning to stand beside the bed. He looked down at his brother, noting his face was very white but peaceful, looking much younger than his 52 years. He placed one hand on the younger man's shoulder, and clasped his right hand in his own, shaking hands one last time before bending to kiss him on the cheek. "Bye Sam."

Turning slowly, he walked out to join Kath.

You will go out in joy and be led forth in peace;
the mountains and hills will burst into song before you,
and all the trees of the field will clap their hands. Isaiah 55:12

Part Two

*The LORD will guide you always; He will satisfy your
needs in a sun-scorched land and will strengthen
your frame. You will be like a well-watered garden,
like a spring whose waters never fail.
Isaiah 58:11*

CHAPTER 11

The Saddest Goodbye

*"In everyone's life, at some time, our inner fire goes out.
It is then burst into flame by an encounter with another
human being. We should all be thankful for those people
who rekindle the inner spirit." Albert Schweitzer 1875- 1965*

Sam's body was taken back to Queensland. He was buried in the Dalby lawn cemetery on the outskirts of town, with only the family in attendance. It was a beautiful sunny day with a light breeze. Recent rain had greened up the grass, and freshened the well-maintained gardens. Kath noticed none of this; completely lost in her own world of grief and despair.

Jack and Edith never left her side, while Craig and Rosemary comforted Jessica. Jarrod and Majella, and Bryce and Sally, stood huddled together with their cousins. Nate and Angela had flown up from South Australia with their 2 sons. Their daughter was working overseas and was unwell, so she couldn't fly home for the funeral. The foursome from down south

had travelled out from Toowoomba with Josh and Bronwyn. It was a subdued gathering of a heartbroken family farewelling a beloved son, husband, brother, father and uncle. They were all still shocked, and struggled
to come to terms with their great loss.

After a brief message from Pastor Bob, they slowly moved forward,
one by one, to lay a rose or a handful of soil on the casket, before it was
slowly lowered into the black earth. Kath broke down at this point and
sobbed into Jack's shoulder, tears also streaming down his pale weathered
face. Edith, too, was overwhelmed and grateful for the support of Nate
and Angie who stood beside her; Nate's strong arm supporting her in the
immense sorrow of burying her son. The cousins stood united, supporting
Jarrod and Majella, Bryce and Sally, and Jessica, dark glasses hiding their
red rimmed eyes.

When, at last, the casket reached its resting place in the soft earth, they
slowly turned and moved to stand in the shade of a nearby gum tree. Jarrod,
Bryce and Jessica went to their mother and, together, they hugged and cried
by the open grave, finding it all so surreal, but trying to draw strength from
each other. They didn't want to leave their father alone in the ground; the
finality of death was brutal, their grief raw and heart breaking.

After a while, Nate came and gently ushered them to the waiting cars.
They were driven to Jack and Edith's home where they were able to rest, and
have a light lunch. The break allowed them to regain their composure as
best they could, before attending the 2pm memorial service at their church.
Kath managed to drink a cup of sweet tea, and nibble on a sandwich, but
she spoke little and remained pale and wan. However, she managed to rally
herself and put on a brave face as she entered the church, where she and
Sam had been married. They had been so young and naive about life in
those days, imagining a lifetime of growing old together.

The memorial service was bittersweet, a beautiful tribute to a loving family man, and a very well-known and respected member of the local community. It honoured Sam and celebrated the life he had lived, and gave his many friends an opportunity to speak, some causing more tears to flow while others a few laughs at the memories of good times past. It all passed in a blur for Kath, lost as she was in her grief; still struggling to believe that her beloved husband was gone. Jessica had put together a slideshow of pictures of her father from his childhood onwards, snaps of him with family and friends; it was a mixture of sadness and joy as they saw a caring, good natured and fun-loving man, called home way too early.

The song that Jessica chose to have played during the slide presentation echoed throughout the church, the words enabling all present to imagine the wonder of Sam's arrival in Heaven:

> *Surrounded by your glory*
> *What will my heart feel?*
> *Will I dance for you Jesus?*
> *Or in awe of you be still?*
> *Will I stand in your presence?*
> *Or to my feet will I fall?*
> *Will I sing hallelujah?*
> *Will I be able to speak at all?*
> *I can only imagine*
> *I can only imagine*

It was a very poignant service, and afterwards there was an endless line of people all wanting to pay their respects to Kath. She feared it would never end. As much as she appreciated their love and kindness, in her fragile state she just wanted the formalities to be over so she could seek the refuge of her home and be alone. Again, it was Nate who came to her rescue, and walked her to the car where his parents were already waiting with Angie. After making sure Jessica was okay, Kath gratefully got in the car and they returned to Jack and Edith's home; a quiet group all mentally and emotionally drained from the day's proceedings.

Kath sat quietly on the verandah, staring out into the garden while she waited for the rest of the family to return. She heard muffled conversations from inside, but paid little attention, and was grateful when Angie came to tell her that Nate was ready to drive them back to the farm. Josh, Bronwyn and their three girls were staying in town with Jack and Edith, while Bryce and Sally and their cousins from South Australia were going to drive out to stay with Jarrod and Majella at Oakleigh. Hugs and kisses were exchanged all round, as everyone took their leave.

Jessica had the week off work, and was going to stay at the farm. She stepped wearily into the car and settled on the backseat next to her mum, relaxing back into the soft upholstery. Jack and Edith both looked totally worn out, and Kath was relieved to see that Rosemary was fussing over them and would make sure they were resting before leaving them in the care of Josh and Bronwyn.

Jess took her mother's hand in hers, and Kath smiled sadly at her, thankful for the comforting touch of her darling girl. They drove to the farm in silence, the four occupants lost in their own thoughts. Kath closed her eyes, not opening them until the car pulled up in the carport, Little Tink's shrill bark welcoming them home. Old Nipper barked too and ran to the car, eager to greet his master. Not finding him there, he ran off down the driveway looking for the ute but, not seeing or hearing any other vehicles driving on the gravel road, walked back dejectedly to his favourite spot under the jacaranda tree to faithfully wait for his master's return.

They all entered the house quietly and, after declining the offer of another cuppa from Kath, ever the thoughtful hostess; they all disappeared to their respective bedrooms to rest. Kath picked up her little dog and walked slowly down the hallway, old floorboards creaking comfortably as she passed. She kicked off her high heels, and sank thankfully on to the bed with a loud sigh. Tink sensed her mistress' need for quiet, and curled up beside her whimpering quietly as if to assure Kath that she was not alone. Kath welcomed the little dog's company, and simply stared at the ceiling thinking over all that had happened in the past few months; trying to comprehend the enormity of her loss. She was totally absorbed in her thoughts when there was a soft knock on the bedroom door. She turned to see Jessica looking in.

"Are you awake, Mum?"

"Yes, Jess. Come on in."

"There's a phone call for you, and I thought you would like to take it. It's Gertrude. She rang my mobile. You must have yours turned off still. She's somewhere in Europe." She finished explaining, and handed her phone to her mother.

"Thanks sweetie. Of course I'll talk to her. Hello Gertrude?"

"Oh, Kath darling," a loud voice gushed. "I'm so sorry we're not there. We've been on a cruise to see the Northern Lights. We only just arrived back at our hotel, and received the message Nate sent. Oh, you poor girl. I can't believe your darling Sam is gone, and we're not even there to support you!"

"It's alright, Gertrude, I'm fine really. The family is all here, and everyone has been wonderful. I can't believe he's gone either. I really can't believe he's gone," she ended, her voice choking.

"Oh, my darling. My heart is breaking for you, really it is, and so is Max's. We both loved Sam, and we both love you. Oh, I wish we were there right now, not on the other side of the world. We would do anything for you darling, you know that!"

"Yes, I know that." Kath smiled sadly as her dear friend spoke loudly and quickly, and she could imagine Gertrude waving her free hand around dramatically as she spoke. There was no one quite like Gertrude.

"We're flying home next week, darling, and I'll call as soon as we get back. Just rest now and take care of yourself. We're praying for you."

The call suddenly ended. Typical of Gertrude, when she had no more to say she simply hung up. Kath felt somewhat energised by her friend's call, Gertrude always had that effect on her. She scratched Tink's ears. She decided to have a shower and freshen up, and see to her guests. When she entered the kitchen sometime later, she found Nate and Angie sitting at the kitchen table with Jillian.

"Oh Kath, you look much better, you've got some colour back in your face. Did you have a little rest?" her good friend enquired.

"Yes, I did. And then Gertrude rang from overseas. It was good to hear her voice; she'll be home in a week or so. I didn't hear you arrive, Jillie. Something smells good." She looked enquiringly around the kitchen.

"Oh, I've brought some casseroles over that the church ladies have made."

"How thoughtful. You've all been so good." Kath hugged her friend.

"No problem at all. Well, I'll leave you to it. I'll be in touch, Kath, but call me if you need anything, won't you?"

"Yes, of course. Thanks again, Jillie."

Nate, Angie, Kath and Jessica enjoyed a quiet evening together. The meal provided was delicious home cooking, with a sweet dessert supplied as well. Kath actually felt hungry for the first time in a while, and enjoyed her meal. Afterwards they sat out on the verandah as the cool easterly breeze blew across the fertile plains; soft music playing in the background that Jess had put on. No one was in the mood for conversation, and they quietly drifted off to bed.

Jessica was the last to leave, reluctant to leave her mother's side, and Kath was comforted by her daughter's presence. They shared a special bond, the two girls in the otherwise male household. They had similar natures although Jessica was far braver and more confident than her mother had ever been. Kath was so thankful for that. Jessica had been an A grade student all through school and university where she had completed a Bachelor of Business, majoring in Accounting. She had her father's head for figures, and was very analytical, lacking her mother's artistic flair and creativity. Mother and daughter were of similar height and build, although Jessica's body was tanned and well toned as she, like Bryce and Sally, liked to play sport and keep fit. She had her mother's dark hair, only longer, which she normally tied back in a high pony tail or a loose bun.

"Are you okay, Mum?" she enquired softly, snuggling close.

"Yes, I'm okay I guess. Still trying to take it all in. Did you think it was a nice service? I must admit I struggled to focus on much of what was said."

"It was a beautiful service, Mum, and it was recorded so maybe one day you might want to watch it again? When it's not so overwhelming?"

"That's a good idea. You should go to bed. I won't be long. Goodnight."

"Night Mum. Love you."

"Love you too, Jess."

Kath picked up the order of service from the memorial service, staring for a few moments at the picture of Sam's smiling face on the cover, looking up at her. Shaking her head sorrowfully, she opened the program and began to read it slowly. The Bible reading summed up Sam's life. He hadn't been perfect, but it was still so appropriate for him:

Marks of the True Christian
Let love be genuine; hate what is evil, hold fast to what
is good; love one another with mutual affection; outdo

*one another in showing honour. Do not lag in zeal,
be ardent in spirit, serve the Lord. Rejoice in hope, be
patient in suffering, persevere in prayer. Contribute to
the needs of the saints; extend hospitality to strangers.*

*Bless those who persecute you; bless and do not curse them.
Rejoice with those who rejoice, weep with those who weep.
Live in harmony with one another; do not be haughty, but
associate with the lowly; do not claim to be wiser than you are.
Do not repay anyone evil for evil, but take thought for what is
noble in the sight of all. If it is possible, so far as it depends on
you, live peaceably with all. Romans 12:9-18*

It was a beautiful piece of scripture, but it gave her little comfort on this dark night. She did not weep, however. She just felt sad, so very sad, and desperately heartbroken. Later in bed, she lay awake for a long time, her thoughts finally drifting to Gertrude and Max. That, at least, was something to look forward to; seeing them again.

* * *

Gertrude and Max Bianchi were both larger-than-life sort of people. Friendly, outgoing and wonderfully creative. They were well respected in the art world for their expertise, and their two very successful galleries on the Sunshine Coast – Bianchi's at Noosa, and Serendipity Place in the hinterland. Max and Gertrude were Majella's uncle and aunt. Kath and Sam first met them at Jarrod and Majella's engagement party, held at Serendipity Place, which was also the Bianchi's home. They met up with them again at Jarrod and Majella's wedding. Sam warmed to them instantly, but Kath was hesitant at first. Intimidated by their extroverted personalities – well

Gertrude's for sure – but thankfully Max was not as loud and outgoing as his wife. Their warm caring natures soon put her at ease, and their common interests in art and family soon formed the basis for a friendship that quickly grew strong, as if they had known each other for much longer.

Gertrude was quite a tall woman, standing 180cm, with a full curvaceous figure. Her long, thick hair had begun to grey when she was in her 30s, and she had not denied the change in colouring. By 50 she had been quite silver. She had embraced her new look, favouring brightly coloured clothing and equally bright lipstick and nail polish to match. Now in her 60s, her wardrobe and makeup remained flawless, a stylish ensemble that suited her perfectly.

Everything was 'plus size' for Gertrude – her clothing, hairstyles and jewellery and, most importantly, her love for her husband, their two boys, Toby and Julian, and their extended family and friends. The fountain from which all this love and nurture flowed was none other than the faith she had been raised in by her devout parents. God's love was the foundation of her life. She was outgoing, effervescent and vivacious, but nothing concealed her kind and loving heart. 'Love God and love others' was her motto.

Serendipity Place had once been a grand farmhouse, but the property had long since been subdivided and sold, with Max and Gertrude purchasing the home block, with the old house and a number of outbuildings on it. They had renovated extensively and, in doing so, had breathed life back into the beautiful old Queenslander with its wide wrap around verandahs, and its 3-metre-high ceilings, polished timber floors and brick fireplaces. The gardens were also carefully restored and extended.

The pathway from the car park meandered through a cottage garden full of blooms, releasing scents of lavender, rosemary and honeysuckle. White standard roses in vibrant pots graced the sides of the front stairs, while geraniums, petunias and pansies, with their ever-cheery petals, smiled happily in the warm sunshine. A huge jacaranda tree stood as if it were the king of the garden, resplendent in royal purple, providing shade as well as magnificent beauty. Flowering wisteria threaded gracefully through the verandah rails, and up the posts, its lavender blooms contrasting starkly with the red climbing geraniums, spilling out of the many pots hanging from the overhead beams.

Max was responsible for the design of the garden, his attention to detail and creativity in evidence everywhere. There were numerous secluded spots, where chairs were carefully placed to ensure the occupants would enjoy the unique focal spot for that particular area. These varied from water features, bird feeders, native bee hives, to fish ponds. Guests could also enjoy a coffee seated on one of the verandahs; there was a special place for everyone, no matter the weather. Max originally took care of his beloved garden himself, with the help of a casual maintenance man, but on his 60th birthday he employed a full-time gardener to keep it looking its best. However, if Max could not be found, Gertrude knew he would be somewhere in the garden.

The kaleidoscope of colour that was Serendipity Place continued when one entered the boutique itself, and many a visitor stopped on the threshold and simply stared in wonder at the sight before them. The boutique section contained a rather eclectic collection of arts, crafts, gourmet foods, natural skincare, homewares, books, and a range of clothing. The art gallery was in two large large rooms that adjoined the boutique, and beyond that was the café and dining area.

The old barn at the rear of the farmhouse had proved to be a perfect foundation to create a light and airy two-storey townhouse in the country. Not overwhelming in size, but large enough to have three bedrooms. It was perfect for Max and Gertrude, and was tastefully furnished in a way that reflected their love for antiques and fine art. It provided the perfect escape from the noise and bustle of the business; a private space where they could relax and unwind. Their oldest son, Toby, was qualified in Business and Marketing, and was working in Sydney. Julian in contrast had started two different degrees but had dropped out of each at the end of the first semester, much to his parent's dismay. He then spent 12 months backpacking around Europe, but had returned home broke, still with no ambition or enthusiasm for work or study.

He was a constant cause for concern, and fought continually with his father who could not comprehend his son's attitude to life. In particular, Max could not understand Julian's complete lack of work ethic, and resolutely refused to support his lazy whimsical lifestyle. His mother had been his main defender but finally, when she was called to the local police station for the second time to pick him up after a night of drinking and driving, she too had had enough. Both parents attended Julian's court hearing where he was heavily fined, and lost his driver's licence for 12 months. Thankfully, to their knowledge, he was not doing drugs. A very unhappy Max paid the fine, with several conditions clearly outlined; namely the money was to be repaid in full and he was to find a job, any job, immediately.

The following few weeks passed under a cloud of tension which only lifted when Frank, an old Italian friend of Max's, provided a solution agreeable to them all by offering Julian a job at his restaurant in Brisbane. The position was for a waiter/kitchen hand, with a minimal wage, but was sweetened by the offer of accommodation in a small flat at the back of the restaurant at a very reasonable rent. Surprisingly, Julian accepted the job, apparently eager to escape the family home and become independent.

Old Frank was a bachelor and entrepreneur, and had known Max for many years. He was familiar with Julian's history, and hoped to not only help his old friend, but to also endeavour to give Julian another chance to make his way in life. Frank was small in stature, barely 162cm tall, totally bald with a raspy voice. He looked quite fearsome, with steely black eyes and a large nose, but his ready smile softened his features. He was not to be trifled with though, as he could be quite intimidating if he chose to be, and did not suffer fools lightly. First impressions may have been of a gruff little man, bossy and commanding, but he was actually very kind-hearted, and chose to see the best in everyone. He was respected by his staff as a fair boss. He spoke softly, using his hands to wildly emphasise his key points, and when handing Julian the key to the little flat, he told him very clearly what his expectations were of him as a tenant and an employee.

"You slack off, or behave bad, you go. Understand? You are in charge of your life. You always have choices in front of you, and you must decide what to do."

Every 'you' was punctuated with a pointy finger jabbing into the younger man's chest. "But remember, Julio, there are always consequences to deal with. Understand? You got to start making good decisions. You work hard, you get rewards. Understand? Choices, decisions, consequences! Very important!"

Julian nodded in agreement, not quite sure what to make of this little man, or his new name Julio, but replied politely, "Thank you, Frank. I'll do my best, I promise."

Strangely enough, it was a turning point in Julian's life, allowing him to break free from the self-absorbed hole of apathy he had dug for himself. He respected his new boss, and actually enjoyed the work and got along well with the other employees. The staff were all aged in their 20s and 30s, and there was an easy welcoming camaraderie between them all. A lot of their customers were regulars, and they all seemed to be close friends or relatives of Frank, who was a little gnome-like figure presiding over the kitchen and the guests. He ensured his restaurant ran smoothly, and everyone enjoyed their dining experience in the friendly relaxed atmosphere. So, Julian's life began to slowly improve as he settled into his new job in the city. He worked hard, watched others, listened carefully and began learning new skills.

Frank was pleased with his work, and the initiative he was displaying, and rewarded him with more responsibility and an increase in wages, simply saying, "Good work, Julio, very good work."

For the first time in his young life, Julian was leading a healthy and productive lifestyle. Even his bank balance was steadily growing, thanks to the pay rise and taking advantage of working extra hours when he was offered them. He couldn't believe it when he realised he had been working there for 12 months, and that he was content and enjoying life. Other employees came and went, but he felt that at last he had found his niche in hospitality, and he intended to keep moving upwards.

He had two mottos stuck on his bedroom wall, the first was written in his own hand, in big black letters, and was from his favourite childhood author Dr. Suess:

> *You have brains in your head and feet in your shoes.*
> *You can steer yourself any direction you choose.*

The second was a canvas wall hanging, a gift, from his mother:

> *With man this is impossible, but with God all*
> *things are possible. Matthew 19:26*

Julian's parents had raised him in a Christian home, and were disappointed with the direction his life had taken over the years since he'd left high school. They still loved him, and had never turned their backs on him, and he knew they never would. He alone was the one responsible for taking the rebellious step to fold to the pressure of his mates at school and uni; ignoring the values and Christian faith his parents had taught him. His time of fun and free living had not ended well as he had nothing to show for it – no money, no job, no qualification but, thankfully, by the skin of his teeth, no criminal conviction.

He was so thankful for the unconditional love of his parents and his brother, for even Toby had not given up on him. He knew he had hurt them all, and it would be a while before he could prove his worth to them. But they were still there for him, and encouraged him on his road to redemption. He knew Jesus was still there too, only a prayer away, but he had not sought forgiveness from Him, yet.

Looking back over the past year, he could see how God had been working in his life, preparing him for a new beginning. He had his parents' prayers, Toby's too, to thank for that and now, of course, he had Frank in his corner as well. He could hear the lively worship music from a nearby church every Sunday morning, and in the evenings too. He could feel a stirring deep within his spirit, and knew that Jesus was waiting to welcome him back into sweet fellowship once again.

He could no longer ignore what his heart was telling him to do, so one afternoon, sitting alone in a park looking at the river flowing by in front of him, he simply whispered a short prayer from his heart into the wind, knowing that fancy words were not necessary,

"I'm sorry Lord; I know I'm saved by your sacrifice on the cross, that you died and rose again. Please forgive me."

By the peace and joy he felt, he knew Jesus had heard him.

* * *

Meanwhile, back at Yallaroo, another young man, a good mate of Julian's, was struggling to come to terms with his father's death. Bryce, too, had been a rebellious teenager, getting into all sorts of trouble at school and with his parents. His father had spent a lot of time talking to him, trying to help him figure out the questions of life that most boys struggle with. Sam and Bryce had formed a close bond during those years and it was only now, when his father was gone, that Bryce realised just how much his dad had helped him, and how much he respected his wise counsel. Bryce had first met Julian at Jarrod and Majella's engagement party. Bryce was the oldest by a few years, but he could empathise with where Julian was in life. They still kept in touch by phone and social media. Bryce had stuck by Julian throughout his various scrapes and indiscretions, trying to help and encourage the younger man when he could.

Julian had taken time off work last week to attend Bryce's dad's funeral. He had been deeply moved by the memorial service, and the broken hearts of the family. Afterwards, when he was back in his flat in Brisbane, he had phoned his parents. They had finished their trip, and were staying with family in Florence before flying home. It was difficult but, through tears and with a broken voice, he had managed to apologise to them for all the pain and disappointment he had caused, and thanked them for never giving up on him. He told them that his job was going well, and of his time spent with Jesus by the river. He promised to prove to them that he was a changed man. It was a very emotional conversation for them all. One his parents had hoped and prayed for, indeed trusted in God to bring into being, for many years.

See, I can never forget you…
I have written your name on the palms of My hands.
Isaiah 49:16

CHAPTER 12

The Walls Crumble

*The greater your knowledge of the goodness
and grace of God on your life,
the more likely you are to praise Him
in the storm." Matt Chandler*

The peace of the early morning was broken by heavy footsteps, as Bryce thundered down the hallway and into his father's office where a metal gun cabinet stood. Unlocking it, he considered the small collection of guns, before taking out his favourite .22 rifle.

Whistling to his dog, Butch, he walked quickly to the old Toyota Hilux he used for bush bashing and shooting. Hardly waiting for Butch to jump in the back, Bryce slid behind the wheel and slammed the old ute into gear. He roared off in a cloud of dust that was nearly as dark as his mood.

Kath watched her son drive off. Wiping a tear from her eye, she said quietly to Nate as he sat with Angie at the kitchen table. "I thought he was spending the day at Jarrod's? Poor boy. He feels so lost, confused, we all do. Do you think he'll be all right? He shouldn't be shooting in his present state. Oh, Nate, I'm so worried about him. He used to be such a hothead, remember? Always in fights at school and with Jarrod."

"He'll be okay, he just needs to blow off some steam. He won't do anything stupid. He's matured a lot since then. I'll go check on him, though. I've a fair idea where he'll be," her brother-in-law answered.

He turned to Angie and gave her a quick hug before grabbing an old felt hat off the hat rack, and going down the back stairs into the garden.

Bryce's head cleared a little, as he drove along the rough track to a little clearing on the far side of the property. He skidded to a halt at his destination, and sat for a few minutes looking at the targets set about 50 metres away in a steep sided gully. It was a perfect bush shooting range, where his father had taught both Jarrod and Bryce, and Jessica too, how to handle guns safely and shoot straight. Bryce got out of the ute and slammed the door behind him. The dog wisely made no move to jump down from the tray. He could sense Bryce's mood and decided to stay well away from both man and gun.

Bryce quickly loaded the rifle and, taking aim, fired a round into the first target. Re-loading, he took out his fury on the second target. His aim was good, but not perfect, considering the mood he was in. But Bryce didn't care, he just wanted to hit out at something. He kept re-loading and firing and, with each round, his anger lessened and his aim became straighter. It was sometime later when a movement caught his eye as he turned around to get some more ammo. He was surprised to see his uncle sitting on the quad bike some distance away, under a shady tree. Bryce had not even heard the bike arrive, he was so focused on his shooting and dark thoughts.

Not bothering to reload the .22, Bryce waved to his uncle and leaned against the ute, as he waited for him to ride over.

"How long have you been here, Uncle Nate?" he asked.

"Oh, a little while." Nate answered quietly as he got off the bike and walked over to scratch Butch's head.

"You know, it's not a good idea to tear off with a firearm when you're not thinking clearly. It's an easy way for an accident to happen."

"Yeah, I know, sorry. I just needed to get even at the world somehow. It's all so unfair. Me and Dad," he continued waving his fist in the air, "well, we didn't always see eye to eye, but he was a good dad, a really good dad. But," Bryce kicked a rock angrily with his worn work boot, "I just don't get why he didn't tell us he was sick. He was forever telling us to be truthful, that honesty is the best policy. I must have heard him say that a thousand times, and Grandad always says it as well! But he lied to us, Uncle Nate!"

The older man was slow to reply, feeling the pain of his nephew's anguish.

"Bryce, you're right. Your father was a good man, and a very good father, and he was most certainly a man of honesty and integrity. No doubt about it. I suppose it's a fine line between withholding facts, and telling an untruth, but I know for sure that he never wanted to lie to you, or hurt you or any of the family. He sorta got himself boxed into a corner you know? First he had to come to terms with finding out he was going to die, and then he was trying to figure out how to break the news, how to protect you all. He was going to tell you all." He emphasised the point by pointing a finger at Bryce.

"Well, why didn't he? He could have at least told Mum first and then the rest of us," the younger man questioned, still angry.

"He told me he was going to tell you everything. He just didn't think for a minute that there would be an accident that very day when we went fishing. The telling was taken right out of his hands. He thought he had more time, Bryce."

"Yeah. I get that I suppose," Bryce replied, less heated now.

"You and me," his uncle continued, "well, we've never been in a situation like that. Being told a cancer you thought you beat years ago had come sneaking back, and was really going to kill you this time. I don't know how I would react if it was me, and I'm pretty sure you've never thought about it either, hey?" Bryce shook his head.

"We gotta try and understand what he was going through," Nate continued. "Let's go easy on him; cut him a bit of slack, the last few months were pretty rough on him. Don't let your anger spoil the good memories, or change the course he set you on. He was proud of you, Bryce, proud of the man you've become. He wanted nothing more than to be around to see you marry and settle down, have a family of your own. Don't let bitterness worm it's way into your heart."

"I know you're right, but it's all so hard to figure out!"

"We don't always understand how God has things planned out for us, but we can know for sure that He knows what's best and He has His reasons. We've got to keep moving forward, that's what your dad would have wanted, and we all need to be strong and support your mum. This is all terribly hard for her. I know it feels like we're in a battle, and you want to go out and fight someone, or something, for making us feel this way. So damn wretched but, remember, the bigger the battle the bigger the victory. It'll be okay. God's got this. When you get a chance look up 1 Peter 5: 6-10; your grandfather often got us to read it when we were younger."

Bryce nodded his head sadly, wiping a tear away before his uncle gave him a quick man hug, and some hearty slaps on the back.

"Come on now, must be time for smoko. I'm hungry!"

Humble yourselves, therefore, under God's mighty hand, that He may lift you up in due time. Cast all your anxiety on Him because he cares for you. Be alert and of sober mind. Your enemy the devil prowls around like a roaring lion looking for someone to devour. Resist him, standing firm in the faith, because you know that the family of believers throughout the world is undergoing the same kind of sufferings. And the God of all grace, who called you to His eternal glory in Christ, after you have suffered a little while, will Himself restore you and make you strong, firm and steadfast. 1 Peter 5: 6-10

* * *

They returned to the farmhouse, with Nate following the younger man's ute at a slower pace on the quad bike, with Nipper sitting behind him. After washing up in the laundry, and taking off their hats and boots, Nate joined the others on the verandah while Bryce returned the rifle to the gun cabinet and securely locked it away. He then went to the kitchen, where he found his Mum. He simply gave her a big long hug which was lovingly reciprocated, no words needed, before making himself a strong coffee with way too much sugar. After taking a seat at the outside table next to his sister, he helped himself to a large piece of chocolate cake that had arrived with Jillian the evening before. Jessica patted his knee affectionately, before taking a sip of her own coffee.

Conversation flowed easily around the table as plans for the day were discussed. Bryce was to return to Jarrod and Majella's farm to collect Sally, and drive her back to town so she could then make her way back to Toowoomba where she was on roster for night shift. Nate and Angie and their boys were going to have lunch with Jack and Edith, Josh and Bronwyn, and their girls. Kath and Jessica were happy to have a quiet day at home together. They would all be together for dinner that night, with Jarrod and Majella coming to join them also.

Nate and Angie and their sons left later that week to fly back to South Australia, with Bryce driving them to the airport in Toowoomba. Josh and Bronwyn had returned home a few days earlier for work commitments. Kath was sorry to see them all go as they had been such amazing stalwarts for her; she could never have coped without them. Nate and Angie in particular had gently taken control, and had efficiently handled most of the funeral arrangements. They had shared so much of the whole awful experience with her.

"How can I ever thank you both?" she enquired as they hugged goodbye.

"No thanks necessary. You know that," Angie assured her. "We're family, and that's all there is to say. But you will stay in touch, won't you? Promise?"

"Yes, yes, of course. Oh, Nate. Thanks for everything. You've been amazing. Truly!" She hugged her brother-in-law again. "I couldn't have managed without you."

"Call me anytime. There'll still be a lot to work through. Me or Josh, we're both happy to help."

Kath nodded, tears welling up in her eyes. She was indeed blessed to have loving family around her. These two people were especially dear to her, and she felt quite indebted to them. She was thankful that she still had Jessica for company. She could totally relax with her daughter, chat openly and honestly or just sit in a comfortable silence. No need to fulfill the role of hostess. Not that Nate and Angie had expected that of her. They had been very easy-going house guests, always caring and considerate. However, both Kath and Jess were glad to have some time alone together, to share their thoughts and begin processing their overwhelming grief. If such feelings of shock and despair could be processed.

"How about a nice cuppa, Mum? You sit out here on the verandah, and I'll put the kettle on."

"Sounds lovely, Jess." Kath smiled as she sank gratefully into the old wicker chair, which creaked its welcome as she settled comfortably, with Tink curling up at her feet. She and Jessica had always been close and, after they had navigated the somewhat turbulent early teenage years, they had drawn closer still. Jess was very intuitive, and had often surprised her parents with her perceptiveness. Her input into any conversation was welcomed, although her dry sense of humour often caught them off guard. The boys teased her mercilessly, as brothers do, but they were certainly valiant protectors of their baby sister when the need arose.

She was a typical farm girl though, able to drive all the vehicles and farm machinery, ride the motorbikes, and she was a pretty fair shot with a rifle too. She had learnt to cook standing on a stool at the kitchen bench next to her mother and grandmother. They had both shared in teaching her to sew and knit, and Edith also taught her to play the piano. Now that the older woman's arthritic fingers made playing difficult, Jess was often summoned to visit her grandparents and play for them.

Jess was also stubborn, competitive, and fiercely independent. She succeeded in many things, not always because she was naturally gifted, but because she applied herself and practiced relentlessly, often to prove a point to her older brothers. Being Daddy's little girl meant she had been able to convince her father to give her extra driving lessons in cars and tractors, and extra sessions shooting at targets in the back paddock. Her relationship with him had held a special richness, and they often had long conversations about politics, religion or current affairs.

Sam's patience, and easy-going nature, ensured their encounters ended amicably, each enjoying the sharpness of the other's mind. Jess usually rang her father a couple of times a week for a chat, or to bounce ideas off him, or ask his opinion on something. Kath had loved their easy communication, something she had never experienced with her own father. She was now worried about how Jess would cope without her father to talk to.

"How are you going, Jess? Really?" she enquired gently when her daughter returned with two cups of tea, and some biscuits Angie had baked yesterday.

"It's all so unbelievable, Mum," was the soft reply. "First, that he is actually gone, and second that he never told us he was sick. Not even telling you! I just keep going over and over it in my mind. It was just so out of character for him." She shook her head sadly, a tear escaping to roll slowly down her cheek.

"I know it's all hard to comprehend. We'll never understand what he was going through, or what he was thinking. If only he had let us in. I'm sure we could have helped him. I know he thought he was protecting us, but we should have been there to support him." Her voice ended on a sob. She took her daughter's hand in hers. "Sorry darling. I'm trying to support you, and here I am crying again."

"It's okay, Mum. We need to remember that Dad told Uncle Nate that he was going to tell you that week in Cowell. That's why he booked the cottage, so you could be alone."

"Yes, I know. But he kept it from me for far too long. He deceived me!"

"Out of love, Mum. He did it out of love. Don't hold it against him. He didn't for one second think he was going to have an accident on that little fishing trip."

"It was no accident! He dived in purposely to save that woman."

"Yes, because that was the type of man he was. We should be proud of him, putting others first, not thinking of himself. He'll always be my hero, Mum. I know that's very clichéd, but it's true."

"I know you're right. I just wish everything had been so different. I miss him so much. It's like walking in a thick fog, going round and round with nothing making any sense. All I can do is believe that he's up in Heaven, healthy and happy. Up there with Jesus, waiting for me to join him one day."

Jess smiled at her mum through her own tears. "Don't forget, Mum, we're not alone. We have the Holy Spirit. Somehow, with His strength, we'll get through this."

"Oh Jess, my gorgeous girl." She reached over and enveloped her in a big hug. "How did you ever get so wise?"

The following week passed quite quickly. With many friends and family visiting, the kettle was constantly on the boil for numerous cups of tea and coffee, consumed along with endless plates of scones and cakes. All too soon it was time for Jess to say goodbye and drive back to Toowoomba. Her firm had been very accommodating, but she felt she needed to return to work after 10 days off.

"Will you be okay, love?"

"I have a close circle of friends, Mum. A great Life Group at church, and good work colleagues. I'll be fine, and I promise I'll keep in touch and come home often."

Sadly, Kath waved her off, realising now that she really was on her own for the very first time in her life. Bryce had left the weekend before to go back to his flat in town and his job. In some ways she appreciated the time alone, to gather her thoughts and reflect on everything that had happened in the last few weeks. But she also had moments when she felt quite bereft, and panicked about how she would cope. Tears always came readily, as she thought about the end of her marriage. She had contemplated growing old with Sam, never considered a life without him. But now she was a widow, a broken, shattered woman trying to come to terms with the loss of her husband. She was alone and her darling man was gone from her.

That night, after a long day of moping mournfully around, she stood on the verandah and looked up at the clear night sky. It was magnificent; thousands of stars shining brightly. She had managed to pick out a couple of constellations, but astronomy was definitely not one of her strong points, so she just went back to gazing in awe at the beautiful night canvas. For the first time since the catastrophe had unfolded in South Australia, she experienced a strange sense of peace and had felt, in that moment, close to her beloved Sam. The beauty and serenity of the night sky seemed to envelop her, the stars reaching down, the moonlight guiding her to the heavens above. Like a spiritual communication of encouragement and love from her Heavenly Father.

Kath went to bed and fell asleep without too much trouble, only to be wide awake at 1am. She tried to walk silently to the bathroom without disturbing Tink, but the little dog woke up and watched her leave the bedroom. She waited with sleepy eyes, before snuggling back into her doggy bed when she saw her mistress return. Sadness again filled Kath's every fibre, and she tossed and turned for a long time before falling into a restless sleep.

Her scream woke her up, with Tink barking shrilly in fright at her bedside. The same old nightmare had returned, complete with the screeching wind, the rattling door, and a roaring beast coming to get her! She reached instinctively for Sam, but the other side of the bed was cold and empty. There was nobody there; no one to comfort her. In confusion, she pulled the little dog up onto the bed and, as realisation finally swept over her, she turned her head into her pillow and sobbed in bitter anguish until she fell into an exhausted sleep. She woke a little later than usual, with Tink curled up beside her and remembered the horrors of the night. With teary eyes, she looked upon the emptiness of the bed. Desolation once again washed over her.

In another bedroom, close by in town, her beloved mother-in-law was at that same moment standing in the morning light praying to the God who had faithfully upheld her for many years. She knew His presence and comfort and that His ways are perfect, even when hard to understand. She knew He would not desert her now,

"Dear Heavenly Father, your love is as wide as the oceans, as deep as the sea, and as tall as the heavens. I pray, Lord, that your Spirit will rise like a mighty wave and restore Kath's broken heart. You are the water of life, a fresh spring. You are the healing rain that she needs. Indeed, Father, we all need you right now. Wash over us, Lord. Fill us with your presence. Be our comfort and strength today and, in the days ahead, as we mourn our dear Sam. In the name of Jesus, Amen."

Wiping tears away from her wise and wrinkled face, pale from lack of sleep, she nevertheless walked slowly but purposefully to the kitchen to begin her day.

* * *

The next couple of weeks after the funeral were excruciating. Despite her best efforts, Kath languished in the depths of despair; wondering over and over how her husband and soulmate could be gone. Sam's death swirled around her like an ever-present fog, dark and suffocating, difficult to break through. It was easier to sink into its cold embrace, succumbing to the numbing despair, than to engage with the world around her. She had thought she could cope with anything once she had God and Sam by her side. But Sam was gone now, and God seemed far away.

Her family rang her daily, but she fobbed them off saying she needed some time alone to adjust and process what had happened. She had received numerous visitors in the week after the funeral, but now she felt abandoned. This was ridiculous because she was the one forcing people away. She kept saying that she knew they had their own lives to lead, and appreciated how busy they all were, and that she was just fine. Jack and Edith in particular were very concerned about her, but wanted to respect her wishes.

Finally, one afternoon she found herself in her studio, sitting in her favourite chair looking out the window to the mountains beyond. She had put one of her favourite playlists on, and let the soothing music surround her. The words of a particular song wafted over her, soaking into her soul. The lyrics kept jumping out at her, and speaking to her parched soul in a powerful way:

> *You've been down long enough*
> *You can rest in His presence*
> *You can trust in His name*
> *All we have to do is just ask seek knock*
> *Watch the doors swing wide open*
> *Jesus, You change ev'rything*
> *When You pour Your Spirit out*
> *Just like Silas singing with Paul*
> *Praise can break down prison walls*
> *Jesus, You can have it all*
> *Won't You pour Your Spirit out*
> *Oh, pour Your Spirit out (Pour Your Spirit out)*
> *Pour Your Spirit out (Pour Your Spirit out)*

When the music finished she sat in silence for several minutes, deep in contemplation, and then she closed her eyes and, in a trembling voice, prayed in desperation,

"Help me, Lord. I'm sorry for blocking you out. Please pour your Spirit out on me. Cover me with your presence. Comfort me, be my strength and courage. I can't do it by myself. I just can't! I feel like I'm in a prison. Please set me free, and show me the way forward. I can't continue like this. Please, dear Lord, help my mind to dwell on you always, and help me to sleep well. Please help me, Father. Pour your Spirit out on me, I pray."

She must have dozed off because it was dark when she stirred. Standing and stretching she startled Little Tink who had been sleeping soundly on the floor beside her. Picking the little dog up, she crooned, "Sorry Tink, didn't mean to scare you. Let's close up, it's getting late."

After satisfying her hunger with some leftovers from the fridge, Kath wandered down the hallway intending to take a shower but, for some reason, she stopped at Sam's office and opened the door slowly, switching on the light. The room still smelled of him. The favourite aftershave he had used for years, mingled with his favourite shampoo. The two combined to make his unique scent. The boys had always teased him about his penchant to smell nice, but Kath had always appreciated it. Now it nearly caused her to swoon with the pain of missing him, not seeing him sitting behind his big desk, reading glasses on, frowning at his computer screen.

Holding the edge of the desk to steady herself, she walked slowly around and sat in his big office chair. On one side of the desk, her own face smiled back at her in a photo taken some years earlier. A photo of their children on the same day sat on the other side. She shook her head sadly and, again for no apparent reason, opened the desk drawer on her right. Putting her hand in, she moved a few things around absently, not looking for anything, just trying to experience her husband, having seen him fiddle in that drawer a thousand times.

"Oh, Sam, my darling," she whispered to the empty room. As she was about to withdraw her hand she looked down and her name jumped out at her, written in Sam's distinctive writing on the front of an envelope. It was not sealed and, of course, she curiously opened it and sat back in his chair to read the letter. It was dated back in April, a week or so after he came home from hospital after his fall from the header.

My Darling Kath,

This is about the fifth time I've started this letter. It's the hardest thing I've ever tried to do and for one reason; I love you so much, with every fibre of my being. I don't want to hurt you, and I certainly don't want to leave you or the kids either. We made great kids didn't we? I'm so proud of them all. You're an amazing mum and you have been the best wife a man could ever ask for. I'm not really sure why I'm even writing this letter when the obvious thing is to simply talk to you, tell you what's on my heart, what's churning me up. But I just can't. Not yet. I nearly did last night but, again, I just couldn't do it. I know I'm cowardly, I just can't explain it.

I want to take you away to visit Nate and Angie, and have a great little holiday together, something really special for you to remember. I want to tell you when we're away from the farm so that it can just be you and me coming to terms with it. Then, when we get back, we'll go and see Rose, my new oncologist. You'll like her, and she can answer all your questions. After that we can sit down together with the kids and tell them too.

I know you will all be upset and angry with me for doing it this way, but it's the best I can manage at the moment. I'm so sorry my love, so very sorry. Please don't stay mad at me for too long. We've had such happy times together, so much fun with the kids.

Kath paused, a little frown creasing her brow, trying to comprehend what he was saying. Shaking her head and taking a deep breath, she continued reading:

I suppose the fall off the header gave me a fright, and I realised that I needed to have something in place in case I don't wake up one morning. I hope you never actually read this, that we'll talk it all out in South Australia. Make some more happy memories together. For some reason though, I just feel I should write this letter to you. Sorry, my darling, I'm not really thinking clearly at present. This is all jumbled up, I'm afraid. But I'm not writing it out again.

The cancer is back and, this time, there is no escaping death. I've looked into every possible treatment but there's nothing that will help. I've accepted it now. I'll be gone in a few months. It's a funny thing knowing that you're dying, so surreal. I'm not angry anymore, I have trusted in God's will for my life for a long time now, and I'm not about to stop. I don't understand it, or agree with it, but He is God and that's all there is to it. I know He loves me and my family, and I just have to trust that He will look after you all. I know He will.

Kath, my darling, you will be okay. You are stronger than you think and you will get through this. Allow yourself time to grieve for me, that would be nice ☺, but please, for your sake and for the children, rise up and move on. You're still young and beautiful and, one day, perhaps, someone else will come along. When that happens, follow your heart, with all my blessing. Stay close to Jesus, and let the Holy Spirit guide you. That's where all the wisdom is. We found that out together lots of times, didn't we? And, Kath, keep painting, you really must. Paint something wonderful to remember me by.

I love you,
Sam xxx

In all your ways acknowledge Him, And He shall direct your paths. Proverbs 3:6

Kath re-read the letter several times, trying to understand her husband's heart and mind at the time.

"Oh, Sam. Why didn't you just tell me?" she whispered to the empty room, before putting her head down on the desk and sobbing like never before.

It was some time before she was able to pull herself together. After blowing her nose noisily, and wiping her eyes, she carefully folded the letter, placed it back in its envelope, and put it back where she had found it.

She leaned back in the chair as clarity returned to her mind. She acknowledged that the letter answered some of the questions that had been nagging at her. Yes, Sam had considered all options before making an informed decision regarding treatment, or rather not having any treatment, and he had intended to tell her and the children. It was touching that he wanted to have one final holiday that would be a special memory for her.

Suddenly, she felt like a weight had been lifted off her shoulders. She could understand his thinking better now, and she didn't feel so deceived. She also felt somewhat encouraged about the future, as daunting as it was, and she was rather relieved that he had mentioned her painting; what a brilliant suggestion to paint something to remind her of him. She knew already that it would be a landscape that included the crops, blue sky, and the mountains in the background.

Closing her eyes and bowing her head, she prayed,

"Oh, Heavenly Father, I know you led me into this room tonight, just as you led Sam in here not so long ago. Thank you for the wisdom of your Holy Spirit, for answering my cry for help. I can't do this on my own but, with your help, I will try to keep going, keep busy and honour you in all I do. Thank you for my darling Sam, the time we had together, and for the words he left for me. Please keep guiding me, be my strength and my courage. In Jesus' name, Amen."

* * *

Feeling a little like her old self, and determined to get on with life, Kath returned to the classroom for the beginning of Term 3 after the winter break, praying that focusing on her work would keep her mind occupied and help her to move forward. A pregnant Jenny welcomed her back to their shared role, but that was short lived as after the second week she was asked to meet with the Principal in his office. There she learned that, on doctor's orders, Jenny needed to take sick leave and rest for the sake of her baby. So, when Warren asked to her to increase her hours to full-time instead of the part-time she usually worked, she could hardly refuse.

Initially she enjoyed being back with the children, and was happy to be planning lessons, interacting with the students and the other staff and parents. People were incredibly kind and thoughtful; children often arrived at school with flowers or fruit for her, and the mums even came to her classroom after class with home-baked cakes and biscuits. Friends in town often invited her for coffee at the end of the school day and, although she didn't always accept their kind invitations, she appreciated the efforts they were making to support her. She felt very cared for.

It was little things such as these, blessings worked through other people, that strengthened and sustained her as she struggled through the long dark tunnel of grief and loneliness. There was still much she couldn't understand about Sam's behaviour, and his untimely death, but Kath knew she simply had to trust God, believing that He would bring about His good purposes for her and for her children.

But she found it very hard. It was often difficult to muster the energy, and find the motivation to get out of bed and tackle another day. As the weeks rolled by, she found less and less joy in the classroom, and found her patience with her students waning, often feeling irritated by little things that once would never have bothered her. She found herself eager, along with her students, to mark off the day with a big red cross every afternoon on the calendar hanging on the wall in the classroom, indicating one day closer to the end of term. Of course, the children were excited about the countdown, which meant the Spring holidays were getting closer and there would be no homework for two weeks, but Kath just wanted to escape.

At the end of one particularly exhausting day, she was sitting at her desk in an empty schoolroom staring dejectedly out the window, when Jillian stopped by. Kath turned to look at her friend and, with big sad eyes, stated, "I can't do this anymore, I can't focus on teaching or anything else for that matter. What am I going to do, Jill?"

Jillian perched on the edge of Kath's desk and, taking her hand she patted it affectionately. "You, my dear, are going to see a friend of mine in Toowoomba; a wonderful counsellor who will help you work through your feelings, and make a little map to help you navigate your way forward. You okay with that?"

Kath burst into tears and nodded her head in agreement as she accepted the proffered tissue.

"I'll be back in a few minutes. Wait here for me, would you?" Jillian left the room and returned 10 minutes later. "Right. You have an appointment on Saturday morning. She's actually booked up until the end of next month, but she managed to make a little exception for an old friend of yours truly. I've known Renae for a long time and she owes me a few favours, so I'll drive you down and then, after your appointment, we can have lunch and hit the shops."

"Jillie there's no need for you to drive me, especially on a weekend. I'm perfectly capable of taking myself there. Thanks anyway."

"No, I've got it all planned. I'm driving you. Dave's taking the boys to soccer, and then to Maccas for lunch on Saturday, and then they're watching car racing on TV." She pulled a face. "They won't miss me, and I'd much rather do lunch and shopping with you!"

Sweet friendships refresh the soul and are like the anointing oil that yields the fragrant incense of God's presence. Proverbs 27:9

CHAPTER 13

It's a Whirlwind

*"If you hear a voice within you say 'you
cannot paint', then by all means paint,
and that voice will be silenced."*
Vincent van Gogh 1853-1890

Kath sat on the verandah, shielded from the August westerlies, her
hand cradling a half empty cup of cold coffee and her thoughts a
million miles away.

Suddenly, both dogs began barking loudly, startling her as they
announced an approaching vehicle on the driveway. She watched the sleek
car arrive with a frown of annoyance creasing her brow. As it parked under
the Jacaranda tree, she continued to wonder who dared to come and interrupt her quiet misery. She had no interest in conversing with anyone today.
But then the passenger door was thrust open and a familiar figure, larger

than life, emerged. Kath could not suppress the quick smile that burst on to her pale face.

"Gertrude", she whispered and, rising quickly, she walked, half running, down the path to greet her dear friend. She was soon embraced in a giant bear hug, her body held tight against the other woman's enormous soft bosom. No sooner had Gertrude released her when Max captured her face and kissed her soundly on each cheek, before he too enveloped her in a rib squeezing hug.

"My dear, you are so thin and pale!" he exclaimed before adding. "Don't you worry, my Gertie will soon fatten you up. It is so good to see you." He hugged her again before his wife pulled Kath free and, linking her arm through the younger woman's, announced loudly, "Come along, that's a lazy wind blowing, it's going straight through me! I sure hope you've got the fire burning, we've got lots to talk about."

The Bianchi's had arrived like a force of nature, drawing Kath in to their whirlwind personalities, showering upon her their combined zest and vitality for life, enabling her own depleted energy levels to be renewed. How could she resist them? Loud, caring and protective, their initial exuberance calmed. Or perhaps the warmth of the heat radiating from the wood stove finally subdued them as they settled comfortably around the kitchen table, sipping water while Kath prepared hot coffee and warmed some of Edith's pumpkin scones that she had thankfully found in the freezer.

"We're so sorry we couldn't get here earlier darling," began Gertrude apologetically. 'I know it has taken us such a long time to visit but, with the cruise, our flights home delayed, and then we both became ill with some wretched virus. Then would you believe, poor Max ended up with pneumonia? We just couldn't get to you sooner. But we are here now!"

"That's okay; really. I'm just so pleased to finally see you. It's so much better than just talking on the phone."

They sat at the table for the next few hours, talking and catching up while they ate the toasted sandwiches Kath prepared for lunch, asking endless questions about all that had transpired in the last few months. Kath didn't mind speaking to them. In fact it was a relief to tell everything to fresh ears, and hear their perspective. Gertrude must have murmured 'Poor Sam' a hundred times, while simultaneously patting Kath's hand and cooing 'Oh, darling'. She oozed understanding and empathy, and did not seem surprised by Sam's secrecy.

"What a burden he carried darling. He loved you so much. There was no duplicity, just a desire to protect you."

"Yes, do not be angry with him, my dear. He acted out of love. What a shock his diagnosis must have been," Max said sadly, shaking his head. "And then to dive in to save that poor lady with no thought for himself. Now that was heroic! I know he would not have hesitated. What a sacrifice he made. You should be so proud, my dear!"

Kath looked at them both with eyes full of tears. "Yes, but now he's gone. My husband's gone."

Gertrude stood quickly, and walked around the table to pull Kath into her arms.

"Yes, our dear Sam is indeed gone. But you're still here. I can barely imagine the pain you're suffering in your grief. My poor angel. Now enough talking, we are all tired and need a rest. Then we will make plans. Max, come darling, we know where the guest room is. Kath you must lie down for a little while too."

Like obedient children, Max and Kath followed the indomitable figure of Gertrude down the hallway to their respective beds.

* * *

"So, Kath," said Gertrude in her businesslike manner, sitting on the verandah while sipping yet another cup of coffee later that afternoon. "What are you planning to do after the school holidays?"

Kath was caught off guard, not expecting such a direct question about something she had been mulling over constantly in her mind since she last spoke with the counsellor some weeks ago. Thankfully Renae had turned out to be a very warm and compassionate woman, whom Kath had felt very much at ease with. They had been having regular Zoom meetings, which Kath found positive and helpful regarding moving forward with her life. But she wasn't quite ready for her friend's question.

Before she could answer however, Gertrude continued. "I don't want to rush you, darling. You'll know when you're ready, of course. But I want you to consider something. Your art is amazing. You're talented and have a lot of potential, as I've told you so many times. I would not hesitate to display your work at Serendipity House. I know it would sell."

Kath sat still, chewing her lip as she looked out across the crops, to the mountains beyond. "I think you overestimate my abilities."

"Nonsense, you have great talent. You're just afraid to see it."

The sharp comments made Kath turn her head quickly to look at Gertrude before replying. "You may well be right. I don't know, but I'm just not prepared to give up my secure teaching job to find out. It's too risky to try and forge a new career, especially one dependent on my art work. And at my age too."

"You are certainly not old," snorted Gertrude. "And the risk is minimal if you go about it the right way."

Kath, becoming defensive, replied, "I'm back teaching full-time at the moment until Warren finds someone to take over Jenny's role, so I'll just buckle down and keep on teaching until my position at school changes, which might happen next term. It'll keep my mind occupied, and I need to support myself and not rely on the farm. That's the boys' future now. I won't have time to concentrate on painting and, besides, I have never sold anything of substance. Just a few cards and tiny landscapes."

"Why can't you do both, darling?" The question came gently. "Continue teaching, but do it part-time and then you could paint as well. Didn't you say earlier that teaching five days a week is proving too much? You also said Bryce still has his apprenticeship to finish in town, and he's not married or ready to farm full-time yet, so you have time to test the waters."

"Yes, I suppose," was the soft reply. A frown creased the younger woman's brow as she continued candidly. "I've always dreamt of painting a landscape. You know, something really wonderful that someone somewhere would pay big dollars for and be pleased to hang in their home. But really, Gertrude. Do I have that in me? I guess I'm afraid to try in case I can't live up to my own expectations, and end up painting something really pitiful instead."

Gertrude nearly choked on her Anzac biscuit and reached quickly for the remains of her coffee.

"Pitiful?" she gasped at last. "Oh, Kath, you are funny! Can't you see that you have talent? You could paint beautiful pieces that would be snapped up! Start small by all means, with little things that the tourists will buy, but as you paint more; your name will become known. You could enter some art work in an exhibition, in a gallery over at the coast, or in Brisbane. I can help you with all that of course. I would be thrilled to display your work at Serendipity Place. As I said earlier, I know what sells, and I know your work will sell very well. Really you need to trust my discernment. I would not be encouraging you in this if I didn't believe in your potential. I am a business woman after all, and there needs to be something in it for me too." She grinned impishly at Kath. "Just kidding darling, I will not impinge on your profits in any way, well not until you are world famous anyway," she teased. "I believe in you, Kath. You just need to believe in yourself too!"

Kath smiled at the older woman, her dear friend and confidante. Standing slowly, she walked along the verandah thinking about her future. Was she brave enough to embark on a new challenge. To break free from her safe, conservative life? She thought not. It could all end so badly, go completely pear shaped in a hurry, she mused; worried that she may be left with no secure income, and some paintings that no one would want to buy. She turned to look at Gertrude, knowing her friend was exceptional in her field of expertise, someone she could trust. The idea of painting both excited, and terrified her.

"Oh, Gertrude. I'm just not as brave as you! I can't burn my bridges and leap into the future believing it will all work out."

"I'm not asking you to leap anywhere, darling. I said part-time. Remember? You can still teach, have a regular income, but you can also paint seriously as well. We could work out some goals to aim for, milestones to meet, if you like. Flexible ones, mind you."

"Now you sound like Renae, my counsellor. She asked me to draw up a timeline of things to achieve, just baby steps to keep me motivated and kicking some little goals. I must admit, I put painting some landscapes on it. As much as I enjoy painting with water-colours, I really want to try other mediums, and on a larger scale than I have been doing."

"Well, there you go. I'm just reinforcing what you already know would be valuable steps to take," Gertrude added triumphantly. "Commit to some scheduled works, and teach part-time. You'll still feel safe and secure, but you'll be expanding your wings at the same time."

Gertrude's enthusiasm and persuasiveness was hard to ignore. Kath's mind was racing, daring to believe she could perhaps realise her dream of one day, painting full-time.

"Well, I suppose I could give it a go. I'd have to speak with Warren at school, and see if he's found someone to take Jenny's position first. I know the farm's in a good position financially, but there's so much to work through with Sam's will, and the farm business. I'm really struggling to get my head around it all, I've been leaving everything up to Josh and Nate, and poor Jarrod, which isn't fair I know but they don't seem to mind. I have an unfinished painting I need to complete and some ideas for some others. It'll all take time, of course."

"And that is exactly what you have. Time! You can take as long as you like, there's no urgency, darling. I just don't want you to bury yourself in the class-room and give up your dreams. Keep teaching, you're comfortable doing that, but put your toe in and test the waters. No deadlines, no pressure, just experiment and enjoy what each day has to offer."

"Everyone is being so patient with me. I know I'm just muddling along at present. It's like I'm stuck in a holding pattern, and I can't go anywhere. I haven't been able to function properly since I lost Sam."

"You haven't lost him completely, darling." Gertrude stood before her friend and put a hand on each of Kath's shoulders. "No one is lost who is not forgotten, and Sam Wilmont will never be forgotten."

The younger woman stepped closer and wept in the older woman's embrace. "Oh, I miss him so much."

"Of course you do. That's understandable but, as I said earlier, you're still a young woman with a life time ahead of you. You'll be able to forge a new path, no doubt in my mind at all. Just believe in yourself Kath. You'll work it out as you go. Remember; just take one day at a time."

The Bianchi's stayed for several days, continuing to buoy Kath up with their warmth and energy.

Just before they left, Max hugged her and gave her a piece of paper. "Perhaps this will speak to your heart, my dear? Help you to know that Sam is truly at peace? I can't begin to understand the pain you feel, but please reach out to us at any time."

> *Life is but a stopping place*
> *A pause in what's to be*
> *A resting place along the way*
> *To sweet eternity.*
> *We all have different journeys*
> *Different paths along the way.*
> *We all were meant to learn some things*
> *But never meant to stay.*
> *Our destination is a place*
> *Far greater than we know.*
> *For some the journey's quicker*
> *For some the journey's slow.*
> *And when the journey finally ends*
> *We'll claim a great reward.*
> *And find an everlasting peace*
> *Together with the Lord.*

* * *

The Bianchi's had succeeded in motivating Kath, giving her much to consider. Her thoughts were dominated by the possibility of reducing her teaching role, and focusing more on her art. She decided to think on it for the remaining two weeks of term. She needed to pray about it, and seek God's guidance. Was it the right thing to do? Would her art work be good enough? She asked Jarrod those very questions when he dropped by one afternoon the following week. They often discussed the farm management, not that he really needed her, she was certain. But he always made sure she was involved and aware of everything going on, and she appreciated him doing that.

"Mum," he said, after she had shared her quandary about teaching and painting. "You don't need to work at all, if you don't want to. We're in a good position at present. The farm can support you. We're still working through things but, if you want to take a break from school or quit teaching all together, it's okay by me. And the only way to know if your art is good enough is to give it a go. I know that's what you would say to me if I was in your position."

Kath smiled at her firstborn, so much like his father. "Thank you, Jarrod. That's very sweet, but I don't want to stop teaching completely. I think I need the routine and security it offers, and I want to earn my keep. But I think I'll talk to Warren about reducing my hours next term."

"Good idea. Can you talk to him before the holidays? Then you might know where you stand."

"Yes, you're right. I'd like to get it sorted sooner rather than later. Thanks, love."

"No worries. I'd better head home, time's getting on. See ya, Mum."

Kath did spend a lot of time praying about it and also managed to speak to Warren before the end of term, and he was quite supportive of her request. "Would you believe Gayle Roberts came to see me this morning asking if she could have more hours, and now you want to have less. Funny how things work out, isn't it? Leave it with me. I should be able to work something out."

Kath received a phone call from Warren a few days later when she was grocery shopping after work. He enquired if she would be happy with only two days a week for Term 4.

After a moment's hesitation she said, "Yes. Thanks, Warren. That'll be fine. Can we re-negotiate next year, if necessary?"

"Yes, should be able to. No promises at this stage though. But there are always lots of changes with each new school year. As you know."

Kath drove home that afternoon with mixed feelings. She had received positive responses from her son, and her boss. She believed that God had answered her prayers and coordinated everything, giving her an opportunity to explore something other than teaching. But she still worried that her creative skills were not good enough, despite what Gertrude said. She looked heavenward and thought, '*Oh, Sam, I wish you were here to help me. How I miss your calm assurances and encouraging smile*'.

She felt the Holy Spirit answer her. '*Don't be afraid, trust in the Lord.*'

With a cautious smile, she kept driving.

Later that evening she rang Gertrude.

"Hello darling. I've been wondering how you're going? Have you thought anymore about what we discussed?" It was typical of Gertrude to get straight to the point. No preamble.

"Yes. I have thought about it, prayed about it, and discussed it with Jarrod and my boss."

"All very good steps to take. And what is the outcome, darling?"

Kath took a deep breath, before saying quickly, "I've decided to cut back to two days teaching next term, so that I can concentrate more time on painting."

"Oh, that's wonderful news. Bravo darling!"

"I'm still very nervous about it, and I hope I'm doing the right thing."

"Of course you are! It's a big step for you. But, remember, you still have your teaching to fall back on. But I'm sure you won't need it."

"I just wish I had your confidence."

"I'm very proud of you. I know it's not an easy decision for you to make. Just focus on your art, and see what comes next."

They chatted for a little longer before saying goodbye.

* * *

Kath settled into her new weekly routine for Term 4, working at the school on Mondays and Tuesdays, while Gayle worked the remaining three. Her first project was to complete a painting in memory of Sam. It was truly a labour of love. She thought about him constantly as she worked, often having to stop to wipe tears away. The distant mountains and the cropping lands she could see out the window formed the basis for her work. It surprised her just how quickly it all came together, and how much she enjoyed painting it. She was always eager to start each morning, and spent many hours each day in quiet contentment with only the birdsong and soft worship music to distract her.

While she was waiting for the oil pigments to dry one day, she brought a half finished piece out of storage and looked at it critically. She had begun painting it last year, but had never actually completed it. She remembered going to FarmFest with Sam on a very chilly day, and coming home with a cold that had lingered on. The unfinished painting of a storm brewing in the western sky, with dark clouds swirling in the wild wind, had been put away for another time. After examining it from all angles, she decided it was worth completing. She did some sketches of how the finished work might look, and was determined to start on it once she had finished Sam's painting.

The final months of the year flew by, with Kath feeling stronger emotionally, her grief nowhere near as raw and tangible as it had been. However, there were still many difficult days when she longed for Sam, and hoped to see him walk through the door, and always the long, lonely nights to get through. The school term finished; another year of teaching completed.

Christmas came and went. A quiet affair, as Jarrod and Majella went up to their family at Tully, and Bryce stayed with Sally's family in Brisbane. It was only Kath and Jess who joined the Dalby Wilmonts at Craig and Rosemary's home for a traditional Christmas dinner; roast meats and baked vegetables, followed by plum pudding and custard.

As Kath and Jess drove home in the late afternoon, Jess asked her mum, "How are you coping today, Mum? The first Christmas without Dad."

"I must admit I've been a quite down at times. It's just not the same, is it? I know he would want us to be happy, so I'm trying not to get too down-hearted. I'm glad you suggested coming home early though as I do feel I've had enough of people for the day. Yourself excluded, of course," she ended, with a little smile towards Jess.

"Yeah. Me too. I think we should have a quiet drink together on the verandah this evening, and play Dad's favourite music. Grandad gave me a bottle of his special Christmas ginger beer and Granma's given us enough food for a week!"

"They're a pair of old sweeties, aren't they?" Kath smiled. "A quiet evening on the verandah sounds wonderful, and hopefully it'll cool down a bit by then. It's been a hot day."

Jess left a few days later, and Kath was disappointed to wave her off as she had enjoyed her company. However, Jess was keen to leave as she said she had a friend in Toowoomba to catch up with, but promised to be back the following week. Kath returned to her work in the studio. She had finished Sam's painting, and had it framed. Jarrod had hung it for her in the living room, in pride of place, before he went away. She was still working on the storm painting, as well as a garden scene. She hadn't worked on more than one painting at a time before, never having had so much time free to indulge in her passion. But she was really absorbed in her art at the moment, and liked to have something else to concentrate on while she waited for paint to dry.

It was towards the end of the Christmas school holidays when Bryce invited her to join him and Sally for a weekend away at the Sunshine Coast. Kath deliberated for a day or two before giving him her answer. She had actually finished the other two paintings, much to her amazement but, instead of feeling pleased with herself, she became a little depressed again. *'Do I just keep painting? What am I really aiming for?'*

A meeting with Warren about class allocations for the new school year had not gone how she had hoped it would. Instead of returning to her three days a week, he could only offer her the same two days a week for the term unless she wanted to return to a full-time position, which she did not. Uncertainty crept back in, and she questioned her decision to focus so much time on her art. Was she really doing the right thing?

She was at a crossroads again, having fulfilled her immediate painting goals. How she wished she could talk it over with Sam. He would help her see things clearly so she could choose the right direction. Would she ever be able to move through life without missing him so much, she wondered sadly? A familiar question filled her mind; why had God taken her husband away so early? They should have had so many more years together.

Later that evening, before she went to bed, she stopped by Sam's office. It had taken quite some time for her to feel at ease in the small room. Initially, an overpowering sense of grief and loneliness had enveloped her every time she walked through the doorway. She had made some minor changes to tone down the male décor, and make it more welcoming. Nothing too dramatic; just a scented soy candle, some of her favourite water-colours of birds and flowers on the wall, a couple of bright cushions, and a mohair throw-rug in warm autumn tones placed casually on the armchair in the corner.

These small touches gave a more feminine feel to the room, and brightened it up considerably. It was still Sam's office, with his desk and chair, bookcase and cabinets, but now it felt more like a shared space, more comforting than overwhelming. She was thankful for God's grace in easing her pain, and now looked forward to spending time there most evenings. She opened her Bible to the devotion and reading for the day. She focused on one particular verse:

Your word is a lamp for my feet,
a light on my path. Psalm 119:105.

The words reminded her that she had been neglecting to spend the time with God that her soul needed. She had only been giving Him brief acknowledgements, quick prayers, and cursory readings of His Word as she'd been totally focused on working in her studio. She knew she needed God's input into every area of her life. He was the strength and wisdom that would sustain and guide her, and help her grow in confidence. Bowing her head and closing her eyes she prayed a quiet prayer,

"Thank you, Father, for your patience with me. Please forgive me for not giving you the time you deserve. I need to make spending time with you a priority; to slowly meditate on your Holy Word. Help me to trust in you and your timing. Guide me through the coming year and help me to honour you in everything I do. In Jesus' name, Amen."

With a lighter heart she went to bed, making a mental note to accept Bryce's invitation to go to the coast. Perhaps the time was right to show her paintings to Max and Gertrude, and see what they thought of them. When she spoke to Gertrude last she had said they would be home for the following few weeks. With plans forming in her mind, she drifted off to sleep.

Therefore I live for today-
Certain of finding at sunrise
Guidance and strength for the way.
Power for each moment of weakness,
Hope for each moment of pain,
Comfort for every sorrow,
Sunshine and joy after rain.

-Anonymous

CHAPTER 14

Promises on a Mountain

*"A joyful heart is the inevitable result
of a heart burning with love."*
Mother Teresa 1910-1997

*B*ryce pulled into the carpark at the base of Mt. Tibrogargon, one of the five peaks that make up the Glasshouse Mountains some 70kms north of Brisbane.

He remembered his primary school history lessons where he learned that these mountains were remnant volcanic plugs. They were named by Captain Cook in 1770 because, with the Queensland sun shining on them, he was reminded of glasshouses back in his home country of England. Although Bryce was keen to get to the coast, feel the warm sand between his toes, and inhale the salt air, he had an undeniable urge to stand on the summit of the big mountain.

Known fondly by locals as the 'Gorilla', as that is what it resembles from the eastern side, it is a challenging climb. Bryce last climbed Tibrogargan with Jarrod, his father and uncle about five years ago. His family had been holidaying at Caloundra with Nate and Angie, and Kath had kindly given the men a choice between a shopping trip to Sunshine Plaza at Maroochydore or going mountain climbing. Before the opportunity was lost the men had quickly put on their joggers, thrown some water and fruit into a few back packs, and roared off down the road.

Bryce would have enjoyed Jarrod's company again today, but he knew Sally's climbing experience and skills were more than up to the task. He was really looking forward to climbing the mountain with her. Bryce looked at her lovingly as she put on her shoes, admiring her fit, lean body, and knew she was the only climbing companion he wanted with him at the moment. He couldn't really say why, but he just knew he needed to climb the mountain today. Having Sally with him was an added bonus.

"Are you sure you don't want to come with us, Mum?"

"I'm absolutely positively certain that I do not want to climb that mountain, Bryce. I'm very happy to sit here in the shade and draw some of the beautiful birds and trees. I have everything I need," she added, pointing to her art supplies, camp chair, binoculars, water bottle and snacks. "You know I don't like heights. But I do appreciate nature, so this is where I'll stay. You two go and enjoy yourselves. Take your time, and do please be careful. Have fun," she finished with a smile.

"Okay then. We'll be off."

Bryce pulled on his cap and backpack, put his car keys in Kath's bag, grabbed Sally's hand, and headed for the start of the track. There was something about pitting one's own strength and skill against the elements that needed to be satisfied in Bryce's restless soul. He didn't understand the urgency he felt to complete the climb, and stand triumphant on the top.

He just knew that he needed to tackle the mighty Gorilla. The first part of the climb was relatively easy, just a steep walk really, so Bryce upped the pace and jogged to the first rock wall, Sally right behind him. The steep parts were challenging and required a good level of fitness and climbing skills, definitely not for those afraid of heights.

They climbed steadily, hardly aware of their surroundings. They just focused on the path before them, determining the best places to obtain secure foot holds and hand grips, and walking when the path allowed. At one stage they were warned of falling rocks by a cry above of 'Look out below.' They were yet to encounter anyone, but they were obviously gaining on those above.

Bryce climbed with cat-like ease, his fitness and flexibility not letting him down. He kept a careful eye on Sally, and slowed his pace to allow her to keep up with him, her smaller frame no match for his long arms and legs. At one stage, as he climbed up a steeper section, his feet slipped on the loose rocks underfoot.

"Hey, careful up there," Sally cried out as she was showered in dirt and gravel. The rock wall beside the track was worn smooth by the passing of many hands and feet, and thankfully a small tree root was within her grasp. It was strong and secure, and also very smooth, its bark having long been worn off by the hands of climbers. Sally held on to it for balance as she wiped grit off her face.

"Sorry! Are you okay, Sal?"

"Yes. I'm fine; just let me catch my breath."

The slip was a good warning for Bryce, as his mind had wandered off elsewhere, thinking of times and places that were best left in the past. He shook his head, and berated himself out loud: "Be careful, you fool! It's a long way to the bottom!"

Once his breathing had settled, he began his ascent once again. About 10 metres higher, he came upon a middle-aged couple sitting on a couple of rocks, their backs against the rock wall. They looked reasonably fit, but were obviously doing it tough if their ragged breathing was any indication. The man smiled at Bryce, and indicated that he should pass by.

"Yes," gasped the woman. "You go. I'm waiting here for the SES helicopter."

Bryce raised his eyebrows in question and the woman laughed. "Just kidding, but I do need a rest. I didn't realise it was so steep."

"Now come on, Caroline," her husband replied. "You've done really well, and we're nearly there."

"That's what you said last time we stopped, James," she answered in a shaky voice.

Bryce intervened. "You are nearly there, you know and, once you've made it to the top, you'll be able to tell people you climbed a mountain 364 metres high. That's the same height as a 50 storey high-rise building!"

The tired woman smiled kindly at Bryce. "50? Really? I certainly believe you! Thanks for the encouragement, though. But if I do make it to the top, I would still have to get back down. And I don't see a lift anywhere."

"Coming down is much easier; you just slide down on your back-side, nice and steady in the steeper parts. You'll feel like you've won a million dollars when you've conquered this mountain. Not to mention the fabulous view and the coffee shop at the top."

"Cccoffee shop?" stammered the woman. But she had seen the twinkle in Bryce's eyes before they looked past her, as Sally came up the path to join them. Bryce greeted her with a hug before asking, "How're you going, Sally? All good?"

"Yes. Aren't the views amazing?" she replied with a wave to the other couple sitting in the little clearing, before reaching for her water bottle.

"Sure are, and we aren't even at the top yet!" Bryce waited while Sally quenched her thirst and caught her breath before taking her hand. "Right to go?"

Sally smiled and nodded, keen to reach the summit as well.

"See you up there," Bryce called to the others as he took Sally's hand, and disappeared with her along the path.

"Come on love, you can do it," the older man coaxed his wife. "We're in this together, a team. Let's go." He held his hand out to help her up and, feeling somewhat rested, her flagging confidence buoyed, the woman began to slowly climb upwards once again.

Bryce progressed quickly up the rocky track, tackling the steeper inclines with care, keeping a close eye on Sally. Before long they were walking on a rocky path, through the spiky native grasses that grew on the mountain top.

A group of six young people were sitting in a small clearing, preparing to begin their decent by the look of it, as they were pulling on back packs and adjusting shoelaces. They greeted Bryce and Sally, who smiled in return as they walked a little further to where a ledge with a magnificent view to the coast line was. They stood together with arms around each other, the hot sun on their faces enjoying a mutual feeling of satisfaction.

Bryce checked his watch. 8:40 It had taken them about 45 minutes to complete the climb. They were hot and sweaty, and needed a few deep breaths to slow their heart-rates down, but both were enjoying the euphoria of reaching the top of the mountain. Bryce removed his backpack and took out a couple of mandarins. They gazed at the panoramic vista before them, slowly peeling and eating the fruit. Below them were pine plantations, eucalypt forests, pineapple and macadamia farms and open fields. In the distance was the coast line. The air was clear, and fluffy clouds floated lazily over the hinterland.

"What a magnificent country," Bryce spoke quietly. "We live in paradise here. Australia, the Lucky Country all right."

"Yes, it sure is pretty special."

"You're pretty special," he countered kissing her lips and tasting mandarin on them. "I'm so glad you're here with me right now, Sal. Sorry I raced ahead of you back there, not very gentlemanly of me. Just had this terrible urgency to get up here."

"That's okay. No harm done. Was something chasing you, or were you running towards something, I wonder?"

"Good question. A bit of both I think. I've been thinking a lot about Dad lately. Still trying to escape the pain of his death, and find some way of understanding it all, I guess."

"You know, sometimes we never understand why things happen. Sometimes we just have to accept that it has. I think the important thing is to just keep moving forward with our lives. You know your dad loved you, and he didn't want to leave you."

"Yes, he was a great dad, even though we argued a bit sometimes. But I know he loved me, that's for sure. How come you're so wise, Sally?" he teased, stealing another kiss.

"I'm not wise." She shrugged. "But sometimes it's easier to see things when you're watching from the sidelines, not part of the family, you know? Your dad was an awfully nice man, and I know he really loved your mum, and all of you. It's so sad that he's gone, but he'll always be a part of your life, Bryce. Don't be angry at him for dying. Try and be thankful that he was your dad, and that he taught you so much."

Bryce turned and stared into Sally's face with a strange look in his eyes.

"Bryce what's wrong?" she whispered feeling suddenly afraid.

"I had a dream the other night," he started, then looked away shaking his head.

"Go on. What was it about?"

"This mountain. I raced up here like the devil was after me and, when I got to the top, I stood on that ledge over there." He pointed to the wide ledge the young group had been standing on earlier.

"Yes. Then what?"

"I was really angry and lonely, even though I've had friends and family around since Dad died. And you too of course." He smiled. "But I didn't think anyone really cared. I remember taking a step closer to the edge of the cliff, and staring into the bush below. There was a roaring sound in my ears and I began to sway."

Sally's eyes widened and she listened in horror as the full weight of his words sank in.

"But suddenly, I heard a voice. I think it was Dad's, or maybe God's, I'm not really sure. It said loud and clear: *'Bryce, No! You have so much to live for!'* I spun around in surprise to see who had spoken, but there was no one there. I was alone on the ledge with only the sound of the wind. That's when I woke up. It seemed so real!"

"Oh Bryce. What a terrible dream! But don't you see? It's true. You do have so much to live for; a whole life ahead of you. Your dad was so proud of you. Your whole family loves you!" And leaning in very close, she kissed him gently before saying softly, "I love you!"

Bryce drew Sally to him in a tender hug, and kissed her back gently at first, and then more passionately. Finally, he drew back and stated the obvious. "I love you too. and I'm so glad you're here with me right now." They were kissing again when voices startled them and, turning around, they saw the couple they had met on the path earlier walking towards them.

"Hello again. I made it!" the woman greeted them triumphantly.

"Good for you. It wasn't so bad, was it?" smiled Bryce in return.

"Are you kidding? My legs are like jelly and I'm sure I'll be so stiff tomorrow I won't be able to move!"

"It's all worth it, Caroline. Look at that view!" beamed her husband, placing his arm around her shoulder and kissing her on the cheek.

Bryce studied them closely, as they moved away, taking in their easy camaraderie, realising that their obvious closeness reminded him of the loving comfortable relationship his parents had enjoyed. Turning back to Sally, he looked at her thoughtfully, suddenly realising how precious this young woman was to him. He had been so intent on finding solace that he had completely overlooked what was right there in front of him all the time. Sally was his soul mate, the person who would complete him, and make him whole. He had been taking her friendship, indeed her love, for granted. The pain of grief had blocked her out of his reality. Yet she had been there all the time, caring for him and supporting him without expecting anything in return. He felt guilty about how he had failed to truly appreciate her patience and kindness.

Cupping her lovely face in his hands he whispered, "Oh Sally, I'm so sorry."

"For what?" she asked confused.

"I haven't treated you very well since Dad died!"

"Oh, really? Why do you say that?"

"I've been so caught up in my own misery, and feeling sorry for myself, that I've been neglecting you and you've not once complained or got angry at me."

"Don't be silly, Bryce. These last six months or so, have been really hard for you and your family. I know that. Besides you haven't been that bad." She punched him on the shoulder. "Although you've blocked me out I knew you'd snap out of it, sooner or later. Actually, I did talk to your mum about it one day."

"Really?"

"Yeah. She saw me looking a bit gloomy one day after lunch, and asked if everything was okay. I told her you were being a bit distant, not your usual self. She suggested I give you time, and you'd work things out."

Bryce threw back his head and laughed out loud.

"What's so funny?"

"What hope did I have? With a mum like mine, and a girl like you on my side? Oh, Sally. You are the best!"

He pushed her away suddenly and jumped to his feet. "I've had an epiphany!"

"You've had a what?"

"An epiphany. You know a revelation. A light bulb moment!"

"I know what an epiphany is. I'm just surprised you do," she laughed.

"Well, I heard someone at work say it, and it sounded really cool, so I googled it."

"You googled it?" Sally hooted. "Really, Bryce! You crack me up!"

"Don't move, and stop laughing at me!" He winked at her before saying, "I'll be right back." He then disappeared into the bush.

Sally watched him go, wondering what he was up to. At least he had gone in the opposite direction to the cliff, she thought with relief. It wasn't long before he came crashing back up the path towards her.

"Bryce, you're crazy! What's going on?" she laughed.

He took her hands and pulled her to her feet. "Close your eyes."

"What?"

"Just close your eyes and don't open them until I say so!"

"Okay, okay. Whatever you say."

"Righto, open your eyes."

Sally opened her eyes to see Bryce kneeling on one knee before her, with the beautiful Sunshine Coast vista in the background behind him.

"Bryce, what…" she began to ask.

"Shhh. I love you, Sal. And I want to marry you."

Sally's eyes filled with tears, and she looked up at the clear blue sky above while she let his words sink in.

Bryce interrupted her thoughts by gently tugging on her hand. She looked down and saw him take something out of his pocket and place it on her left ring finger, saying as he did so, "Sally, will you be my wife?"

Sally's eyes widened further as she realised he had made a ring out of grass. Giggling with delight she whispered, "Oh yes, Bryce. Yes, I will. I love you so much!" She knelt down and threw her arms around his neck. "Oh yes. I love you, my crazy spontaneous man. Are you sure though? Really sure?"

"Absolutely! Now I know why I had to climb this mountain. I had so much stuff to deal with. You know, what's happened in my family. I can't be angry or upset any more. I need to accept Dad's death and move forward. I need to make plans for my future, a future that totally includes you. This feels so right, Sal. You're my epiphany." He enveloped her in a huge bear hug and, laughing and kissing, they fell over in a tangle of arms and legs, neither noticing the hard ground beneath them.

It was some time before they gathered themselves, and made ready for the trek back to the car park. Neither one could stop smiling, happy and excited to have found a partner to share the highs and lows of life with. Someone to love, and to be loved in return. With a final kiss and a hug, they began the descent down Tibrogargan. It was easier than climbing up, but still required concentration and care because there was little to stop a climber's fall as quite a number of ill-fated adventurers had found out.

A broken leg or worse was the last thing the happy couple needed to burst their bubble of excitement, but they had no trouble negotiating the descent and, even travelling at a quick pace, had no slips. They had to wait several times to allow other climbers to pass by but, before long, they were walking towards the car, hand in hand eager to share their wonderful news.

Kath looked up from her sketch pad, stretching her back in the warm sunshine. She was pleased with what she had accomplished in the last few hours, and was feeling relaxed and content. She heard Bryce and Sally talking and laughing before she saw them. She smiled and waved when they came into view, noting how happy they both looked.

"Hi, Mum," her son called when he drew closer.

"Well, hello there. I'm pleased to see you both made it back in one piece. Enjoy the climb?"

"Oh yes," laughed Sally looking at Bryce and digging him in the ribs with her elbow.

"Ow, steady on," he laughed back in mock pain, before kissing her cheek.

"What's going on with you two?" Kath asked curiously, with a big smile on her face. Their happiness infectious.

"Mum, I would like you to meet my fiancé!" Bryce announced as seriously as his delight would allow him.

"What? Really?" Kath questioned, looking from one to the other and then at the hand Sally held out towards her with the woven grass ring on it. "My goodness, how wonderful! And wow, what a ring!" She laughed, standing to hug them both.

"Well, of course, it's just a temporary ring," Bryce explained the obvious. "But I couldn't propose without one!"

"It was so romantic," gushed Sally, gazing in awe at her finger.

"Well, I'm so very happy for you both. Now we have a wedding to look forward to!"

"Oh, we haven't even thought about that yet. Just getting engaged is so amazing," the ecstatic Sally replied, looking at Bryce with eyes full of love.

You have captured my heart, my treasure, my bride.
You hold it hostage with one glance of your eyes,
with a single jewel of your necklace.
Song of Songs 4:9

CHAPTER 15

I Can Feel Him in the Air

"We ask ourselves: "Who am I to be brilliant,
gorgeous, talented and fabulous?"
Actually, who are you not to be? You are a child of God."
Nelson Mandela 1918-2013

They were soon on the Bruce Highway, travelling north to the Sunshine Coast. Bryce and Sally chatted nonstop all the way, bubbling with excitement after their mountain top experience. Kath was so happy for them, she really was, but for some reason she also felt the familiar feelings of sadness wash over her.

Bryce had briefly explained his sudden realization, and how he finally felt free to go on, enjoy life, and build a future with Sally. Kath understood what he was saying, and was relieved that he had overcome the negativity that had haunted him since his father's death. She was so proud of him but, though it pained her to admit it to herself, she knew she was envious of her son's happiness. She too wanted to be free to live and laugh again, not just superficially as she had been doing during the long months since Sam had died, but to really experience joy in every new day and in every new circumstance. If Bryce had managed to find true happiness and embrace the future, and all that it offered, then surely she could too. Why was she allowing her sadness and loneliness to hold her back? Hadn't she just read this morning that God was her refuge and her strength?

She was very careful to mask her melancholy mood during the journey, and contributed appropriately to the conversation in the car, not wanting to dampen the elation of the young couple. But she needn't have worried; Bryce and Sally were so enraptured with each other that they failed to notice how quiet and subdued their back seat passenger was.

When they reached their accommodation, a small Airbnb holiday house that Sally had booked, Kath was relieved to escape to the solitude of her room. But she could not relax, her mind raced at an unprecedented pace. She needed to walk off some energy, and feel the sand between her toes. Grabbing her hat and phone, she called out goodbye and quietly pulled the door shut behind her. As she drew closer to the beach, the roar of the waves became louder, intoxicating her senses. She picked up the pace, and walked quickly through the soft sand to the harder surface near the water's edge. She could not help but smile. The surging waves, the circling seagulls with their piercing cries, and the rising salt mist all attacked her mind and body, urging her onwards. Not for a swim though; the cold water rolling over her feet did not entice her at all.

She turned south and walked quickly along the beach, enjoying the wind in her face. She headed towards a rocky area where a boardwalk provided a detour around a cliff to the beach on the other side. She had been walking steadily for about 20 minutes, so she was glad to stop at the top of the path to rest and take in the view. Out to sea, where the aqua hues of the water were topped by little white capped waves whipped up by the wind, a loaded tanker was making its way along the shipping channel. Glorious rays of sunshine peeked through white cumulous clouds, spun like fairy floss. It was a true reflection of Creation's glory. She was not oblivious to the beauty before her, but something was suppressing her joy. Shaking her head, she prayed silently for guidance.

A jogger interrupted Kath's thoughts with a cheerful "G'day. How're ya goin?" as he ran past.

Kath nodded in response, and walked over to the railing at the top of the cliff where the roar of the wind and waves was deafening. Without warning, a mighty gust of wind tore her cap off, tossed it through the air and over the side of the sheer rock face. She stood still, hesitating, with her hand on her head before edging closer to peer down to see what had become of her favourite hat. The wind had dropped it on a tiny ledge about 40cms beneath where she stood. She looked fearfully at the wild foaming waves crashing far below. Taking a deep breath, she crouched down on her hands and knees, and then lay on her stomach. Just as she was about to reach over and reclaim her property, strong hands grabbed her ankles and hauled her backwards over the rocky surface. She cried out in pain and twisted to see who had hold of her.

"Let go of me!" she yelled angrily at the jogger.

The man released her ankles but grasped her firmly by the arm, allowing her to sit up.

"There's no need to end it all, lady. There's gotta be a better way!"

"What in the world are you talking about? I just wanted to get my cap! That hurt! Look at my knees!"

The jogger looked over the edge and saw Kath's cap within arm's reach and, after looking back at her sheepishly, he released her arm before reaching over and quickly grabbing it.

"I'm sorry; but it's a long way down. There've been a few nasty accidents here. Well, actually, a few blokes have jumped. That's what I thought you were going to do."

Kath looked at him horrified before saying, less harshly now, "Well, thanks for thinking of me, but that was not my intention. I can assure you, if I was going to do myself in I would take a running leap, not crawl over the edge on my belly!"

"Yeah, I suppose so. I really am very sorry. I didn't mean to hurt you. Must be the Boy Scout coming out in me. Are your knees okay? Eddie's the name," the 'would be hero' stated, holding out his hand.

"No worries, Eddie. Just a bit of skin off. You gave me a fright, though." There was a little sparkle in her eyes now as the funny side of it began to emerge. "But thanks anyway, you're a good man to think of saving me." She smiled at him and held out her hand. "I'm Kath."

"Nice to meet you, Kath." He smiled in return, shaking her hand.

They moved away from the edge and sat down on a rock, two strangers now sharing a unique experience.

"Great view, isn't it," offered Kath.

"Yeah, sure is. Can't understand what would drive someone to want to end it all."

"I guess some people just aren't as happy as others. Missing something, or someone perhaps," Kath replied thoughtfully.

"My old man always said life is what you make of it."

"True."

"My mum says that the Lord gives and the Lord takes away. It's not up to us to decide. We've just got to do the best we can with what we've got. I reckon we have to ask if the glass is half empty, or half full? And if it's half empty, you can always fill it up again. Right? That's my philosophy anyway. Well, I've gotta go. See you around some time, Kath."

Kath waved the jogger off, noting that he was a good-looking man, fit and suntanned. His words echoed in her mind, *'if the glass is half empty you can always fill it up again'.* Memories of Sam flooded her mind. He had been a real glass half-full sort of person; his positive attitude always lifting her up. She felt like there was a struggle going on inside her, with dark forces wanting to keep her subdued and imprisoned by grief and despondency, but she knew that more powerful forces of light and hope were fighting for her.

As she prayed fervently for God's strength and courage, her thoughts began to spin as her body became heavy. Suddenly, there was a release of tension and deep emotional pain, so intense that she shuddered and leant backwards against the sun-baked rocks. She relaxed, completely still, her eyes closed. Slowly a smile formed on her salty lips, as a great peace at last enveloped her. Then, looking up at the bright blue cloudless sky, she knew that her cup was indeed filling up again with God's goodness and joy. She could almost see the angels in Heaven smiling back at her.

'Thank you', she prayed silently, knowing her plea had been heard. She rested contentedly for a while before slowly standing.

Breathing deeply of the ocean air, and then feeling totally pumped, she began the walk back. By the time she reached the surf club, the euphoria of the cliff-top experience was wearing off and a healthy tiredness was starting to creep over her. She entered the building, and ordered an icy cold lime and soda before settling at a table overlooking the beach.

On the tables outside, willy-wag tails flitted about. The little birds were finishing off some chips that had been left behind by the previous occupants. They were happy and chirpy, without a care in the world, simply looking for crumbs to eat. Kath felt that a bright new season was just beginning for her, and she believed it would be good. She vowed to herself that she would move forward in a more positive way, and hopefully cope with whatever life would bring. She was not naïve enough to think that everything would be perfect, but her confidence had been given a huge boost.

Her stomach growled loudly, reminding her that breakfast had been a very long time ago. She added grilled fish and salad to her order. While waiting for the meal to arrive, she picked up her mobile and called Gertrude, who answered on the third ring.

"Kath, darling. How lovely to hear from you."

"Hello, Gertrude. How are you?"

"I'm wonderful. All's well here."

"This is very impromptu, and I apologise for not calling earlier, but I wonder if you're free tomorrow?"

"Darling, I will always make time for you. What do you have in mind?"

"Well, actually, I'm at the sunshine coast with Bryce and Sally, and I was wondering if we could pop over and visit you?"

"Oh, how marvellous! You must join us for morning tea. Lunch too. I'm dying to meet Sally!"

Kath smiled into the phone. "That would be great. And Gertrude, guess what?"

"What, darling?" she asked curiously.

"I've brought some paintings to show you."

"Really, you finished them? How very exciting! Max will be thrilled too!"

"You might not be when you see them. But I'm pleased with them, one in particular."

"Well, I can't wait to see you all and your work. See you tomorrow morning, darling."

The call ended. Kath smiled to herself, but felt a few little butterflies flip in her empty belly, as she wondered anxiously what her friends would say about her work.

She took her time with the delicious meal of local fish served with avo-cado and cous cous salad, the view of the beach and pounding surf relax-ing her further. After paying the bill, she walked slowly back to the house where she enjoyed a long, hot shower. She hummed happily as she towelled herself dry, and dressed in shorts and a strappy top. It was only then, when her gaze fell upon the beautifully made-up bed, that she realised how tired she really was. *'Just a little nap'* she thought to herself, before laying down and immediately falling into a deep dreamless sleep.

When she woke and looked at the bedside clock through sleepy eyes, she was at first horrified to see that over three hours had passed. But then she smiled to herself, knowing that such a sleep was just what her exhausted body and mind had needed. Rolling over, she wondered where Bryce and Sally wanted to go for dinner tonight?

* * *

The following day, Bryce and Sally drove up to Serendipity Place with Kath sitting happily in the back seat. She was excited to see her good friends, but she was especially keen to show Gertrude the paintings that she had brought with her. Sam's painting in particular, filled her with joy every time she looked at it. It was a view from the verandah at Yallaroo, looking across the crops to the distant mountains. It embodied so much of what was important in her life; the farm, her garden, the countryside; and of course, memories of her husband.

After eating way too much at a very authentic Thai restaurant the eve-ning before, the trio had agreed to skip breakfast and wait to have morning tea with Max and Gertrude. Kath and Bryce knew there would be no escap-ing a scrumptious 'tuck in' as Bryce described it, teasing Sally and keeping her guessing as to what that might actually entail.

"Scones? Waffles? Muffins?" she queried.

The light hearted bantering concerning many mouth-watering delicacies assured they were all well and truly salivating by the time they arrived, with Bryce's belly rumbling loudly right on queue as they pulled into the car park.

Moments later they were greeted exuberantly by their hosts; bear hugs all round. Sally received a smothering embrace from Gertrude, almost disappearing completely in the folds of the brightly coloured caftan the older woman was wearing. Bryce laughed out loud at the expression on Sally's surprised face. Max rescued her by pulling her towards him so he could plant a kiss on each of her now crimson cheeks.

"Look at her finger!" Kath directed them and poor Sally was once again smothered and gushed upon, by not only Gertrude but now Max joined in before exclaiming, "You are family now! Excellent!" Kissing her again before turning to Bryce to give him the same treatment. "Congratulations, Bryce! What a lucky man you are. Winning the hand of such a beautiful young woman."

The scene provided much entertainment to the people sitting on the verandah above them, as the newcomers hadn't even managed to enter through the gate before the welcoming and congratulations had begun. Max turned to the onlookers and, holding Sally's hand aloft, her finger still wearing the woven grass engagement ring, shouted: "They're getting married!"

The announcement received much applause and whistling. When at last she was free, as Max and Gertrude turned to escort Kath inside, Sally turned to Bryce and punched his arm. "You could have warned me!"

"What! And miss seeing the look on your face? Sorry, babe. But it was priceless! I wish I'd recorded it!" He laughed at his fiancé as he hugged her. "What can I say? They're very loud and affectionate people, with hearts of gold. You were such a good sport though! Love you, Sal." His kiss mollified her somewhat.

"I think I have some broken ribs," she exaggerated with a small smile.

Bryce put his arm around her shoulders. "My beautiful, brave girl! Come on, honey. I'm sure a nice morning tea will help."

A further surprise greeted them inside when Bryce saw Julian coming towards them, a big smile on his whiskery face. "Hey buddy, haven't see you for ages."

Bryce replied, "Hi Julian, it has been a while, good to see you." Shaking the offered hand warmly he said, "Julian, I'd like you to meet my fiancé, Sally."

"Nice to meet you, Sally." He too kissed her on both cheeks. "I just heard Dad shout out that you're getting married," he laughed. "When's the big day?"

Sally giggled, showing him her ring. "It's only just happened, as you can see, so nothing planned yet."

"Oh, nice indeed." He smiled, admiring the grass ring. "Good on you, mate. Nothing like being prepared." He laughed, giving Bryce a hug and slapping him on the back. "Let me know when the engagement party is."

They all sat down around a large table in the back garden, ready to enjoy the promised morning tea. Some of Max's friends were visiting from Italy, so of course they were introduced and invited to join them. The aroma of strong espresso coffee filled the air, and a selection of goodies appeared from the kitchen; a variety of pastries, pistachio and raisin biscotti, almond macaroons, spiced fig cookies and basil and parmesan scones. There was much laughter, with multiple conversations taking place at once, some in English, some in Italian. Each was vying to be heard over the other, voices getting louder and louder. Sally's eyes were as big as saucers as she took it all in.

By the time they were ready to embark on a tour around the gift shop, gallery and garden, it had been decided that Bryce and Sally's engagement celebration would be a pizza garden party held at Oakleigh in a month's time. Julian had assured them that Majella would not be able to resist being involved. He remembered going to a pizza party at her family's cane farm, for her younger sister's birthday, a couple of years ago. A phone call by Julian to his cousin had confirmed the arrangement as Majella was, as he knew she would be, delighted to be asked to host the party. Julian made another phone call, this time to Frank, and managed to secure the hire of the restaurant's outdoor pizza oven. Bryce offered to bring both Julian and the oven out to the farm in his ute.

"Well, that's everything sorted," Bryce announced happily.

"Well, not quite," his mother replied, pointing to Sally's ring finger. "That grass ring won't last the distance I'm afraid. You'll have to go jewellery shopping, Bryce."

"Oh, yeah." He laughed again, and kissed Sally before saying, "We're off to the big smoke next weekend to see Sally's parents, and find the perfect ring."

"What! You mean you didn't speak to her father already?" Max asked horrified.

"Yes, yes. I did. Don't worry, Max. I spoke to him on the phone last night. All done properly, I can assure you."

"Good boy. That's okay then." Max visibly relaxed, hearing that the correct traditions had been observed.

While the younger people went off to explore the premises, and the Italian visitors left for a drive around the local area, Kath had opportunity to show the paintings she had brought with her to Max and Gertrude. First, she showed them Sam's painting, and then the one of her garden with beautifully detailed finches in one corner and the Jacaranda tree resplendent in the other. Gertrude, of course, raved over both of them, while Max studied them carefully and quietly. Kath explained tactfully that while she respected and valued their opinions, she really felt she needed her work to be critiqued by a wider audience.

"But of course, darling. That's very wise. You must arrange to exhibit them."

"Oh, I wasn't really thinking of going that far just yet. I thought you might know some people who could just have a look at them and give me their opinions as well?"

Gertrude shook her head adamantly. "No, you must exhibit them. Don't you agree, Max?"

"Yes, I do think that would be the best thing to do, and they are certainly of a high enough standard. Gertie what about the art exhibition Henry is having at his gallery in Mooloolaba next month? Is it too late to submit work for that?"

"Oh Max. That's a marvellous idea. It would be the perfect opportunity. I'll call him immediately." She pulled a phone out of a pocket, secreted away somewhere amongst the voluminous vibrancy of her floating dress, and sailed away.

Max stayed with Kath and turning to her he said softly. "These really are very good you know. I'm sure they'd sell easily."

"The one with the crops and the mountains." She indicated the one on the left. "Well, I don't think I can part with it. It's really my memorial piece to honour Sam. I just brought it over to show you."

"Then don't even consider selling it, my dear. You must keep it if it is of great sentimental value to you. Such things of the heart must be cherished and held close. But, if my memory serves me right and my wife will no doubt correct me if I'm wrong," he smiled ruefully, "all displayed work must be available for sale. So you might want to keep that in mind."

"But really, Max. I don't think I need worry about my work being snapped up. I'm a very struggling artist with so much to learn," she answered derisively.

"Tut, tut. You underestimate yourself, my dear. You certainly do," he said turning to study her work again. "Have you anymore at home?"

"Actually, I do have another one similar to the cropping one. I started painting it some time ago. It's in the boot of the car actually. I thought it was a bit presumptive of me to bring three paintings in to show you."

"Presumptive? Really? Three is not too many. Don't be silly. Run along and fetch it."

So Kath, like a chastised school girl, rang Bryce for the car keys, only to discover that he was standing outside on the verandah. He simply pressed the unlock button when his mother reached the car so she could open the boot and remove the other painting. A few minutes later, Max was carefully studying it.

"Kath, Kath, Kath," he murmured shaking his head.

"Well, now you know why I left it in the car." She sighed before turning at the sound of Gertrude's voice.

"It's all settled, the exhibition is in three weeks so there's no problem, and you must display at least two pieces, which you have, and be prepared to sell them..." Her voice trailed off momentarily as she noticed that there were now three paintings. "Where did that one come from?"

"The poor woman didn't want to overwhelm us, so she left this one in the boot of the car!"

"Really?" Gertrude looked at Kath in astonishment. "But, I think I like this one most of all!" She studied it more intently, moving back a few steps. "Oh my, it's quite extraordinary!"

"Yes, it is. Isn't it, Gertie?" Max clapped his hands together gleefully.

"What? Why?" Kath asked, surprised at their praise.

"Because it has more depth of colour I think. Look at the shadows, Max. Don't they create a most wonderful effect?"

"Yes, indeed. How long ago did you paint this one, my dear?"

"I started it about 18 months ago, but I lost interest in it, I think. Then I looked at it again and found some more inspiration. I only just finished it recently. Why?"

"All exhibited work in the show next month must have been completed within the last two years. The others are marvellous, of course. But there is something distinctive about this one. What do you think it is, Max darling?"

"It's partly the colours. You're right, Gertie, but it's more than that. Perhaps the contrasts between the lighter and darker aspects. But then they merge so powerfully. The eye is drawn to the sky and the cloud formations, a storm building. Yes, this one must definitely be exhibited." Looking up at his wife from where he was now seated, straight in front of the painting, he asked, "Don't you agree, my dear?"

Gertrude kissed the top of her husband's balding head. "I certainly agree. The brushstrokes and the texture of the oil create the most hypnotic effect, drawing one in. I can almost hear thunder," she laughed.

"Oh my, you two!" Kath exclaimed. "Now you really are getting carried away! But I'm happy to display the garden scene and the storm one. Actually, I call that one," indicating the one they admired most, "*Storm Brew*, because I was inspired by a huge storm rolling in across the plains one afternoon. The lightning and thunder were incredible. The other one is simply *Garden Peace*."

"Fabulous! That's settled then," Gertrude exclaimed loudly. "But Kath darling, you really should start to promote yourself and your work, you know, on social media and such. You must have confidence in yourself, and your talent. There are online galleries and forums you could be involved with also. Oh, there are so many possibilities for you!"

"I think one step at a time will suit me just fine at the moment. How about I put these two in the exhibition and see what happens from there?"

"But of course, darling. That would be splendid, a great starting point," she agreed. "But mind you," she wagged her finger at Kath, "when your career takes off, and one day it will, I will most certainly say 'I told you so'. Just you wait and see!"

Laughing at the light-hearted interaction between the two women, Max gathered each one by the arm and said, "Come now, enough about art. It's time for lunch, I believe."

* * *

Thankfully, lunch was a light meal of cold meats and salads, and a delicious antipasto platter. No one needed a big meal after the delightful morning tea. Finally, good byes were said, accompanied by lots of kissing and hugging, and the country threesome began the journey back to the farm. The lovebirds chatted away quietly in the front seat, leaving Kath to enjoy being alone with her thoughts in the back. She was happy to have Sam's treasured painting safely stowed in the boot, and excited that her other two paintings would be placed on exhibit at the art show in Mooloolaba in a few weeks' time; an event she was really looking forward to attending. It had been a wonderful long weekend away and, as she sat contentedly watching the passing scenery out of her window, the words of a song kept repeating in her mind, encouraging her as she endeavoured to keep her life moving forward:

> *One day at a time, sweet Jesus*
> *That's all I'm asking of you.*
> *Give me the strength to do every day*
> *What I have to do.*

Yesterday's gone, sweet Jesus
And tomorrow may never be mine.
So, for my sake
Teach me to take one day at a time.

Kath kept herself busy at home, painting small works for the Information Centre, and teaching on her set days. She was nervously looking forward to the art exhibition but, much to her dismay, she was unable to attend. She was forced to spend that week at home with a bad cold, which progressed to bronchitis, requiring antibiotics and bed rest. Bryce came home for a few nights, to keep an eye on her, and managed to cook some simple yet tasty meals for them both. Not that his mother had much appetite, but she was impressed with how capable he had become from flatting in town.

"What a wonderful husband you'll make," she teased him between coughs.

"That's what I intend to be, Mum. A wonderful husband, and all-round nice guy," was his cheeky reply.

An excited phone call from Gertrude the following night buoyed her spirits greatly. "Kath darling. Wonderful news. Both your paintings have sold, and for very nice amounts, I must say! And what's more, you won't believe this, darling, but a gentleman from Brisbane was very upset that he missed out on acquiring your *Storm Brew*. He asked me to enquire of you whether you would paint another one for him, similar but larger! Can you believe it darling? I'm so happy for you! It's quite a feather in your cap, you realise? High praise indeed, and only after your very first showing too!"

Gertrude happily continued talking, hardly stopping to take a breath. She was so full of energy, riding high on Kath's success, prattling on and on about online galleries, radio interviews, and writing a blog. Kath, in her weakened state, had no hope of taking it all in; she was actually beginning to feel dizzy from the sound of Gertrude's animated voice. But the one fact she certainly did grasp was that someone wanted to commission a piece of artwork from her. How amazing? When Gertrude finally ran out of words, and Kath started to cough, not that she had been given much opportunity to speak during the nonstop monologue, the phone call abruptly ended after Gertrude said, "We'll talk some more when you're feeling better, darling."

Kath lay back on her pile of pillows smiling. "Well Tinkerbelle, how about that?" she whispered to her little bed fellow. "How about that?"

CHAPTER 16

A Break in the Clouds

*"Life is 10% what happens to you and
90% how you react to it."*
Charles Swindoll

Pastor Bob and his wife Stephanie chatted easily as they left the built-up area of the town. They drove along the highway, which was bordered by crops on each side. They commented on the weather, the colour of the crops, and the change they could see coming, if the buildup of clouds in the west was anything to go by.

When an easy silence settled between them, Bob began to hum softly, interrupting himself to pray as thoughts came to mind. These were directed, he knew, by the Holy Spirit. He and Stephanie had spent time together that morning in prayer, committing to the Lord this visit to Kath Wilmont. Asking His direction for the words they would share with her, and asking that He would prepare their friend's heart and mind so that she might be open to receiving the message they felt led to share.

They had known Sam and Kath for many years, and had always considered them to be close friends. When Sam had been called home, Bob, in particular, had felt the loss keenly as he had not only lost a great mate and confidante, but someone whose opinion he often sought and respected.

Bob's heart ached for Kath, as she continued to mourn her husband's death. Both he and Stephanie had thought she had begun to move forward, and was coping reasonably well. She had been excited to tell them about reducing her school hours so she could concentrate more on her art, but her happiness had disappeared and she was obviously not in a good place at present.

Her regular church attendance had become spasmodic, until it stopped altogether. She kept making excuses when they had tried to arrange a catch up with them both. Even refusing to meet for a coffee with just Stephanie, something they had been doing quite regularly in recent months. Other mutual friends were also worried about her and, although she was pleasant to everyone who met her at school or at the shops, she was keeping everyone at a distance. None of Pastor Bob's recent phone calls had been returned.

Bob had not spoken to her about the visit today, and didn't even know for sure if she would be home. He confidently believed she would be, however, as the prompting of the Holy Spirit to drive out to Yallaroo and speak with her today had been very strong. He had woken from a dream at 3 o'clock that morning when he had clearly seen a picture of Kath's face and the number 18 written on a raggedy old piece of material, like a flag, fluttering in the breeze on top of a funny little house. There had been tears on Kath's cheeks, and she had looked quite upset. Bob had prayed for her then, in the early hours, and asked God to direct him further. After writing her name and the number 18 on the little pad he kept beside his bed, he managed to go back to sleep. He hadn't really been surprised later that morning, when he looked at the calendar hanging in their kitchen while he made his morning coffee, to see that the date was the 18th. He chuckled at the resourcefulness of the Holy Spirit as he drove, remembering the conversation that had unfolded with his wife earlier that morning.

"Hey Steph," he had called happily to his sleepy wife when she wandered out a few minutes after him. "Can you come for a drive with me this morning?"

After kissing her good morning, he had filled her in with the day's scheduled visit as planned by God. Stephanie's eyes had grown wide, and she became instantly wide awake as she listened to Bob's description of his dream. Not that she was at all surprised to hear about the dream, as God had used this method and many others to give them instructions in the past. But one little detail had really caught her attention.

"Bob, you won't believe this, but..." She had stopped mid-sentence, rolling her eyes before continuing. "Silly me, of course you will believe it!" And, laughing at her husband's curious expression, had run to her desk in the adjoining room.

"Now you've got me really intrigued," was his smiling response, as he took a sip of his coffee and watched her triumphantly enter the kitchen waving a sheet of paper in the air.

"Sorry, I'll explain." She kissed his forehead. "Last week, at the craft morning, old Mrs. Coates read out a poem, well just a few lines actually, and it's been going round and round in my mind ever since. And now I think I know why."

"Really? What is it?"

"It was written centuries ago. This is it: *Narrow is the mansion of my soul; enlarge it, so that you may enter in. It lies in ruins; repair it.* It was written by St. Augustine who lived between 354 and 430."

"Wow, that's deep. And he died in 430? What do you think he's saying?"

"Yep, long time ago," she had agreed before adding. "Well, I think he's saying that his soul had become weak and small, with not much room left for God, like a broken-down house needing repairs. He's suffering, lost his way, maybe, and he wants God to come in and make his inner house strong again. To mend it, like a spiritual transformation. An act of grace maybe, something that only the Holy Spirit can do. It's a real cry for help, I believe. And I think it also sums up where Kath is at the moment. The clincher to all this is the little house in your dream, with the ratty flag flying from it! This is our message for Kath. She needs help with her housekeeping, or rather her soul keeping." She had smiled at her husband. "She needs some encouragement, and a boost to help her clean out her inner house, and let God back into the number one place He needs to be in, so that she can find peace and happiness again."

They had sat in silence for a few moments smiling at each other, wondering at the workings of God, the mighty choreographer, the one who never sleeps and who always provides for His children.

* * *

The arrival at the farm was, of course, announced loudly by Nipper and Little Tink. Kath appeared on the verandah to see what the commotion was all about, calling to the dogs to settle down. She greeted her visitors. "Hello Bob. Hi Stephanie. How are you both? I wasn't expecting you."

"Hi, Kath. Bit of a surprise visit I'm afraid," replied her pastor. "I hope you don't mind?"

"No, of course not. You're always welcome." Her smile did not quite reach her eyes.

"No chance of sneaking up on you though, with your watchdogs on duty," Stephanie remarked, as she greeted her friend with a warm hug.

"No hope of that. They both have very good hearing and, once one starts barking, the other tries to make even more noise. Come inside and I'll put the kettle on. Actually, why don't we sit out on the verandah, its lovely there at the moment."

"Sounds great. I've brought some slice I made yesterday." Stephanie indicated the Tupperware container she held.

"Thanks, Steph. That'll be a treat. I don't seem to bake much anymore."

They meandered through the garden, admiring the shrubs and flowers before going up the steps and settling around the big timber table. It wasn't long before they had hot cups of tea before them, as well as the chocolate slice Stephanie had baked. The conversation flowed easily as they discussed safe topics, such as the weather, school, the children, and Jack and Edith's health. Kath baulked a bit when asked how the farm was going, simply saying that the boys were doing a great job.

When questioned further she added, "Bryce works part-time in town now. He wants to work full-time on the farm, once he finishes his apprenticeship at the end of the year. He's a big help to me, and spends a few nights here every so often. He even does the lawn mowing now." She smiled sadly. "Something he rarely did before."

"Oh, wasn't Bryce and Sally's engagement party wonderful? You looked so radiant that night." Stephanie steered the conversation to a happier topic. "Jarrod and Majella did such a great job decorating Oakleigh and hosting the party. I never knew there were so many variations of pizza toppings!

Sally's a beautiful girl, inside and out. You must be very proud, Kath? Both your boys have found lovely young women to share their lives with."

Kath's smile finally reached her eyes, as she remembered the festive occasion of the engagement party. True to his word, Julian had worked most of the night over the hot oven, cooking a variety of pizzas. His parents had come out for the night, and stayed with Kath. "Yes, it was a wonderful night. Sally was so excited to show off her beautiful diamond ring, and Bryce is so proud of his lovely fiancé. He's matured so much; I can't believe he's going to get married."

"His father and brother have set great examples for him to follow."

Kath smiled ruefully at Steph, the sadness back in her eyes. "Yes, Sam would be so proud of our young men. Jarrod works so hard. It's a lot for him to manage both the properties. Of course, Bryce helps out a lot more now, and we can employ contractors if needed…" Her voice trailed off and a faraway look stole over her countenance, which both her guests picked up on immediately.

Bob leaned forward, placing his elbows on the table. Folding his hands together and resting his chin on them. "So, Kath. Tell me. How's your walk with the Lord going?"

Kath spun her head around to look at the pastor, obviously startled by his direct question.

"Well, actually, seeing as you ask. I'm having a bit of trouble connecting with Him lately," she answered quietly, with a hint of annoyance in her tone.

Bob was not the least perturbed. "Oh really? How do you mean?"

Kath exhaled loudly, a sad sighing sound. "I used to see God in everything. The sky, the flowers, the birds, everything. And I prayed all the time. An ongoing conversation, if you know what I mean?" Stephanie nodded her agreement as Kath continued. "I had a wonderful experience with Him a few months ago at the coast. I thought I had really changed, been set free from all my worries, ready to start afresh. But now…" Kath's voice quivered and trailed off, as tears began to spill down her cheeks. She wiped them away angrily, turning her head away from her guests to look towards her beloved mountains.

Stephanie moved closer and put a comforting hand on her friend's shoulder. "What's it like now Kath?" she asked gently.

"I seem to be all alone. I can't hear Him anymore."

"He's still here, you know," Bob reminded her.

"No, not now. Not for me," she countered, turning back to face them. "He was there when Sam first died. He got me through those first dreadful weeks, the first lonely months. He gave me courage to start afresh. To not give up, which I could have done, so very easily. I really wanted to just curl up in a ball and let the world go by, but I know Sam wouldn't have wanted me to do that. He said as much in his letter to me."

"So, what did you do?" Bob queried.

"I started painting again," she smiled. "Gertrude and Max were my big encouragers. They were very supportive, and made me believe I could do it. Paint seriously, I mean." She looked from one to the other; to check they were following her.

Stephanie agreed. "Yes, you have wonderful friends in them. And you told me about the letter Sam left you, and how you painted a landscape to remember him by as he'd suggested."

"Yes, that's right. I painted two more actually, and Gertrude and Max encouraged me to enter them in an art exhibition over at the coast. I couldn't bear to part with Sam's landscape, but I put the other two on display." She grinned sheepishly at them. "I didn't think anything would come of it, but it was nice to be invited to show something. Anyway, they both sold for quite a bit of money, would you believe? An art collector from Brisbane was disappointed that he had missed out on buying the one I called *Storm Brew*, so he asked me to paint another one similar to it. Only bigger! I couldn't believe it! You could have knocked me over with a feather! I was so excited, and started work right away on my days off. The paint seemed to fly off my brushes. Mind you, it still took quite a while but I was consumed by it, and spent every spare minute on it. I was thrilled with how it turned out, my best work yet. I called it *Thunder Roll*." The animation suddenly left her voice. "Then there was the fire," she choked out the words.

"Oh, Kath," Stephanie gasped in horror. "A fire? Where? Not in Gertrude's gallery?"

"No, not there. My painting was in her gallery for a little while because the buyer was going to collect it from there. But then he couldn't get up to the coast, so he asked Gertrude to send it to another gallery in Brisbane. Apparently, he was held up in Sydney for a week or so."

"Was it insured?" Bob interrupted.

"Yes. Gertrude made sure it was insured and transported properly. I had a signed contract as well, and I did receive some payment up front, but it's not really about the money." She shook her head dismally. "So, anyway, I came home and the painting went to Brisbane. A short time later I received a phone call from poor Gertrude. She was so upset. She told me that there had been a fire in her friend's gallery. Some things in a back room were saved, but my painting, *Thunder Roll*, couldn't be found. The office and all their records were destroyed too."

"Oh, how awful for you. Your painting was burnt?"

"Yes, Steph. It was burnt. Pretty much everything in the gallery was destroyed. All that work, all that time and effort I put into it. My first commissioned piece, my chance to be seen as a respected artist, gone. Up in smoke, literally. It was devastating. I just couldn't believe it. My painting was gone. I received the money from the insurance pay-out, but that was a small consolation. No-one really got to see it, only Max and Gertrude and, of course, they said it was amazing, so much better than the first." She shrugged miserably. "But I wanted the opinion of the buyer, the poor fellow who commissioned it; he's well respected in the art business. I don't believe I'll ever be a world-renowned artist by any stretch of the imagination, but I seem able to paint things that others want to buy and, if that helps pay the bills and I don't have teach full-time, I would be more than content. But it all got snatched away from me! I had a great opportunity, and it was ruined through no fault of my own!"

Kath banged her hand on the table in frustration. She jumped to her feet, and walked to the verandah rail. "I'm just not strong enough, not tough enough to make it on my own. I was foolish to think I could've been a serious artist; I was aiming way too high. So now I'm just concentrating on teaching, doing what I know best, and trying to help the boys on the farm where I can. I know I'm languishing in self-pity, but I don't seem able to move on from the disappointment."

She blew her nose and wiped tears away before continuing quietly, "My life, since Sam died, has just been one of ups and downs, highs and lows. I feel like I'm stuck on some sort of emotional roller coaster. I thought the nightmare, that I've experienced on and off since I was a child, had stopped. I thought the Lord had heard my prayer, but I've been having the same old dream again, waking up terrified. One day I feel so close to God, flying high spiritually, but then something happens and I just come crashing down, a disillusioned, blubbering mess."

Bob and Stephanie sat looking at their friend's back, her shoulders slumped in resignation. After a few moments, taking in everything she had told them, Stephanie blurted out, "But why not paint another one? There's nothing to stop you painting more pieces and putting them on show too." She nodded to the canvas, Sam's painting, hanging inside in the living room, on view through the open window and added more gently, "You could do it again, you know?"

Kath turned around to face them. "No. I had my chance and it didn't work out. If God wanted me to paint, my picture would not have been destroyed. Besides, it hurts too much to lose something of value; it just rekindles the pain of losing Sam all over again."

They sat in silence again before Bob said quietly, "Tell me Kath, when you give your students a test, do you talk while they're completing it?"

"Bob, really? What does that have to do with anything? And no. Of course not!" she answered crossly.

"Why not?" he persisted.

"Because, I want them to focus on the test, to concentrate and remember what I taught them. Hopefully, they've studied the text book and can complete the tasks."

"Are you available to help your students during the test?"

"Yes, of course I am. They just have to raise their hand and ask. I can't tell them the answer, but I can help them understand what's required. What are you getting at?"

"Well, I was thinking that it's exactly the same for us. God gives us tests, certain trials that we need to work our way through and, like you with your students, He is quiet while we navigate the path. He's still there, of course, and we can ask Him for help at any time, things like strength, courage, patience, direction, and so on. Sometimes we get so caught up in all our problems, everything that's gone wrong, that we forget to talk to Him and we think He's abandoned us. But remember the meme: 'when you're going through something really hard, the Teacher is always quiet during the test'. It's just like you are in your classroom. We can raise our hand and ask for help at any time. Jeremiah 33:3 says we can call on Him at any time and He will hear our call. That's our emergency phone line, available 24/7. God is always with us, and He promised that He'll never leave us or forsake us. Remember, that's in Deuteronomy 31 verse 6."

"Yes, but I failed. My first big test without Sam! I crumpled in a pathetic heap. I feel so guilty, ashamed, you know, for being so weak. I was given a great opportunity when I was asked to do that painting, but then everything went wrong, the fire and everything. I just couldn't handle it. I gave up. I say I'm a Christian but, at the first hurdle and without Sam here to bolster me up and push me along, I just give in to all my old insecurities and fears. So very pathetic." She slowly returned to the table and sat down dejectedly beside Stephanie.

"I think you're being rather hard on yourself." Stephanie patted her hand comfortingly. "You're still grieving, Kath. It hasn't been that long since Sam died. You don't become superwoman overnight, you know. You're still vulnerable, finding your way forward on your own. The apostle Peter says that the devil prowls around like a lion, looking for someone to attack. And he always goes for our weak spots. He's a thief, he wants to steal your joy, and destroy your confidence. You may have opened a door for all his lies and negativity to enter in and pull you down, but it's your house, your heart and mind, and you can easily ask for God's help. He wants to make everything clean and fresh again so you can live life to the full."

"Yes, that's right," agreed Bob. "And you know what is really amazing?"

Kath shook her head; listening intently to what her friends were telling her.

"God welcomes us back gladly, lovingly, at any time, no matter how far away we've moved from Him or how long we've been gone. You're not pathetic, Kath, far from it. You just need some help from Jesus. He wants to take your pain and disappointment, and fill you anew with His hope and promises. You lost your painting, and your dream was destroyed, but remember Christ lost His life for you, He knows your pain. Give Him your heartache and brokenness and let Him build you up again, fill you with His love. Who knows what He might be preparing you for? We all go through different seasons in our lives. When you're not sure what to do, lean on Jesus, soak in His presence, read the Word and wait. You might not think you're being productive, but drawing closer to God is one of the most important things we can do in our lives. Remember, He stands patiently at the door, just waiting for us to open up and let Him in, ready to graciously forgive our waywardness, our weakness, our doubting. He wipes our sins away, and fellowship is restored. But you need to ask Him, Kath. You need to make the first move."

Kath put her face in her hands and began to sob. The dam had burst. All her pent-up sadness, disappointment and confusion rushed out in a healing flow. Bob and Stephanie both put their arms around her, and held her until the worst of the emotional storm was spent. Then they shared a time of prayer together, where a broken-hearted daughter was restored to fellowship with her loving Father. She was blessed by the love of her friends; caring, obedient servants of the Lord.

Later Stephanie gave Kath a copy of the words penned by St. Augustine that she had shared with Bob earlier in the morning. Such special lines of a poem, written by a faithful disciple of the Lord so very long ago; heartfelt words, a cry from a burdened heart that was as relevant today as it was then. The words of a man who wanted his soul to be restored, made richer and stronger by the grace of a loving God; the same God who drew Kath back into His warm presence that sunny morning.

Later, as she was clearing the table after her guests had departed, she saw that her caring pastor had written a Bible verse, in his very bad hand-writing on a serviette which he had left on the table, held down by the sugar bowl.

Because of the Lord's great love we are not consumed,
for His compassions never fail.
They are new every morning; great is your faithfulness.
Lamentations 3: 22-23

CHAPTER 17

Baby Steps

"If you look at the world, you'll be distressed,
If you look within, you'll be depressed,
If you look at Christ, you'll be at rest."
Corrie Ten Boom 1892-1983

$\mathcal{K}$ath walked purposefully toward her little studio, the gravel crunching beneath her quick steps. Little Tink sensed excitement in the air and pranced around happily, yapping at shadows and butterflies. Kath turned the door knob forcefully, and pushed the door wide-open.

Standing with her hands on her hips, in a determined stance, she surveyed the interior. Memories began to fill her mind of Sam and his father remodelling the little building for her, and how pleased she had been with her interior decorating that had never failed to inspire her creativity.

She thought of the day she had bought the beautiful old chair, and the thousands of times she had looked out across the crops to admire the distant mountains. Oh, how she had missed being in this space – her own studio. It had been like turning her back on a close friend. It had been far too long. She offered up a silent prayer of apology: *'Oh, I've been so silly, Lord. Forgive me please. Let the gift you have given me flow from my paint-brushes once again.'*

She made a mental note to ring Max and Gertrude, and apologise to them for her behaviour since the fire. She had pushed them away, politely but firmly, as she just couldn't bear to talk about art projects. But she knew they were hurt and saddened by how she had treated them. They, too, had encouraged her to continue painting, and couldn't quite understand why she had completely shut down and turned her back on her art. It had just been too difficult to share with them the heartache and loss that had once more consumed her, taking her back to the dark days after Sam's funeral. She bent down and picked up Tink, ruffling her soft fur.

"I have bridges to mend, little one, but first we have work to do here, this place smells very musty; time to let the fresh air in again."

Placing the little dog on the floor, she first went to the CD player. Not bothering to find something on Spotify, she found a favourite CD to play. Then she opened all the windows, and began dusting and checking out her art supplies, humming happily to the lively music. It felt good to be back in her special space, thinking about projects, colours and textures. The right side of her brain, full of creativity, going into overdrive.

The Information Centre in town had called several times asking for more of her post cards and small water-colours to sell. She had, of course, ignored the requests, but now she was keen to paint again. Only small things, she decided, as the thought of starting another big project like the dreaded landscape, as she referred to the one that had been destroyed, was just too overwhelming.

"Baby steps", she cautioned herself out loud. "Just start with what you know you enjoy doing, and go from there. No need for deadlines, I don't need the pressure, especially as I'm busy most of the week."

Tink looked up at her, and whined.

"Oh Tinkerbelle, did you hear me talking to myself?" She laughed out loud, feeling the happiest she had for many weeks. Realistically, she did not have time to commit to a big project, even though her teaching role was still only four days a fortnight, teaching Year 3 students Mondays and Tuesdays. Wednesdays and Thursdays had been free, but she had agreed, or rather she had been skilfully coerced by dear sweet conniving Jillian, to care for two little girls while their mother worked on those days. Kath had not been at all keen when the idea was first suggested to her, as she didn't want the commitment.

Thankfully the days of moping around the house, bemoaning the things she had lost, were mostly over. However, she was keeping busy and enjoying working in her studio again, and in the garden, reading her Bible and daily devotional, and she was once more meeting with Stephanie and some other friends on Fridays.

"Please consider it?" Jillian had pleaded over coffee when she had met her in town last week. "Both the parents are doctors, lovely people. You would have seen them at church, surely? Anyway, they've both taken jobs at the medical centre and you know how desperately we've needed more doctors in town. Sarah's parents are moving here too. Isn't that exciting?" Jillian's words were tumbling out quickly. "But now they've been delayed, something to do with the sale of their house, or was it health issues? I can't remember. Apparently they used to live here years ago, but now they can't look after the girls. They're twins, you realise? Only three years old. So adorable and well behaved. Sarah and Cliff, that's her husband, are in a real bind. It'll only be short term of course; just to get them out of the pickle they're in."

"Okay, okay. I'll do it." Kath raised her hand in a gesture of surrender and to stop her friend's verbal onslaught. "But just temporarily, you understand. Just until the grandparents arrive," she added.

"Oh, that's wonderful!" Jillian clapped her hands together. "You're the perfect person to do it. I'll let Sarah know. She'll be so excited."

Whether the arrangement resulted from Jillian's urging, a visiting preacher's message on servant ministry, or the prompting of the Holy Spirit to help others, probably a combination of all three, Kath quickly became Aunty Kat, besotted babysitter of little Isla and Holly. The girls were indeed a delight, and the hours spent with them flew by. So many books to read, puzzles to put together, block towers to build and then knock over, games to play, snack time, lunch time, more books to read, nap time and, before she knew it, delighted cries of "Mummy's home!"

The time spent with the twins was like a balm to Kath's weary soul. She began to see the world through their big innocent baby-blue eyes. Everything was interesting and exciting; pointing at clouds while lying on the soft lawn, chasing butterflies, picking flowers, singing silly songs, building sand castles. All of which reminded Kath of precious times spent with her own children when they were little.

Isla and Holly re-energised her, and made her laugh and smile more than she had for many months. She cherished their hugs, when chubby arms were circled around her neck, their soft hair tickling her nose. Her life settled into a steady rhythm; teaching in the classroom for the first part of the week, babysitting the twins for two days, concluding with meeting her friends from church at a café every Friday afternoon. The long weekends were then spent catching up on chores around the house and garden and, of course, working in her studio.

It was not a demanding routine and, for the most part, enjoyable. She was kept busy, and her mind occupied. The children in her class at school were engaging and stimulating, and she still liked teaching them new concepts and encouraging them to do their best. They were generally well-behaved, although some days she looked at the clock regularly, waiting for the 3 o'clock bell to ring. The twins, however, were a joy to be with, and she looked forward to every hour spent with them. They squabbled sometimes when they were tired, but their bickering rarely amounted to much and they were easily distracted. They had already developed a great appreciation for books, thanks to the time and patience their parents had invested, and Kath was only too happy to indulge them in reading book, after book, after book. They each had their favourites, which Kath now knew word for word, narrating the stories off by heart while the girls, seated on either side of her, turned the pages with their little fingers.

Of course, Kath also encouraged them in other more tactile artistic activities. She once again found herself adept at making play-dough, and even slime, which proved a great backyard 'messy play' activity. The bubble bath which always followed, was gleefully anticipated by both little slime monsters. Puzzles and colouring books were favourite indoor activities, and Kath loved to sketch the girls while they concentrated on their work. They, in turn, drew pictures for her, which she gladly took home promising to put them on her fridge, just as her sketches of them were displayed on their fridge where everyone could see them. Looking after the girls was a real highlight of her week, and she was visibly disappointed when, after six weeks, Sarah announced that her parents would be arriving in two weeks.

Seeing Kath's crestfallen face, Sarah quickly added, "Oh Kath, the girls have become very fond of you, they'll miss you terribly, so please don't become a stranger. You know you're welcome here anytime. I can't thank you enough for helping us out. You have such a wonderful way with children. Isla and Holly were instantly at ease with you."

"Thanks Sarah. I'll certainly miss them too, and I would love to stay in touch, that's for sure. You and Cliff are doing such a good job of balancing your busy work lives with your little family."

She drove home feeling rather upset that her time with the twins was coming to a close. After greeting the dogs, she put the kettle on and was sitting on the front verandah sipping her hot cuppa, feeling quite weary, when the phone rang. Seeing it was Jarrod, she rallied and answered with a smile in her voice. "Hello Jarrod, how are you?"

"Fine, thanks Mum. Hey, just wondering if we could come over for dinner tonight? We're long overdue for a visit."

"Of course," she replied without hesitation, mentally wondering what she could rustle up for a meal at such short notice.

"Don't worry about cooking, we'll bring everything. We're in town at the moment so we'll pick up some take-away on our way home. See you about 5:30. Okay?"

"Yes, of course. That'll be lovely."

She was going to say more but he had already hung up. Looking at Tink, she smiled at Jarrod and Majella's spur of the moment idea.

"Overdue for a visit indeed. They dropped by just last week for a coffee."

However, she enjoyed their impulsiveness; they were always full of surprises. Her tiredness vanished as she looked forward to the arrival of her guests. A hot shower further revitalised her and, after picking flowers to arrange in a vase to decorate the dining-room table, she was feeling very relaxed as she put the finishing touches to the table settings.

Jarrod and Majella's arrival was heralded by the usual loud barking from Nipper and Tink. Kath went outside to greet her son and his wife in the fading light. The days were growing shorter, and the air cooling down with the autumn temperatures. She was enveloped in an enormous bear hug by her son, and received an equally warm embrace from her beautiful daughter-in-law. They were both grinning madly. Jarrod reminded her of when he was a young school boy, bursting with excitement to tell her a big secret.

"Whatever's going on? You're both behaving very mysteriously!"

"All in good time, Mum. I'm starving, let's eat. We've brought curries and rice."

"Yes, they smell divine. Come on in."

"We ordered mild, medium and hot. Something for everyone." Majella smiled as they took seats around the dining-room table.

"That's a lot of food!"

"You know me, Mum. I'll polish off whatever you two don't want. Nothing goes to waste when there's a pig around!" Jarrod laughed.

The conversation around the table was light and easy, focusing on the usual topics – the weather, crops, school, and what Bryce, Sally and Jessica were up to. Majella asked lots of questions about her time spent babysitting the twins, and even Jarrod was surprisingly interested in how she spent her time with them. She regaled them with some of their funny antics, and they all laughed together at the stories. Kath's mood changed when she told them that she wouldn't be required in a couple of weeks when the girls' grandparents arrived. She jumped up quickly to clear the table to hide her emotions. When she returned, there was a little gift-wrapped parcel sitting on the table at her place setting.

"Well now, what's this?" she enquired, raising her eyebrows as she looked at the giggling duo.

"Open it and see," they said in unison, before erupting in laughter and kissing each other soundly on the lips.

Kath joined in the merriment. "You two are incorrigible! Whatever have you been up to?"

The innocent question only made them laugh harder, a blush appearing on the younger woman's cheeks.

Kath just shook her head in bewilderment, and opened the wrapped gift. Inside was a little white garment with red writing on it. After she read the words, and realisation dawned on her, she gasped, "Oh, really?"

Together the beaming couple nodded their heads.

"When?"

"Well, we thought we'd give you something really special for your birthday this year."

"My birthday? In September? Oh, how wonderful!"

"Yes, but Mum, you haven't finished opening your gift. There's more."

"What?"

"Keep going," Jarrod prompted again.

Confused, Kath lifted up the tiny jumpsuit with the words 'My Grandma Loves Me' written across the front, only to see another identical suit folded neatly beneath.

"Oh, you can't be serious? You're having twins?"

Majella squealed delightedly. "Yep, I knew I was pregnant, but I never for a minute imagined twins. We had an ultra-sound today, and there are two!"

"But I had no idea you were even pregnant. I didn't suspect a thing. How have you hidden it from me?"

"Well, I haven't been sick at all. Just a bit tired, and I'm tall, so it's not as obvious. I've also been wearing fashionably loose clothes that have kept my little bump tucked out of sight." She shrugged before adding, "I'm not that far along, but my doctor thought I seemed bigger than normal so she suggested a scan. Especially since I had the miscarriage last year."

"Pretty crazy, hey Mum? I'm still trying to come to terms with it all. Two little bubs at once! Wait until we call Majella's parents. You'll hear Dafne scream from here!" he laughed.

The newly informed grandmother-to-be rose and went to hug them both. They all stood together and enjoyed a group hug, smiles and kisses all round.

"Well, you certainly took me by surprise! That was the last thing I was expecting. Jarrod, weren't we discussing babies a few weeks ago when I was telling you about Isla and Holly? You said you wanted to wait a while before trying again?"

"Just trying to throw you off the scent, Mum." He winked mischievously.

"Well, it certainly worked! Not that I'm too hard to fool, I know." She smiled good naturedly. "I think this calls for some celebratory dessert. I found a chocolate cheese cake in the freezer this afternoon. How's that sound?"

"Any ice cream?"

"Yes, of course there's ice cream! Your brother would never forgive me if there wasn't."

"All's good then!"

* * *

After the excited couple had left, Kath sat in Sam's favourite chair, a habit she enjoyed in the evenings, remembering when Jarrod had told her about Majella's miscarriage last year. She had only been eight weeks along but they had been quite devastated nonetheless, and Kath had not been there for them.

Physically she was just down the road, but emotionally she had still been lost in her own world of grief after Sam's death. Jarrod and Majella had known that, and had chosen not to confide in her then. It was several months later, in fact, that she heard about it.

She had felt dreadfully guilty about her failure to support and console them at their time of loss. So she went into her studio and found an appropriate card, blank with remembrance lilies on the front and, in her beautiful calligraphy, wrote the following verse:

> *For you created my inmost being,*
> *you knit me together in my mother's womb.*
> *Psalm 139:13*

Kath then drove to town and purchased a beautiful white rose bush, a bouquet of flowers and a box of fine chocolates. Next, she went to visit her daughter-in-law. After apologising profusely to Majella and offering her words of comfort, the two women had cried and hugged and then, together, walked outside into the glorious sunshine and planted the rose in the garden as a remembrance for the little baby that was now in Heaven, safe in the arms of Jesus.

She stirred herself from the memory and her eyes settled on a little plaque sitting on the nearby chest of drawers:

> *I don't know much, but three things I do:*
> *There is a God,*
> *His Word is true,*
> *Stay close to Him and He'll bring you through.*
> *Amen.*

She was instantly reminded of how blessed she was to have a Saviour who walked with her and watched over her every day. She didn't know what the future held, but He most assuredly did. She didn't understand why things happened the way they did, but she believed her loving God has a purpose for everything.

A little babe was lost, but now there was a double blessing of twins on the way. She had been upset to learn she was no longer needed as a baby-sitter for Isla and Holly. But now, she shook her head incredulously, she would have the joy and privilege of helping to care for her very own twin grand-babies. God is good, all the time.

Children are a gift from the Lord.
Psalm 127:3

CHAPTER 18

Movement Afoot

*"People become really quite remarkable when they start
thinking that they can do things. When they believe in
themselves, they have the first secret of success."*
-Norman Vincent Peale 1898-1993

There were times when Kath swore she could hear Sam's voice, or his
laughter, wafting through the open windows on the breeze. She wandered slowly around her lovely old farmhouse, every room held a story, lots
of stories actually, memories beckoned from every nook and cranny.

Most days they were comforting and seemed to envelope her, like a
warm embrace. But there were times when they were like sharp arrows
straight into her heart, causing feelings of grief and loneliness to rise up
again like an incoming tide. The tsunamis that used to knock her off her
feet, and into her bed to lay in misery under the blankets, rarely came anymore, but nonetheless the memories could still be painful.

She often toyed with the idea of moving somewhere else. But where would she go? That was the big question. A house in town didn't hold much appeal as she was too used to the peace and quiet of the country. A quaint little cottage nestled in the rainforest up at the Bunya Mountains captured her imagination, but she felt it was too far from town and her family. Driving up and down the narrow windy road was something she didn't want to do on a regular basis, and certainly not at night. So, she waited and prayed about it, asking the Lord to guide her, to show her what she should do and, in the meantime, she just sat tight. It was far too big a decision to rush into and, even though she was only painting small items for the information centre, she still wanted a place with room to set up her studio.

Gertrude and Max were always encouraging her to move to the coast and, as much as she would love to be near the beach, it was way too busy over there and even further from her family. She needed to be close to them and, now that there were grandchildren on the way, she could not possibly move away. But move into another house nearby? Well, maybe, she thought. In time Bryce and Jessica would marry. They had yet to set a date and, as Bryce wanted to work full-time on the farm, it was obvious that they should move to Yallaroo.

"But what about me, Tink? Newly-weds won't want me living here as well," she mused to her ever-faithful companion. "Where will I go?"

The little dog looked up and whined, as if to say, 'You mean what about us? You're not leaving me behind!'

Gertrude, of course, did not give up easily and had many ideas. Some quite reasonable, others rather way-out compared to Kath's less fanciful way of thinking. She rang quite regularly to share her latest scheme. "Kath darling, there's a gorgeous little cottage for sale just down the road a bit that would be absolutely perfect for you!" It was very quaint but situated on a busy intersection over 75km from Serendipity Place.

Another idea was, "Kath darling, I've just seen the sweetest pole house over at Noosa and it would suit you wonderfully!" It was huge, and the price was astronomical! The latest phone call began with, "Kath, darling, Max and I were thinking," Kath doubted that Gertrude's long-suffering husband had even been consulted, "that we could renovate the old shed down the back and make it into a superb studio apartment for you." From memory, the old building was mostly collapsed and very tiny.

All Gertrude's suggestions were well meaning and had some merit. But nothing really beckoned to Kath, and she felt no compulsion at all to move to the coast. Truth be known, as much as she loved Gertrude, she felt living too close to her might put a strain on their relationship; the eccentric loud extrovert and the peace-loving introvert. So, Kath determined she would not make any hasty decisions, but opted to continue with the pray, wait and see approach, believing she would know the right course of action when it appeared.

However, Jack and Edith then became quite vocal about all the positives of living in town, and they too started ringing often to tell Kath about a house they just happened to see for sale. She was, of course, very gracious in declining to inspect them, and had many reasons for doing so – too close to the highway, might flood there, too much dust from the sale yards, the motor-cross bike track was very noisy. She had become quite adept at thinking up excuses on the spot, and surprised herself with her quick responses, most of which were true. She continued to pray about it daily, and was content to wait upon the Lord, believing that He would show her if and when, and indeed where, she should move.

It came as quite a surprise when something Majella said, during a conversation they were having over morning tea at Oakleigh one day, caused her to prick up her ears.

"We went for a drive up the hill yesterday. I hadn't been up there for a long time. Jarrod needed to get something out of the old cottage. It was so lovely up there. I'd forgotten how beautiful the view is. You look right out over to the mountains. Funny isn't it, that cottage, tucked away on the far side of the hill? Out of sight, but only a few minutes away."

Kath stared at the Italian beauty, her pregnancy seeming to add a fresh glow to her olive complexion.

"The old cottage! You know I haven't been up there for years either. I'd forgotten all about it. I suppose it's starting to fall down now; it's been empty for so long."

"Actually, you'd be surprised at how good a condition it's in. They certainly built things to last back then, hey?" Majella continued innocently with no idea that she was stirring something in Kath's imagination. Or rather was the Holy Spirit planting a seed in response to Kath's many prayers, using Majella as the messenger?

"The trees on the western side of the hill are just beautiful too. I felt a real peace up there. There's even a big Jacaranda tree. Jarrod told me one of his great uncles used to live up there."

"Yes, that's right. Jack's brother Ian. He was a lovely gentleman apparently. He built it for his bride and they lived there for a few years before he moved away for work. I'll have to ask Jack the whole story. He has some photos of it, I believe."

"There's even the remains of a garden. Some shrubs of some sort, I don't know what, but they sure must be hardy. The fence is okay, Jarrod said he fixed it up a while ago when the neighbour's cows got out and were roaming around. He fixed the roof up a bit too, and boarded up some broken windows so they could keep using it for storage. Gosh, I'm tired." She yawned, patting her burgeoning bump.

Kath stood up and gathered their empty coffee cups, clearing the plate of biscuits off the table. "Why don't you go and lay down for a while? I'll get the washing in, and then I might walk up the hill and check out the cottage for myself. It's such a lovely day, and the exercise will do me good."

"Sure thing. Thanks Kath. Jarrod will be home in an hour or so." Yawning again, she wandered off down the hallway to rest her weary body.

Kath quickly brought the washing in from the clothesline, and folded it up, leaving it in neat piles on the laundry bench. Smiling secretly to herself, she put her hat and sunnies back on, pulled on her boots, and set off along the worn track that led to the hill. There was a definite spring in her step as something deep inside her had sparked when Majella had mentioned the old cottage. She couldn't wait to see it, and cautioned herself that she might be very disappointed. But she had learnt not to disregard the still quiet voice of God that often manifested itself as spontaneous thoughts from the Holy Spirit.

The hill was not very high, nor very steep, but compared to the otherwise flat landscape of the farm, it was an impressive sight in its own right. The last time she had been up there was with Sam, of course, in his old ute. He too had wanted to find something stored in the old building.

She remembered sitting in the shade of an old belah tree, which her knowledgeable husband had told her was a native in the area and a member of the sheoak family. He thought it was probably where Oakleigh had got its name from. There must have been many more on the property before the land was cleared for cropping, he had explained further.

The very memory of the tree, and the view, made her quicken her steps. She felt like something was drawing her forward. About ¾ of the way up the hill from the western side, the track veered to the right and headed around to the eastern side. She was breathing harder now, and stopped when the old cottage came into view. It was perfectly positioned to take in the morning sunrise over the mountains. The thought brought a smile to her face, bombarding her mind with ideas.

She walked forward unhurriedly until she was once again standing beneath the old belah, still standing tall and proud. It was about 15 meters high, its pendulous branches weeping down and swaying gently in the breeze. Her gaze was drawn again to the vista spread out before her, the mountains standing like sentinels in the distance.

Moving forward more slowly now, taking careful notice of everything before her, she removed her phone from the back pocket of her jeans and began taking photos. The jacaranda that Majella had mentioned was old and neglected, its trunk gnarled by the passage of time, but it was growing still and would no doubt herald in the spring with its purple covering of flowers, or at least it would if it had some TLC, she thought. She was surprised that she hadn't recalled the bottle trees, and the vibrant bougainvilleas and oleanders that were growing in wild abandon. '*Thank you, great Uncle Ian, for planting these trees,*' she thought to herself.

The fence was barely fulfilling its purpose, but it had evidently kept the wandering cattle out. The remnants of the garden beds were evident, just, and a rusty old tap stood not quite upright beside an old wooden trough, obviously hewn out of a giant log. It was once used to water stock. She stared at it incredulously, wondering where the water had come from? She shook her head, filing that question away for Jack.

The cottage was bigger than she expected, with full-length verandahs on both the eastern and western sides. The walls were made of weatherboards, horizontal boards that overlapped each other to cover the exterior of the cottage. The timber used in the cottage looked like cypress pine, not that Kath was an expert, but she knew it was one of the most termite resistant timbers available in the area. Sheets of old iron covered the roof. There were glass window panes; surprisingly some were still intact, while others had been boarded up.

The door opened, after much pushing, to reveal the dusty, dirty interior. The front half had obviously been the kitchen and living area with an old wood stove, a wooden bench with a sink in it on one side, and a brick fire place further along on the adjoining wall. The back half was divided into two bedrooms, with a lean-to built on the northern side, outside the kitchen for the laundry. Old cement wash tubs sat on a wobbly wooden frame. Kath's imagination was on fire, with Gertrude's words about other old properties echoing through her mind: "Oh, Kath darling, imagine the possibilities! Some slight renovations, some modern touches and the place would come alive!"

She could indeed see the possibilities! Was it really achievable though? She would need some professional opinions, and a building inspection by someone not wearing rose-coloured glasses like she knew she had. But still she thought that the potential was huge. The question was how big a project would it be, and what would it cost? She believed the old cottage could become a wonderful home once again where she could live contentedly. It wouldn't be big, but really there was only her and Tinkerbelle. Two bedrooms would suffice; one for her, and one for guests. Other family could always stay at either Oakleigh or Yallaroo. An art studio would be a must though, so she would need to figure that out.

'But was it all doable?' she wondered again. She sure hoped so! The idea had so many positives to recommend it; close to family, close to town and school, still on the family property. In fact, nothing would change really except she would have the opportunity for a fresh start and be independent; allowing the boys to raise their families in the other houses and work the farm.

When she emerged into the bright sunshine after pulling the old door shut behind her with effort, she stood on the front verandah, careful to avoid the broken boards. For a few minutes she looked thoughtfully out at the mountains, before praying quietly, hands clasped together in front of her,

"Oh Lord, is this the place for me? Please guide me, help me make the right decision. If this is the right path, please provide other people to confirm it for me. Show me how to manage the finances and the land ownership. I want to do what you want me to do, walk the path you have prepared for me. I promise I won't rush in. I will wait upon you, Lord. But, oh Father, it feels so right. Thank you for bringing me up here today. Bless you, Lord."

Kath walked down the track from the old cottage much slower than she had ascended. Visions of morning sunrises, and birds and bees buzzing around vibrant flower beds, were running through her head. It would be a small but adequate home, a project she could oversee while still working part-time. It sent a thrill of excitement through her body, resonating into her very bones.

She had not felt so alive in a very long time. However, there was lots of research to be done, and questions to be answered. *'Slowly, slowly'* she kept telling herself, as she neared Jarrod and Majella's house. Her son's work ute was parked at the back gate, so she knew her firstborn was home. Taking a deep breath, she forced herself to curtail her enthusiasm, so she could have a calm and considered conversation about her scheme.

Upon entering the kitchen, she found Jarrod and Majella sitting at the table, deep in conversation, but they stopped mid-sentence, and greeted her arrival with welcoming smiles.

"G'day Mum. I heard you've been hiking up the hill. I was just about to send out a search party. Want a cuppa? The kettle's just boiled."

"Yes, thanks. But I'll get a glass of water first."

"Did you enjoy your walk?" queried Majella, looking quite refreshed after her rest.

"Oh yes, it was wonderful. Um, I need to run an idea by you both," she ventured, with a somewhat nervous smile.

"Oh, really? Shoot then. We're all ears!" her son encouraged.

"Well," she said, putting down the now empty glass, the cool rain water satisfying her immediate thirst, and accepting the hot cup of tea her son offered her.

"I've been thinking for a while now that I need to make a fresh start. You know, move somewhere new. But I haven't been able to think of anything that appealed to me, something that felt right."

"Oh no! You're not thinking of moving away, are you?" Majella was quite shocked.

"No, I don't want to move away. I've given that idea a lot of thought, and I definitely want to stay around here. Don't worry, I'm not going anywhere." She smiled reassuringly.

"Phew, that's a relief. You really had me worried for a second there."

"How could I leave now that my grandbabies are on the way?" she questioned with a smile. "I'm so excited about them, and I want to be around to help out when you need me. But I do have something else in mind." She hesitated, wondering how to proceed, wanting to express her thoughts clearly.

"Bryce and Sally will be getting married at some point, when they decide on a date that is. Of course, you know, he wants to come back and work the farm full-time with you, Jarrod. The logical thing would be for them to live at Yallaroo, and I think that would be great, but I don't want to get in their way."

"Well, Bryce and I have discussed this quite a lot, Mum, and no one wants to make you feel unwelcome in your own home. We were going to have a chat with you at some point and see what your thoughts were. We were sort of wondering if you might want to move in to town? The farm would support us all, I'm sure, especially after the last couple of good seasons," he finished quietly.

"I know I wouldn't get pushed out, and I would fully support you boys running both properties. I know you work well together but, no, I don't want to move to town. I have another idea. It's about the old cottage up on the hill."

"The old cottage? It's just a storage shed now, and a good one I might add. Dad and I mouse-proofed it a few years ago; no vermin get in at all. It's weather-proof too."

"I was thinking I could renovate it, and make it into a new home." She looked from one to the other. "For me to live in."

She looked anxiously at them, awaiting their responses. Majella, with raised eyebrows, looked questionably at her husband who seemed to be studying something on the far wall.

"It's doable, you know," Kath added quietly after a few moments had passed.

"I think it's a great idea!" Jarrod and Majella said simultaneously which, of course, resulted in an outburst of laughter and an obligatory kiss.

Kath smiled, expelling the breath she hadn't realised she was holding. "Really?"

"Oh yes, it's a marvellous idea." Majella continued. "You'll be close, but you'll be independent. I was so worried you were going to leave us."

"Yeah, very happy to have you here on the property, but it will be a big project, Mum, and you couldn't do it on your own, you know."

"Yes, I realise that. There's an awful lot to consider, but I wanted to get your opinions first. After all, I would be living quite close to you."

"Don't you worry. With twins on the way we'll be very happy to have you nearby." He smiled, squeezing his wife's hand.

"If it is possible, things might get a little busy for a while, with people and vehicles coming and going."

"Actually, there's another track that veers off about 20 metres in from our mailbox. It's hard to see 'cos it doesn't get used much, but I'm sure I could tidy it up with the tractor and blade. It might need a bit of gravel here and there, but then you'd have your own separate driveway."

"Oh, this is so exciting!" Majella chimed in, clapping her hands together. "I would love having you live up there, Kath. Close, but not too close. We won't disturb you, and you'll have peace and quiet. But are you really sure you can leave Yallaroo though? It's been your home for such a long time."

"Yes, it will be hard to leave that lovely old place. But sometimes the memories there are too hard to bear. I had this discussion with your grandparents a few weeks back. I love Yallaroo, I really do, but it's just not the same anymore without your dad. I see him everywhere, so many memories. Sometimes, I swear I can even hear his laughter coming through the window on the breeze. I just feel I need a fresh start. Your father will always be with me, forever in my heart, but I'm just rattling around in a big empty farmhouse all on my own now."

"You're quite sure you don't want to think about buying a nice house in town?" Jarrod questioned again. "A lot less work."

"Your grandparents suggested that too, and I have given it a lot of thought, but I really don't want to live with close neighbours all around me. This way, at the old cottage, I'd still be on the property with all my memories and family nearby, and a bit involved with all the happenings of life on the farm. I can take all my special things with me, and whatever furniture I'll need. The only thing I will really miss is my art studio."

"Well, surely we can build another one. We'll work something out," Jarrod answered thoughtfully.

"The main thing I need is a clear view of the night sky."

"Oh, really. Why is that so special to you?" Majella was intrigued.

"Well, that's when I feel Sam's presence the most. When I look up at the night sky. I know he's in Heaven, but the night sky, with all the twinkling stars, just seems to bring Heaven so much closer. And you know what else?"

Majella shook her head, smiling, encouraging her to continue.

"The cottage faces the Bunyas, and you know how much I love those mountains. They were always our special place, your father and I," she added softly looking at Jarrod, wiping tears away before smiling into Majella's equally moist eyes. "I'm not running away, I'll be taking special memories with me. I need a fresh start, for me. I feel this is what the Lord wants me to do."

She blew her nose, and they sat in silence for a few moments before Kath added, "I need to discuss all this with your grandparents next, and see if they approve. After all, it's their land, and the farm business still has the share-farming agreement in place."

"Do you want me to come with you?" Jarrod offered.

"Thanks, but I'll be right. I'll pop in tomorrow and see them. I'm so glad you're both in favour of my crazy scheme. Now I've just got to see if I can make it a reality."

"I'm sure we can make it happen, Mum."

After kissing them both good bye, she drove the few kilometres home to Yallaroo, a smile playing on her freckled face. She knew it would be an enormous task, but she felt she could handle the challenge with the support of her family and friends. Indeed, she knew she needed the challenge;

something major to achieve by herself. Thoughts of the dreaded painting that was destroyed, along with her dreams of becoming an accomplished artist, entered her mind but she quickly pushed them away, refusing to let the pain and disappointment resurface. Any painting ambitions she had taken seriously over the course of her life had been forcibly stopped, snuffed out like a candle in the wind. She refused to allow herself to become vulnerable to any other disappointments where her art was concerned.

Would she ever fully recover from the hurt her father had caused her? She had forgiven him, but the fear of chasing her artistic potential lingered on. The gallery fire had devastated her, and confirmed her thoughts that she would never be good enough. She was done with big art projects; she had firmly closed that door. Renovating the old cottage would fulfil her creative desires, she told herself. She had money in the bank, and was confident she could secure a bank loan. *'One step at a time,'* she cautioned herself, thinking about her visit to Jack and Edith, and wondering what their reaction would be.

Before Kath went to bed that night, she went into Sam's office. Stephanie had invited her to a new Ladies Life Group at church some time ago. It was dedicated to journaling and, although she had been very reluctant to attend at first, she had been very surprised to discover that journaling was something she really enjoyed and looked forward to attending the meeting each week. She had always attended a weekly Bible study with Sam, but now she found this particular group was just what she needed. Everything discussed was kept in confidence, and they were able to support and encourage each other about whatever path life was presently taking them on. It was lovely to sit with other women, and feel relaxed and accepted. There was certainly great therapy in having a good laugh. Age was irrelevant. They all had different pasts and experiences to share, and they were certainly all on different journeys.

Stephanie had taught the ladies in the group how to write a journal entry based on four simple steps – Scripture, Observation, Application and Prayer, or SOAP for short. It focused on understanding what the scriptures said, and asking the Holy Spirit to speak into their lives. They were following a Bible reading plan that gave a daily reading suggestion of a chapter from the Old Testament and one from the New Testament. That night, sitting in Sam's office, Kath laughed out loud when she began the designated reading, Psalm 127. The first verse read:

Unless the Lord builds the house, they labour in vain who build it.

Immediately, she began to pray, "Oh, Heavenly Father. Thank you for your Holy Word, inspired by your Spirit so long ago. Thank you for this verse tonight. I feel you have been guiding me today. Everything in my heart and mind has been leading me to that little old cottage. I feel the Holy Spirit directing me. Thank you that Jarrod and Majella are all for it. I pray that you will continue to show me the right path. Please go before me on my visit to Jack and Edith's tomorrow. I pray that they will be home, and that they will be positive about my idea as well. Then, Lord, I need the rest of the family to be supportive too and, of course Father, I pray you will help sort out finances and the practicalities of all the planning and building stages. Father, you know me so well and you know how easily I get anxious and overwhelmed. Be my strength and courage, please Lord. Help me to be obedient to your will, and trust in you in every step. Bless you Lord. In Jesus' name, Amen."

After reading the rest of the Psalm, and completing her journal entry, she sat for a few moments, feeling a wave of peace wash over her. She knew she could rest, worry free, trusting that her Lord would guide her. She stood slowly, blew out the fragrant candle, turned off the light and, with a thankful heart, went to bed.

CHAPTER 19

Going Forward, Going Back

"When one door of happiness closes, another
opens; but often we look so long at the
closed door that we do not see the one
that has been opened for us."
Helen Keller 1880-1968

K ath slept deep and dreamlessly, waking with the first rays of sunshine peeping through her bedroom window. Her good mood had not dissipated overnight, and she happily started her morning routine, somewhat earlier than usual. She laughed as Tinkerbelle chased some big moths off the verandah in a fearless display of courage, only to jump and whimper in fright when a big green frog leaped off the step to land beside her on the dewy grass.

"Oh Tink, you are such a fraidy cat. It's just an old Freddo."

Tink yapped loudly, as if taking umbrage at the insult, which made Kath laugh even more. "You are so good for me, little Tinkerbelle. Like a good tonic! Now enough playing around, I haven't had my morning cup of tea yet." Together they went inside to the warm kitchen, closing the door behind them against the chilly air.

A phone call later in the morning confirmed that Jack and Edith would indeed be home, and they invited her to join them for morning tea. While she did her morning chores she kept thinking about the old building on the hill. She wandered around, touching furniture, caressing photos, remembering so many things that had happened within the old house over the years.

Could she really leave? Was she abandoning Sam? The home they had shared together for so long, since they were first married, and where they had raised their children. She was surprised that she really did feel, in her heart of hearts, that it was time to move on. The first six months after Sam's sudden death had been spent under a cloud of grief and despair, so heavy she had often wondered if she would ever really live again.

Thankfully, the fog had slowly begun to lift and the pain had eased. Then she had begun to paint again, thinking that becoming a respected artist would be the purpose and fulfillment she craved. She shook her head sadly at the thought of her beautiful painting that was lost. Why did her thoughts always return to that wretched painting, she thought, angry at herself for allowing it to happen?

She took her exasperation out on the floors, vacuuming them with great gusto. But when she entered the kitchen she looked at the old kitchen table, and pictured her children sitting there as youngsters doing their homework. She always seemed to fall back on teaching and, really, she told herself that was no bad thing; being a skilled educator after all and, generally speaking, she loved it. Her present part-time arrangement suited her very well, and she hoped she didn't need to go back to full-time in order to pay for the cottage renovation.

Round and round her thoughts went, until she realised she was wasting time and mental energy on something that was a long way from being confirmed. She looked forward to talking it through with her in-laws, respecting their wisdom. It would be good to discuss it with Nate and Angie too, she thought, as they were always great sounding boards.

She left home earlier than necessary so that she could buy Edith some flowers, and a sweet treat for Jack, probably some of the chocolate liquorice that he liked.

"Not that I'm trying to soften them up, Tink," she told her travelling companion for the morning. "I just like to give them little gifts when I see them, you know that." She smiled. The little dog loved car rides, well the first five minutes anyway, before she fell asleep. As Kath drove into town, she prayed,

"Dear Heavenly Father. Be with me today please, and help me to express my thoughts and ideas clearly, and to respect their opinions, whatever they may be. Thank you for blessing me with such good in-laws. In Jesus name, Amen."

"Kath, love. How good it is to see you," her father-in-law greeted her, rising from the comfy chair he favoured on the front verandah where he had obviously been waiting for her.

"Hello Dad," she kissed his cheek. "How are you?"

"Just fine, all the better for seeing you. And what's this? Little Miss Tink has come for a visit too!" The little dog was bouncing around his feet and eagerly stood on her hind legs for a pat, before being lifted into his arms where his face became an easy target for her quick tongue. "Stop that, you little rascal," he laughed before calling through the front door. "Mother, come see who's here."

Edith appeared and she, too, received a boisterous greeting from Tink, except that Jack held the poodle firmly in his arms so that she wouldn't scratch his wife.

"Goodness gracious me, Tinkerbelle. Have you missed us that much?" The older lady laughed as she patted the fluffy bundle of energy.

"You obviously both rate very highly with her! But, that's enough now, Tink. Settle down," her mistress scolded the little dog.

Tink obliged, responding to the firm tone and, once Jack put her down, seemed to indicate that her welcoming repertoire was completed anyway by stepping inside and walking haughtily down the hallway to the kitchen. She knew exactly which room the best smells came from.

"I see she's still a little prima donna," laughed Edith, her welcoming arm still around her daughter-in-law's shoulders. "Such a lovely surprise to have you visit dear. I know I saw you at the shops the other day, but sitting down over morning tea is so much better."

"Yes, you're right about that, and we haven't had a good chat for quite a while. I can smell something delicious. You've obviously been baking."

"Just a date loaf and a few scones."

"Edith, your date loaf is an award winner! I am privileged!"

"So are the scones. First place in my book, every time," Jack added enthusiastically, patting his belly. "I'll put the kettle on. Hey, Miss Tink. I think I have a treat for you somewhere."

The little dog barked, already sitting in front of the cupboard where she knew the dog treats were kept. After she sat and shook hands, then gave a high five with her other paw, she was rewarded with a treat. Then, seemingly satisfied with her grand entry and performance, she turned in circles twice before curling up on the mat.

"Oh, you are gorgeous. Aren't you?" cooed Jack as he ruffled her fur. "She certainly has a personality all of her own." He smiled at Kath.

"Yes, and she also knows who always spoils her," she countered.

The conversation flowed easily from one topic to another; the weather, school, Majella's pregnancy.

"Twins, no less. A double blessing from the Lord! How exciting. I can hardly wait!" said Edith. Then changed the subject to Bryce and Sally's engagement.

"Wonder when they'll decide on a wedding date?" Jack asked scratching his head.

Next, an update on Jessica.

"No boyfriend yet?" wondered Edith.

Then they chatted about many other family members, and also the local town news. When at last there was a lull in conversation, and the tea pot was empty, many slices of date loaf and several scones had been consumed, Kath broached the topic that was burning in her mind.

"There's something I want to run past you both. An idea I've got. Something I feel I'd like to do, need to do in fact. I would really value your opinions."

The two older people leaned forward; their attention totally focused on her face.

"Really love?" said Jack. "Sounds very mysterious. We're certainly eager to hear what it is, aren't we Edie?"

"Oh my, yes, of course. Is everything okay, Kath?" her mother-in-law enquired quickly.

"Yes, there's nothing wrong, I didn't mean to alarm you. In fact, I feel the best I have since Sam died. And it will be 12 months soon."

"Nearly a year," sighed Edith. "Mind you, I think it's been a very long year for all of us. You especially, of course."

"You're right about that, Edith, and I believe I'm finally moving forward in a positive way. It's been a difficult journey, and I didn't cope well at first, I must admit. I've had to learn how to do a lot of things for myself that Sam used to do. But I have certainly become much more capable and independent, and I've also learnt to lean on God so much more too. And you two have been wonderful to me, always so encouraging and supportive."

"Hush now, you're like a daughter to us. You know that." Embarrassed by her praise, Jack hurried the conversation along. "Now, what's this idea of yours?"

Kath took a deep breath before saying, "It concerns the old cottage up on the hill at Oakleigh. That your brother built."

They were both surprised. "Ian's old place?" Jack clarified.

She nodded. "I was wondering what you would think about me renovating it, and making it into a place where I could live?"

"But it must be practically falling down by now?" Edith said.

"Well, I know the boys have been using it as a storage shed for quite a while, but it can't be in very good shape, I wouldn't think." Jack scratched his head again, as he always did when pondering something.

"It still seems quite solid. Of course I'd need a builder to look at it, and give me an honest opinion. But I think it's possible to fix it up," Kath countered.

"I know we had a discussion about you moving a while back, and we fully understand why you would like a fresh start. Really we do. We were hoping you would move into town, but we also respect your reasons for wanting to stay out on the farm," Edith added quietly.

"I just feel more relaxed out there. No traffic noise, loud neighbours or barking dogs, except my own, of course," she smiled. "It's where I feel closest to Sam, you know?"

The older couple nodded in understanding.

"Also, I look forward to seeing Bryce and Sally married and living at Yallaroo. I know I'll be able to visit the house whenever I want, and then there's the two little babies on the way at Oakleigh! I'd be close enough to help when needed, but far enough away to give them their space as a new family. But I do feel God is telling me this is the change I need. Something to strive for and build, for me." She looked from one old face to the other, pleading with glistening eyes for them to understand.

After a minute or two of consideration, Jack said enthusiastically, "Well, I think it's a grand idea! Don't you Edie?"

She nodded her greying head, placing her wrinkled hand over the younger woman's smoother one. "Yes, actually I do. I can imagine how you must feel, my dear. I often think of you out there alone with all those memories. A comfort mostly I'm sure, but you mustn't feel held captive by them. Sam wouldn't want that."

"It's probably a better option than moving to town. It did take us a long time to adjust when we left Oakleigh, but it was the right thing for us to do at the time. You're right in that you'll still have family around and, once the twins arrive, your presence will be very welcome no doubt." Jack smiled at her. "But won't it be a huge undertaking, making that old place liveable again? It was beautiful you know, when Ian first built it. He was quite the craftsman. He built it to last, and to impress his new young bride, of course. I've got some photos somewhere. Edie, where's that big biscuit tin with the old photos in it?"

"Look in the sideboard in the lounge room, left side door, I think. Ian and Patty had a nice garden up there too, and the view was glorious. They were so sad to leave it all behind, but Ian had a job offer in Goondiwindi that was too good to refuse. They passed away several years ago now."

Jack returned triumphantly, waving an envelope with several black and white photos inside. "Looky here what I found!" he chortled happily.

He passed a photo to Kath. "Oh, look at it; all nicely painted with clean shining windows. There's even smoke coming out of the chimney!"

"Oh yes. Patty was a great cook, and charmed all sorts of goodies out of that old wood stove!"

The second photo showed Jack standing beside his brother near the veggie garden.

"Look how young and handsome you both were," remarked Kath.

"What do you mean 'were'? I still am!" He teased mischievously, causing his wife to swat him on his arm playfully.

They discussed the photos for some time, Jack and Edith getting lost down memory lane, meandering down many sidetracks and roundabouts.

Finally, Jack said, "You know, it really would be nice to see that old place turned into a happy home once more. Are you sure you're up to the challenge, love?"

"Yes, I believe I am. Jarrod and Majella are happy for me to live there, close but out of sight, and I needed to know you were both agreeable to the idea, seeing as you still own the property and we're just share-farming it."

"But that's only for another few months and then 'Wilmont & Sons Farming Company' will own it."

Kath looked at him in confusion. "But Jack, it will be quite some time before we can afford to buy the whole property from you. I was thinking maybe you would agree to sub-dividing a small portion where the hill paddock is, and I could buy that from you. I haven't actually looked at the property map but Jarrod thought that area of land might be on a separate portion."

"Kath love, Sam sorted all this out with us a month or so before he died."

"Sorted what out?"

Jack leant forward, his elbows on the table. "Sam rang me one day to discuss paying off Oakleigh. He wanted to make sure the properties were secure for you and your family. I said there was no rush but he was insistent about finalising it all. Not that I knew he was sick of course but, in hindsight, I see that he must have received the terminal diagnosis and that galvanised him into action. Actually, I believe the good Lord even tried to warn me in a dream that Sam was soon to be called home, but I didn't understand it at the time. But that's another story for another day." He smiled at Kath, while Edith nodded in agreement.

"Okay, another day then." She looked at him still confused. "But I still don't understand. What action are you talking about exactly?"

"Well, Sam came here one afternoon and spoke to us about buying Oakleigh. I told him that as we hadn't needed all of the income from the share-farming arrangement, Edith and I had kept some money in a special account, basically as a down payment on Oakleigh for when you decided to buy it. Anyway, Sam was adamant that everyone must agree on the financial arrangement, so he arranged a phone hook up with Nate and Josh, and asked Rosie to come around. So we all discussed the price for the farm, and that we had kept some of the share-farming money for you to put towards the payment. Of course, everyone was happy as Sam and you, and the boys of course, had worked hard for many years running both properties. Sam also said that he had sold the old unit you had at the Gold Coast. The unit itself wasn't worth much, but the land had increased greatly in value. So with the proceeds from that and, we all agreed, two more share-farming payments, the property would be transferred to your farming business."

"But I know nothing of this! Neither does Jarrod, I'm sure"

"I'm sorry, love. We honestly thought you knew all about it."

"Well, we did sell the land at the coast. It got snapped up very quickly before we went to South Australia, but he told me that he intended to invest the money."

"Oh, he invested it alright." Jack smiled. "To secure Oakleigh."

"And Nate, Josh and Rosie all agreed with this?"

"Yes, it was all very fair and businesslike. Acceptable to everyone."

"I just can't believe it. I just assumed he invested the proceeds from the land sale in shares, or our Super Fund. I've never even checked the accounts. Sam was always the financial head of the farm business, and I didn't pay much attention to the financial details. Josh did send me some documents, but I obviously didn't read them very carefully, just filed them away. Jarrod and Majella handle the farm accounts now, and transfer a monthly amount to me. Plus there's what I earn teaching. Oh, how ignorant I've been with our financial matters! Nate and Josh must think me a fool!" She finished, horrified.

"What nonsense, girl! You've had a terrible shock and bereavement to come to terms with, and Nate and Josh have been only too happy to help out. The boys put a succession plan in place years ago after we left the farm, and this is perfectly in keeping with that. They all have their own livelihoods and families, separate from the farms. We, thank the Lord, are financially secure, and Sam certainly made sure that you and your children have a secure future. It hasn't been mentioned because there's been nothing to discuss, really."

"What about Jessica though?"

Edith laughed. "Oh, Sam didn't forget his daughter. Did he Jack?"

"Forget the apple of his eye? Of course not! I believe there's a small block of vacant land still in your name at the coast?"

"Oh yes. It's quite a bit further inland though. Something else I'd forgotten about."

"Yes, but apparently it's situated in a very good area and, when the time is right, will sell for a good price. Sam bought it a long time ago when it was sitting in the middle of nowhere, miles from anywhere. But now there's new developments going up all around it. I remember telling him he was mad to buy it at the time. The same with the unit, cheap though they were." He laughed. "Just shows you how much I know about real estate, and speculating on markets."

"Oh my," Edith spoke quietly. "I'm so proud of all our children. They work hard, and have prospered so well."

"Kath, love, would you mind running out and watering my veggie garden please while I have a quick word with Edith?"

Both women looked at him with raised eyebrows, somewhat surprised by his request, but neither objected. Kath called Tink, bending to kiss the balding head of her father-in-law as she walked past him to do as he asked. She stood in the backyard and reached up, stretching her limbs before walking to turn on the garden tap so she could water Jack's plants. She had grabbed one of Edith's gardening hats from the verandah, but still squinted in the sunlight. Her mind was awash with thoughts and mixed emotions, all swirling around together as if in a washing machine.

Dear darling Sam, how good was he to put so many things in place when he was coming to terms with his illness, facing his own death. He would have told her all about the property dealings, she knew, but the fishing trip and untimely accident had put a stop to that. Thankfully, the remaining men in the Wilmont family were of the same ilk; kind, caring and compassionate. They too, were also savvy businessmen. How blessed was she to be surrounded by such a family. She didn't have to worry about buying the land the cottage was on. Sam had already secured it for her through the farming business. *'Thank you darling.'* She blew a kiss heavenward.

After ensuring the veggies were well watered, she turned her attention to the adjacent flower beds which were Edith's pride and joy, and rightfully so. Their beautiful fragrances filled the air as the brightly coloured blooms swayed gracefully in the light breeze. Tinkerbelle was enjoying herself, chasing the butterflies that the water disturbed, yapping merrily as she danced around on the soft green lawn. Their time in the garden was interrupted by Jack calling, "Lunch is ready."

Kath washed up in the laundry before entering the kitchen, where Edith had placed plates of cold meats, salad and bread rolls on the table.

"My goodness, hasn't the morning flown by! What can I do to help, Edith?"

"Just have a seat, dear, all done. Just simple fare. Say grace would you please Jack, and then we'll just help ourselves."

After the blessing, they enjoyed the meal together, chatting easily, mostly about the beautiful garden outside. It wasn't until they were again sipping hot cups of tea that Jack brought up the subject of the cottage.

"Kath, love. Edith and I would like to give you some money which, we believe, you are quite entitled to."

"No," Kath interrupted quickly. "I didn't come here looking for money."

"Sshh, we know that," he answered gently, patting her hand. "But we want to. You see, Sam insisted on paying us more than we wanted him to for the share-farming. Much more. But he always wanted everything to be fair and equitable with his siblings, as he was farming the home property. Anyway, to placate him, we finally agreed and accepted what he determined was the right amount. Anyway, we have always put a certain percentage of it into a separate account, planning to give it back to you both when you wanted to buy the property, as I explained before. Now there are two share-farming payments due, as I mentioned, but there is still quite a tidy amount in that account, which Sam insisted we keep for a rainy day. Now,

I've just had a quick chat to Josh, as he advises us on all our financial matters, and he sees no problem with our intention, as it's our money after all."

"But…"

"No buts about it. Edith and I would like to give you some funds to put towards the renovation of the cottage. The money was earned by you and Sam in the first place, so it's only fair." He wrote a figure on a note pad and showed it to her.

She gasped, covering her mouth with her hands. "Oh no, it's too much, I couldn't."

"No, it's not," Edith assured her firmly. "We always felt Sam was paying us too much, and now we can make amends, to our way of thinking anyway. We have everything we need, and then some. And just so you know, we are not showing you any favouritism. Everything we do for our children, we do equally in one way or another. So, no fuss. The money will be returned to you. Start planning your renovations, Kath, with our blessing." She smiled and, standing, she held her arms out to her daughter-in-law.

Kath was quite overwhelmed with emotion, and could not speak. She simply hugged the sweet woman whose arms were wrapped around her, before turning to Jack and hugging him too, wetting his shoulder with tears of love and gratitude.

✳ ✳ ✳

After thanking them profusely again, and then saying farewell to them both, she gathered Little Tink in her arms and settled them both in her car. She then drove out to the cemetery, a place she didn't visit all that often, but today she felt particularly compelled to go to Sam's graveside.

The sky was a vivid blue, not a cloud in sight. A soft easterly breeze was blowing across the black soil plains, the wheat crops nodding their heads as if drowsing in the sunshine. She walked to Sam's grave with Tink on a leash beside her, and knelt to brush some leaves off his memorial plaque:

Samuel Matthew Wilmont
22/01/1969 – 27/05/2021
Beloved husband of Kath.
Dearly loved father of Jarrod, Bryce and Jessica.
Sadly missed by family and friends.
Forever in our hearts.

She made a mental note to bring fresh flowers next time, berating herself for not giving it a thought today. She removed the dried-out flowers from the vase beside the grave, the final resting place for his body. The gardens at the lawn cemetery were beautiful, but she never felt close to Sam here. The night sky, especially from the farm, was what always brought him close to her; the stars twinkling and seeming to wink at her, and as he so often had.

'What is it about the Wilmont men and winking?' she thought to herself, smiling. They were all so good at it, while she had never managed to master the skill.

"Oh Sam, my darling. I know you're not here, that you are wonderfully alive and well up in Heaven." She spoke quietly, but loud enough for Little Tink to hear and prick up her ears. "Thank you for looking after me and the children so well. You made sure everything was paid off and secured. You had so little time, yet you managed to achieve so much, put so many things in place."

She alternated between speaking to his grave and raising her hands upwards to the sky and the heavenly realm above. "You were constantly thinking about your family. I'm so sorry I was upset at your secrecy, mad at you for not confiding in me. I still don't really understand why didn't tell me, but I do know how much you loved me and the kids."

She was walking around the grave now, talking to Sam and praying, arms outstretched and tears streaming down her face. "Oh Sam, we all miss you so much! You must be pleased my darling though, that I'm moving forward at last with some joy in my heart. Thank you, Heavenly Father, for being my strength; for blessing me with such a caring and thoughtful husband, and his equally caring family. Thank you that my future is clearer now. I have a plan, Sam, a project. It's rather daunting, I must admit, but I'm looking forward to it and I think I can do it."

Poor Tinkerbelle was trotting round and round in circles beside her mistress, looking up frequently, wondering what kind of silly walk this was. But she was happy as she could sense excitement in the air. A pair of butterflies flew past, causing a sharp yap from the poodle which caused Kath to glance down quickly at her and laugh. "Oh Tink, I must look like a crazy woman, turning circles, crying, talking and praying." She looked around the cemetery quickly, thankfully seeing no one else around. "It's alright, little one. Everything is going to be okay."

She kissed her fingers, bent down and placed them gently on Sam's engraved name, whispering good bye before she and Tink returned to where the car was parked in shade amongst the trees. As she was driving back into town her phone rang. Seeing the name on the car's screen display, she answered with a smile, "Hello Jillian."

"Hi, I'm at the skate park watching the boys, and I thought I would give you a ring. How're you going?"

"Oh Jillie, I have some exciting news! I'm just driving home so I'll stop by and tell you about it. Okay?"

"Sure, can't wait to hear what's going on. See you soon."

The two friends sat in the shade at a picnic table while Jillian's two boys practiced their tricks on the hot concrete. Kath waved to them as they flew past, Riley on a scooter and Jayden on a skateboard. "Wow, must be so hot out there. Look how red their faces are!"

"Yeah," answered the boys' mother unconcerned. "But they love it, and it wears them out. A stop at Maccas drive-through on the way home, and I'm assured of a few hours' peace and quiet this afternoon while they watch a movie. Method in my madness, hey?"

"A win win situation all round, I reckon," laughed Kath.

"Mind you, they had to do their chores this morning, and make sure they're up-to-date with their homework and assignments. I still think there's a place for bribery and blackmail in parenting." She grinned audaciously. "Now tell me what's going on with you. You look like you're going to burst, or lay an egg. I can't decide which!"

Kath leaned in toward Jillian and began filling her in on everything that had recently transpired; the expected twins, the need to find somewhere else to live, the old cottage, and finally today's news about Sam's financial dealings with his parents.

"Wow wee. That's quite a story! Oh, I'm so pleased for you! Twin babies! Good thing you just acquired all that experience looking after Isla and Holly! The cottage reno will be the perfect project for you. And dear sweet Sam, bless his cotton socks. What a wonderful man he was. Not to mention Jack and Edith; all the Wilmonts in fact. What a wonderful family you have!"

"Yes, I know, I am truly blessed. If I had had my wits about me, I would have worked a lot of things out for myself earlier, but I just left all the financial concerns to Nate and Jack. So very slack of me, I'm sorry to say."

"Well, no harm done. It's all just been a matter of timing really. You had to work through a lot of stuff before you could get to this point. Sometimes the journey is more important than the arrival. You've discovered a lot about yourself along the way, and grown a lot too, emotionally and spiritually.

Who would have imagined you tackling a renovation project six months ago? Look how confident you're becoming! I'm so proud of you!"

They stood and hugged each other, and then did a happy dance together, giggling like a pair of eight-year-olds. Little Tink joined in with excited barking, which made the women laugh even more.

"Mum, what are you doing? You can be so embarrassing!" Riley sounded quite horrified.

They turned around to see Jillian's boys standing behind them, watching them wide-eyed.

"Oh, lighten up fellas. We were just celebrating some good news."

"Can we go to Macca's now?" Jayden asked hopefully.

"Yes, in a few minutes. After you've both had a drink of water and cooled down a bit. Now go and get your water bottles." Shooing them away, she turned back to her friend. "So glad we caught up today, Kath. You'll have to keep me posted on all your developments."

"Yes, of course. It could be a long and bumpy road, but I'll never, never know 'till I have a, have a go," she beamed, quoting another of Bryce's favourite sayings.

"That's the spirit! Oh, when are you going tell your kids about all this?"

"Well, Jessica is coming out for lunch tomorrow, so I might ask them all over. Jarrod and Majella should be right. I don't know what Bryce is up to, or if Sally is working this weekend, though. It might be short notice for her. Jack and Edith would probably be available. I'll see what I can arrange this afternoon, and work out what I'll feed everyone. I should make some calls before I leave town, I guess, in case I have to pop into Coles for a few things. I'll figure it out."

"Yes, of course you will. See you later. Oh, before I go, Stephanie asked me to give you something." Jillian rummaged in her large carry bag before pulling out a folded sheet of paper, albeit rather crinkled. "It's a Divine

Reading. Just insert your name into the blank spaces. It's really special, you'll love it."

"Thanks Jillie," Kath said, taking the paper and hugging her friend. "And thanks for everything. You've been such a good friend to me all along the way. I couldn't have managed without you."

"Don't be silly, of course you could've. Besides what are friends for?"

Kath waved good bye, before resuming her seat at the picnic table and taking her phone out. She was surprised to see a missed call from Jessica, as she hadn't heard her phone ring. She returned the call.

"Hi sweetheart. Sorry I missed your call. I was catching up with Jillian."

"No worries, Mum. I was just wondering if I could bring a friend along tomorrow?"

"Of course you can, but I was going to ring you and let you know that I was going to invite your brothers and the girls over for lunch as well, if you don't mind? Oh, and your grandparents too. There's something I need to tell you all."

"That's fine by me; a good chance to see everyone. Is everything okay, Mum?"

"Yes, everything's fine. In fact, I have some very good news to share with you all."

"Oh really. No tit bits for me now?" Jessica quizzed, hoping to get some more information.

"Nope. I'll tell you tomorrow when all the family is together."

"You are being very secretive! Are you sure it's a good time for me to bring a friend along then?"

"Well, it does concern the farm business. Would your friend mind sitting on the verandah, or going for a walk, if we had a little family meeting? What's her name, by the way? Do I know her?"

"Oh, it's Lane and, no, you haven't met. I'm sure a walk in the garden would be fine."

"You don't hear that name very much. I only know of Layne Beachley, the surfer."

"Well, you're going to meet another one tomorrow." Kath could hear the smile in her daughter's voice, and something else she couldn't quite put her finger on.

"I'll be home in the morning if you want to come earlier."

"Okay, sounds good. We might come for morning tea then."

"That'll be lovely. See you tomorrow."

A few more phone calls confirmed that all of the others were, indeed, available for lunch, so she headed back to the supermarket to do a super-quick grocery shop, considering she had to leave poor Tinkerbelle locked in the car. At least she found a shady park and left the windows down a bit.

✳ ✳ ✳

Just before she went to bed, she obeyed Jillian's instructions and wrote her name in all the blank spaces on the typed sheet she had been given, and then she read it out loud in Sam's office,

> *"Isaiah 43: 1-3*
> *But now this is what the Lord says, <u>Kath</u>,*
> *He who created you, <u>Kath</u>, He who formed you, <u>Kath</u>;*
> *Do not fear, for I have redeemed <u>Kath</u>.*
> *I have summoned <u>Kath</u> by name; <u>Kath</u> is mine.*
> *When <u>Kath</u> passes through the waters, I will be with <u>Kath</u>;*
> *And when <u>Kath</u> passes through the rivers, they will not sweep*
> *over <u>Kath</u>.*
> *When <u>Kath</u> walks through fire, <u>Kath</u> will not be burned;*

For the flames will not set <u>Kath</u> ablaze.
For I am the Lord, <u>Kath</u>'s God, the Holy One of Israel,
<u>Kath</u>'s Saviour."

'*Oh, how beautiful,'* she thought as she began to pray quietly, thanking God for all her many blessings. Sometime later she fell asleep in her warm bed, still thanking and praising God for all He had done for her. She knew He would be with her in this next chapter in her life.

CHAPTER 20

Bold New Beginnings

*"What you are is God's gift to you, what
you become is your gift to God."*
Hans urs von Balthasar. 1905-1988

*R*ain fell across the flat plains, making a soothing melody on the old
tin roof of the farmhouse. At first, Kath's sleep-muddled mind, half
awake, didn't recognise the sound. Its gentle constancy lulled her back to
sleep and, when she did wake up fully thirty minutes later and realised that
it was raining, she was at first disappointed. "Oh no. Everyone's coming for
a BBQ, and it's raining!"

Tink seemed to sense something was wrong and jumped up onto the
bed. A warm arm revealed itself to cuddle the little dog closer. "Morning
Tinkerbelle, I wasn't expecting rain, were you, hmmm? Maybe I should
have checked the forecast before planning my menu? What do you think?
What sort of farmer am I?" She laughed as Tink turned her head sideways

and whined. "I think it's a good thing you can't talk. You would tell me a thing or two, wouldn't you? Come on, lots to do."

Happy barking followed her to the French doors opening onto the verandah. "Oh dear. It does look like it's set in. Not to worry, we'll just have to make the best of it."

After a cup of tea and a hot shower, her disposition had improved immensely, and she dressed carefully, wanting to look her best today. She finally decided on some new jeans she had recently bought, a light jumper and a silk scarf that Jessica had given her last Christmas. It matched her outfit perfectly. Leaving her hair hanging loose around her shoulders, and applying some light makeup to her face, she was ready and looking forward to the day, wet or not. The rain didn't really alter her plans, as the BBQ was set up on the verandah outside the kitchen, and she knew the boys would happily do the cooking.

With a potato bake, a salad and the fresh rolls she bought yesterday, the main meal was organised. Edith was bringing a trifle for dessert. She had custard in the fridge, and the essential ice cream in the freezer. It wasn't a really big gathering with only the three men, Jack, Jarrod and Bryce, and the six women, Edith, Majella, Sally, Jessica, Layne and herself, so she felt she had plenty of food to satisfy all appetites. Everyone was bringing their own drinks, Majella was making a slice, and Jessica was bringing some chocolates, so afternoon tea was sorted as well. She was so looking forward to seeing Jess as she hadn't seen her for well over a month. She seemed to be busy most weekends lately, with one thing or another.

After finishing all her preparations, Kath sat in her favourite chair in the living room. She was glad that she had cut flowers yesterday, instead of today as they now looked waterlogged and forlorn, petals bowed down towards the wet earth. She opened her Bible to Romans 8:28, for her morning devotion:

And we know that in all things God works
for the good of those who love Him,
who have been called according to His purpose.

Oh, how faithful He was! Despite the pain and turmoil she had experienced since Sam's death, and then the lesser tragedy of the loss of her painting in the fire, here she was today, happy and excited, wiser and stronger on the cusp of a big adventure. Oh, there was still pain in her heart, but the grief was easier to bear. She was quietly praying, asking the Lord to bless the family gathering, and thanking Him for her loved ones, when Nipper sounded the 'there's a vehicle coming' canine alarm. Little Tink, of course, joined in eagerly, having no idea what she was barking at, but she certainly sounded impressive.

Bouncing out of her chair, Kath went quickly to the window to look down the driveway, expecting to see Jessica's white Rav4, but she didn't recognise the oncoming vehicle. Frowning, she looked at the black Toyota Hilux. She only knew what make it was because Rosemary's husband, Craig, drove a similar work ute. The dual cab vehicle stopped near the front gate, and she was surprised to see Jessica get out of the passenger side. A tall young man then exited from the driver's side, and walked around to where Jess was standing to hold an umbrella over her. Jessica waved at her mum before reaching back into the vehicle to gather some bags. She said something to the fellow, and they both laughed. He closed the door for her and then opened the garden gate, still protecting her from the rain with the brolly as they walked along the path and up the front steps to where Kath was standing.

Jessica greeted her mother warmly with a hug, before turning to take hold of the young man's hand and pulling him closer said. "Mum, I'd like you to meet my friend, Lane."

Kath, her manners impeccable, kissed the young man on the cheek saying, "Lane, how lovely to meet you. Welcome to Yallaroo."

The sideways look she gave her mischievous daughter over his shoulder, left Jessica in no doubt that she would receive a good-humoured castigation later, when they were alone.

"It's great to meet you too, Mrs. Wilmont. Jess has told me all about your lovely home."

"Sorry it's such a wet day, but we do welcome nice steady rain like this. I wasn't expecting it though, so it'll be an indoor BBQ. Or rather, a verandah BBQ."

"It'll be fine Mum," said Jessica, cuddling Tink. "There's lots of space out here, and we can always eat inside if it gets any cooler. Lane, meet Tinkerbelle, otherwise known as Little Tink or just Tink."

"I hope you like dogs?" Kath ventured.

"Yes, I'm a dog lover. I've got a staffy at home. He thinks he's human."

Tink seemed to think Lane was okay as, after he finished rubbing her back, she yipped loudly and when he leaned closer, his dark brown, wavy hair falling forward over his forehead, her pink tongue quickly emerged and licked his nose in rapid movements, causing him to close his dark brown eyes as he drew back, laughing in surprise. "You sure are fast, Little Tink! Got me good."

Jessica too laughed at the scene. "Now you've been properly welcomed by the most important member of the family, and received the official lick of approval! You're a cheeky puppy, Tink! Hey Mum, is the kettle hot? I'm starving."

"It was. Just turn it on again for a minute, or would you prefer the coffee machine? Lane what would you like?"

"Tea will be fine, thanks."

"Okay, I'll make a pot then. Jess, you might want to give Lane a quick tour of the house while I get things ready."

"Sure." Holding hands, they wandered down the hallway, Kath watching them go with warm eyes, pleased to see her daughter so happy, and looking forward to getting to know her friend and finding out some more details about him.

When they returned, morning tea was ready on the verandah table.

"Oh, hummingbird cake! My favourite. Thanks Mum."

"Special occasion. You haven't been to visit me for so long," she teased.

"Sorry, been a bit busy." The reply was accompanied by a light blush, as she looked at the man sitting beside her.

"So, Lane, tell me about yourself." Kath turned her attention to her daughter's friend. "You're not a surfer, I gather!" Lane looked at Jessica, and they both laughed loudly.

"No, I'm an electrician actually," he finally replied. "I work for a company in Toowoomba. My family all live there. Mum's a nurse and Dad's a dentist, and I have a younger brother and sister. I met your daughter at church."

"He's an amazing singer, Mum, and he plays the guitar. I joined the music team and that's how we really got to know each other."

"You have a lovely voice, Jess. I miss hearing you sing."

"I'm not that good at singing, Mum. I'm happy just playing the piano."

They continued to chat generally for some time. Lane was easy to talk to, and seemed knowledgeable on a range of subjects. He was confident, but not overbearing, his smile always at the ready. There was an easy camaraderie between him and Jessica.

"So how long have you actually known each other," Kath asked, thinking how white and even his teeth were. But then his father is a dentist, she recalled with an inner smile.

"Well, we met last year but we've really only been seeing each other seriously for the last few months."

"Hmm, you've been very secretive. I didn't suspect a thing."

"Sorry Mum, nothing much to report. We're just good friends, hey buddy?" she raised her eyebrows in question at the young man sitting beside her, who merely grinned back at her, saying nothing, his arm draped casually along the back of her chair. "But we're here today, and Lane will get to meet everyone."

"Yes indeed. I'm very happy you're both here," replied her mother, reading the situation perfectly. Rising she began to clear the table. "The rain has stopped for a bit, it seems. You might get a quick walk around the garden if you hurry. Looks like there's another shower coming."

"Great idea. Can I show Lane your studio, Mum?"

"Of course, though there's not much to see in there at the moment. I'm just working on a couple of little projects. Oh, and the light's not working for some reason, so you'll have to turn on the lamp in the corner."

No sooner had Kath finished tidying up the kitchen, putting the potato bake in the oven, and ensuring that everything else was ready for lunch, than a heavy downpour began. She heard a loud squeal in the backyard and looked out the window to see Lane and Jess running through the rain making a dash for the back steps, the young man's arm around her daughter's waist holding her back. Tink growled from where she had fallen asleep in the kitchen, woken by the commotion.

"It's all right Tink. They're just friends, you know?" She smiled at the little dog as she left to get towels for the young couple. "I thought the others might have been here by now; they'll get caught in the rain," Kath said, handing them each a towel.

"They won't mind, Mum. It's been a while since it last rained. It's quite a novelty actually."

Right on queue, Nipper started barking again, with Tinkerbelle's shrill voice joining in, a near deafening crescendo as she competed with the rain pounding on the tin roof.

Great activity quickly followed, as three vehicles arrived within minutes of each other. Edith was surprised to be carefully escorted to the house by a handsome young man whom she had never seen before. Majella, looking very pregnant, received the same treatment with equal gratitude and curiosity. Bryce and Sally shared a tiny fold-up umbrella that did little to keep either of them dry, while Jarrod covered his grandfather with his big golf umbrella, ensuring they both arrived on the verandah relatively unscathed by the downpour. Jessica was happily introducing Lane to her family, and Kath was busy making sure everyone was warm and dry. It took some time for the noise to settle and, thankfully, the rain eased to light drizzle, so they didn't have to raise their voices to be heard. A relative peace descended on the gathering.

The BBQ was soon fired up, with Jarrod and Bryce taking control of the cooking as their mother had requested. When Lane had answered all the questions from the inquisitive womenfolk, and chatted for a little while, he joined the men at the barbie where he visibly relaxed.

"Survive the interrogation, mate?" Bryce questioned jovially. "You were quite the centre of attention."

"Yeah, that's for sure. Got a bit intense for a minute or two, but no worries. Glad to finally meet you all."

Jack, too, escaped the women and joined in the conversation with his grandsons and the newcomer.

"Grandad, Lane's an electrician. Are Uncle Craig and Aunty Rosie coming out today?"

"No, they're away this weekend. Craig would enjoy meeting another sparky. Another time I'm sure, hey Lane?"

"Sure. I look forward to meeting them."

The men stayed around the BBQ talking while the steak and sausages cooked, the smell making them all hungry. The women chatted while sitting at the outdoor table, Jessica also being asked a seemingly endless barrage of questions about her friend. Sally and Majella teased her about keeping her good-looking boyfriend a secret for so long. Jessica soon gave up trying to assure them all that they were just good friends, especially when her grandmother said, "My dear, a young man doesn't look at a mere friend the way that fellow keeps looking at you!"

The conversations continued once the meal was ready, and Jack said grace. There was, of course, plenty to go around. Dessert was then received with equal enthusiasm and, once their appetites had been satisfied, the younger men all managing seconds of dessert, the table was cleared, the dishwasher packed and started, and they all retired to the living room. Lane was noticeably absent as Jessica sat on the couch beside Jarrod and Majella.

"Where's your young man Jess?" Jack asked.

"Oh, he's got some work calls to make so he's out in Mum's studio. Mum said she wanted to discuss some business concerning the farm with us."

"That's right, as long as he understands. We don't mean to be rude to your guest."

"No, its fine. Mum told me yesterday that we'd be having a family meeting, so he's fine with it."

Kath took that as her cue and, from her seat in her favourite chair near the window, she began by saying, "Well, some of you know my idea and

some of you don't so I'll just start from the beginning and explain it all."
She began with telling them why she felt the need to move, wanting a fresh
start and how the idea of renovating the cottage came about.

Bryce was the first to interrupt her saying, "But Mum, don't think Sally
and I want to push you out. We were thinking about renting in town when
we get married."

"And when will that be exactly?" Majella asked cheekily.

To everyone's great surprise, Bryce replied. "Well, as a matter of fact,
we were going to tell you today, seeing as we're all together." Smiling at his
fiancé, he continued. "We've decided on November 29, if that suits you
all."

The announcement was greeted with claps and cheers.

"Of course it suits us all." Kath smiled at the lovebirds.

"Wonderful news, a wedding to look forward to, as well as new babies,"
Edith said excitedly.

"Well, it certainly suits me," Majella said rubbing her expanding belly.
"The babies will be a few months old and I won't be waddling around like
an old duck."

"Quack, quack," said her husband, nibbling her ear and receiving a
playful slap in return.

Bryce looked at his mother again. "There's still no rush for you to move
out, Mum. The renovation might take quite a while you know. That old
cottage is in pretty bad shape."

"Thanks Bryce. Let's just see how things go. There's an awful lot to do,
I know, and it will be a steep learning curve for me. Really, I have no idea
how long it will take."

Kath went on to explain how she had discussed her initial plan with
Jarrod and Majella, and then she had visited Jack and Edith to get their
opinion and discuss buying the land. She then continued to reveal all that

Sam had done for his family. and what he had managed to put in place before his death. Jack added information, and clarified some points along the way. When she had finished speaking, there was silence in the room. It was a lot for her children to take in.

"Wow!" Bryce said quietly at last. "I didn't know what this meeting was about, but I certainly wasn't expecting to discover that Oakleigh would soon be part of the farm business, debt free."

"Yeah, I had no idea either," his brother agreed. "Although I did wonder, Grandad, why you said we were nearly there when I checked if you had seen that I had deposited the payment into your account last month? I meant to follow up with you and see what you meant, but then it slipped my mind."

"Sorry, Jarrod. Your grandmother and I thought you were all aware of the situation, so we were rather taken aback when your mother came asking to buy some land off us. But I think we've cleared everything up now," he said, looking around the room.

It was then that Jessica spoke up. "I'm happy for the boys, that their futures are assured, and I'm blown away by everything Dad did when he was obviously so sick. He really was amazing." She stopped to wipe a tear away. "But, and I know this will sound very petty, I have to ask. What about me? I know the boys are working the farms, but don't I get anything? I know I'm the girl, the only daughter, and I've started my own career, but don't I count for anything?"

"Oh Jessica, pet, of course you do," her grandfather replied quickly, leaning towards her. "Forgive me for not explaining everything. Your father did not forget you, not at all. He would never overlook you. Now, all property in his will was in joint names, and has now reverted to your mother. But he left very clear instructions about what he wanted to happen. Right, Kath?"

"Yes, absolutely. Jess, I owe you and your brothers an apology. I have been very negligent in taking responsibility for your father's affairs. I just left everything to Nate and Josh and, of course, your poor grandfather to handle. I trust them completely, and they have done an admirable job. I've only just grasped the entirety of all this myself. How I forgot about the Gold Coast properties, I don't know. Your father bought them when we were first married but, as you heard, one block has been sold and those funds were used to help secure Oakleigh. Now there is still the other smaller block, quite a bit further out, and that block is to go to you Jess. It was your father's intention and, of course, I will honour his wishes. He has left me very well provided for. In fact, he made sure we are all very well provided for. He was so clever, a shrewd businessman, with a handy share portfolio as well. So, Jessica, you are indeed provided for."

Kath stood and held her arms out to her daughter. Jessica went and hugged her mother. "I'm sorry Mum. I should have known Dad wouldn't forget me. I wasn't expecting a block of land at the coast though."

"Well, it is for the future, so maybe keep that bit of information to yourself for the time being, hey?" her mother cautioned.

Jessica's eyes widened, but she nodded, knowing she was referring to her relationship with Lane, and understanding the hidden meaning. Jack, who had come to stand beside his granddaughter, one arm placed lovingly around her shoulders, said quietly, "Your Father loved you very much Jess. From the moment you were born, from the hair on your head to the soles of your feet. Never doubt that. He adored you!"

"Thanks, Grandad."

The other members of the gathering were all standing, talking amongst themselves. Kath looked at everyone and said to no one in particular: "Time for afternoon tea I think. I'll go and put the kettle on".

Jessica went out to her mother's studio to fetch Lane and was surprised to find him kneeling on the floor with a tool box beside him.

"What on earth are you up to?" she asked, putting her arms around his neck.

"Oh, I just thought I'd see why the light wasn't working in here. It just needed a new switch. The power point for the lamp was pretty dodgy, so I replaced it too. I was able to turn the power off for this building on the electrical panel I found on the back verandah. I just need a dust pan and brush to clean up my mess. Your mum won't mind, will she?"

"Of course she won't mind. She'll think you're very sweet, just like I do," she said softly, kissing him on his full lips.

"Well, that was my intention, to impress your mother," he replied, kissing her.

"What about me?"

"I'm always trying to impress you!" Another kiss confirmed the fact.

"Mmmn, you're succeeding! Hungry?"

"Always, you know that," he laughed. "Good meeting?"

"Oh yes, Bryce and Sally have finally announced their wedding date, and Mum is going to renovate an old cottage on Oakleigh for herself to live in."

"Really? Well, good for her. I wonder if she'll need a sparky?" he teased.

"I don't know any good ones," she quipped, receiving a kiss on her noise for her sassy comment. "Come on, let's tidy up. Afternoon tea is ready."

He gathered his tools, while Jess found a little hand-held vacuum cleaner that her mother kept in a corner cupboard, and cleaned up the floor. Then, hand in hand, they returned to join the others, where the old cottage was the hot topic of conversation.

"Are you sure it will be big enough, Mum?" Bryce asked before taking another piece of cake.

"Well, it won't be huge by any means, but it's actually quite roomy inside. I was quite surprised how big it was when I went in the other day."

"Ian thought that he and Patty would live there for some time, you know," Jack informed them. "We were all working the farm together, Dad, Ian, Fred and me. Fred didn't enjoy farming much so he left to work on the railway, and then Ian was offered the job in Goondiwindi as a builder. It was too good to refuse working for a mate there, and he was obviously a good carpenter. Otherwise that old cottage wouldn't be in such good order today, I imagine."

Edith continued the story. "Poor Patty loved the cottage though, and thought they would raise a family there. She had plans to extend on to it, of course, when they needed to. She was a bit upset to leave but, of course, Ian built her a lovely new home in Goondi on a block they bought just out of town. That's where they raised their family of five boys."

"Five boys, my goodness," gasped Majella.

"Only three more to go after the twins, honey," Jarrod teased, rubbing her swollen belly, only to receive a fiery look in response, much to the amusement of everyone present.

"Are you having twin boys?" Jessica asked excitedly.

"Maybe yes, maybe no," was the cryptic answer. "We're not telling anyone the sex of the babies. Are we Jarrod?" she asked her husband very pointedly.

"Absolutely not! I was just imagining us with a family of five children, that's all."

"Well, you can imagine all you like. It won't be happening!" Majella's smile did not quite reach her tired eyes.

Kath tactfully brought the conversation back to the cottage. "I'm trying not to get too ahead of myself. I need to find a good builder to inspect it first, before I go much further."

"Well, what about that mate of Uncle Craig's? What's his name Grandad? You know the builder he plays golf with all the time?"

"Oh, Ted, you mean? He's a good honest fellow, with lots of experience, and I know he does renovations as well as new houses. He'd be worth talking to, I reckon."

And so the talk continued, with plenty of ideas and suggestions being thrown around. Great anticipation filled the air; twins on the way, a wedding to plan, a cottage to renovate, and a new romance blossoming between Jessica and Lane.

The afternoon passed very pleasantly, and soon it was time for the guests to leave. Before they all rose from the verandah table, Kath made a suggestion. "I was thinking about going up to the Bunyas at the end of next month for a picnic. It will be the first anniversary of Sam's death. The 27st will be a Saturday. What do you all think?"

Jack and Edith nodded their immediate approval, with Edith saying, "That would be lovely, dear."

The younger generation all pulled their phones out to check their calendars, but everyone was able to say that the weekend was free and they were available, much to Kath's delight.

The rain had finally stopped, so Jarrod and Majella said their goodbyes to the family and left, followed soon after by Bryce and Sally. Lane and Jessica also made ready to travel back to Toowoomba but, before they did, Jess had a quiet moment in the kitchen with her mother. She leaned in to her mum and whispered. "So what do you think? Do you approve?"

"Oh Jess, I'm so happy for you. He seems a lovely fellow. You kept him a secret for a long time though."

She shrugged. "Well, everyone's been waiting for me to get a boyfriend for so long, you know how the boys tease me! So, I just wanted to make sure before I brought him home. Sorry Mum."

"Nothing to be sorry about. It was a wonderful surprise." She hugged her daughter.

Arm in arm they walked together, out to Lane's vehicle where he was waiting. Jessica said, "Oh, by the way, Lane fixed the light in your studio and replaced a power point while we were having our meeting."

"Oh, Lane," she turned to face him. "You fixed my light? That was very good of you. Thank you so much. I must owe you some money then?"

He held both hands up. "No, certainly not, it was an easy fix and my pleasure. Thank you for having me here today."

Kath hugged him. "It's been so good to meet you. I have a feeling I'll be seeing a lot more of you."

Jess blew her mother a kiss as the ute pulled away, a final toot of the horn and they were off down the long driveway.

Kath walked back to the verandah to find Jack and Edith waiting there with Tink.

"What a nice young man Jessica has found. You must be very happy, dear?"

"Oh yes, Edith. Don't they make a great couple? It's good to see Jessica so happy. Thanks for your help today."

"Don't be silly, I hardly lifted a finger. Sally, Jess and Majella are very capable young women."

"It was good to catch up with everyone," Jack said as she hugged him goodbye too. "And your renovation plan seemed to be very well received."

"They were all very supportive, weren't they? I just hope I can make it all happen."

"Of course you can, love. You've got a dream in your pocket, just follow it through!" And, leaving her with one of those endearing Wilmont winks, her sweet father-in-law escorted his smiling wife to their car.

* * *

Later that evening, after a light snack for dinner, Kath rang Gertrude to fill her in with all that had transpired.

"Why, Kath darling. That sounds absolutely wonderful. So clever of you to come up with the idea! It will be magnificent, I'm sure of it. I can't believe everything that's on your horizon at the moment! Oh, and dear Sam, what a wonderful man he was! He thought of everything when his world was crumbling all around him! God obviously sustained him, and gave him the strength he needed to put everything in place for you. It's just so sad that the accident took him away even earlier, and he didn't have the opportunity to spend more time with you. But, look at you now! Twin grandbabies, a building project, a wedding, and dear sweet Jessica has a young man!! I am sooo excited for you, darling! Wait till I tell Max! Oh, I've just had the most marvellous idea! Max's nephew, Alberto, is here at the moment, actually." She lowered her booming voice a fraction. "He's driving me crazy. He's looking for work, he's a builder, you know. Well he does interior things mostly, like kitchens and bathrooms, but he's nearly got Max convinced that we need a fountain and, of course, a pizza oven, which would be quite nice I suppose. He's built lots of them apparently. He says our place needs freshening up; he wants to redo everything! But really darling, he could be a great help to you. He's really very gifted you know, a great craftsman. I could send him over."

Kath's head was beginning to spin at Gertrude's fast paced narrative. Then warning bells began ringing loudly in her ears at her suggestion of sending Alberto over. "Well thanks. But I'm nowhere near that stage," she replied quickly, fearing Gertrude was about to steamroll her way into the project. "First I need a building inspection, to see if the whole project is even viable. Then I'll have to get plans drawn up and get council approval, and probably lots of other things I haven't even thought of! But thanks again, Gertrude. I'll keep Alberto in mind."

After chatting a bit longer, Kath said goodbye, smiling to herself at her friend's enthusiasm. Gertrude had such a zest for life but, as much as Kath loved her and respected her opinion, she wanted to take things slowly, one step at a time. Calling Tinkerbelle, she wandered outside onto the verandah and looked heavenwards, as she further reflected on the activities of the day and began to wind down. How enjoyable it had been to have her family all here. Such a special time together. The sky had cleared and a bright moon shone down, highlighting the water droplets that still clung to the plants and spider webs in the garden, making it look like a fairy land.

A satellite, passing by in the night sky, caught Kath's attention, and then she saw a most beautiful shooting star streaming through the myriad of other stars twinkling down at her. Her thoughts immediately went to Sam, his wide smile, blue eyes twinkling with merriment and, of course, his cheeky wink.

"I see you, Sam," she whispered softly to the wonder of the night sky. "I see you up there with Jesus."

A tear rolled down her cheek as she called Tink, and they went inside, closing the French doors behind her and walking quietly into the office to light her candle and play some peaceful music. She refused to let sadness spoil her positive day, but rather stored the memory of the shooting star in her heart. Something else to treasure and ponder. She let the soothing sounds of worship wash over her soul, as the candle's sweet fragrance filled the air. Turning on the desk lamp, she opened her Bible, reading and praying before writing in her journal.

Sometime later she crawled into her bed, feeling tired, happy, and very much at peace. Promises from God's word swirled around in her mind as she drifted off to a deep dreamless sleep.

The LORD your God is with you,
He is mighty to save.
He will take great delight in you;
He will renew you with His love,
He will rejoice over you with singing. Zephaniah 3:17

Do not worry about tomorrow. Matthew 6:34
I am precious in God's eyes. Isaiah 43:4
I can do all things through Him who gives me strength.
Philippians 4:13
Fear not, for I am with you. Isaiah 41:10

CHAPTER 21

The Transformation Begins

"Faith is unseen but felt, faith is strength
when we feel we have none,
faith is hope when all seems lost." Catherine Pulsifer

"The foundations are certainly solid. Whoever built this place intended it to last. Look how substantial these posts are. They're sure not going anywhere!"

Kath smiled at Ted's large frame, thinking he looked more like a lumberjack with his blue overalls, checked flannelette shirt, and bushy beard. He looked very awkward crouched down low, looking under the old cottage.

"Jack's brother built it, and went on to work as a builder after he left the district."

"Well, he knew what he was doing. Chose good timber too."

The big man stood up and dusted himself off, before continuing his walk around the exterior of the building, stopping frequently to tap here, push there and write things down in the little notebook he pulled from his pocket. The building inspector had visited a fortnight ago, and Ted had read the favourable report. His own personal inspection so far agreeing with its findings.

They entered through the front door. The inside had been cleared of all rubbish and cleaned up considerably, thanks to a mini working bee when Jarrod, Bryce and Sally had come over one Saturday and worked with Kath. Ted stood still and surveyed the interior, Kath silently by his side, the top of her head barely reaching his shoulder.

"It's quite a good-sized space, and would lend itself to an open-plan kitchen, dining and living area. You could take out part of the front wall, and close in half of the verandah, to give it more area too. Depends if you want a full verandah, or a smaller porch with a bigger living area inside, I guess?"

"Oh, I hadn't thought of that."

"You should come up with a few ideas to give to your architect, so they can draw up some options for you." He moved about slowly, studying the rooms. "Bedrooms are a good size. That lean-to laundry could be made into a nice laundry-bathroom combo, you know. Like what we do in a lot of the retirement units now-a-days. You'd have enough space for a laundry tub, washing machine, and fold-down ironing board hidden behind sliding doors, and a cupboard here, beside them." He pointed with his big hand. "The rest would be big enough for a vanity unit, shower and toilet. Don't think you'd fit a bath tub in, though. There's a nice unit in town we've just finished that I could show you if you like. To give you some ideas. Lots of clever space-saving ideas on the internet, too."

"Yes, I have been looking online, but I would like to see the unit you mentioned."

"Sure, no worries. We'll work something out next week."

They spent another hour or so, walking around measuring and discussing ideas, Kath becoming more optimistic and excited by the minute.

Finally, Ted glanced at his watch and realised the time. "I better get going. Got another job to look at in town. I'll be happy to give you a quote once you've got your plans sorted. Now, if you decide to offer me the job, I'm not sure what my time-frame will be, though. The bloke who usually works for me broke his leg last weekend. Fell off his horse, would you believe? So, I'll have to find another labourer, and that won't be easy. I've got plenty of work on the go, too," he ended sadly, running his hand through his scruffy hair.

Gertrude's loud voice boomed suddenly in Kath's head as she remembered their conversation several weeks ago.

"I might know of someone," she mentioned cautiously. "A nephew of my good friends over at the coast. He's experienced, and looking for work. I can ring and see if he's interested, if you like?"

"Sure, tell him to give me call. What's his name?"

"Alberto."

"Righto. I'll keep an ear out for him. See you later."

The following weeks were full of meetings, phone calls, council applications, and endless decision-making, causing Kath to often wonder if she had actually bitten off more than she could chew, a saying she remembered old Tom had been fond of. Many nights she felt quite overwhelmed, and missed Sam's cool, calm presence to discuss various options with. Thankfully, Nate didn't mind her calling him for advice, and he was always a great listener and helped her work through many things concerning the planning process. Plus, he gave her some good suggestions regarding the actual building and renovations.

"Remember, Kath. This is actually the hardest part, making all the initial plans and decisions. The rest will be much easier."

"I sure hope so. My head is spinning already, and I'm only at the first stage."

"You'll be fine. Call anytime."

"Thanks Nate."

Still, she wondered how she would get through the whole renovation process when the initial planning stage was proving very stressful. Gertrude was keen to help, but her ideas, although very modern and on trend, differed quite a lot from Kath's more conservative preferences. Jessica's input was invaluable, as she always managed to find the middle-ground between what Gertrude suggested, and what she knew her mother liked and could afford.

Kath still had an online counselling meeting once a month with Renae and, although she knew she wouldn't need them for much longer, during this busy period Renae's calm and logical advice helped her to keep everything in perspective and to be mindful of taking care of herself. Poor Jillie was often the one who provided the listening ear when she needed to vent her frustrations. Jillian didn't mind at all, however, and continued to provide unlimited enthusiasm and motivation to keep the dream alive by helping Kath to work methodically through issues.

"How do you eat an elephant, Kath?"

"One bite at a time, Jillie."

* * *

Kath knew she couldn't do life alone, much less manage the renovation by herself but, as Stephanie reminded her one morning after church when they were chatting in the car park, she was not alone. She had a big God, and a big circle of friends who had already formed a rich supportive web of social fabric around her. They provided so much of what she needed;

emotional support, encouragement, listening ears, nourishing food, laughter, friendship, shoulders to lean on and, sometimes, cry on.

These were the things that had kept her chin up and heart full for the last few months, and now they fuelled her determination. Buoyed by their strength, she struggled on valiantly, having never felt so determined about anything in her life before. She needed this project, needed to see it through and make it a success. She was quite driven, even more so than she had been when she was painting *Thunder Roll*, and that surprised her.

Everything was nearly in place for the renovation to begin, but first there was an important anniversary to observe. As Kath had suggested on the day of the farm business meeting at Yallaroo, the whole family journeyed up to the top of the Bunya Mountains for a picnic to remember the first anniversary of Sam's death. Everyone was able to join Kath in the pre-arranged spot, a place where many family picnics had been held over the years.

The picnic area was partly shaded as the sun filtered down through the leaves of the nearby trees in the thick rainforest, which also protected them from the chilly easterly wind. Jack and Edith sat comfortably on the folding chairs they had brought with them. Jarrod, too, had brought some chairs which he set up for Majella and himself, while Bryce and Sally sat at the picnic table with Kath, and Jessica and Lane rested comfortably on a picnic blanket spread on the soft green grass.

When the various foods they had all brought were set out on the picnic table, Kath asked Jack to say grace. The patriarch of the family stood as straight and tall as his aging body would allow, looking at each person gathered around him before he began to pray,

"Heavenly Father, we thank you for the privilege of meeting here today in this beautiful part of your creation. We thank you, Lord, for all you have blessed us with. Thank you for providing us with this food today, and we ask that you bless it to our bodies, and us to your service. But, today, Father, we particularly thank you for the wonderful memories we have of Sam. We thank you for the honour and blessing of having had him in our lives. We know that he is not really dead because, when you called him home, he became more alive than he ever was here on Earth. He's with you now. Fit and healthy, living his best life and, Father, we so look forward to seeing him again when we arrive in Heaven. Thank you, Lord, for your love, your promises, and your faithfulness to us. In Jesus' name, Amen."

There was silence following the closure of the prayer, except for the chattering of a nearby satin bower bird that was giving a series of loud descending whistles. After a few moments when moist eyes were wiped and noses sniffed, Jack added, "Come now, let's eat. No need to become melancholy. Let's be glad we had the privilege of knowing such a man. Jarrod, pass me that potato salad!"

The moment passed, and hearts full of emotion were soon joined by stomachs full of good food. After enjoying Edith's cheesecake, and Kath's mini apple pies for dessert, Bryce and Sally as well as Jessica and Lane, decided they needed a good long walk to aid their digestion. Jarrod declined, saying he would stay with Majella, but she convinced him to go on the hike, declaring she would be happy to stay in the company of Jack and Edith who firmly declared they were not going anywhere anytime soon. After clearing the picnic table, and making sure everyone was comfortable, Kath said she was going on a short walk on the nearby track. She left her in-laws and Majella resting peacefully, and quietly slipped into the cool rainforest.

Deep in thought, she wandered slowly along the well-worn track, her mind mulling over all that had transpired in the last year. A butterfly flew past, just inches in front of her face, and she realised she had left her camera behind. However, she decided not to return for it, not really in the mood for taking photos. She continued on, stopping to simply admire the towering trees and beautiful foliage all around her, soaking in the serenity.

After a while she came to a clearing that provided views out across the countryside far below her. She sat down on the soft earth, and hugged her knees to her chest as the reality of her present situation settled over her. She was alone. It was twelve months since Sam had died. Twelve long months since her best friend, her stalwart, her beloved husband had disappeared from her life. Tears coursed down her cheeks, but not the distraught and shocked ones of a year ago, just poignant reminders of all she had lost.

However, grief no longer dominated her life. This time last year she had been totally bereft, barely able to breathe from the ache of her broken heart, and the deep constant pain in her chest from her overwhelming sorrow. She hadn't known how she would go on alone; just wanted to be with her beloved Sam. Initially, life without him had seemed meaningless, or so her anguished mind had led her to believe. Certainly, the past year had been one of ups and downs, moments of triumph followed by swift and painful plummets into the depths of despair. Nevertheless, with God's help, here she was today having once more clawed her way to the top. Well, to the top of her little world at least. Forging a solo life, coping somehow on her own, not being defeated by sorrow and hopelessness.

"Can you see me, Sam?" she whispered into the mountain air. "Can you believe what I'm doing? Thank you, my dear sweet man, for all your support and encouragement over the years. You always believed I was capable of doing something amazing. I think you would approve of my plans. I hope you are proud of me."

She knew she had made a triumphant step forward concerning her future, having finally made a decision about where she wanted to live, and setting a major goal to achieve. She was now coordinating a building project. A major renovation that would give her a new home, one steeped in family history and sentimentality. She wiped her tears away, and a smile lit up her face. She couldn't believe she was feeling happiness on this day, of all days.

Sam would always be a part of her. She thought about him every day, but it didn't hurt quite so much now. The renovation was exciting, so right in this season of her life – and what a season it was proving to be! Her grandbabies were due in a few months. Bryce was going to marry Sally, and Jessica was in love with Lane. She was healthy and happy, and so were her children. So much to be thankful for.

Her only regret was that her painting career had not developed to the extent she had hoped or dreamed, but she had come to terms with that disappointment. Art would always be a major passion, and a very enjoyable activity, but not the focal point of her life. Her days were presently full with teaching, a little painting, overseeing the cottage project, plus commitments she had once again made within the church, school, and local community.

Her walk with the Lord had grown so much deeper and closer, the Holy Spirit was her friend and sweet companion. Family members and friends surrounded and supported her. She felt loved, and grateful that she had survived the journey since Sam's death, thus far at least. Her mindset had become so much more positive. She consciously sought to find the good in every situation, and in every person she met. She knew that she would never, and indeed, had never, her father included, looked into the eyes of a person that God did not love. Jesus had died to save everyone, shed His blood for all people everywhere, no matter who they were or what they had done. How very humbling to have such a Saviour in her life. Standing up, she stood tall and stretched her arms heavenward, blowing a kiss into the cloudless blue sky above. "I love you, Sam."

The words were her farewell whisper to a private and very special anniversary moment on the mountain top. Turning, she continued on the path which she knew was a loop that would take her back to the picnic area. Before long she was once more walking beneath the enclosed canopy of the thick rainforest.

Stopping a short distance in, Kath closed her eyes and lifted up her hands, as if in worship, and slowly twirled around in a circle. When she opened her eyes, she gazed up into the green branches above, imagining angels sitting aloft, their warmth and radiance shining down in the dappled sunlight that managed to find its way through the intricate weavings of the branches and vines. It was like an emerald cathedral secreted away amongst the majestic Bunya Pines. The cool wind blew softly, rustling the leaves above and stirring the dry matter on the ground, the sounds combining with the bird songs of the forest to form a soft dulcet refrain.

She felt blessed. She knew she was blessed. She knew she was precious, honoured; chosen and anointed. She was a child of God, a daughter of the King. There was so much she didn't understand, but she knew, without any doubt, that she was loved and that she would never be alone. God was with her and He would not leave her side.

She also knew that Sam would, indeed, be proud of her. After another happy twirl, she smiled heavenward and laughed out loud with joy, before slowly retracing her steps to the picnic area.

✳ ✳ ✳

The following months were crazy busy. A copy of the plans for the renovation had been sent to Ted, and a price for the job agreed on. Alberto had indeed contacted the older builder, and arrived in town one afternoon towing an old caravan he had purchased over at the coast. Ted had agreed to give him a two-week trial, and had shown him a block of land that he owned on the edge of town where he could stay with his van. The house on the small acreage property was rented out, but there was plenty of room for Alberto behind the shed which Ted used for storage. Power and water were available in the shed and, as the van had its own ensuite, Alberto was more than happy with the arrangement.

"He seems a decent young bloke," Ted had told Kath on the phone one morning early in June. "He gave me some referees to ring, and they both spoke quite highly of his work. So I'll give him a go. There are a few little jobs in town he can help me with before we start on your place."

Apparently, Alberto had proved himself a valuable employee because they were both soon busily working on the cottage. Kath visited nearly every day, excited to see the progress, and there always seemed to be decisions to make and new ideas to discuss. It amused her to see the two men working together.

Ted was loud, somewhat gruff and slow moving, while Alberto was lean and wiry, and seemed to almost run everywhere with a big smile permanently plastered on his swarthy face. Ted spoke with many Australian colloquial terms, the Aussie slang causing ongoing confusion for his new labourer but, to his credit, Alberto just smiled and asked for clarification. He even tried to teach Ted a few words in Italian.

There was a lot of good-natured laughter on the work site. Their preference for music genres was the only sticking point, although everyone else found it very amusing. Ted was a country music enthusiast; he never listened to anything else, while Alberto loved classical music, especially opera. Ted had an old radio and always had it tuned to the country music station, while Alberto had an iPhone with his classical playlists on it and a little boom speaker.

First on site, usually Ted, started his favourite music but, as soon as an opportunity arose, the genre was quickly changed. If Ted left to go to town for parts or supplies, or to take a phone call, Alberto quickly turned off the radio and started his music. But when Ted was back working, the opera music was quickly drowned out by loud country music. Kath always wondered who would greet her when she arrived at the old cottage, Slim Dusty or Luciano Pavarotti.

Regardless of the music playing, the renovation progressed steadily, even with the limited workforce of just Ted and Alberto. Jarrod and Bryce helped out when they had time available, but mostly it was just Ted and his Italian off-sider. But, even so, the transformation of the old building slowly took place. Floorboards were replaced, walls were knocked out, and old windows and doors were replaced. Ted arranged for another tradie to clad the exterior of the cottage, while he and Alberto concentrated on insulating and lining the interior.

Plumbers were tasked with replacing the old roofing iron, and putting guttering on to run rainwater caught on the roof into the rain water tanks that were yet to be delivered. That would be the only water supply for the cottage, as Jack and the boys had checked out the old tap and discovered that it was no longer connected to a water supply. The best advice was to order the delivery of three large poly tanks. Kath knew there might be dry times that necessitated having a load of bore water delivered but, being on her own, she thought she could manage the water supply for the cottage and the garden. The plumbers weren't available for several weeks, so they had to wait patiently until they arrived to do the roofing job, thankful that the old iron still kept the rain out. Ted declared there was no way he was climbing up onto the roof.

"I'm far too old to be climbing about like a monkey. Happy to let the young fellas do the high stuff. Last thing I need is a broken neck!"

Power had been connected to the old cottage many years previously, and had long since been disconnected. Kath was very relieved when it was once more connected after the lines and poles were checked out, and some fittings replaced. It proved to be a rather straightforward process, and much less expensive than she had anticipated. Ted and Alberto were certainly pleased to have power on the work site. Ted was very professional and careful with everything he did. He seemed to be really enjoying the project, obviously putting a lot of thought into it, because one Thursday morning he rang Kath and asked her to come to the site to discuss some ideas he had. On arriving, he greeted her with sketches and new ideas for the kitchen and bathroom

"You see," he explained. "A mate of mine over at the coast has some Caesarstone bench tops, and some tiles left over from a job. I think they would blend in nicely here. There's just enough for a small job like this. We just need to alter the kitchen bench configuration a little. The tiles would be a good match for the bathroom, and will get us out of a pickle seeing as the ones you originally chose are out of stock at present."

Kath agreed. His ideas were great, but she was worried about the extra cost. "I haven't found the pot of gold at the end of the rainbow, you know!"

"No worries, love," he chuckled. "We won't go over budget, well not by too much anyway! If you like the colours, I'll get them sent over with another mate, and Bob's your uncle!"

Kath knew she could trust his judgment; the unit that he had taken her to see in town was beautifully finished. Before long the new kitchen was being installed, the bench tops were indeed wonderful, and the soft-closing drawers were quite a delight after her heavy kitchen drawers at the farm. The old wood stove, which Kath couldn't bear to have removed, was lovingly restored by Alberto. Not quite to its former glory, but it would certainly add the ambiance of a by-gone era to the cottage. She opted for electric hotplates on the bench top, and intended to use her air fryer for a small oven as she would be mainly cooking just for herself. The oven in the wood stove would be a good back-up if needed. Alberto also restored the fireplace, spending many hours on the weekends working on his pet projects. Kath was amazed by his attention to detail and the results he achieved, making a mental note to purchase something special for him as a thank you gift.

"Oh Alberto, what wonderful work you've done! You really are a gifted craftsman. I'm so very glad Gertrude suggested you to help out here."

Looking proud of his work, but embarrassed by her praise, the younger man blushed beneath his dark whiskers. "It is my pleasure, Mrs. Kath. The old stove and the fireplace deserve to be cared for. They will add warmth to this little home for many more years."

Split air conditioning units were added to the main living area, and in the main bedroom. Ted's idea for the combined laundry and bathroom worked very well, and she was delighted when the modern taps and shower fittings were installed with the new cabinets. Ted had indeed utilised every square inch of the combined area, squeezing many practical ideas into the efficient user-friendly space. The result was light and airy, the walk-in shower allowing the room to appear more spacious than it really was.

Electricians from Craig and Rosemary's business came, and Kath made sure she had enough power points positioned where she wanted them. She was very pleased with the light fittings she had chosen, simple but well suited to the cottage. The painters arrived next, and it didn't take them long to undercoat the walls. They had another job on the go, but planned to come back the following week to complete the final coats.

The delay with the painting had a flow-on effect, which meant that the carpet could not be laid on schedule. Unfortunately, there was another delay with the vinyl planks Kath had chosen, as they were currently out of stock. The company had said new stock was expected the previous week, but that had not eventuated. There were other options, but Kath felt they were all too dark or too light. She decided to wait for what she really thought would suit the cottage best.

Moving slowly from room to room, she assessed the interior with a critical eye. The overall effect was very pleasing so far, and she hoped the neutral tones of the paint colours she had finally decided on and the floor coverings, if they ever arrived, would form the perfect backdrop for the colour she intended to add with her furniture and soft furnishings.

She was amazed at how well everything was falling into place and thankful that the weather had remained mostly fine, not hindering progress. There was nothing she could find fault with. Enlarging the living area by enclosing part of the verandah had proved an excellent idea. The remaining porch was still a perfectly usable area, certainly big enough for a small outdoor setting. It was an ideal place to view the sunrise and enjoy the warmth of the morning sun, as well as seeing who was coming up the driveway.

Jarrod's decision to work on the old track had proved fortuitous, considering the amount of traffic on it during the recent few months. It was an exciting day when three big poly tanks were delivered and settled into place on the levelled pads of crusher-dust. Jarrod had prepared them after he removed the old rusted-out tank and pulled down the old tank-stand.

Jack and Edith were frequent visitors, and took great interest in the work. They seemed just as excited in the project as their daughter-in-law. Edith always arrived with a picnic basket full of delicious treats from her oven, and a thermos of hot coffee and another full of hot water for tea. Ted and Alberto were always quick to down tools when they saw Jack's old

Commodore driving up the hill track. Edith was such a calming influence, nothing seemed to ruffle her and she could always point out the positives in every situation. How grateful Kath was to have this delightfully wise and poised older woman in her life.

The fear of the Lord is the beginning of wisdom; all who follow His precepts have good understanding. To Him belongs eternal praise. Psalm 111:10

CHAPTER 22

One plus One equals Two

*"You don't choose your family. They are
God's gift to you, as you are to them."*
Desmond Tutu 1931-2021

*K*ath was woken from a deep sleep by a distant sound. She slowly registered that it was a phone ringing, seemingly from a very long way away. Tink jumped up on the bed and licked her face, alerting her to the disturbance in the pre-dawn light.

Finally, she realised that it was her phone, ringing and vibrating simultaneously on the dressing table on the far side of the bedroom where she had left it last night. Slowly, still not fully awake, she pushed back the blankets covering her warm body and walked blearily to pick up the phone.

"Hello?"

"Good morning, Mum. Just ringing to wish you Happy Birthday."

"Jarrod?" she queried before yawning. "Thanks love, but I'm pretty sure it's not my birthday. What are you doing up this early? It's cold and it's still half dark." She yawned again as she snuggled back in her bed.

"Actually, I haven't been to bed yet."

"What?" The fog in her sleepy head began to clear. "Is Majella in labour? Do you need me to come over?"

"Nope, stay where you are and she's not in labour. Well, not anymore," he quipped.

"What? Where are you?"

"Toowoomba, and everything's great. I just wanted to congratulate you."

"Congratulate me? Jarrod, stop speaking in riddles, it's far too early!"

He laughed at her confusion. "Your birthday presents have arrived, Mum. They came early."

"What?"

He laughed again, obviously enjoying himself. "The babies are here, Mum!"

"The babies are here? Oh, really? Is Majella okay? Are they okay? What are they? When were they born?" Her excited questions tumbled out as she quickly sat up in bed, now oblivious to the cold, fully awake.

"Majella is fine, she was amazing. Everything went well. It all happened very quickly at the end. We have two beautiful sons, Mum."

"Two sons! Oh, darling, that's wonderful. Congratulations to you!"

"Thanks, Granny!"

"Are they okay?"

"They're perfect, small but healthy, absolutely fine, both around two-and-a-bit kilos, that's about five pounds, I think. They were born soon after 3 this morning. I can't remember exactly. It's been quite a night."

"Oh, I can't believe it! Two baby boys!"

"Yep, two boys! Hey, can you ring Granma and Grandad for me? I'll ring Bryce and Jess."

"Of course I'll ring them. It's such great news."

"Sure is. Gotta go."

"Okay, I'll call you later today. Give my love to Majella, won't you?"

"Sure thing, Mum. See ya."

Kath lay in bed wide awake, too excited to go back to sleep. She was a grandmother of two tiny baby boys! It was too early to ring anyone yet but, when the first chorus of bird calls started, she knew that it would not be long before the first glow of the rising Sun would appear. Throwing back the covers quickly, she startled Tinkerbelle. Gathering the little dog in her arms she cooed softly, "Sorry Tink. I didn't mean to scare you, but I can't stay in bed any longer!"

Putting the little dog on the floor, Kath quickly pulled on her Ugg boots and dressing gown before heading to the kitchen to put the kettle on, humming happily to herself as she went. While waiting for the kettle to boil she thanked the Lord again for the safe arrival of the babies. What a wonderful start to the day! Once she had a hot cup of tea in her hand, she went outside on to the verandah to enjoy the early morning, the crisp morning air unable to dampen her spirits.

It was a beautiful morning, the early sunrays were shining on the dew, and reflecting on the spider webs scattered throughout the garden. Little Tink tiptoed out cautiously at first, but soon found a cheeky wren to chase. A flock of corellas flew from the direction of the shed and silos, and then over the house, their raucous squawking somehow combining into a beautiful out-of-tune bush rhapsody that brought a smile to Kath's face, and caused a lot of noisy yapping and barking from both dogs. They were certainly all wide awake now.

When she returned inside, Kath picked up her phone to call Jack and Edith, and saw that she had a text message from Jarrod. Just four lovely words: Alexander Samuel, Nicholas Angelo.

The babies' names! Each boy to honour a grandfather. Tears trickled down Kath's cheeks. How proud Sam would have been today; how nice to have his name live on. After a little while, when she had composed herself, she rang her parents-in-law, knowing they would be up by now. Edith answered on the third ring.

"Good morning. How are you today?"

"Just fine thank you, dear. Is everything okay? You don't usually ring this early."

"Yes, everything is just fine. I have some wonderful news to share."

"Oh, do tell. I can hear the excitement in your voice!"

"The babies are here! Two baby boys. Born this morning."

"Oh, my goodness! That is wonderful news! Are they okay, and their dear mother too?"

"Yes, yes. They're all fine."

Kath went on to tell her everything she knew, which wasn't much, but enough for now. Health status, weights and names were all that mattered at the moment. Promising to pass on any more information as it came to light, she finished the conversation, smiling at being able to pass on such happy news. After she had finished breakfast and the hour was more respectable, she rang both Jillie and Gertrude, and shared the announcement with them. Such loud happy conversations! When she had finally put her phone down and tidied the kitchen she looked down at her faithful dog.

"Well, Tink, that was fun, hey? Now, I think I had better get ready for the rest of the day. We've got a lot of gardening planned." Turning, she headed down the hallway, still humming and thanking God for His goodness.

* * *

Some time back, Bryce and Sally had offered to help Kath dig up the garden beds, and prune the shrubs and trees growing in the cottage house yard. Now the time had come to make a start. They met at the cottage at 8am, along with Jack and Edith, who wanted to help too. After the three women had talked excitedly about the new babies, they started tidying the yard. Jack and Edith were more in advisory roles, although Jack was very handy with a pair of secateurs, and a battery-operated reciprocating saw that was ideal for trimming small branches. They worked steadily until smoko time, when they joined Ted and Alberto on the front porch for a hot cuppa. The men all eager to see what baked goodies Edith had brought for them. Of course, she didn't disappoint, and produced pumpkin scones and homemade rosella jam.

Once they had rested and enjoyed a good chinwag, as Ted liked to call their friendly chatter, they returned to bringing order to the long-neglected garden, while Ted and Alberto continued working inside the cottage. Thankfully, it had rained a few days previously, so the soil was still moist and soft enough to dig up and turn over. The women spread fertiliser and mulch on the garden beds, and around the base of the shrubs and trees, all under the watchful eyes of Edith.

Bryce used the tractor to pull out the old fence posts, his grandfather helping by placing a chain around each one before it was pulled free from its hole in the earth. The old wire was placed on a pile to be removed at a later date. New fence posts and wire netting would make a more aesthetic border around the house yard. The four corner posts were quite substantial and still standing firm, so it was decided to keep them.

By midday they had achieved a great deal, and were well satisfied with their efforts. Bryce and Sally were going to continue working on the fence after lunch. Once again they sat on the porch, surveying their efforts, when Bryce said, "Well, Jarrod managed to escape the gardening. As if the arrival of twins takes precedent over digging and fencing!"

"Yes, he'll be extra pleased today. Gardening is certainly not his favourite activity." Kath smiled.

"Yeah, I reckon. He sure sounded pretty chuffed when he called this morning!"

"It's certainly a very exciting time for them." The new great-grandmother added.

"When are you going to visit, Mum?" Bryce enquired.

"I'll call tonight and see how Majella is, but I hope I can visit tomorrow. I won't be able to wait much longer! I think Jess will pop in this afternoon."

"Yeah, nothing will keep her away from two baby nephews," Bryce laughed. "What is it about you women and babies?"

"Careful, lad. You're on thin ice," Jack chuckled. "Just be thankful God made women so good at loving and nurturing. Sally might want a big family, you know!"

"That's right, Bryce. You're going to have lots of nappies to change, so you better start practicing on the twins!" Sally teased.

"I'm hungry, let's all go and have lunch. Coming back home?" Kath enquired of her in-laws.

"Yes, for sure love," Jack answered, and Bryce and Sally nodded in agreement.

A short time later they were sitting on the verandah at Yallaroo, eating ham and salad sandwiches washed down with hot tea, when Edith enquired innocently,

"So, what's next on your list, Kath? Apart from going to Toowoomba to visit the babies." Her eyes twinkled brightly. "You know you're not going without us!"

Kath laughed at the two expectant faces gazing at her. "Of course, I'll take you," she said, patting Edith's hand in assurance. "And then when we get back, I guess I had better start packing up what I want to take to the cottage."

"That'll be a big job, with lots of decisions to make. What to take, what to get rid of, and what to leave," Edith commented.

"You're right and, honestly, I've been putting it off. I've thought about it a lot, but haven't actually filled a box yet. So many memories here."

"You'll always be welcome here, Mum. Any time you like. You know that," Bryce said quietly. "And what you leave behind will still be yours, if you decide you to want to come back and get something else."

"Thank you. I know I'm leaving everything in good hands with you and Sally. I better get organised though, so I'll be ready to move in once the painters have finished and the floors are done."

"We're happy to help, dear," Edith added. "Aren't we Jack?" She looked directly at her husband.

"Of course we are. Just say the word and we'll be here with bells on." He smiled and gave his daughter-in-law one of his beautiful winks.

Later that afternoon, long after her guests had departed, Kath wandered into the large walk-in robe in the main bedroom. She still thought of it as 'their' bedroom, although she was the only one sleeping in it now. Quite a few months back she had asked the boys to take any of their father's clothes they wanted, and they had both chosen a few things. There were two RM Williams leather belts that they had been especially keen to have, as long-lasting mementos of their dad. His good Akubra hat was claimed by Jessica, who wanted to keep it on display in her living room.

Kath had left everything else as it was the day Sam left the house for the last time. But now she knew the time had come to bag up all the clothes and shoes, and give it all away to charity. She had, of course, filled a box with some special sentimental items that she would always cherish; like his watch, cufflinks, cologne, an engraved pen, his Chess set, Bible, and favourite books.

She had known it would be a very difficult task, hence the long period of procrastination, but nothing prepared her for the memories that the scent, lingering still on his clothes, evoked. She battled on through her tears, determined to finish what she had started but, when the last box was sealed, she sank to the floor and gave in to pent-up sobs.

She cried long and loud until finally she was exhausted, lying curled up in a ball on the carpet. It was then that Little Tink approached cautiously, and started licking her salty face.

"Oh, Tink. Did I scare you?" she whispered. "I'm okay, puppy. Just got a bit overwhelmed."

Slowly she rose to her feet and, stripping off her clothes, she turned on the shower and let the warm water soothe her weary body.

"I must be more tired than I thought," she said to herself, surprised by the overpowering release of emotion. She had not cried like that since the early days after Sam's death. But the dam had certainly burst today.

Turning off the water she towelled herself dry, and put her pyjamas on. Although she was very tired, she actually felt revived, as if she had just experienced some sort of cleansing. While she was still trying to rationalise what had just happened, her phone rang. It was Jillie.

"Hi. As usual, you know just when to call."

"Really, why's that? What've you been up to?"

Kath told her about clearing out Sam's belonging from the bedroom, and then her emotional break-down.

"Don't be too hard on yourself. I'm not at all surprised. You've been under a lot of stress, what with the cottage reno and working at school as well."

"Yes, but I didn't think I'd react as badly. My hysterical sobbing nearly frightened my dog away!"

"As if that devoted pooch would ever leave you! I think you needed a good cry, Kath, to clear the way to pack up the house and start a new life at the cottage. You're taking a momentous step forward, and there are bound to be times when you feel sad and lonely. Be prepared for that, and have some strategies to deal with it up your sleeve."

"Hmm. Like what, Jillie?"

"Like my phone number on speed dial of course." Kath could hear the smile in her friend's voice. "And the phone numbers of others who will understand, like your counsellor Renae, and Pastor Bob, and Stephanie, and the other women in our Life Group. Of course, you can always call on Edith too, or go visit Jessica. Just don't go it alone, Kath. You've come so far."

"Thanks, Jillie. Your wisdom, as always, is very timely. I think if I get a good sleep tonight I'll be able to tackle the rest of the house. Anyway, enough about me and my woes. How are things with you?"

The two friends chatted on for some time before saying goodnight, and then Kath suddenly realised how hungry she was. On opening the fridge she noticed that Edith had sneakily put a chicken casserole in there for her. Smiling, she closed her eyes and whispered a prayer of thanks to her Heavenly Father who provided all her needs, including a debrief with Jillie and a meal from her mother-in-law. After she had eaten and fed the dogs, she walked to the office, lit her candle, and sat behind Sam's desk to read her Bible and write in her journal.

"I'm certainly not leaving this house without this desk," she told Tinkerbelle, who barked in agreement.

She read the passage in her Bible from the reading plan she followed, and wrote her thoughts and a prayer in her journal. As she stood to blow out the candle, a piece of loose paper fluttered from the desktop to the floor. She picked it up and sat down again. It was a list of verses that make up a morning prayer of gratitude to God that she had written down at one of their life group meetings. She had been meaning to type it up and laminate it. She silently read each verse again, marvelling at their power to lift her up:

Lord, I give you thanks today. (Psalm 107:1)

I am blessed. (Jeremiah 17:7)

A child of God, a daughter of the King. (Psalm 82:6)

A woman of faith; holy and dearly loved. (John 15:13, 1 Peter 1:16)

I am precious and honoured, chosen and anointed. (Proverbs 31:10, 1Samuel 2:30)

My sins have been forgiven and my wounds have been healed. (1 John 1:9, Isaiah 53:5)

Because of Your sacrifice on the Cross, I am clothed in righteousness. (2 Cor. 5:21)

The Holy Spirit strengthens and empowers me. (Luke 4:18)

I will sing your praises today because You, Lord, are good and your love endures forever. (Psalm 100:5)

Your steadfast love never ceases. Your compassions never fail, they are new every morning. Great is your faithfulness. (Lamentations 3:22-23)

I ask that you will supernaturally infuse me with your strength and power to face this new day that you have blessed me with. (Ephesians 6:10)

In Jesus' name, Amen.

With a full heart, and her spirit singing, she retired to her bed and slept soundly until the morning birdsong woke her.

CHAPTER 23

Happy Days

"It's one thing to be grateful. It's another to give thanks.
Gratitude is what you feel. Thanksgiving is what you do."
Tim Keller

*K*ath picked up her in-laws at 8 the following morning, and they enjoyed an easy drive along the Warrego highway to the hospital in Toowoomba to meet the latest additions to the Wilmont family. Jess had rung her mother the night before. She was already besotted with the babies and had gushed about how tiny and beautiful they were and now Kath couldn't wait to see them. Jarrod rang just as they were parking the car, and said the doctor had just arrived so they would have to wait a little bit longer.

"No worries, love," Jack replied when Kath relayed the message. "I could do with a cup of tea. How about we find the cafeteria while we wait?"

"Good idea," agreed his wife.

They were just finishing their morning tea when Jarrod rang again to say they could come up. Hurriedly, they gathered their belongings and headed for the lift, following the signs to the maternity ward. When they finally found the room, having to ask for directions at the nurse's station, they knocked quietly on the door. It was opened by a beaming Jarrod.

Kath hugged him, and kissed his cheek. "Congratulations, daddy!"

Edith hugged and kissed him also, before Jack shook his hand and then enveloped him in a bear hug, slapping him on the back. "Congratulations, Jarrod."

"Majella did all the hard work." He smiled at them. "Come in and see."

Jarrod held the door while the trio walked quietly into the room to stand at Majella's bedside. She looked tired, but a beautiful smile lit up her face and nearly chased her weariness away.

Kath leant forward and kissed her daughter-in-law's cheek. "Congratulations, I hear you did a splendid job."

"It was the hardest thing I've ever had to do; I think. But look at them. It was so worth it! Can you believe how perfect they are?"

Kath quickly put the flowers she had picked from her garden early that morning on the bedside cabinet, and went to peer into the two little cribs on the other side of the bed.

"Oh, aren't they gorgeous! Perfection indeed." Tears welled in her eyes as she stared lovingly at the little faces, both babies fast asleep.

The great-grandparents both congratulated the new mum, and then they too looked in wonder at the newborns.

"Oh, my. Aren't they tiny?" Edith exclaimed. "And you're sure they're both fine?"

"The doc just checked them over, and said they're absolutely perfect. I've counted their fingers and toes, and everything is in A1 condition," Jarrod answered.

"You can hold them," Majella invited.

"Oh, are you sure?" Kath questioned quietly. "I'd forgotten how small new babies are. And these are smaller than most, although, for twins, they're a good weight."

Edith and Kath each sat in the chairs Jarrod indicated, and the proud Father gently handed each of them a tiny bundle.

"Are they identical?" Jack enquired as he watched on proudly.

"No," their mum answered. "They're fraternal twins, because they had two separate placentas and each was in their own amniotic sac. They may look quite alike, or be quite different."

"Yeah. We'll have to wait and see," Jarrod added. "It should be easy to tell them apart anyway. At least I sure hope so."

They stayed for about 30 minutes but, when one of the babies started to cry and the other one began to stir, they decided to take their leave and let Majella feed them.

"It's all a bit daunting, I must say. We're all learning to breastfeed."

"Well, I'm not," Jarrod interjected with a wry grin.

"No. But you're going to become an expert at changing their nappies and burping them, I can assure you." His wife laughed, pointing a finger at him.

"When is your mother coming down, dear?" asked Edith.

"Both Mum and Dad are driving down. I think they were leaving this morning, and it'll take a couple of days, so they'll be there when I get home. Dad's going to stay for a week or so, and then he'll go back. Not sure how long Mum will stay."

"She'll be a great help. And don't forget to let us know if we can do anything for you. I've got some baking in the freezer for you." She smiled before adding, "A good excuse to come and visit."

"You don't need an excuse, Granma," Jarrod smiled at his grandmother. "You're welcome anytime. You know that."

After final looks at the now wide-awake babies, and quick hugs for the happy parents, they left the room.

* * *

An art studio for Kath had been a dominating topic of conversation for many weeks until one morning, during smoko at the cottage, Ted casually announced the obvious solution.

"No need to build another one. We'll just move Kath's studio from the farm to here. I had a look at it yesterday, and discussed it with a mate in town. We reckon it shouldn't be too hard to lift it onto a low loader and bring it up here. He's got a crane and a prime mover that should do the job nicely."

Ted had mates everywhere and they were always willing to help him out and vice versa, usually at very reasonable mate's rates.

"We could set it up beside the back verandah, joining the roofs together to make a great north south breezeway. Here's the quote, Kath," he added, handing her a piece of paper. "What do you reckon? That old building worth it? It's pretty solid, and just sitting on stumps where it is. This really is a lot cheaper than building something new."

She considered the figure for a minute before looking up and saying, "This is such a brilliant idea, Ted. I would love to have that old building moved up here! Jack and Sam created that studio for me years ago. It really is very special to me. Thank you, for thinking of it." Her eyes welled and she could say no more.

Ted cleared his throat, impacted by her emotion.

"Right then. My mate said he could probably be available in a fort-night's time, so we'd better get cracking and get everything ready. You boys able to give us a hand?" he asked, looking at Jarrod and Bryce.

"Sure thing!" they replied in unison.

"Goodo. I'll sort things out with the council, but that should be pretty straight forward as we're only going a few kilometres up the road. We'll still have to get approval, and prepare the foundations and footings. Hopefully, council won't hold us up. It's a pretty tight schedule. Won't need water connected, but you might want power, hey Kath?"

"Yes, Ted. Power would be nice." She smiled back at him.

He nodded in reply before adding, "We'll need the sparky at your place to disconnect the power from the building too, before we can move it."

True to his word, Ted had everything organised; council, electrician, crane operator, and new stumps put in place within the two weeks. Kath didn't know how he managed to get everything approved and organised but, somehow, he did and she was rushed to pack up her art studio so that the empty building could be transported up to the cottage. When the last box was sealed, and she closed the door, she walked along the garden path to the kitchen.

"Oh, Tink. Can you believe all this? I'm so tired. I'll be very glad when this renovation is finished. You will be too. Won't you?" She scratched behind the little dog's ears. "Let's find something to eat and go to bed, hey?"

After her meal, she sat at the kitchen table thinking, too tired to move. She was a woman who needed purpose. Before starting the cottage project she had felt like she was moving along on a conveyor belt to nowhere. Sure, she had her teaching, but there was a void in her life that she had thought painting would fill. Now she was worried that once the cottage was completed she would have no major goal in her life. But she heard a quiet voice in her spirit say:

Don't worry about tomorrow, I know the plans I have for you,
plans to give you a hope and a future. Trust in Me. Live one
day at a time. I will never leave you or forsake you.
Matthew 6:34. Jeremiah 29:11. Psalm 9:10.

Once again, a peace descended and her worry abated. She whispered a thank you to her friend, the Holy Spirit and, after tidying the kitchen and turning off the light, she headed to her bedroom. After a hot shower, she crawled thankfully into her warm bed, feeling guilty that she had not written in her journal that night. She whispered a simple prayer,

"Forgive me Lord, I'm just so very tired tonight. Thank You for Your goodness. Everything is falling into place so wonderfully. I'm having trouble keeping up with You! Bless you Jesus."

She was asleep within moments.

✳ ✳ ✳

She woke early the following morning as usual. It was her birthday, and she immediately felt rather sad to be home alone. This time last year had been her first birthday without Sam waking her with a kiss, and wishing her Happy Birthday. He had always made a big fuss of her on her special day, and not once had he ever forgotten. Last year she had been absolutely miserable, and nothing any of her friends or family had done had brought her any real joy. She had tried to be gracious but there had been a total absence of happiness in her heart and mind.

How glad she was now that the terrible shock of Sam's sudden death no longer weighed her down and pervaded her every thought. But she still felt quite downhearted on her special day. However, she was not forgotten as the phone first rang at 7am when Jess called to wish her Happy Birthday, and then rang constantly for the next hour. It certainly lifted her spirits to know so many people were thinking of her.

A bit before 9, Nipper let them know that a vehicle was coming. Kath looked out from the verandah, and her eyes widened at the sight of not one vehicle but a convoy of vehicles coming up the driveway.

First was Ted's work ute, driven by the builder with Alberto as passenger. Then came a prime mover pulling a long flat-bed trailer. Behind that was a large crane mounted on a big truck, then a tractor, followed by Jack's car and Jarrod's ute. She recognised the farm tractor and wondered who was driving it as Bryce was supposed to be working in town today. It wasn't really a surprise though, to see her youngest son behind the wheel. He would have been very disappointed to miss out on all the action. The cavalcade drove past the house and around the back to stop near the old building they intended to move.

Quickly, she went inside to put the kettle on. Edith and Jack walked in a short time later, the smell of warm scones preceding them. The women hugged, as Edith wished her daughter-in-law a happy and blessed birthday, and Jack kissed her cheek before giving her a prettily wrapped gift.

"Just a little something I made for you," he said modestly, as she carefully unwrapped the present. She gasped in delight at what was inside; a pair of polished wood photo frames. They were joined together by tiny gold hinges that allowed the frames to stand. In one frame was a photo of the Yallaroo farmhouse, while the other one had a photo of her and Sam.

"A little memento to take to your new home."

"Oh, Jack. It's beautiful! I'll treasure it," she whispered wiping tears from her eyes. "This house and Sam; they'll both be coming with me."

Taking a deep breath, she brought her emotions under control and said briskly, "We better get this morning tea started!"

Before too long, smoko was being enjoyed on the back verandah. The group of men stood together discussing the logistics of the task at hand. Between sips of hot tea, and mouthfuls of scones and jam and cream, Ted and Ralph, the crane operator, and Syd, the semi driver, explained their plan and made sure everyone understood what they were required to do.

After thanking the women for smoko, the men all donned their hats and proceeded to get everything in position. Bryce had removed part of the house-yard fence during the week, to allow for easy access so the trailer and crane could be maneuvered into position. Chains were put in place under the little building, and everything double checked.

Syd positioned the long trailer into the required location and the other men all took their positions so that all angles were covered, before Ted signalled to Ralph that they were ready. The crane's boom was raised, and then the jib lowered the wire hoist rope and large hook into position over the building. Bryce climbed onto the roof of the building, and attached the chains to the big heavy hook. After giving Ralph a thumbs up signal, he quickly climbed back down onto the ground.

With relative ease the crane lifted the old building, which creaked and groaned in protest as it left its resting place of many decades. Dust filled the air, and Kath held her breath, hoping the shed wouldn't fall to pieces. Slowly Ralph raised the building further, and maneuvered it over the trailer, guided by Ted and the other men on the ground. When it was in the correct position, Ralph slowly lowered the boom and the building settled gently on to the trailer. Kath and Edith gave great sighs of relief. The whole process had gone very smoothly. Ralph, Syd and Ted then set about securing the load on the trailer, ready for the short trip to the other property.

When Syd was satisfied that his load was ready to go, he climbed into the cab of the big truck and turned the long load around, ready to follow Ted and Alberto to Oakleigh. The convoy assembled again; although Bryce left the tractor there so later on he could tidy up the site where the building had been. He hopped in his mother's car and chatted happily to her as he drove her to the cottage, following slowly behind his grandparents.

"Rather eventful morning. Hey, Mum?"

"You can say that again! It'll be easy to remember when the old building was moved; same day as my birthday! By the way, how come you aren't at work today?"

"I swapped days, of course. Boss didn't mind and I didn't want to miss out on this." He grinned.

They continued talking in general conversation for the rest of the short drive.

"Grandad sure won't get a speeding ticket today," Bryce remarked dryly. "Maybe I should round him up?"

"Don't you dare, you'll scare your grandmother! We're nearly there," his Mum laughed.

When they arrived, Syd, Ralph and Ted were standing together, looking at the prepared site and discussing their plan to unload the building.

"I hope this part goes as smoothly as the first," Kath said, as they pulled to a stop under the jacaranda tree.

"They seem to know what they're doing. So nothing to worry about, Mum."

Bryce's words were quite right and, before long, the whole procedure was reversed and the old building was settled on its new footings. After Ralph and Syd had rumbled off in their heavy rigs, Ted walked over to Kath. "Well, what do you think?"

"It looks like it belongs there. So glad you thought of moving it, Ted. I can't thank you enough!"

"Just remember that when you get the bill," he chuckled. "Let's go and inspect the inside and see how she handled the move."

Together they entered the empty building. There were a couple of cracks in the sheeting the interior had been lined with, and one of the windows wouldn't budge. Nothing that couldn't be fixed, Ted assured her. The view from the southern window was panoramic; not as perfect as the vista from the front porch, but the distant mountains could still be clearly seen. Jack and Bryce joined them inside.

"Oh, this is a great spot, love," exclaimed Jack. "You'll have it all set up in no time."

"Yes. I'll give it a good clean, and move everything back in as soon as Ted says I can."

"You won't have to wait long. It's a bit low on the northern side, but we can adjust the footings so no worries there. The timber for the breezeway floor to join it to the cottage arrived yesterday, so Alberto and I can get cracking on that after lunch. Not sure when the sparky can come back, but I'll chase him up for you. Bryce, you can finish putting the rest of the fence posts in whenever you like."

"Lane and Jess are coming out on the week-end. Perhaps I could ask Lane to finish the electrical work?"

"Good idea, Kath. That'd solve the problem quick smart," Ted replied.

Edith interrupted their conversation as she called them all to the front porch. She had set up a small folding table, complete with a lace tablecloth, upon which sat a beautifully decorated birthday cake.

"I thought it would be nice to have your cake up here, dear," she commented, as her gaze took in the cottage and the view to the mountains.

"Oh, yes indeed. What a lovely surprise Edith. You are naughty though! I did say no fuss for my birthday," she scolded with a smile.

"Did you dear? I must have forgotten," her mother-in-law answered innocently. "And besides, we're not fussing at all, just enjoying some cake up here on this beautiful day."

"Struth, no complaints from me! Happy Birthday, Kath," Ted agreed.

"Buon compleanno, Mrs Kath," Alberto added happily.

After they had all enjoyed cake, and some of Jack's ginger beer, it was time for Ted and Alberto to go back to work.

"Nothing'll get done if we keep sitting here. Come on, Alberto. We're wasting daylight," Ted remarked dryly. "Great cake. Thanks, Edith."

The rest of the week flew by, as Kath was asked to fill in for another teacher who was away on sick leave. What free time she did have was spent sorting out cupboards and drawers, and packing up what she wanted to take with her to the cottage. Her mind wandered off constantly, often thinking about her baby grandsons. She always made time to visit Majella and the little twins, who were totally irresistible. Majella was settling into motherhood very well and, although always tired, she was full of love and enjoying her new role in life.

Kath was so grateful that the babies were healthy and doing well, but couldn't help but imagine what it would be like if Sam was with her to share the joy. He would have been a wonderful grandfather. She smiled at the thought, and then shook her head to clear it so that she could get back to the task at hand.

A friend had told her that it only takes two days to pack up a house, and here she was taking months! She knew she was procrastinating, unable to make decisions about what to keep and then what to do with everything else. She was about to close the door on a large chapter of her life, her entire married life with Sam. It was much harder to do than she had anticipated.

She tried to be methodical and practical as she moved slowly through the house, studying each room.

Surveying the dining room and its contents, she concluded that the lovely dining-room suite would be too big for the little cottage, but thought the kitchen table and chairs would be okay. They actually held more sentimental value for her anyway.

There was a small buffet with a beautiful bevelled mirror that she didn't want to leave behind, as Sam had given it to her for Christmas years ago and, of course, his desk and book case. She definitely wanted their bedroom suite, their two favourite recliner chairs, and another bedroom suite for the spare room. A small couch and coffee table from the living room were also must haves, as well as a collection of outdoor furniture for the front porch and the breezeway. Fridge, washing machine, TV, reading lamp and an antique clock completed the list for the present, along with an assortment of artwork, kitchenware, crockery, appliances, photos, linen and, of course, pot plants.

The last thing Kath wanted to do was clutter the limited space, so if she wasn't happy with something it would be coming straight back. The old farmhouse would have lots of empty spaces for Bryce and Sally to fill, but they were happy to make the house their home with their own personal touches when they moved in.

It was nearly a fortnight before she finally went up to the cottage to check on progress. She met Ted standing on the front porch. "Hi Ted. How's everything?"

"Everything's just tickety boo!" he smiled broadly. "Come and have a look."

Kath was thrilled to see what had been achieved during the last two weeks. The breezeway floor and roof were complete, and connected her art studio to the cottage, making the cottage look much bigger than it really was. Lane had been happy to connect the power to the studio, and the painters had finished the final coats on all the interior walls. Ted had even asked them to fix the cracks in the interior walls of the studio, and paint the walls again.

"Hope you don't mind, but they were here and had it done in a jiffy. I heard you were busy packing so I didn't want to bother you. Bryce brought up the leftover paint you had in the laundry at Yallaroo one day when you were at work."

"Oh, did he? He didn't mention it, but of course I don't mind. It looks brand new! Once the exterior walls are clad with the same boards as the cottage, it really will look like it's all one beautiful home. I hope there's more of the same cladding available?" she asked worriedly.

"Yep, all good. I checked on that and put an order in. It's gotta come up from Brissie, but at least they have some."

"Well, that's a relief. Any word on the floor coverings?"

"You'll be pleased to hear they arrived in town this morning, and the bloke is coming out first thing Monday. Actually, two blokes are coming out, one to do the carpet and the other the floor planks, so they should be done pretty quick. I reckon you could start moving in at the end of next week," he smiled.

"Really? So soon? How exciting! I'm working Monday and Tuesday next week, but I should be organised by Thursday or Friday." But then her face fell. "Oh, but you know what?"

"What's wrong?"

"I've completely forgotten about booking a removalist! Originally the boys were going to do it for me with the farm truck, but that's been hired to a neighbour for a few weeks while his truck is being repaired. I won't get anyone at such short notice now."

"Leave it with me. I might know someone," Ted said as he pulled his phone out of his pocket and walked away.

True to his word, the infallible Ted did know someone who had a truck and was experienced with moving furniture.

"Jacko used to be in the furniture removal business, but he retired last year and only does a few jobs now and then. I told him it would only be a small job and, it just so happens, he's available on Saturday of next week," he grinned.

"Oh Ted. I don't know how you do it!" she laughed. "That'll be perfect."

✳ ✳ ✳

The days passed by quickly, as Kath continued sorting and tidying cupboards and rooms, surprised by how much 'stuff' she had accumulated over the years. She was beginning to stress that she would not be ready in time. She could easily come back to clean once she had moved out, but she wanted to make as clean a break as possible, not wanting to leave any mess or disorder behind.

Thankfully, Jess was able to take some time off in lieu of overtime and came out to help for a day. "Mum, you really have to do some disciplined de-cluttering," she said firmly.

"Oh, really. And just what do you mean by that exactly?"

"Put all the undecided things and everything you don't really need, together in one spot, like out on the verandah, and go through it one item at a time. Keep only the things that speak to your heart and get rid of the rest."

"Speak to my heart?"

"Yes. Ask yourself 2 questions. When was the last time you used it? And, is it beautiful? You've packed all the main things you want to take. All this stuff," Jessica waved her hands at the piles of miscellaneous objects, "needs to be ruthlessly graded."

"Graded?"

"Yep. Keep it, give it away, or dump it."

"That's quite harsh, Jess. But I know you're right. You'll have to help me though; I didn't realise I had become a bit of a hoarder."

Jessica was a tough taskmaster and kept her mother on track, asking the same questions over and over: "When did you last use that? Why on earth would you want to keep that?" And often saying: "That is certainly not beautiful!"

By the end of the afternoon, they had laughed a lot and had a few disagreements. They compiled a load for the op-shop, one for the women's shelter, and another smaller one for the dump. A couple of packed boxes were to remain in storage at the house. Kath had found a few items that she declared were indeed beautiful, and she didn't know how she had overlooked them.

To her mother's great amusement, Jessica even had a number of things that she wanted to take home with her. They had achieved a great deal, and enjoyed a cool drink and some lamingtons at the kitchen table, as they celebrated their good work.

"Thanks so much for coming out today, Jess. You really helped me with that last part. I think I'm nearly ready. Can you believe I'm about to move?"

"Yeah. It's all happened faster than I thought it would. Are you ready to go? I mean are you really looking forward to it?"

"I've thought about that a lot, and I can honestly say that I am. It feels the right thing to do, the right time to go, especially as Bryce and Sally's wedding is coming up fast. It's less than a month away. Goodness knows what I'm going to wear!"

"Well, I think a day shopping with me in Toowoomba is the answer to that. Um, Mum?"

"Yes?"

"Was wondering if you still have those awful nightmares?"

Kath looked at her daughter blankly for a few seconds. "No, actually I don't. I had quite a few in the months following your dad's death and then they stopped for a while. But they returned after the gallery fire when I was so upset about losing my painting. I let all my old fears and insecurities back in. You know, I haven't even thought about that terrible dream for a long time."

"Really? They just stopped?"

"Well. It was by divine intervention, I believe." She smiled. "Pastor Bob and Stephanie helped me through that rough patch, and prayed over me, right here on this verandah. I was feeling really down, nearly back where I was just after your father died. They asked the Lord to lift me up and be my strength and prayed that the blood of Jesus would erase that nightmare once and for all." Kath paused as she remembered the powerful time of prayer. "I had distanced myself from everyone, including God. I asked Him to forgive me and to help me to focus more on Him; to trust Him completely, with everything. And you know what? He did! My relationship with Him is closer now than it ever was and I've been sleeping peacefully. I haven't even thanked Him for it. Thanks for reminding me."

After she had waved goodbye to Jessica, Kath walked around the garden praying and thanking God for His goodness and for delivering her from the nightmares that had plagued her for such a long time. Despite the fact that she didn't understand His ways, she knew they were perfect and that His timing was impeccable; never early, never late. With a thankful heart she continued her stroll until she was looking at the site where her art studio used to be.

In the dimming light she could still see where Bryce had tidied it up, removing the old stumps, and even putting a load of good garden soil on the area, with the intention of making another garden bed. Kath shook her head as she considered everything that had taken place during the last six months.

Soon she would be leaving this place and starting a new life in the cottage. It was exciting, but also a little daunting. She called to Tink and went to sit in her favourite chair on the verandah, the little dog content to curl up at her feet. She looked up into the sky, and smiled as she saw the evening star appear. Quietly she whispered the rhyme her mother had taught when she had been a little girl:

Star light, star bright, first star I see tonight.
I wish I may, I wish I might, this is the wish I wish tonight.

She didn't believe wishes came true; certainly none of the hundreds she had wished as a child had. But now, without doubt, she knew where the power lay; in God Almighty, the Mighty Healer and Redeemer. Her Heavenly Father, who watched over her and showered her with daily blessings. She quietly recited a favourite scripture passage, "When I consider your heavens, the work of your fingers, the moon and the stars, which you have set in place, what is mankind that you are mindful of them, human beings that you care for them? You have made them a little lower than the angels and crowned them with glory and honor."

She smiled and thanked the Lord for His great love, and His beautiful grace and endless mercy, not wanting anyone to perish. Without Him she was nothing, could do nothing. He alone gave her the strength that propelled her forward, and the peace that calmed and comforted her. She smiled as she thought of old Tom sitting in the morning sun, eyes closed, quietly singing in his raspy voice a few lines from a lovely old hymn, over and over:

> *"What a friend we have in Jesus, all our sins and griefs to bear,*
> *What a privilege to carry everything to God in Prayer.*
> *Can we find a friend so faithful, who will all our sorrows share,*
> *Jesus knows our every weakness, take it to the Lord in prayer."*

CHAPTER 24

A New Season

*"May your joys be as bright as the morning, your
years of happiness as numerous as the stars in the
heavens, and your troubles but shadows that fade in
the sunlight of God's love." Old English Blessing*

*T*he day of the big move was finally upon her, and Kath was so busy she
had little time to dwell on the enormity of what she was doing. This
was a good thing, as it prevented any last-minute nervous over-thinking.

There seemed to be people everywhere; all the family plus Lane, and
Jillian and Dave and their boys, and Pastor Bob and Stephanie. Furniture,
appliances and boxes were carried out to the removalist truck while the
smaller items and pot plants were deposited into the other vehicles and
trailers.

Rosemary and Edith tidied and vacuumed rooms as items were removed.
Jillian took charge of supervising the kitchen and, under her watchful eye,

the fridge and freezer contents were packed into big eskies. The kitchen items that Kath had been using, and wanted to keep, were packed in a box ready for the short trip to the cottage.

Kath seemed to be everywhere at once, answering questions and giving directions until all the loading was complete and the vehicles all headed down the driveway enroute to the little cottage on the hill. Nipper rode on the back of Bryce's ute, while a very confused and rather anxious toy poodle sat on the seat beside Kath in her car, wondering what was going on.

"Don't worry, Tinkerbelle. You're not being left behind, and I promise you'll like your new home," her mistress crooned as she ruffled her woolly coat. The little dog didn't seem too reassured by her words and whined sadly. She spent the rest of the day in either Kath's or Jess's arms, quite overwhelmed by all the activity. Nipper, too, was moving to the cottage, as Bryce had two dogs of his own and besides, Kath couldn't leave Sam's faithful companion of many years behind.

The unpacking all happened with quick efficiency, with Kath once again directing where to put the furniture, and where the marked boxes should go for easy unpacking. By 1pm everything had been unloaded, and then several ladies from town arrived with lunch for everyone. It was so good to be part of a wonderful caring church family. A merry feast of fresh sandwiches and cake was held on the breezeway, amid packing boxes and collections of pot plants. Majella even drove up with the twins to join in the celebration. There was no shortage of eager arms to cuddle them, while their mother enjoyed the picnic lunch.

"Well, what do you think, Mum?" Jess asked quietly when she caught her mother's attention.

"I don't think I've had time to think. This has been like an army operation, everyone doing their bit so efficiently. So much was achieved in such a short time. I can't thank you all enough." She looked around the gathering, her eyes misting up.

"No thanks necessary," Bob answered easily. "You and Sam never hesitated to help any of us when we needed it. It's nice to be able to reciprocate."

"So, Mum." Jarrod said wiping chocolate icing from his mouth. "What are you going to call this place? It needs a name, or did old Uncle Ian give it one?"

"No. I checked that out and, for some reason, he didn't give it a name. But I have decided what I want to call it."

"Oh, you have? Do tell," Jillie asked excitedly.

Kath looked at the enquiring faces around her. "Bonnie Brae."

"Bonnie Brae? That sounds a bit too Scottish!" Jarrod teased.

"Yeah," Bryce chimed in. "Next thing we'll hear bagpipes echoing across the paddocks."

"Well, you've got enough hot air to blow 'em," his older brother laughed, as he poked the younger man in the ribs with his elbow.

"Ouch," Bryce protested in mock pain.

"Come here, poor babe," Sally laughed.

Kath smiled at their tomfoolery before stating, "It's actually Gaelic."

"What does it mean?" Jess asked.

"Beautiful Hillside. I've always loved Bonnie as a name. It's so cheery, and I wanted something that incorporates the hill. It's exactly what this spot is – a beautiful hillside."

"Well, I think you've hit the nail on the head, love. I like it," Jack said enthusiastically.

"Yes, it's absolutely perfect," Jillie agreed, before raising her paper cup, signalling an impromptu toast. "To Kath and Bonnie Brae."

Everyone joined in and repeated the toast, with Stephanie adding, "May you know great peace and happiness here. God bless."

Gradually, people began to leave. Kath hugged everyone, as she thanked them for their kindness and help. Bob and Stephanie had placed the outdoor furniture where they thought it should go, and moved the pot plants so that there were attractive displays on the front porch and in the breezeway. The greenery instantly brightened the area, giving it a homely appearance.

"You can move them where you really want them to go when you have time, but it's a start at least," Stephanie said as they were leaving.

"You've been terrific. Thanks so much."

Jillian and Dave had done a great job unpacking most of the kitchen boxes, and re-filling the fridge and freezer, while their boys had unloaded various items from the trailer. They were all hugged and thanked profusely for their help, as they took their leave.

"There's a meal in the fridge for you too. Enough for guests if your kids want to stay."

"Oh, Jillie. Your blood's worth bottling!"

"Really?"

"Sorry. I think I've spent too much time around Ted! He's got a one liner for everything!" A tired Kath laughed, and hugged her good friend.

Jack and Edith left after they each had a little nap in the chairs on the front porch, where they enjoyed the cool afternoon breeze. Edith had enjoyed unpacking some of the books and putting them in the bookcase, before Kath made her sit and rest. Jack had busied himself in the laundry, before helping Jarrod and Bryce put the beds together and move some furniture around a few times before Kath was happy with their positioning.

Finally, only Bryce and Sally, and Jessica and Lane, were left. The two girls, taking a still upset Tinkerbelle with them, closed the bedroom door, after telling Kath that they would unpack her room. Kath simply nodded happily and continued arranging the living area. Sometime later, Jess and Sally appeared smiling and, each taking a hand, tugged Kath into her bedroom.

"Ta-da!" they exclaimed together, indicating the beautifully styled room.

Kath put her hands over her mouth as she looked around. The bed was made with a new doona cover and matching pillows; a contrasting throw-rug placed fashionably at the foot. Her bedside tables had her old favourite lamps, and her dressing table was tastefully adorned with her favourite knick knacks, a new scented soy candle, and the photo frames that Jack had made for her birthday. All her clothes were unpacked and put away, with the hanging space in the wardrobe full. Her cherished bedroom-chair graced the corner near the window, with a crocheted throw rug draped carefully over one arm.

"Oh, girls. You've been busy. And doesn't it look divine! It's like something out of a magazine." Kath turned around slowly, before drawing both young women to her and hugging them. "Thank you so much. It's beautiful, just right!"

"You'll have fun trying to find everything," Sally giggled merrily.

"Nah. Just think logically, or send us a text," Jessica grinned. "I hope you don't mind, Mum, but you really did need a new doona cover. Your other one was pretty daggy."

"No, I don't mind, Jess. I know it was rather old and worn, but I couldn't decide what to replace it with. You've chosen the perfect one. What a makeover! I love it!"

The two couples stayed on, helping Kath until the sun began to set. Then they all enjoyed an early dinner together of lasagna and garlic bread, courtesy of Jillian's big heart. At about 8pm, Kath, holding Tink, waved farewell to her visitors and watched as the red tail-lights of the vehicles disappeared down her driveway. It was suddenly very quiet. She turned and stood in her front doorway looking into the cottage. A little smile of pleasure and satisfaction lit up her tired face. The room before her looked modern, but with an old-world charm. Jessica had also bought her mother a new rug for the living room floor.

'She certainly knows my tastes,' Kath thought approvingly, vaguely remembering a conversation about floor rugs a few weeks back; not realising at the time that her scheming daughter had been contemplating a new rug for the cottage. It all looked so comfortable and inviting. She was keen to keep unpacking, but knew that her energy levels had plummeted throughout the evening. She decided that checking out the efficiency of the shower would be the wisest course of action. The basic items had been unpacked, and the remaining boxes would certainly wait for another day.

The shower proved to be both hot and therapeutic for her tired body and, as she towelled herself dry, she assessed the practicality of her combined laundry/bathroom. With the doors pulled shut in front of the laundry section, it was like being in a lovely ensuite, quite spacious and certainly very modern. After she had put her pyjamas on, she wandered back into the open-plan living area, and filled the kettle on the kitchen bench.

Once her cup of tea was made, she walked to where Sam's lovely old desk sat in the section of the living room that was once part of the old verandah. In the daylight she would be able to sit at the desk and look out the new window. His office chair was very welcoming, and she looked forward to finding her scented candle. She had, however, known where her journal and Bible had been packed, as she had found them earlier and placed them on the desk for this moment. She just needed to debrief with the Lord before she went to bed.

The reading for the day was John chapter 15. She read it through slowly, meditating on the verses. Many thoughts began to swirl around in her mind. In verse 5, Jesus said:

> *I am the vine, you are the branches. He who abides in Me and I in him, bears much fruit, for without Me, you can do nothing.*

Slowly she wrote the following words in her Journal;

> *I can't do anything in my own strength, but I am amazed at what I can do with God's help. I know I can't do life alone. I need Jesus, my family, my school community, my church family, my local community, my neighbours, and my friends near and far. I need their support, fellowship, friendship and encouragement. I recognise this great need in my life, and I embrace it. And I thank Jesus for where He has brought me today, to Bonnie Brae. I pray that He will continue to help me, as I seek to develop an ever-deepening relationship with Him.*

Her gaze returned to her Bible and she read verse 13 again, several times:

> *Greater love has no one than to lay down his life for his friend.*

She thought back to the day in South Australia when Sam, not caring about his own life, dived into the cold, salty water to save a woman from drowning. She picked up her pen again:

> *My Darling Sam gave his life for a stranger. He knew he had a terminal illness, and that selfless act greatly accelerated his death. Jesus gave His life for all mankind. We're not strangers*

to Him. He knows everything about us, and yet He loves us unconditionally. He willingly died on the Cross, for me! Because He loves me. My Sam is gone. I know I'll see him again one day, but he's gone from my life and I can't talk to him or hear him. But I still have Jesus. He truly is my greatest friend and He will never leave me or forsake me. And now I have a new home and a new season of my life, beginning from today. His eye is on the sparrow, and I know He is watching over me. Thank You, Lord, for all You have done for me. Bless You Jesus.

With a full heart, she turned off the desk lamp, the kitchen lights and, with Little Tink right behind her, entered her new bedroom to rest and sleep contentedly.

CHAPTER 25

The Cup Overflows

"He has no design upon us, but to make us happy...
Who should be cheerful, if not the people of God?"
Thomas Watson 1620-1686

*T*he little restaurant had never looked so beautiful. From where she sat on the far side of the room, Kath admired the flowers and fairy lights that adorned the main dining area, flowing out into the adjoining garden, making it one big fairyland.

Frank had been fastidious with his arrangements, overseeing every detail in order to create the perfect atmosphere for the wedding reception. Kath had dined there several times with Sam, and the little establishment had always made a good impression on her. But tonight, the ambiance was exceptional.

Bryce and Sally had invited a large number of people to their engagement party, with the intention of having a smaller, more intimate wedding reception with just their families and closest friends. Frank's restaurant provided a wonderful venue for such an occasion.

Kath thought back to the moment when she turned and saw Sally enter the church earlier in the afternoon, walking down the aisle on her father's arm. She truly did look beautiful, in a simple yet elegant white sheath wedding gown. It was a fitted, straight-cut dress, nipped in at the waist, suiting her slim figure perfectly. The gown didn't have a train, and neither did she wear a veil, but she held a stunning bouquet of a mixture of traditional and native flowers in a burgundy and white colour palette.

Her two bridesmaids, friends since her school days, wore A-line dresses in burgundy that were fitted at the waist, with flared skirts. Sally's blonde hair was woven into a low bun, with some lovely relaxed waves sweeping around her face. It was a simple yet classic look. Placed above the bun was a filigree comb in a rose gold tone, embellished with diamantes and pearls in a floral motif.

Kath's eyes misted at the sight of the young women, and she couldn't help but think of the day she walked down the aisle to become Sam's wife. She turned to look at the groom. How handsome Bryce looked in his navy suit; no longer her little boy, but a grown man. Jarrod stood beside him as best man, with Julian as groomsman. Oh, how Jarrod resembled his father!

Tears began to fall unheeded down her face. Jess gently took her mother's hand and squeezed it in support, intuitively knowing that mixed feelings of joy and sadness were flooding through her heart.

The service was well thought out by the young couple. The minister who married them, used the theme of God's love for all people, weaving it throughout the service; a perfect love, which forms the foundation for the love between a man and his wife.

Dear friends, let us love one another for love comes from God. Everyone who

loves has been born of God and knows God. Whoever does not love,
does not know God, because God is love. I John 4:7-8

Kath had mopped her eyes constantly throughout the service, espe-cially when Jessica read the beautiful well-known chapter on love from 1 Corinthians 13, which had been the reading from her wedding with Sam. She knew verses 4-7 and 13 off by heart:

Love is patient, love is kind. It does not envy, it does not boast, it is not proud.
It does not dishonour others, it is not self-seeking, it is not easily angered,
it keeps no record of wrongs. Love does not delight
in evil but rejoices with the truth.
It always protects, always trusts, always hopes, always perseveres.

Concluding with the words:

And now these three remain: faith, hope and
love. But the greatest of these is love.

Oh, but how she had loved Sam, and she knew that love had been recip-rocated. She no longer asked God 'why?' but simply trusted in His wisdom. With great determination not to break down, she had given a speech earlier in the evening as mother of the groom, prepared with the help of Stephanie and Bob. She hadn't wanted it to be too soppy but she wanted to convey how proud she was of her children, especially Bryce on his wedding day.

She also wanted to welcome Sally into the family, and pay a special tribute to Sam for the wonderful father and role model he had been to his children. She had managed to present it all with her voice only breaking during the last sentence. Speech-making was certainly not something she enjoyed, and this one had been especially difficult.

She was glad when she was able to resume her seat for the rest of the formalities, and the cutting of the cake. She was feeling quite relaxed now as she sat with Jessica, watching the dancing.

Jarrod and Majella walked over to where they were sitting, and deposited a baby in each of their laps. Laughing, the two women happily placed their arms protectively around the little ones.

"Would you mind holding them while I dance with my beautiful wife?" Jarrod asked needlessly.

"They've just been fed so you might need these," Majella added, handing them each a burp cloth.

"Enjoy yourselves," Kath replied, cuddling her little charge.

The boys were just over three months old, and growing quickly. With full bellies they were content to receive adoring attention from their grandmother and aunty. Kath held Alexander, and spoke baby talk, receiving big smiles in return that lit up his big blue eyes. Jessica was doing the same with Nicholas, but she had to work harder to earn a smile as he was much more reticent than his brother who was 7 minutes older.

The twin's parents enjoyed their time on the dance floor, obviously still very much in love as they gracefully slow-danced to the final song in the bracket, looking deeply into each other's eyes when they weren't stealing peeks in their babies' direction.

When they returned, Jessica enquired, "So, how did you manage to give the right name to the right baby?"

"What do you mean?" Majella asked with raised eyebrows.

"Well, Alexander's middle name is Samuel, after his father and grandfather, and he has blue eyes and fair hair, obviously favouring the Wilmonts. Nicholas, on the other hand, has brown eyes and dark hair, clearly taking after your side of the family. And his middle name is Angelo, after your dad. I'm just curious how you named them so perfectly?"

Jarrod laughed. "Don't ask me! Crikey, I couldn't even tell them apart for the first month!"

Majella added, "We didn't know who they would look like, or what sort of little personalities they would have when they were first born. We only agreed on names a few days before they arrived. But I'm so happy with how it's turned out."

Jack and Edith came to sit at the table with them. They were beautiful dancers, who still moved together with ease and elegance, their aging bodies now favouring a slow waltz.

"You've still got the moves, Granma," Jessica teased as Lane came to sit beside her.

"I'm just glad your grandfather can hold me up," Edith smiled. "He's always been a great partner on the dance floor."

They were all sitting and chatting easily when Gertrude hurried over, the brightly-coloured cape, attached at the shoulders of her turquoise gown, billowing out behind her like a parachute. She arrived quite breathless.

"Kath, darling. You won't believe what I just found out!"

Pulling a chair out for her, Kath said, "Here, sit down. What are you so flustered about?"

"I just had the most incredible phone call from Tyrone Patterson. That's what!"

"Hmmn, okay. And who's Tyrone Patterson?"

Gertrude rolled her eyes theatrically as she stood up again. "Darling, he's my good friend, the owner of the gallery that burnt down."

"Oh yes, of course. I've tried to forget about that disaster."

"But, darling. Guess what he told me?"

"I have no idea."

Max had sauntered over, and pulled up a chair near where his wife was standing. He had heard most of the phone call, and knew the telling of the saga would be most entertaining. Julian also wandered over to stand behind Jessica and Lane. He smiled at his father as he too could tell that his mother was excited and ready for a melodramatic story telling.

"Your painting, *Thunder Roll*, was not destroyed in the fire."

"What?"

There was complete silence around the table as all eyes focused on Gertrude, who was now enjoying the attention enormously.

She continued. "Tyrone was away at the time of the fire. His assistant, Reagan, was working that day. Now, Ivo Bronson, the man who commissioned your painting, sent his son, Donald, to collect two paintings for him. Now one of the paintings, called *Forest Song* or something like that, had not arrived. Some delay with the courier, I think it was. Anyway, Reagan took payment for your *Thunder Roll*, but the silly fellow," an exaggerated eye roll followed, "recorded the transaction as being for the *Forest* painting by mistake. Apparently, they were having a somewhat heated discussion as, understandably, Donald was not happy about not being able to collect both of the paintings as arranged. Reagan said he was trying to placate him, and was not fully concentrating on what he was doing. Actually, I don't think Reagan is the best person for that position. I've told Tyrone many times he should find someone else. But did he listen to me? No, of course not! Reagan would be better suited to another role elsewhere. He should…"

Kath held her hands up to stop Gertrude from rambling off on a tangent, and get the conversation back on track. "Yes, yes. So, you're saying the other artist received payment for my painting, while I was told it was destroyed?"

"Yes, that's exactly what I've been trying to tell you!" Gertrude waved her hands in the air in animated exasperation.

"But it doesn't make sense! How could the figures for each painting be exactly the same? And why didn't Mr. Bronson realise the mix-up earlier? The fire was over six months ago, longer in fact!"

"I know, darling. I asked Tyrone those exact questions," Gertrude replied, dramatically shrugging her shoulders. "Apparently, there was a discrepancy with the funds, which Reagan somehow covered up. Quite dishonest of him, mind you. And Ivo asked his son to pick the paintings up because he had to fly to London on urgent business. He thought his son had collected the *Forest* painting, as per the receipt that was emailed to him, so he didn't give the matter another thought. Donald was meant to pick the other painting up the following day but, of course, the gallery burnt down that very night. Anyway, while Ivo was in London, he had a major heart attack, poor man, and spent quite some time in hospital before going to his sister's place to recuperate for several months. Then he went on a cruise around the Mediterranean. He only returned to Australia last week and, when he entered his home, he found your *Thunder Roll* there and not the *Forest* painting," Gertrude finished breathlessly.

"My, my, what a story," Edith interjected.

"I'm struggling to take it all in," Kath said quietly.

"Yes. But wait, darling. It gets even better!" Gertrude clapped her hands together gleefully, getting her second wind and laughing loudly.

Jarrod and Majella looked at each with broad smiles, enjoying the show immensely. Even the baby boys, now in their parent's arms, appeared spellbound. Gertrude, in full flight, was quite a sight to behold.

"Ivo is quite the entertainer, so he threw himself a little homecoming soiree last week and was showing his art collection, including *Thunder Roll*, to his guests and…" she paused for dramatic effect looking around the table, "two of his friends want to commission paintings from… you!" She pointed her finger dramatically at Kath who went quite pale and looked like she was about to fall off her chair.

Jessica took her hand. "Mum, this is wonderful news! Here, drink some water."

Kath drank deeply before slowly placing the empty glass on the table, still trying to come to terms with what she had heard. "But, it's still a bit of a mess, isn't it? I mean, I received insurance money for a painting that wasn't destroyed. And some other artist, who was paid, is now going to be told that their work was burnt in the fire."

"I know, darling. The fire has been very upsetting for everyone. But don't worry, I'll help you sort all of that out. Don't give it another thought, especially not now. Tonight, you have very good news. Enjoy it, and be happy."

"Oh, I am. I think." The colour was beginning to return to her face.

"Congratulations, love. What a way to end the day!" beamed Jack.

"Yes, Kath. Congratulations. I knew it was only a matter of time before your talent was recognised." Max rose, and kissed her soundly on both cheeks.

"And I have never doubted from the first moment I saw your work, years ago, that you would become a well-known artist one day. Didn't I say that, Max?"

"Yes, yes, you did Gertie dear. Right as always." Max kissed his wife, placing his arm around her shoulders. "I think this party should continue. So much to celebrate today; the wonderful wedding and now this exciting news."

* * *

The following day, Kath sat in the back seat of Jess's car, as Lane drove her and Jessica back to Toowoomba. Her thoughts were still in a whirl, as she tried to process everything that had taken place over the weekend. A beautiful wedding, a new daughter-in-law, and an artistic career primed to unfold once again. She couldn't hold back the little smile that kept tugging at her lips. Her painting had not been destroyed! *Thunder Roll* had been found! Her work was in demand; a small start, but it was a start nonetheless, and a huge boost to her confidence. They stopped at a café once they reached the city at the top of the range, and found a table outside in a shady garden area.

"So, what are your plans now, Mum?' Jessica asked over lunch, as she started on her risotto once her mum's quiche and salad had been delivered by the young waiter.

"Well. I guess I need to meet with the people who want me to paint something for them, and see exactly what they want. And what the time frames will be. Then there's the mix-up business at the gallery. I won't relax until that, and the insurance mess, is straightened out. But Gertrude is adamant that she'll be on top of that in no time."

"I sure wouldn't like to do battle with her!" Lane grinned as he began devouring his steak sandwich.

"Oh, she's actually quite a softie, and wouldn't hurt a fly. But she sure can look pretty formidable." Jessica smiled at her boyfriend. "Are you going to keep teaching, Mum?"

"Well, that's the million-dollar question! I'll see how all the discussions go, and decide after Christmas, I think."

"Good idea. Take things slowly. Granma would tell you to pray about it, and see what the Holy Spirit says," Jessica smiled.

"Wise words indeed," her Mum agreed.

Once back at Jessica's unit, they hugged goodbye. Kath then started the drive back to Bonnie Brae in her car, which she had parked in Jess's front yard for the weekend. She was looking forward to picking Nipper and Tinkerbelle up from a friend's place. Tink never liked being left behind, and she smiled at the joyful reception she knew she would receive from both dogs. She played some upbeat worship music to match her mood, and enjoyed the country drive, constantly shaking her head at the amazing revelation of the night before. She kept thanking the Lord for His goodness.

Eighteen months before she had been a shattered woman. Now she was a proud grandmother with a new home, a newly married son, a new daughter-in-law, and Jess was in a relationship with a lovely young man. After all the ups and downs since Sam's death, she had now been properly presented with an opportunity to focus on what she really enjoyed; painting in her art studio. Her work had been seen, critiqued, and definitely passed muster. She was so blessed!

When she was nearly home, driving down the last long straight before her turnoff, she noticed flashing lights in her rear-view mirror.

"Oh, no," she groaned as she put on the indicator and pulled over to the left, shaking her head in disbelief. Of course, it had to be Ricky again.

"Mrs Wilmont, I haven't seen you for a while. Well, not in this situation anyway," he smiled.

"Hi, Ricky, you'll be pleased to know I have actually been a very responsible driver of late."

"That's good to hear."

She knew the drill, and had her driver's licence ready to hand to the young police officer.

"Thank you. Shouldn't be too long," he said, as he took the licence and returned to the police car to do the required checks, and issue her speeding ticket. When he returned, he said cheerfully, "Well, at least you weren't too far over the speed limit, so it's not too big a fine."

"Thanks, Ricky. I'll keep an eye on my speed. I promise."

"Enjoy the rest of your day, Mrs. Wilmont."

As she slowly drove off, she could have sworn she heard familiar laughter wafting in through her open window. She looked through the windscreen at the late afternoon sky.

Golden sunrays sparkled through stormy looking clouds, radiating brilliant beams of light. She smiled as she whispered, "I see you, Sam. I will always see you."

The End

Notes

All Scripture from the New International Version unless otherwise specified.

Part One
1. Isaiah 40:26, New Living Translation

Chapter 1
1. "Safe in the Arms of Jesus," 1868, Fanny Crosby
2. Bunya Mountains National Park. Nature, Culture and History. www.http.parks.des.qld.gov.au

Chapter 2
1. Proverbs 31:10-12, Amplified Bible

Chapter 3
1. Psalm 23, New King James Version

Chapter 5
1. "Amazing Grace," 1772, John Newton
2. John 3:16, New King James Version

3. "A Poem", by Ruth Bell Graham 2006, From "Sitting by My Laughing Fire," 2006

Chapter 7.
1. "House of Miracles," by Brandon Lake, 2020

Chapter 9
1. Romans 8:26-28, Contemporary English Version

Chapter 11
1. "I Can Only Imagine," by Bart Millard, MercyMe, 1999
2. Marks of the True Christian, Romans 12:9-18, English Standard Version
3. "Oh, the Places You'll Go", by Dr. Suess 2012
4. Isaiah 49:16, New Living Translation

Chapter 12
1. "Pour Your Spirit Out", C. Gall, T. Gall, C. Phillips, J. Fay, K. Williams, Thrive Worship, Integrity Music, 2021
2. Proverbs 3:6, New King James Version
3. Proverbs 27:9,The Passion Translation

Chapter 13
1. "Poem of Life", Author Unknown
2. John 15:4-5, New King James Version

Chapter 14
1. Song of Songs 4:9, New Living Translation

Chapter 15

1. "One Day at a Time Sweet Jesus", by M. Wilkin & K. Kristofferson 2020

Chapter 16

1. The Confessions of St. Augustine of Hippo, (354-430)
2. "God's Not Dead 2", Walter Wesley, 2015

Chapter 17

1. "3 Things About God", Meme, America's best pics and videos, Pinterest
2. Psalm 127:3, New Living Translation

Chapter 18

1. "The Divine Mentor," Pastor Wayne Cordeiro, SOAP Journaling, Bethany House Publishers, 2008

Chapter 23

1. Psalm 8:3-5
2. "Star Light, Star Bright," Author Unknown, 19th Century American Nursery Rhyme
3. "What a Friend we have in Jesus," By Joseph M. Scriven 1855

www.ingramcontent.com/pod-product-compliance
Lightning Source LLC
Chambersburg PA
CBHW031101030726
47496CB00002BA/330